AN AEGEAN APRIL
The Ninth Chief Inspector Andreas Kaldis Mystery

Best Books of 2018 in Crime Fiction—*Library Journal*

Greece's Thriller Writer of Record—*The New York Times*

"The great man behind Greece's crime mysteries."

—*Greek City Times*

"Vivid local color, agreeable central characters, and exciting action scenes make this a winner."

—*Publishers Weekly*

"The ninth case for Siger's Greek detective, brimming with suspense and a distinct sense of place, continues to deepen the back story of its band of heroes."

—*Kirkus Reviews*

"Siger's ninth atmospheric mystery vividly depicts the political and economic issues involved in the European refugee crisis. VERDICT: Fans of Adrian McKinty's Sean Duffy books and other police procedurals that handle violence and political issues with black humor will welcome this outstanding crime novel."

—*Library Journal* (starred review)

"This latest outing also offers a perspective on the Balkan Peninsula and the thorny issue of asylum seekers. A fast-paced international series."

—Karen Keefe, *Booklist*

SANTORINI CAESARS
The Eighth Chief Inspector Andreas Kaldis Mystery

"[This is a] novel that's both a rock-solid mystery and comments incisively about so many issues besetting Europe and the world today."

—Huffington Post

"The eighth case for Siger's police hero has a timely plot and a handful of engaging back stories about its detective team."

—Kirkus Reviews

"As always, Siger provides readers with an action-packed plot, well-developed characters with lots of attitude, breathtaking Greek scenery, and a perceptive take on the current political and economic problems affecting Greece. International-crime fans need to be reading this consistently strong series."

—Barbara Bibel, *Booklist*

DEVIL OF DELPHI
The Seventh Chief Inspector Andreas Kaldis Mystery

2016 Barry Awards nominee for Best Novel

"Siger brings Chief Inspector Andreas Kaldis some very big challenges in his seventh mystery set in troubled contemporary Greece... The final plot twist proves well worth the wait, but it won't take readers long to get there as they will be turning pages at a ferocious clip."

—Booklist (starred review)

"Though the reader is always several steps ahead of the police here, Siger's sublimely malevolent villains make the book a page-turner."

—Kirkus Reviews

"A killer named Kharon (for the mythological ferryman who transports the dead across the River Styx) and bomba, or counterfeit wine, complicate the lives of Chief Inspector Kaldis and his team. The seventh book in Siger's Greek procedural series features a strong sense of place and a devious plot."

—Library Journal

SONS OF SPARTA
The Sixth Chief Inspector Andreas Kaldis Mystery

"Siger paints travelogue-worthy pictures of a breathtakingly beautiful—if politically corrupt—Greece."

—*Publishers Weekly* (starred review)

"Kaldis' sixth case offers a lively, gritty plot, an abundance of local color and two righteous heroes."

—*Kirkus Reviews*

"Filled with local color, action, and humor, this story will give readers a taste of modern Greek culture and its ancient roots."

—*Booklist*

MYKONOS AFTER MIDNIGHT
The Fifth Chief Inspector Andreas Kaldis Mystery

2014 Left Coast Crime Awards nominee for Best Mystery
in a Foreign Setting

"Vibrant with the frenzied nightlife of Mykonos and the predators
who feed on it. A twisty page-turner."

—Michael Stanley, award-winning author
of the Detective Kubu mysteries

"The investigation that follows—highlighted by political interference
and the piecing together of a complicated international plot that
threatens to disrupt the easygoing, anything-goes life that Mykonos
is famous for—keeps the reader engaged, even as it makes obvious
that in Greece it really matters whom you know. The emergence of a
shadowy master criminal bodes well for future adventures."

—*Publishers Weekly*

"Gorgeous Mykonos once again becomes a character when conflicting
forces battle for the resort island's future in Siger's fifth series entry.
Greece's financial vulnerabilities play a key role as Chief Inspector
Kaldis digs in."

—*Library Journal*

"From the easy banter of its three cops to its clutch of unpredictable
villains, Kaldis' fifth reads more like an Elmore Leonard caper than
a whodunit."

—*Kirkus Reviews*

"Acclaimed (particularly by Greek commentators) for their realistic
portrayal of Greek life and culture, the Kaldis novels are very well
constructed, and this one is no exception: not only is the mystery solid
but the larger story, revolving around the political machinations of
the shadowy global organization, is clever and intriguing. Fans of the
previous Kaldis novels would do well to seek this one out."

—David Pitt, *Booklist*

TARGET: TINOS
The Fourth Chief Inspector Andreas Kaldis Mystery

A *New York Times* pick for the summer—Marilyn Stasio

"Thrilling, thought-provoking, and impossible to put down."

> —Timothy Hallinan, award-winning author
> of the Poke Rafferty thrillers

"Nobody writes Greece better than Jeffrey Siger."

> —Leighton Gage, author of
> the Chief Inspector Mario Silva Investigations

"*Target: Tinos* is another of Jeffrey Siger's thoughtful police procedurals set in picturesque but not untroubled Greek locales."

> — *The New York Times*

"A likable, compassionate lead; appealing Greek atmosphere; and a well-crafted plot help make this a winner."

> —*Publishers Weekly* (starred review)

"An interesting and highly entertaining police procedural for those who wish to read their way around the globe and especially for those inclined to move away from some of the 'chilly' Scandinavian thrillers and into warmer climes."

> —*Library Journal*

"The fourth case for a sleuth who doesn't suffer fools gladly pairs a crisp style with a complex portrait of contemporary Greece to bolster another solid whodunit."

> —*Kirkus Reviews*

"Siger's latest Inspector Kaldis Mystery throbs with the pulse of Greek culture...Make sure to suggest this engaging series to fans of Leighton Gage's Mario Silva series, set in Brazil but very similar in terms of mood and feel."

> —Jessica Moyer, *Booklist*

PREY ON PATMOS
The Third Chief Inspector Andreas Kaldis Mystery

"...[a] suspenseful trip through the rarely seen darker strata of complex, contemporary Greece."

—*Publishers Weekly*

"Using the Greek Orthodox Church as the linchpin for his story, Siger proves that Greece is fertile new ground for the mystery genre. Sure to appeal to fans of mysteries with exotic locations."

—*Library Journal*

"The third case for the appealing Andreas will immerse readers in a fascinating culture."

—*Kirkus Reviews*

ASSASSINS OF ATHENS
The Second Chief Inspector Andreas Kaldis Mystery

"Jeffrey Siger's *Assassins of Athens* is a teasingly complex and suspenseful thriller....Siger and his protagonist, Chief Inspector Andreas Kaldis, are getting sharper and surer with each case."

—Thomas Perry, bestselling author

"Siger is a superb writer....Best of all, he creates the atmosphere of modern Greece in vivid, believable detail, from the magnificence of its antiquities to the decadence of its power bearers and the squalor of its slums."

—*Pittsburgh Post-Gazette*

"This is international police procedural writing at its best and should be recommended, in particular, to readers who enjoy Leighton Gage's Brazilian police stories or Hakan Nesser's Swedish inspector Van Veeteren."

—*Booklist* (starred review)

"With few mysteries set in Greece, the author, a longtime resident of Mykonos, vividly captures this unfamiliar terrain's people and culture. Mystery fans who like their police procedurals in exotic locales will welcome this one."

—*Library Journal*

MURDER IN MYKONOS
The First Chief Inspector Andreas Kaldis Mystery

"Siger's intimate knowledge of Mykonos adds color and interest to his serviceable prose and his simple premise. The result is a surprisingly effective debut novel."

—*Kirkus Reviews*

"Siger's view of Mykonos (where he lives part-time) is nicely nuanced, as is the mystery's ambiguous resolution. Kaldis's feisty personality and complex backstory are appealing as well, solid foundations for a projected series."

—*Publishers Weekly*

"Siger...captures the rare beauty of the Greek islands in this series debut."

—*Library Journal*

"Siger's Mykonos seems an unrelievedly hedonistic place, especially given the community's religious orthodoxy, but suspense builds nicely as the story alternates between the perspectives of the captive woman, the twisted kidnapper, and the cop on whose shoulders the investigation falls. In the end, Andreas finds more than he bargained for, and readers will be well pleased."

—Stephanie Zvirin, *Booklist*

The Mykonos Mob

Books by Jeffrey Siger

Chief Inspector Andreas Kaldis Mysteries

Murder in Mykonos
Assassins of Athens
Prey on Patmos: An Aegean Prophecy
Target: Tinos
Mykonos After Midnight
Sons of Sparta
Devil of Delphi
Santorini Caesars
An Aegean April
The Mykonos Mob

The Mykonos Mob

A Chief Inspector Andreas Kaldis Mystery

Jeffrey Siger

Poisoned Pen
PRESS

Published by Poisoned Pen Press, an imprint of Sourcebooks, Inc.
P.O. Box 4410, Naperville, Illinois 60563-4410
(630) 961-3900
Fax: (630) 961-2168
sourcebooks.com

Library of Congress Cataloging 2018959451

Printed and bound in the United States of America.
SB 10 9 8 7 6 5 4 3 2 1

Acknowledgments

Mihalis, Roz, and Spiros Apostolou; Ronnie Bond; Petros Bourovilis; Nellos and Lee Canellopoulos; Beth Deveny; Diane DiBiase; Nikolaos Drivas; David Dyer; Andreas, Aleca, Nikos, Mihalis, and Anna Fiorentinos; Theodora Giovanidou; Paul Greenwood; Donna Harris and Ken Richards; Mark Hartman; Kelly Howe; Nikos Hristodoulakis and Jody Duncan; Flora and Yanni Katsaounis; Olga Kefalogianni; Panos Kelaidis; Alexandros Kolomvotsos; Nicholas and Sonia Kotopoulos; Miltos Kozonakis; Joshua and Kendall Latner; Linda Marshall; Terrence, Karen, and Rachel McLaughlin; Sarah Mucho; Ino Panagopoulou; Phyllis Pastore; Barbara G. Peters and Robert Rosenwald; Bobby Peaco; Kostantina Polychronopoulou; Nikos Raftopoulos; Holli Roach; Kathy "Babe" Robinson; Manos and Irini Rousounelous; Vangelis Savarikas; George Seirinakis; Jonathan, Jennifer, Azriel, and Gavriella Siger; Ed Stackler; Ion Stavropoulos; Hronis, Kate, and Marisa Taboulhanas; Vasilis Tsiligiris; Miltiadis Varvitsiotis; Dimitris Xenarios; Susan Xenarios; Barbara Zilly.

And, of course, Aikaterini Lalaouni.

IN MEMORIAM

Nikolaos Andreas Fiorentinos (1994-2018)
He called me Pappou, as do Anna and Mihalis.

"I am like any other man.
All I do is supply a demand."

—Al Capone

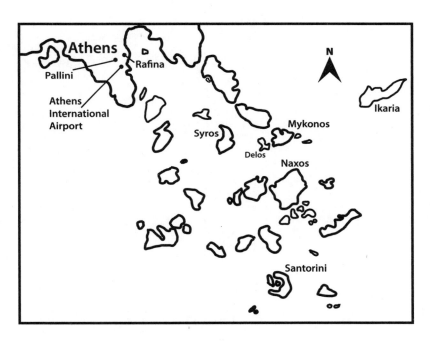

Metropolitan Athens, Cycladic Islands, and Ikaria

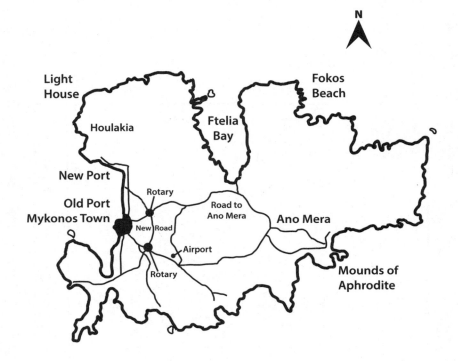

Mykonos Island

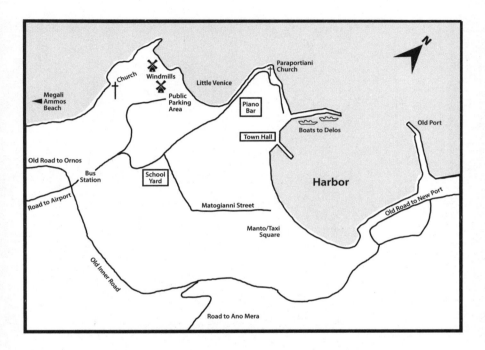

Mykonos Town

Chapter One

He never wondered about the purpose of life or how he turned out as he had. It all just sort of happened. He became a cop because he saw it as the surest way for a kid born into Greece's working class in the tumultuous early 1960s to make a living. He got lucky when, after the fall of the Military Junta in 1974, he joined the youth movement of a left-wing political party that came to power in 1981 and remembered to reward its loyal friends.

As he rose in rank, the more friends and money he made, the more power he amassed. He kept careful track of where the bodies were buried and possessed an uncanny instinct for digging up the ones he needed to achieve his purposes. An effort by the opposition party to paint him as corrupt failed when the prosecution's main witness died in a boating accident. An investigation into the witness' death faded away soon after he announced his decision to retire from the Hellenic Police force with the rank of colonel.

That's when he began to make truly big money, capitalizing on his contacts and former position as head of police for the South Aegean Region, home to Greece's most popular tourist islands for the rich and hard-partying globetrotting crowd.

Tonight, the Colonel was far away from all that glitz and glamour. He sat in a restaurant in a nondescript, middle-class eastern suburb of Athens, virtually equidistant from downtown Athens, its port town of Rafina, and Venizelos International Airport.

"A convenient place for a meeting," said the one who'd arranged it.

The Colonel leaned back in his chair and yawned. The conversation had been as boring as the meal. Everything about the place was mediocre, from its tired, thirty-year-old decor to the hookers at the bar, and the ruddy-faced, pudgy man sitting across the table from him who had yet to say why their mutual business acquaintance thought they should meet.

"Am I keeping you awake, Colonel?"

"Barely."

Ruddy Face smiled. "How do you like my place?"

The Colonel leaned forward. It was long past time to get down to business. "If this is your joint, why don't you just tell me why you wanted to meet? You sure as hell don't need my services to run this operation."

"You're right, it's a dump." Ruddy Face paused. "But I have plans."

"What sort of plans?"

"I'm buying a club on the islands. It's going to be first-class in every way." He nodded toward the bar. "Including the girls."

"Which island?"

"One you control."

"Control is a mighty big word."

Ruddy Face smiled. "Let's just say, I don't like the idea of getting involved in a business where my investment isn't secure."

"That's prudent of you."

"Can you help me?"

"If you're asking for security, the answer is yes."

"I'm talking about *protection* for *all* aspects of my business."

The Colonel shrugged. "It's all a matter of price. You tell me what you want, and I'll tell you what it will cost you."

"I hear you're pricey."

"You heard right. But I make sure things run smoothly."

"How you do that?"

"t have competitors stirring things up, jockeying for

"I maintain order among the chaos."

They might see things differently."

"If by *they* you mean competitors, there are no *they* on my island. I'm the only game in town."

"I get your point," said the man. "I'm sure we'll come to terms."

"If you want to open a club where I'm in business, I'm sure we will."

The Colonel declined an offer of coffee, and the two men agreed to talk again once Ruddy Face had a better idea of what he might need from the Colonel.

He walked the Colonel to the front door, shook his hand, thanked him for coming, and wished him safe travels. "*Kalo taxidhi.*"

But the Colonel only made it as far as the front door of his Mercedes.

Greece's General Police Headquarters, better known as GADA, sat close by the heart of Athens' bustle, next door to a major hospital, down the block from Greece's Supreme Court, and across the street from the stadium of one of Greece's most popular soccer teams. GADA's Special Crimes Unit, charged with investigating potential corruption and other matters of national concern—at least those that piqued the interest of its Chief Inspector Andreas Kaldis—occupied the eastern side of the fourth floor.

Andreas had been at his desk since shortly after sunrise. With two early-rising young children at home, it wasn't unusual for him to flee the morning domestic chaos for the relative calm of tracking down bad actors. His wife, Lila, never seemed to mind when he abandoned her to the ruckus, undoubtedly because she rightly considered him an active accessory to their children's early-morning mischief.

It wasn't as if he were leaving his wife alone to their son and daughter; she did have a maid and nanny, with a decidedly suspicious luxury on an honest cop's salary. Help, of that, and more, had come with his marriage to the daughter of one of Greece's most respected and wealthiest families. He appreciated his good fortune and considered himself a lucky man.

Too bad he couldn't say the same thing for the guy plastered all over the morning news headlines: RETIRED POLICE COLONEL STAVROS AKTIPIS ASSASSINATED. That summed up virtually everything the various news stations had to report on the shooting, though they tried their best to spice up their coverage with references to corruption allegations that had haunted the victim.

All the allegations preceded Andreas' time as chief of Special Crimes, but he'd heard the stories and much more about the Colonel. Instinctively, Andreas believed the victim had been corrupt, for the system far too often brought temptations to one in his position. Yet, if Andreas pursued every case of official corruption brought to his attention, he'd need all the offices in the building to house his staff—not to mention an unimaginable number of additional prosecutors.

Compounding all of that, innovative criminal types from around the world kept introducing new schemes and methods into Greece that added to his caseload. Overwhelmed as his unit was, and Greece a decade into a crippling economic crisis, he knew he'd be wasting his time asking for more support from the government. That left Andreas with little choice but to pursue the most egregious offenders, hoping to make an example of them in a manner that discouraged others from doing the same.

What happened last night to the Colonel, he knew, would be headed straight for his desk, in a file marked NASTY in all-red letters. The Colonel had been murdered for a reason, and it wasn't robbery. His wallet, filled with euros, and an expensive watch were untouched. Three quick bullets to the back of his head as he stood at his car door. No witnesses, and no terrorists claiming credit for the killing. At least none so far.

Andreas held a remote in his right hand, surfing through local news coverage on the wall-mounted TV screen to his right, while drumming the fingers of his left hand on his desktop. He looked at his watch. Detective Yianni Kouros should be at the scene by now. Andreas had called him at home as soon as he'd heard the early morning news. Yianni had been his right-hand man since their days together on Mykonos, back when Andreas was the island's police chief and Yianni a brash young bull of a rookie cop.

Andreas bit at his lip. Killing cops, retired or not, wasn't something even the most hardened criminals undertook lightly, especially when the victim was an ex-colonel. He'd been assassinated for a serious reason, most likely with the blessing of serious people. That's why he'd sent Yianni to the scene. He wanted his own people in on the investigation from the start. Screw-ups early on—unintentional or otherwise—haunted investigations, at times serving as a convenient pretext for bad guys getting away with murder. Not this time, though. Not if Andreas could help it.

Yes, this definitely would be a nasty one.

Early-morning traffic heading east out of Athens wasn't nearly as bad as that going in the other direction, but it still was far from Detective Yianni Kouros' favorite way to start his day. He'd recently moved into an apartment in Kypseli, a staunchly working-class Athens neighborhood only a mile from his office at GADA, and his easy commute had spoiled him.

Athens' eastern suburbs were unfamiliar to Yianni, so he left it to his GPS to get him where he wanted to be. The town of Pallini lay in the central inland portion of the Attica Peninsula, a region known since antiquity as Mesogeia. Once filled with olive groves, fig trees, and grapevines, its fertile plains were now home to one town seemingly blending into the next. All Yianni knew about Pallini was that it lay along the Greek National Road on the way to Athens' port town of Rafina, from which he'd caught many a boat to the Cyclades Islands.

It took about a half-hour for him to cover the twelve miles from his home to the scene of the Colonel's murder, and when he arrived, a local blue-and-white police cruiser sat blocking the entrance to the restaurant's parking lot.

Yianni pulled onto the sidewalk just beyond the entrance and slowly walked toward the cruiser, taking care to pull his police ID out from under his shirt. No reason to make the two cops more nervous than they might already be, having spent all night at the scene of an ex-police colonel's murder by an unidentified assassin for reasons unknown.

"*Yia sas*," said Yianni to the driver through his open window. "I'm Detective Kouros. Special Crimes."

The driver and his partner got out of the car and shook hands with Yianni.

"So, what can you tell me?"

The driver gestured with his head at a late-model black Mercedes sedan parked facing the street ten meters to the right of where they stood, and directly across from the entrance to the restaurant. "That's the victim's car. He was killed at the driver-side front door."

"The body was removed once forensics finished up," said the partner. "The spent shell casings are in evidence bags where they were found." He pointed to three orange cones behind the Mercedes on its passenger side.

Yianni carefully walked toward the rear of the car, studying the ground as he did. He circled the car twice before returning to the cones. Two of the three nine-millimeter shell casings lay in close proximity to one another, indicating that the killer had fired from approximately the same location in relation to the victim, but the third lay several meters away from the other two, in the direction of the restaurant entrance. Yianni knelt to study the casings more closely and looked up at the cops.

"How did this go down?"

The driver answered. "The owner told us he'd said good night to the victim inside the restaurant, standing with him at the door leading out to the parking lot. The owner's back was to the door when he heard the shots. At first he thought it was a motorbike backfire, but after the third shot he turned around and saw the victim on the ground. He ran outside, but by then the shooter was gone."

Yianni looked down at the shell casings. "Do you know whether any vehicles entered or left the parking lot after the victim was shot?"

"The owner said he didn't let anyone leave the parking lot until the police arrived."

"And we were told not to let any vehicles budge until you gave the okay," added the partner. "A lot of aggravated customers went home in taxis."

Yianni nodded. "Thanks. What about vehicles that entered the parking lot after the shooting?"

The partner pointed to the left of the entrance. "They all parked over there, away from the scene."

"And before police arrived?"

"The owner said no one entered or left."

"Is there any other way in or out of the parking lot, besides this entrance?"

The driver answered no in the Greek style of a quick upward jerk of his head. "The perimeter's fenced in, except for a low wall along its border with the front street."

"We checked, and there's no sign of tire tracks anywhere along the front wall," added the partner. "But it would have been simple for anyone to get over the wall on foot."

Yianni stood. "So, no vehicles entered or left the area after the shooting, except for official vehicles, and they parked away from the scene?"

"Yes," said the two in unison.

"What about the ambulance that picked up the body?"

"The attendants used a stretcher," said the driver.

"And kept far away from the cones marking the shell casings," added the partner.

"I see that you get what I'm driving at."

The cops smiled.

Yianni pointed at the shell casing closest to the restaurant's front door. "That shell casing is directly between the front door and the rear of the victim's car. It's deformed at its open end. The others aren't."

"Perhaps the owner stepped on it when he ran to the victim?"

"Perhaps," said Yianni, "but why is it so far away from the other two? Where's the owner now?"

"He's inside," said the driver. "Taking a nap in his office."

"Something I'm sure you'd like to be doing after a night of babysitting the scene."

"At least it pays well," smirked a cop.

"Yeah," laughed his partner.

"Our universal cop lament," smiled Yianni. "I'm going to check in with the owner, and once I'm done, you two can collect the shell casings for forensics and take off." He headed in the direction of the front door, but before reaching it, a small, ruddy-face man opened the door and stepped outside.

"You must be from GADA. I own this place and was told to wait for you."

"I thought you were sleeping."

"Who can sleep with what just happened?"

Yianni extended his hand. "I'm Detective Yianni Kouros. I know you've been asked this before, but I need to hear everything you remember about the shooting."

The owner reached out and shook Yianni's hand. "Everyone calls me Pepe." He matter-of-factly repeated a story consistent with what Yianni had been told by the two cops.

"So, you saw no one?"

"Correct."

"On foot or in a vehicle?"

"No one."

"And no vehicle entered or left the parking lot from the moment you heard the shots?"

"That's correct."

"Do you have closed-circuit TV in your parking lot?"

"No. Though after this, I'm seriously considering the idea."

"Are you expecting more shootings?"

Pepe gave a twisted grin. "I sincerely hope not."

"What about inside, any CCTV there?"

"No, I think it's safe to say we're technologically challenged out here in the suburbs."

"Do you know where the victim lived?"

"No."

"Was he local?"

"No."

"If he wasn't local, why did he pick your restaurant to eat in?"

Pepe ran his tongue across his lower lip. "I asked him to meet me here."

"You knew him?"

"No."

"Then why the meeting?"

"He was recommended as someone who could help me with a new business I'm opening."

"Who made the recommendation?"

Pepe gave a name Yianni didn't recognize. He made a note of it in his pocket notebook.

"What sort of help were you looking for?"

"Security. I'm sure you know who the murdered man was."

"What sort of business?"

"A club on Mykonos."

Yianni made another note. "Did the victim say or do anything in his conversation with you that in any way suggested concern for his safety?"

Pepe gestured no. "Absolutely not."

"Are you aware of anyone else who knew about your meeting with the Colonel?"

"No one I knew, that's for sure."

Yianni drew in and let out a deep breath. "What a terrible thing to happen on the front steps of your place of business."

"Yes, but I can't worry about that. I keep thinking of the poor man and his family."

"Of course," said Yianni. "I just wish you'd taken more care not to step on the shell casings."

Pepe looked at him for a moment. "What? I didn't step on anything."

"How can you be sure?"

He pointed at the cones. "Because when I ran to him, I ran straight for him, and the casings aren't anywhere near the line I took to get to him." He paused again. "And once I realized he was dead, I knew the police would be investigating, so I was careful how I walked back to the restaurant."

"Did you call the police from inside?"

"No, I stood by the front door and used my mobile."

"And you remained outside until the police arrived?"

"And I kept everyone away from his car."

"Thank you," said Yianni. "You've been very helpful."

More than you realize.

● ● ● ● ●

"Morning, Maggie. Is the Chief in?"

"He's down in the cafeteria."

"What! After all these years, he's admitted to being tired of your coffee?"

Maggie scowled. "No, Detective Wise Ass. No one *ever* grows tired of my coffee. He's hungry. He left home without breakfast." She paused, then added with a twinkle in her eye, "Besides, he wouldn't be brave enough to tell me if he were."

"No one on earth is that brave," deadpanned Yianni.

Maggie Sikestes, a sturdy, red-haired, five-foot-three-inch ball of energy and source of all knowledge of GADA's many secrets and intricate ways, had been Andreas' secretary since the luck of the draw landed them together when he assumed command of Special Crimes.

Maggie nodded sternly. "And don't you forget it."

"Forget what?" came a voice from the hallway behind Yianni.

Yianni turned to face Andreas. "Who really runs this place?"

"I already know that answer." Andreas put a covered paper coffee cup down on Maggie's desk. "Here's your skim decaf cappuccino, your Highness, precisely as you told me to order it."

Yianni burst out laughing.

"What's so funny?" said Andreas.

Maggie glared at Yianni. "If you tell him, you're a dead man."

Yianni pointed at the coffee cup and laughed harder.

"Enough," said Andreas. He waved for Yianni to follow him into his office.

Andreas went behind his desk and Yianni dropped onto the couch in front of a row of windows looking out on the windows of an adjacent building.

"What have you've learned about the death of Colonel Akti-pis?"

"It ain't simple, Chief." Yianni told him of his morning at the scene.

When Yianni finished, Andreas picked up a pencil and began tapping its eraser end on his desktop. "I take it you believe the owner is lying."

"If he didn't step on the shell casing, and no one else stepped on it, the only explanation is that someone drove over it. That would also explain why the casing was found so far away from the other two. A tire hit it at an angle that sent it tumbling off in the direction of the restaurant. But the owner insists no vehicles were anywhere near it. I think he's lying because he knows whoever drove over it was the killer."

"Maybe he just doesn't want to get involved. After all, it's obvious this was a hit, meaning whoever's behind taking out a police colonel has cast-iron balls. Taking out a witness like the owner would be a small matter by comparison."

"But why didn't he just tell me he'd stepped on the casing? That would have been the easiest, most believable explanation."

Andreas shrugged. "For reasons I'll never fully understand, liars concoct elaborate, broad explanations but somehow always trip up on the tiny details. It's as if they're trying to create the perfect exculpatory scenario with absolutely no suggestion of potential fault on their part. In this case, the owner has himself doing all the right things—he heard the shots, immediately ran outside, saw no one but the victim, and remained on the scene to make certain it was not disturbed. In that mindset, he simply couldn't bring himself to admit to less than perfect conduct on his part, even though saying he *might* have stepped on the casing was the most logical, innocent explanation."

"Are you saying he wasn't involved in the assassination?"

Andreas shrugged. "He's sure as hell a suspect, but I can see where he could be lying simply out of fear that whoever ordered it might come after him if he admitted to being a witness."

"But that whole dinner scenario smells of an assassination setup."

"Of course it does. Because that's precisely what it was. In fact, it's so obviously a setup that my instincts are screaming the victim wasn't the only target of what went down."

"Meaning?"

"From what the owner told you, he and whoever suggested the meeting are the obvious bad guys. They knew the Colonel would be there. The question is, who else knew?"

"The owner said he'd told no one else."

"That leaves the one who recommended they meet. What's his name?"

Yianni took out his notebook. "Marcos Despotiko."

Andreas stopped tapping his pencil. "Come again?"

"Marcos Despotiko."

"You can't be serious."

"You sound like you know him."

"*Know him.*" Andreas rolled up his sleeve. "Look at the goosebumps crawling up my arm. He's in the deep shadows behind virtually every major criminal activity in Greece. Drugs are just part of it. He's involved in everything from bank fraud to smuggling embargoed terrorist oil from the Middle East into Greece through Turkey. No one talks about him, but even serious bad-asses know not to cross him. They give him a piece of any big deal that goes down in Greece. How could you not have heard of him?"

"You mean he's *the Despot*?" Yianni slapped his forehead. "I only knew him by his nickname. I can't believe I didn't make the connection."

"Don't feel bad. Truth is, I'm more familiar with his real name than are most Greeks, including cops, because I come across it a lot, thanks to Lila. Despotiko's wife is a big-time socialite, and Lila and she sometimes end up on the same committees. Whenever there's a social event that might have me rubbing elbows with her husband, I manufacture some excuse not to attend. It aggravates the hell out of Lila, but I don't want anyone getting the idea I'm friendly with Marcos Despotiko."

"Is that your way of saying you want me to interview him?"

"It's my way of saying I wish you could. But I'm afraid there's no choice now. Besides, I think he'll be more cooperative if I'm along for the interview."

"Even if he has something to hide?"

"This guy has been hiding things for so long it's second nature to him. If he's involved, I doubt there's anything or anyone out there to link him to it."

"Anyone alive, you mean."

Andreas nodded. "Which further explains why the restaurant owner won't budge from his story. He's far more afraid of upsetting Despotiko than of anything we could do to him."

"That leaves us only with Despotiko for answers."

"Precisely. Here's hoping he wasn't involved, and that he'll be angry enough at the thought of someone setting him up as a suspect to give us a lead on who might be involved."

"What makes you think he'll cooperate with us rather than take revenge on his own terms?"

"I have no way of knowing how he'll react. All we can do is question him and hope for the best."

"While wearing a ballistic vest."

Andreas picked up his phone. "I'll have to get Despotiko's home number from Lila."

He called, and after deflecting a barrage of questions as to why he wanted the number of a man he so often went out of his way to avoid, he got it.

He dialed, and a male voice answered, Andreas introduced himself and asked to speak to Mr. Despotiko.

"I'm Kurt, Mr. Despotiko's personal assistant. He said to tell you when you called that he's been expecting to hear from you and is available to meet with you here at his home in Paleo Psychiko at your convenience any time this morning."

Andreas said he'd be there in thirty minutes, hung up the phone, and stared stone-faced at Yianni. "He was expecting my call."

"How could he have known?"

Andreas stood up and started toward the door. "That'll be my first question for him.

Chapter Two

Just north of Athens and west of Kifissias Avenue, the suburb of Old Psychiko stood as a refuge of peace, greenery, and high walls for foreign embassies, exclusive private schools, and the upper echelon of Athenian society. A few more northern neighborhoods and one or two to the south might claim to be equally desirable, but none would dare argue to be greater.

Psychiko's confusing array of one-way streets, winding every which way about its tree-lined slopes and hills, was designed that way for a reason: to keep out casual passersby. But it hadn't worked as well on the new-money crowd. They flocked to the neighborhood, sending prices through the roof for houses they often tore down to build grander homes than their neighbors.' At least until the financial crisis hit.

To Yianni's eyes, this wealthy enclave must seem like a different universe compared to the modest suburb in which he'd spent his morning traipsing about a restaurant parking lot.

For Andreas, it was a reminder of how he'd overcome once-nagging thoughts of being unworthy of the elevated lifestyle that came with his marriage. He no longer lived in the working-class neighborhoods of the Athens that he'd known as the son of a cop. Instead, he now lived in a penthouse apartment on the city's most prestigious avenue, next to the Presidential Palace and across from Greece's National Gardens.

He'd grown comfortable among the crème de la crème of Athens society, in large part because of his wife's down-to-earth attitude toward pretentious societal trappings. In part, too, because of his own merit-earned appointment to a stint as Minister of Civil Protection in charge of all police in Greece—a position he'd relinquished in order to return to chasing bad guys as head of Special Crimes.

Although familiar with the neighborhood, Andreas managed to get lost on the way to Despotiko's house. Ultimately, he found their destination, close by the highest point in Psychiko, on a property more befitting a park than a residence. Between the road and a white stucco house the size of many an apartment building stood a ten-foot-high wrought-iron fence spanning the length of the property. Ten meters of manicured grass separated the exterior fence from an even taller concrete-and-stucco wall mounted with cameras encircling the house.

"Wow, this place is more secure than Korydallos," said Yianni. "Funny how someone who should be in prison ends up living as if he already is."

"I'm sure his accommodations are a bit more upscale." Andreas parked on the sidewalk in front of a double-wide iron-spear gate in the exterior fence. Before he and Yianni left the car, a steel gate in the interior concrete wall sprang open, and two burly men dressed in black walked briskly in the direction of their car.

"Morning," said Andreas, walking up to the gate toward the two men.

"State your business, please," said the taller of the men.

"We have an appointment with Mr. Despotiko. The name's Kaldis."

The man nodded and spoke into his earpiece microphone.

"May I see identification, please?"

Andreas and Yianni showed them their police IDs.

The smaller man unlocked the wrought-iron gate with a key and motioned for them to follow him. The taller man let them pass, locked the gate behind them, and trailed them toward the steel gate.

"These guys even follow prison lockup procedures," whispered Yianni to Andreas.

"Probably comes from firsthand experience."

When they reached the interior steel gate, the shorter man stopped and turned around. "Your weapons, please."

Andreas smiled. "Sorry, no can do."

"Then you can't come inside."

Andreas turned and stepped back so he could see both men and Yianni. Yianni mirrored Andreas' maneuver.

Andreas looked from one man to the other. "Then permit me to make a suggestion for you to pass along to your employer. Either he honors his invitation and allows us to enter on our terms, or please ask him for the name of his attorney, so we can arrange for Mr. Despotiko to turn himself into GADA for questioning." Andreas shrugged. "Of course, I can't promise that we can keep a meeting at GADA regarding your employer's possible involvement in the murder of an ex-police colonel out of the headlines. But, then again, Mr. Despotiko already knows all that. It's why he suggested we meet him here in the first place, away from the media."

The two men looked at each other, pressed at their earpieces, and listened without speaking.

The shorter man glanced at the taller. "It's okay." He stared at Andreas. "Follow me."

Andreas winked at Yianni, waved at the camera above the gate, and said aloud, "Thank you."

Yianni whispered to Andreas. "When did you figure all that out?"

"Like most things in life, as I was saying it." Andreas leaned in and whispered into Yianni's ear. "Considering how hard he works at keeping out of the press, it's the only thing that made sense to me. But there's a downside to being right. It makes the most sense if Despotiko's completely innocent."

They passed through the gate into a courtyard filled with elaborate plantings and classic and modern sculptures, revealing an eclectic but clearly expensive taste.

A short, trim, olive-skinned woman dressed in a pale blue maid's uniform stood between four rose-and-gold marble pillars framing the front entrance to a massive house. "Mr. Despotiko said to show you to his study. Follow me, please."

Andreas and Yianni did as she asked. The two bodyguards did not follow.

She led them into a grand marble foyer bordered by well-cared-for plants, potted in classic Greek shapes, encircling an array of sculptures more delicate than those in the courtyard. An elegant, understated reliance on nature continued inside the house, with plants, organic shapes, and natural fabrics carefully arranged everywhere. Someone with taste had been at work here.

Just beyond what some might call a living room, the maid stopped and pointed to a doorway. "Mr. Despotiko is inside."

"Thank you," said Andreas, clearing his throat and motioning for Yianni to enter first.

It was as if they'd stepped into a different world, one cluttered with mismatched overstuffed furniture, heavy Persian rugs, mounted trophies from foreign hunts, books arranged more for appearance than content, cut crystal decanters filled with varying shades of brown whiskeys, and a pervasive odor of cigar smoke burrowed deeply into the room's walls and fabrics.

"Welcome," said a well-fed, clean-shaven, bald-headed, bear of a man. He sat behind a massive mahogany desk, framed by a world globe on one side and a Tiffany desk lamp on the other.

As Andreas walked toward the desk, Despotiko struggled to his feet.

"Sorry for not standing sooner, but my old knees aren't quite what they used to be." At his full height he stood equal to Andreas but looked easily twenty-five years older. He extended his hand across the desk and Andreas shook it.

Andreas pointed at Yianni. "This is my colleague, Detective Kouros."

Yianni and Despotiko shook hands.

"Please sit." He pointed at two well-worn Chesterfield chairs in front of his desk.

Andreas sat and looked around the office. "Nice arrangement."

"It works for me."

"I'm sure."

Despotiko smiled. "But not for my wife. She calls it my lair. I get to do whatever I want to do in here; she gets to do whatever she wants to do everywhere else."

"A wise arrangement."

"Yes, I'm sure you've come to the same conclusion. I think our wives spend their time together planning such things."

Andreas smiled.

Despotiko picked up a humidor from his desk and held it out to Andreas. "Cigar?"

"No, thank you."

He made the same offer to Yianni, who gestured no.

Despotiko put down the humidor, selected a cigar, and launched into an elaborate massaging, dampening, snipping, and lighting routine. "Cigars are a vice I just can't give up."

Andreas took that as his cue to get to the purpose of the meeting. "Thank you for seeing us on such short notice."

Despotiko nodded, his eyes fixed on lighting his cigar.

"Why don't you tell me why you knew we'd want to speak with you?"

He drew in and let out a tiny cloud of smoke. "Oh, it wasn't all that hard to figure out. As soon as I heard that poor Colonel Aktipis had been murdered at a meeting with that restaurant owner, Pepe, I had no doubt you'd be knocking on my door. I've done nothing wrong, mind you, but as you accurately described to my men, I don't want my name dragged through the mud by the press over this."

"Understood. So, how were you involved in what happened?"

He shut his eyes and sniffed at the cigar. "In what happened, nothing at all. In introducing the Colonel to Pepe, everything. That's what comes with doing a favor for someone."

"What sort of favor?"

He sighed. "My wife loves Mykonos. She spends a lot of her time over there, especially during the summer months. Pepe met her at some chichi island place, and when he said he planned on opening a club on Mykonos, she told him he'd need security. He asked for a recommendation and she said she'd ask me. It was such a no-brainer question for me that I straightaway named the Colonel when she asked."

He fixed his eyes on Andreas. "In retrospect, it was so much of a no-brainer that I wonder why he went to the trouble of having it put to me when anyone on Mykonos could have answered it for him."

"It being a no-brainer because...?" Andreas gestured for Despotiko to finish the answer.

"Because everyone on Mykonos knew security on the island was controlled by the Colonel."

"But aren't there a lot of different companies offering security on Mykonos?" said Yianni.

Despotiko drew in a puff, leaned back in his chair, and let the smoke drift out. "Many people would like to get into the security business there because it offers a lot of side benefits, including money laundering." He drew another puff. "At least that's what I'm told. But on Mykonos every security operation was owned by the Colonel. He just made it look as if he had competition."

"Are you saying the restaurant guy meant to somehow set you up?"

"No, I'm saying that once again my wife got mixed up with a fast-talking idiot. I doubt the man had the brains or balls to try to set me up." He leaned forward. "However, I do think that whoever wanted to eliminate the Colonel used the idiot to set up the meeting and added my name to the mix in order to vouch for the idiot's *bona fides* with the Colonel."

"Any ideas about who that might have been?"

"No."

"Would you tell me if you did?"

"No."

"Are you going to look for him?"

"That's your job, not mine."

"I'll take that as a maybe."

Despotiko stared at Andreas. "What do you want me to say? I'm a responsible citizen with an unblemished record. I'm surrounded by lawyers paid handsomely to protect me from all sorts of scurrilous charges. Why would I possibly be interested in hunting down someone who presents no threat to me?"

Andreas stared back, waving his hand at the trophies mounted on the walls. "Because it's in your blood."

Despotiko laughed. "I like you. We really should get together with our wives."

Andreas smiled.

"Perhaps on Mykonos," said Despotiko.

"Why Mykonos?"

Despotiko studied the glow on the expanding ash of his cigar. "Because we both know you'll be spending quite a bit of time there looking for the person or persons behind the Colonel's assassination." He paused. "At least that's where I'd be looking if I were the hunter."

"But you're not in on this hunt."

Despotiko kept his eyes fixed on his cigar. "True. But there's always fishing."

"And you undoubtedly have a knack for casting precisely the right bait in the direction of whatever you're trying to hook."

Despotiko shifted his gaze to meet Andreas' eyes. "If by that you're suggesting I'm trying to lure you into concentrating on Mykonos, it's only because things there are not as they seem."

"Since when have they ever been?"

"This is different. I get the sense that the island's undergoing a changing of the guard, with the assassination only a start. And no one has any idea who's behind it. Yes, there's the usual gossip-mongering rubbish, accusing everyone from the mayor to the CIA, but no concrete information. And before you ask exactly what I've heard, trust me, whatever I've heard, you'd pick up in your first five minutes on the island."

"Sounds to me like you're overloading your hook with Mykonos bait."

Despotiko shrugged. "It's your case to run, but just ask yourself this question: What do I have to gain by helping you at all?"

"Good question. And one I won't be able to answer unless I start looking."

Despotiko smiled. "So, bite already."

Andreas smiled back. "I just might."

● ● ● ● ●

Back in their police cruiser, Andreas and Yianni sat for a moment, staring at the estate.

"How much do you think a place like that costs?" said Yianni.

"The more interesting question is how many places just like that does he have elsewhere?"

"You mean in Greece?"

"I mean around the world. Our wealthy Greek brethren are prone to acquiring homes in places they like to visit."

"Haven't they heard of hotels?"

"They buy those too." Andreas turned on the engine and eased off the sidewalk onto the street. "So, what did you make of all that?"

"Quite a performance. Despotiko acted as if he didn't care about what was happening on Mykonos. He acted as if he were doing us a favor encouraging us to get involved in whatever mess is over there."

"A bit of an overplayed hand, I'd say," said Andreas. "The guy never has to earn another euro to continue living like a king, but that's not what drives him."

"Control?"

"Bingo. He's been *the man* in Greece for what seems forever, and now someone is challenging his rule."

"At least on Mykonos."

"Mykonos generates a big slice of all the vice money he makes off tourism. He also realizes that whoever is muscling in on Mykonos isn't likely to stop there."

"Hard to imagine he hasn't tried to figure out who might be the new bad guys. Maybe they're not from Greece?"

"I'm sure he's tried," said Andreas, turning onto Kifissias Avenue in the direction of downtown Athens. "That's what really concerns me. If with all his connections and power he really can't ID the bad guys, Greeks or foreigners, then some very serious and disciplined new players are likely moving in on the black-money businesses."

Yianni scratched the top of his head. "Or Despotiko knows who they are, but is unwilling or afraid to start something up with them. So, instead, he's trying to hustle us into doing his dirty work."

"Speaking of Despotiko and dirty work, there's a story about him I think you might enjoy. It gives you a sense of the man, and what he's capable of doing. It's about a favor he did for a friend who'd asked him to recover photos a famous celebrity was using to blackmail a young woman the friend liked. Ever hear it?"

"No."

"The friend came to Despotiko and asked him to recover the photos from the celebrity, but only if Despotiko promised not to beat or kill him. Despotiko promised, then arranged for the celebrity to be kidnapped, made to stand in freshly poured cement for seven hours, taken out in a boat and dropped into the water wearing his new concrete boots. Up until that point they'd not said a word to him about why they were doing what they were to him. Two and a half minutes later they pulled him back into the boat by a rope tied to the concrete. He was unconscious. After bringing him around, he started crying like a baby, and promised to do whatever they wanted. That's when they told him. Needless to say, he destroyed the photos."

"Sounds like a very effective approach."

"The story's not over. When the friend heard what had happened to the celebrity, he complained to Despotiko. Despotiko is reported to have told his friend, 'I didn't beat or kill him.'"

"Quite a story."

"And a good one to circulate if you're Despotiko. Even if it's not true." Andreas braked to avoid a motorcycle cutting in front of them to exit the wrong way onto a one-way street.

"*Malaka*!" yelled Yianni.

"Have you noticed that we're not talking about Despotiko as tied into the Colonel's murder?"

"Yeah," said Yianni. "I don't see him involved."

"Me either. But keep an open mind to that possibility as you poke around Mykonos."

Yianni stared at the side of his boss' head. "I was wondering when you'd get around to that. So, when are we off to Mykonos?"

"Uh, not *we*. At least not right away. I've commitments that will keep me here until the weekend. But you should head over there tomorrow."

"And do what?"

"Start by interviewing Mrs. Despotiko, see where things go from there."

Yianni sat quietly, staring straight ahead.

"What's bothering you?" said Andreas. "You're single and Mykonos is a party island that you know intimately. I thought you'd jump at the chance."

Yianni smiled ruefully. "Mykonos is expensive now. Really expensive. My cop buddies can't afford to live there on a police salary."

"You'll only be there a few days."

"Do you have any idea how much those couple of days will cost me? Nearly a month's salary just for the hotel room. Do I get an expense account?"

Andreas rolled his eyes. "Expense account? These days?" He reached over and patted Yianni's shoulder. "Don't worry. I'm sure you can stay at Lila's parents' house."

"I don't want to impose."

"You won't be imposing. They're away, and your presence will discourage burglars."

Yianni's expression changed to a grin. "If I hustle home to pack, I could make it there by tonight."

Andreas shook his head. "I think I've just been had."

Chapter Three

Andreas surprised Lila by making it home in time for dinner.

He found her in the kitchen, holding their seven-month-old daughter, Sofia, in her arms.

"She's been in a real mood today. Doesn't want me to let go of her."

"I know the feeling," said Andreas, gently pinching Sofia's cheeks and kissing Lila's.

"It must be a slow day for you to be home so early."

"I wish that were true. Truth is, this might be the last chance I have to be home at a decent hour for quite a while."

"What's happening?"

"We have a serious—"

A rolling shout of "*Daddy*," came roaring down the hallway in their direction from the lungs of a racing five-year-old.

"How's my main man Tassaki?" said Andreas, bending down to scoop his son into his arms.

"You're home."

Andreas kissed him.

"Can we play?"

"After dinner," said Lila.

Sofia leaned forward in her mother's arms, reaching out for her father.

"I sense a bit of budding sibling rivalry," said Lila.

"What's that mean?" asked Tassaki.

Andreas tussled his son's hair. "Your sister wants attention."

"Girls," said Tassaki distastefully, hugging his arms around his father's neck.

"Whoa there," said Lila. "Don't say that sort of thing. Boys and girls both want their daddy's attention."

"And their mommy's," added Andreas.

"But Sofia gets to spend all day at home with mommy doing mommy things, and I only get to be with you when you're not at work doing daddy things."

Andreas sensed before he saw his wife's raised eyebrows. "Care to help me out on this?" he said.

Lila handed Sofia to Andreas in exchange for Tassaki. She held him so they were eye to eye. "You know how I always tell you that you can be anything you want to be when you grow up, as long as you always try your best?"

Tassaki nodded.

"Well, the same is true for your sister. Just like boys, girls can be anything they want to be if they try hard enough. Your sister can do daddy things, and you can do mommy things." She kissed him on the forehead.

"But I want to be like daddy and do policeman things."

Lila smiled. "If that's what you want, that's fine."

"So, won't Sofia want to be just like you, and do what you do at home?"

Lila stared blankly at Andreas. "Your turn on the witness stand."

"Your mommy does all sorts of things."

"But you go to the office and she stays home."

"That doesn't make what I do any more important than what your mommy does."

A buzzer went off. "What's that?" said Andreas.

"You being saved by the bell." Lila put Tassaki down. "The chicken's ready."

"Where Marietta? And the nanny? You could use their help."

"It's Marietta's evening off, and Anna's doing laundry. But what's the big deal? It's just plain, everyday cooking, cleaning, baby-sitting, diaper changing, and philosophizing with a five-year-old."

"Right, just mommy things," Andreas whispered in her ear.

Lila offered a forced smile. "A wise decision, keeping those thoughts quiet at this particular moment."

"I value my domestic bliss."

She waved Andreas off into the dining room. "Put the baby in her high chair."

"Can I help you with something?"

"Just do that and keep them entertained until I get them their dinners."

Andreas' cozy evening at home with his family was not going as envisioned. He saw a serious discussion looming on the horizon over careers and role models. Lila had been hinting at a desire to get back into what she called "the adult world." She feared that after so many years of child-rearing she'd lost the spunk that once made her the premier fundraiser in Athens' art-and-museum scene.

Andreas had assured her that she'd not lost a step, but both knew that Greece's ongoing financial crisis had dramatically changed the fundraising world as she'd known it. Austerity had generosity on the wane, and frustration had replaced the "fun" in fundraising. Resuming her old work was a non-starter. She needed to find another career, one that utilized her talents and invigorated her but did not require her to sacrifice the many joyful aspects of being a mom.

Andreas wished he had an answer for her.

• ● ● ● •

Lila knew she didn't have to cook, clean, or, for that matter, do any domestic chores. She led a privileged life, in which money was

not a concern and help readily available. She did what housework
she did for herself, in order to maintain, as best she could, the
sense of self-worth she'd once held as a career woman.

Five years—almost six—had slipped by in the blink of an
eye. Now her son was off to school, and she was back to rearing
another baby. She wondered if she'd be asking herself the same
question in five more years—*Where has my life gone?*

She wanted to cry. But she had a chicken to get on the dinner
table for her son and husband, and an egg to prepare for her
daughter.

*Am I depressed? Perhaps it's postpartum depression. That wouldn't
be unheard of.*

She shook her head. She had no time for such thoughts now.
Maybe after the babies were asleep.

Except Tassaki wasn't a baby anymore.

Her mind wandered, unfocused thoughts jumping in and out.
She concentrated on putting dinner on the table. She'd get into
everything else later. With Andreas. But how could she unload
all of this on him? He had his own problems at work, and hoped
to find peace at home. She couldn't do that to him. But if not to
her husband, to whom? And why were his problems any more
significant than hers?

Yes. We'll talk later.

Lila swung out into the dining room, platters in each hand.
"Dinner is served."

Tassaki took great pride showing off his skills with knife and fork,
and Sofia ate most of her egg. In light of how things had started
out, Andreas considered dinner a major success. He thought
to compliment Lila, but decided not to raise the subject. How
well she was rearing the children touched too closely on what
troubled her. Instead, he stuck to general political and social
gossip, leaving Lila to decide when to bring up what he knew
occupied her thoughts.

When Lila got up to clear the table, Andreas motioned for her to remain seated. "No, you cooked. Tassaki and I will do this. In this Greek household, men share domestic chores with women."

Lila stared at him. "Don't you think you're pushing the point a bit hard?"

"It has to be made when the children are young."

"I'll carry my plate, Daddy."

Andreas winked at Lila. "That's my boy."

"Okay, I'll get Sofia ready for bed. Tassaki already had his bath, so just put him in his pajamas."

"And read him three stories," added Tassaki, carrying his plate toward the kitchen.

Lila struggled to suppress a smile. "Okay, mister negotiator, but only *one* story."

"Two," said Tassaki.

Andreas shrugged. "He *is* helping with the dishes."

Lila sighed through a now-irrepressible smile, "I know when I'm being tag-teamed. Okay. Two stories. But that's my final offer."

"Deal," said Tassaki, raising his right hand to high-five his father.

"Great," said Andreas. "Now let's show Mommy what we can do in the kitchen."

By the time they'd finished cleaning up, Sofia was in bed; Lila joined them for the storytelling.

Tassaki was fast asleep before Andreas had finished the second story. They crept out of his room and crossed over to the other side of the apartment, into a living room offering an unobstructed panoramic view of the brightly lit Acropolis. They sat on their favorite couch and stared quietly out the windows.

"I never tire of this view," said Andreas.

"That's because you don't see it twenty-four/seven."

Andreas patted her thigh. "I wondered when you'd get around to that subject."

She patted his thigh. "Well, wonder no longer."

Andreas drew in and let out a breath. "So, what do you want to do with the rest of your life?"

"How nice of you to put the question so succinctly." Lila leaned her head against Andreas' shoulder. "If I knew, I wouldn't be in this lousy mood."

"Then let me put it differently," Andreas said, kissing her forehead. "Something has your thinking all jammed up. What do you think it is?"

"Same answer."

"But try."

Lila fluttered breath out between her lips, and shut her eyes. "I feel as if I'm irrelevant."

"That's not so. You—"

Lila put her hand over Andreas' mouth without opening her eyes. "I don't need a cheerleader. You asked me to answer a question. So let me do it in my own way."

"Sorry."

"As I said, I'm feeling irrelevant. I see nothing I do as truly mattering, nothing to change the world or even contribute to the world. And, yes, I know one can say properly raising children accomplishes all of those things, but *only* if they grow up to matter, change, or contribute to the world. In other words, I'm kicking my responsibility for having my own meaningful life down the road to my children. I'm putting my burden on them. And that doesn't strike me as fair for any of us."

Andreas said nothing.

Lila opened her eyes. "You can speak now."

He swallowed. "Not sure that I agree, but let's assume you're correct. Are you talking about bringing about change to the world or something more personal?"

Lila paused. "I'm not vain enough to think anything I might do would ever rise to the level of achieving world peace, but I would like it to be significant to a broader swath of society than just our family. My fundraising work gave me that sort of satisfaction."

"It sounds to me that you're making progress. If I'm reading you correctly, you've ruled out any sort of commercial enterprise."

"If you mean selling art, fashion, or tequila, the answer is yes."

"I mean anything where the primary goal is making money for private profit, as opposed to making money for charitable purposes."

"Yes, I must say I'm attracted to eleemosynary causes."

"Are we having one of those, 'You say potato, I say potahto,' moments, à la Ella Fitzgerald?"

Lila offered him a blank stare. Then rolled her eyes. "Okay, I get it. 'You say charity, I say eleemosynary.'"

"Bingo."

"The title of the song happens to be, 'Let's Call the Whole Thing Off.'"

"Whoops. Not intended."

She smiled. "I know." She squeezed his hand.

He squeezed back.

"I need to get back in the world, into the swing of things and see what's out there that might interest me. Teas and charitable events are not doing it. I've got to learn firsthand what other women are doing to overcome these feelings. I can't be the first mother to feel so adrift."

"Sounds like a plan to me. But where do you intend to start?"

"In a place where I can find the kind of women I need to meet."

"In Athens?"

"No. I already know their stories, and, as inspiring as they might be to some, I want to meet new women, from different walks of life and foreign cultures. I won't find them in Athens in summertime."

Andreas shrugged. "Then where?"

"A place that draws successful types from all over the world, and where I have connections to arrange introductions." Lila bit at her lip. "The place that immediately comes to mind is Mykonos."

Andreas sat quietly for a moment. "You know, at first I thought that a silly idea, but on reflection, I think it's a damned good one. Some of the most influential people in the world come to Mykonos on holiday, and they love to go on and on, talking about their work and offering insights on subjects they'd never think of discussing with strangers back home. Come to think of it, it's a *brilliant* idea."

"There you go again, overselling."

Andreas slapped his thigh. "No, I'm not. I'm dead serious. I think it's the perfect way for you to spend the summer."

Lila's face drooped into a pout.

"What's wrong?" said Andreas.

Lila looked down. "You don't seem the least bit upset at the thought of the children and me being away on Mykonos all summer while you're alone back here in Athens."

Andreas grinned. "What makes you think I'll be alone?"

She looked up and glared at her husband. "And what's that supposed to mean?"

"Remember back before dinner when I said something serious had come up at work that would affect my ability to spend time at home?"

Lila cocked her head. "Yes."

"Well, that something is on Mykonos!"

"You mean—"

"I mean all those foreign ladies won't have you to themselves. They'll have to share you with me."

Lila wrapped her arms around Andreas' neck and kissed him. "What can I say? It must be fate."

"Whatever it is, I plan on taking advantage of it at every opportunity."

Lila stood up, pulled at Andreas' arm, dragged him off the

couch, and led him away. "And there's no better opportunity than now."

He glanced up at the Acropolis as they headed off to the bedroom. "Thank you, dear Fates."

Yianni got the last available seat on the early morning flight to Mykonos out of Venizelos Airport, but only because he used his badge and a bit of smooth-talking to finagle a supervisor into putting him into a cockpit jump seat behind the pilots. Though less than a half-hour flight, the trip between Athens and Mykonos held the dubious distinction of being the most expensive per mile route in Europe, and still the planes flew packed throughout the summer.

Approximately one and a half times the size of the island of Manhattan and ninety miles southeast of Athens, Mykonos hosted a population of ten thousand year-round citizens that swelled by fifty thousand visitors in tourist season, plus ten thousand day-trippers who came off behemoth cruise ships that treated Mykonos as the new Mecca for their Mediterranean cruises.

Getting to that point had been a long time coming. As with everything in Greece, the history of Mykonos entwined with the gods. Some said the island's name came from Apollo's grandson, Mykons. Others claimed it just meant "a pile of rocks." Whatever the source of its name, Mykonos' habitation dated back more than six thousand years, virtually all of that time spent as one of the poorest islands in Greece.

Against those millennia of struggle, it seemed impossible that in little more than a single generation the island had achieved worldwide renown as a twenty-four/seven summer playground for international celebrities and the super-rich, drawing in hordes of everyday folk wishing to be in on the glitz of it all and transforming long-impoverished Mykonians into among the wealthiest per capita people in Greece.

But it came at a price. Much of their traditional agrarian and seafaring ways had been sacrificed to cater to the whims, desires, and fantasies of holidaymakers who flocked to their island from around the globe.

Its dozens of breathtaking beaches now boasted world-class clubs and restaurants, many designed to keep sun worshipers and partiers onsite and consuming from morning until well beyond the witching hour. Mykonos and Santorini were practically the only places in Greece untouched by the financial crisis, and everyone in Greece wanted to get in on the action. Good guys and bad.

Yianni hadn't been back to Mykonos in over a year and wondered how much the island had changed. He had no doubt that it had. Locals who'd run traditional businesses out of buildings in town that had been in their families for generations now realized they'd make far more by turning their shops into bars, or renting their spaces to national and international fashion brands, receiving huge under-the-table sweetener payments to do so. Outside of town, farmers found themselves making more from the sale of a parcel of land than they could ever hope to make in a lifetime of farming that same soil.

Yianni stared out the cockpit window at the horizon, where a bright blue sky met a deep blue sea filled with white-edged waves and beige-brown islands flecked with green and white.

At least some things hadn't changed.

Yianni was first off the plane and, with only a carry-on, he was out of the terminal in two minutes. It took another three minutes to cover the hundred meters from the airport to the police station. Police procedures required him to check in with the local police chief.

How much he chose to tell him was another story.

● ● ● ● ●

The police chief turned out to be a decent guy, but that alone wasn't a good enough reason for trusting him. He hadn't displayed the curiosity Yianni expected when Yianni told him that he'd be nosing around the chief's turf on official business. The chief's non-reaction might have reflected polite deference to Yianni's Special Crimes Unit status, or an indifference worn into him by the impossibly frustrating task of trying to maintain order and safeguard the lives and property of so many tourists and locals on an out-of-control party island with fewer than fifty cops available to him for the summer.

Then there was a third possibility: the chief already knew why Yianni was there. Despotiko was nothing if not efficient, and he'd probably informed the chief in advance that cops from Athens would be asking questions about his wife.

Even if Despotiko had beaten him to the police chief's door, Yianni's instincts told him not to ask the man about Mrs. Despotiko. He'd speak to her first. No reason to risk having word reach her about what was on his mind before he had the chance to confront her face-to-face. He knew he'd made the right decision when, out of the blue, he asked the chief for directions to the Despotiko home, and without hesitation or the slightest sign of interest in Yianni's reason for asking, he recited precise, detailed driving directions.

Given the chief's advance preparation, Yianni wondered what he could expect from Mrs. Despotiko. The only way to find out was to ask her, so he borrowed a marked police car and drove in the direction of the Despotiko home.

He didn't bother to call ahead; he assumed the chief would do that for him.

Chapter Four

According to the chief, Despotiko's home lay at the north end of the island, tucked away at the top of a hill overlooking the sea close by a nineteenth-century lighthouse. Once considered undesirable because of its distance from town and lack of ready access to the island's more popular beaches, the sunset side of that hill had experienced a surge in popularity among home-builders who considered those conditions positives. So much, in fact, that the once-neglected area now stood as an enclave for the rich and reclusive.

Yianni turned right out of the police station, headed west toward the rotary at the outer ring road. Also known as the new road, it connected at the sea, both north and south of the old town, with an older inner road marking much of the island's western shoreline, plus the land-based perimeter of the island's old port area. The chief's directions had him heading north along the new road, a major two-lane highway lined with mini-strip malls, gas stations, and squat, one-story stucco homes thrown up to take advantage of the tourist boom.

Traffic seemed exponentially greater than when he'd been here last. The island's vehicle-rental businesses had proven as explo-sively profitable as its hotel, bar, and restaurant operations. Every entrepreneur in Greece, as well as every speculator from abroad, seemed to be getting in on the action. With only thirty taxis on an island of more than sixty thousand daily visitors, municipal buses offering only limited service, and walking or bicycling ranking among the riskiest of extreme sports, the only sane way to get around the island was by renting a motorized vehicle.

Some hotels and beachside clubs offered private bus services to clients, but it was the plethora of private limos and vehicle rentals that clogged the island's arteries. They existed to serve those who stayed in places off the transportation grid, or who desired an independent way to get around on holiday, often renting more than one vehicle per family. Compounding the number of vehicles was their size. VIP vans and large SUVs served as a sign of affluence to many, yet on roads too narrow to allow one to pass the other, they were more of a badge of foolishness.

Yianni turned right at the shore road and continued north, through Tourlos, Agios Stefanos, and Houlakia. Between the old and new ports, hotels lined all but a small portion of the hillside sections of the shore. A half-mile beyond the new port, hotels and tavernas stood grouped around a small beach, but for the most part, from the new port north to the lighthouse, visitors experienced a slower-paced version of the island.

He had no trouble picking out the Despotiko home. Much larger than any of the other whitewashed structures on that west-facing hillside, its stone, bougainvillea-draped, and polished wood veranda encompassed an infinity pool running the full length of the residence. Its sumptuousness was unmistakable, set against the otherwise stark desert landscape.

He'd seen it as soon as he reached the crest of the hill leading down to the private road that would take him up to the Despotiko home. Like many private roads on the island, this one's construction showed little consideration for physics; it looked more like an experiment for determining how steeply a rough concrete road must be angled to overcome a tire's coefficient of friction.

Yianni noticed someone moving in the pool area and slowed down to make sure whoever was up there realized his blue-and-white cruiser was headed their way. No need to unnecessarily heighten tensions by arriving unannounced at the woman's front door, just in case the police chief hadn't warned her of his imminent arrival. He drove slowly up the hill to a driveway, parked in front of a sliding gate made of horizontal wooden slats painted the same deep blue as the rest of the home's wood trim, and sat in the car.

From where he sat he couldn't see over the walls but he assumed whoever was inside knew he was there. He waited three minutes before getting out of the car. He walked over to the gate, and pressed a buzzer while facing a camera.

"Yes?"

"Hi, it's Detective Yianni Kouros here to see Mrs. Despotiko."

"Is she expecting you?"

"I guess you'll have to ask her that."

"What's it about?"

"Highly confidential."

"Sorry, I can't let you in."

"Just tell Mrs. Despotiko her husband sent me."

A minute later the gate slowly slid open. A short, trim, olive-skinned woman of indeterminate age dressed in a pale blue maid's uniform stood in the way, sizing him up. She could have been a sister to the maid at the Despotiko home in Athens.

"Mrs. Despotiko said to show you to the pool."

As soon as Yianni stepped through the open gate, the maid pressed a remote in her hand, sending the gate back the other way. She stood waiting until it closed before saying, "Follow me, please."

She led him along a gray flagstone path embraced by bougainvillea and geraniums, toward a set of steps leading to the pool. She pointed up the steps. "Mrs. Despotiko will see you there." With that, she turned away and disappeared into the main house.

I guess I'm on my own, thought Yianni. He turned and faced the steps, wondering who was about to surprise whom.

Yianni steadily mounted the steps leading to the pool area. At the top, he paused to take in the view. A massive deck area, made of the same non-slip composite material used by luxury yacht-builders to simulate wooden planking in their high-end creations, surrounded a blue-lined pool spanning the west-facing side of the house. From where he stood, the crystal blue hue of the water almost perfectly matched the sapphire sea, into which the pool seemed to vanish.

Almost perfectly, he thought. He'd read somewhere that the ancient Greeks didn't speak of the sea in terms of tint, because sunlight so often changed the hue, but instead thought of it in terms of brightness and movement. To them a "winey" sea did not portray a color but the shine and glimmer of wine inside a cup. Still, he would've been willing to bet that even the most demanding of ancient Greeks would agree this was a pretty impressive, if not almost perfect, interpretation of reality.

He wondered if the same could be said of the tall, slim, bikini-clad blonde lying on a chaise lounge ten meters away from where he stood. She lay facing Yianni behind a pair of Jackie O-style sunglasses, close by a portable bar with a magnum of champagne in a silver ice bucket, a plate of whole strawberries, and a single champagne flute. He guessed her to be in her late thirties, but she clearly worked hard at appearing a dozen years younger. She held a second champagne glass in her right hand, and with her left, beckoned to him.

"It's perfectly all right to come over, Detective. I promise you I won't bite."

Yianni walked toward her, stopping just shy of the lounge. "Mrs. Despotiko, I presume."

She waved at him with her glass, spilling a bit of the champagne as she did. "You're blocking my sun."

"Sorry," said Yianni, moving.

"That's okay, there's plenty more champagne. *Alma!*" she yelled.

"I was talking about the sun."

She didn't reply but concentrated on the maid hurrying out of the house and onto the deck.

"Yes, ma'am?"

She wiggled her glass. "More champagne."

She watched the maid lift the champagne bottle with two hands, and carefully aim for the woman's wavering glass. "And pour a glass for, Detective...uh, what's your name?"

Yianni smiled. "Kouros. Detective Yianni Kouros."

"Yeah, for Detective Kouros."

The department's official guidelines told him to decline, to keep everything strictly professional, but his instincts told him otherwise. She seemed relaxed and, even if this routine was put on for his benefit, playing along with her, getting her to think she was in charge, might give him a shot at getting around what her husband and his minions had undoubtedly warned her: be extremely careful what you say to police.

The maid filled the lone glass on the cart.

"Don't forget the strawberry," snapped her employer.

"Yes, ma'am," and, using silver tongs, dropped a single strawberry into the glass before handing it to Yianni.

"Thank you," he said, nodding to the maid. She said nothing, and hurried back into the house.

Mrs. Despotiko patted the space on the lounge next to her waist. "Sit here."

Yianni hesitated and glanced toward the house.

"Don't worry, no one's filming this."

"It seems inappropriate."

"Damn it, man, we're on Mykonos. I'm just asking you to sit down, not to fuck me."

Yianni wasn't sure what the official guidelines said about this situation, but having gone this far, continuing along seemed the sensible choice, and so he sat on the lounge, but by her feet, not her waist.

As soon as he did, he realized he'd made a huge tactical blunder. He should have sat by her waist as she'd suggested, because from where he now sat, in order to see her face, he had to stare straight up between her legs and over the tiniest string bikini bottom he'd ever seen.

He tried sliding forward on the lounge, but she moved her foot to block him, spreading her legs as she did.

Checkmate, thought Yianni.

All smiles, she said, "So, what can I do for you, Detective Kouros?"

Yianni waggled his eyebrows. "That's now a far more difficult question to answer than it was a moment ago." He raised his glass. "*Salut.*"

She raised hers. "Just start in and let's see where it leads." She sipped her drink.

Yianni took a tiny sip. "I have the sense you've been down this road before."

"What road is that?"

"Answering questions from police about your husband."

She shrugged. "It comes with the territory. But being married to a man who has nothing to hide makes it easy."

Yianni glanced at her bikini bottom. "Speaking of nothing to hide, do you mind if I move up a little closer to you on this lounge?"

She lifted her foot and closed her legs. "Suit yourself."

"Thank you," said Yianni, moving up to beside her waist. "I'm sure you know why I'm here."

She sipped from her glass. "The police colonel who was murdered in that restaurant outside of Athens."

Yianni nodded. "Can you tell me how you met the restaurant owner your husband suggested meet with the Colonel?"

"I assume you mean Pepe?"

"Yes."

"At Easter, I was having lunch at The Beach Club with some girlfriends. Some guy I didn't know was acting like a big shot, talking up the owner and his son, tossing money around. It was Pepe. None of my friends knew who he was, so I asked our waiter if he knew him. He said he was a longtime friend of the owner who planned on opening his own place on Mykonos later this summer or next."

"So, you introduced yourself to him?"

She peered over the top of her sunglasses. "It is not my style to introduce myself to strange men. I was just curious. After all, The Beach Club is the hottest place on the island, and if a friend of the owner planned on opening another place, that new one might be the next hot spot. There's no harm in having connections."

"Agreed," said Yianni. "So how did you meet Pepe?"

"The waiter told Pepe I'd asked about him, so he came over and introduced himself."

"Did he know who you were when he came over?"

She glared at him over her glasses. "Are you suggesting he knew I was *Mrs. Despotiko* when he came over to meet me?"

Yianni blinked. "Excuse me, did I say something wrong?"

She raised her voice. "Do you think men are only interested in me because of whom I'm married to?" She waved at her body with her free hand. "They're still attracted to this." She gulped down her drink. "*Alma!* I need more."

Yianni jumped up and went for the bottle.

"My maid will take care of me."

"No need to bother her. I can handle this." He filled her glass using one hand, and waved the maid back into the house with his other.

Mrs. Despotiko bit at her lip as he poured.

"Would you like a strawberry?"

"No."

He returned to his place on the lounge, placing the champagne bottle at his feet.

"Okay, let's start over again." He leaned in toward her and whispered in her ear. "But trust me, *you're definitely hot*." He sat up and held out his glass. She clinked on his with hers.

"So, did Pepe know who you were when he introduced himself to you?"

"If you promise not to tell my husband, I'll tell you the truth."

Yianni wasn't sure where this was headed. "Not tell him what?"

"About me and that man, Pepe."

Yianni paused.

She stared at him, and laughed. "Oh, my. That didn't come out right. Not even the thought of an affair with that man crossed my mind. He was terribly unattractive." She paused. "Not anything like you."

Yianni forced a grin and patted her elbow.

She sighed. "I told my husband that *I'd* raised the subject of Pepe needing security if he wanted to open a club on Mykonos, and that until I had, he'd had no idea who I was married to." She took a sip. "I wanted to make my husband jealous. I wanted to make him think men were still interested in me, not just using me to get to him." She gulped down the rest of her glass and held it out for more. Yianni reached for the bottle at his feet and refilled her glass.

"Are you saying he knew who you were when he introduced himself to you?"

"I'm sure he did. It's my curse."

"How can you be sure?"

"He said his friend from The Beach Club had just told him he'd need serious security if he planned to open a club on Mykonos, and that the best person to ask for a recommendation was my husband." She took another slug.

Yianni waited until she'd finished drinking. "So, the owner of The Beach Club suggested to his friend, Pepe, that he introduce himself to you in order to get you to ask your husband for a recommendation on which security service to use for his new club?"

"Yes."

"And what happened when you told your husband that The

Beach Club owner was behind Pepe's request for a recommendation?"

She shook her head. "You're not listening. I never told my husband about any of that. I told my husband that a man I'd met at lunch said he was opening a club on the island, and *I* suggested he needed security. When he asked me for a recommendation, I said I'd ask my husband." She drew in and let out a deep breath. "My husband thinks I'm not capable of thinking for myself. I wanted to show him that I could, and that some people—like Pepe—valued my advice."

"When did you ask your husband for a recommendation?"

"That same day."

"He recommended the Colonel?"

"Yes."

"And when did you give the name to Pepe?"

"I didn't."

"What do you mean you didn't?"

"I'd lost his business card."

"Then you never told Pepe about the Colonel?"

"Not directly. A couple days later I was back at The Beach Club and saw the owner's son. I told him to tell his father to pass along to Pepe that my husband recommended he use the Colonel as security for his new business. Whether he or his father did that, I do not know."

She downed her drink, stood up, and stepped toward the edge of the pool. "That's all I know about the Colonel, and I've never spoken to Pepe or anyone else about any of this since passing along that message. Now, if you'll excuse me, I'm terribly hot and must take a swim. Fair warning. I don't want to ruin my suit by wearing it in the water, so if your sensibilities will be offended by seeing me *au naturale*, I suggest you leave now."

Yianni stood up. "Thanks for the heads-up. I better leave and if I have—" Before he'd finished she'd dropped her top and bottom and dived into the pool. "...any more questions I'll get back...." His voice trailed off as he watched her glide effortlessly through the water away from him. He turned and headed in the direction of the steps.

My first day back on the Rock and already a naked interview. Yianni shook his head. *Lord knows what's coming next.*

• • ● • •

Andreas sat in his office, patiently listening to Yianni describe his just-completed interview with Mrs. Despotiko.

"Sounds like you had an interesting morning."

"That's one way to put it."

"Now why don't you tell me what really happened?"

"We ripped off each other's clothes and went at it like rabbits."

"That's better."

"In truth, I think I'm gonna need a few more days to get back in the Mykonos swing of things. I'm still figuring out what it means to be a cop there in this day and age."

"Meaning?"

"The local chief seems a likable enough guy, but he's the head cop in a bordello run by police. My guess is that he and his crew don't bust people for doing what their jurisdiction's establishments advertise as freely available. He also likely keeps its most influential citizens in the loop."

"That sounds like Telly."

"Telly?"

"That's the local chief's nickname, based on his resemblance to Telly Savalas, a Greek-American actor who played the title role of Kojak in an American television cop show popular long before you were born."

"You know him?"

"Yeah. He knows how to go along to get along."

"Are you saying he's dirty?"

"I'm saying he's like many of our brethren who struggle to find a way to make it through to their pensions in treacherous times. I'm not excusing him, just saying it like it is. And on that fine point, permit me to mention that I doubt the police run this particular bordello. It's under new management."

"Why do you say that?" asked Yianni.

"Do you remember what happened to the island's last chief of the Harbor Police?"

"Sure, he lost his job when one of his lieutenants was caught mixed up in narcotics trafficking."

"Correct. Yet everyone on the island knew the ex-chief was cracking down hard on drug dealers, and the big traffickers were desperate to get rid of him. That's when someone in the know came up with a simple plan to game the system and get rid of the chief, without having to raise a finger directly against him."

"I don't follow. His lieutenant was dirty, caught dealing red-handed."

"That was the beauty of their plan. It even won the public relations battle. They found the weakest link in the chief's command, compromised him, then set him up to be caught in a buy orchestrated by national drug enforcement cops. There was absolutely no evidence tying the chief to his lieutenant's drug trafficking, but ministry rules were firm. If one of your lieutenants is caught up in that sort of thing, you go down with him. Period, end of story."

"Damn."

"That little intrigue also had the effect of sending an unequivocal message to his successors: play ball or we'll find a way to cost you your position, too."

"How do you want me to handle him?"

"To be fair, Telly's likely up to his eyeballs battling organized watch-snatchers, break-in artists, pimps, prostitutes, and private-security types thinking they can run the island any way their clients want, but murder crosses a line I can't believe he'd tolerate if it's somehow tied into his jurisdiction. Especially where a high-ranking ex-cop was the victim."

"I repeat. How do you want me to play it with him?"

"Tell him only what he already knows."

"Would you mind putting that in Greek?"

"Don't tell him the owner of The Beach Club suggested to Pepe that he persuade Mrs. Despotiko to ask her husband for a security recommendation. If she was telling you the truth, you and I are the only ones who know that little detail. I don't want Telly passing that snippet on to Despotiko and getting Despotiko thinking that the owner tried setting him up."

"So, you agree it makes no sense for the owner to have put Pepe through the exercise of getting a name from Despotiko, when the owner already knew he'd name the Colonel?"

"For sure. Let's not forget who owns The Beach Club. It's Angelos Karavakis, the most powerful club-owner on the island. He's not in Despotiko's league, but he's still part of that virtually untouchable class of Greek underworld criminals the press likes to call 'the world of the night.' Everyone knows what they're into, but no one dares stop them. Karavakis is big into prostitution and for sure has a hand in drug trafficking and money laundering, if only as part of his club business. There's no question he knew the Colonel was the only security game in town."

"Do you think Karavakis was involved in the assassination?"

"At this point, anything is possible. But since the only bad guy with a solid presence on the island who's tougher than Karavakis is Despotiko, let's not take the chance of doing something that might get them fighting each other."

"Yeah, an island gang war in the middle of tourist season would likely wreck your summer plans with Lila and the kids."

"How'd you know about that?"

"Keen investigative instincts." Yianni paused. "You asked Maggie to set up your computer to work remotely from outside the office, and she asked me to meet with the technician who'd be doing the work at Lila's parents' house."

"Lila just called to tell me she'll be there Friday. I'm going to try to make it over with them."

"I doubt I'll be done by then."

"Don't worry, there's plenty of room." Andreas coughed. "Besides, babysitters with your qualifications are hard to find on the island this time of year."

"I'd rather be spending my time with Tassaki and Sofia than chasing down the parade of assholes involved in this murder."

"Any idea who those assholes might be?"

"Nope," said Yianni. "It just doesn't make sense that a major player like Karavakis would attempt to implicate Despotiko in the murder of an ex-cop colonel in such an amateurish fashion. He left a trail leading straight back to him that a blind man could follow. Only Despotiko's wife's vanity kept her from telling her husband that Karavakis was the one who set everything in motion. If she'd told him, it might have already triggered a war between them, one Karavakis was certain to lose. And there was no way Karavakis could have anticipated that she wouldn't tell her husband."

"All good points. And all in need of answers."

"Why do I sense you're about to ruin my plans to spend the rest of my day working on my tan?"

"As a matter of fact, Detective, suntanning is precisely what I was going to suggest."

"Please, drop the other shoe already. The suspense is killing me."

"Why don't you stop by Karavakis' Beach Club and see what he has to say about all of this?"

"Terrific."

"Interview him in a matter-of-fact way. But be delicate. Nothing serious or accusative, and certainly nothing to get him thinking he might have been set up to look like the one who tied Despotiko into the hit on the Colonel. Just make it seem as if you're following up on his introducing Pepe to Mrs. Despotiko and see where it leads."

"With any luck, to some serious beach time for me."

"Just be careful not to get burned."

Chapter Five

Yianni had been raised in Athens, amid its own form of driving insanity, but here on Mykonos virtual reality met bumper cars, and he never dared take his eyes off what was coming down the road. Afternoons in high season were a particularly treacherous time on the narrow mountainside roads winding down to the popular beaches. He often wondered why it seemed the more popular the beach, the narrower the road and the sheerer the drops.

Yianni was used to maneuvering the island's potholed, uneven roads, but tourist season added a serious additional challenge to the Mykonos driving experience. Now you had to share the roads with drivers who'd never imagine in their wildest dreams behaving at home as they did here, regularly passing around blind curves, turning two-lane roads into one-way whenever it suited their direction, and treating stop signs and rotary rules as advisory only. Toss in drugs and alcohol—and officials who considered it bad business to destroy a vacationer's blissful fantasy of invulnerability with reality—and you had summertime driving on Mykonos.

During Yianni's ski-jump-like final descent toward The Beach Club, a crew of post-adolescents, too busy hanging every which way out of an oncoming Jeep Wrangler and shouting the island's name in sing-song fashion to notice his marked police car, wandered into his lane. Thankfully, he saw them coming and made way for the party crew to pass.

At the bottom of the slope, he steered into a packed, football field-size parking lot. He pulled up to the main entrance and parked next to a row of palm trees directly in front of a large NO PARKING sign. The place had changed a lot from what he remembered of his off-duty, rookie-cop days bouncing from one beach party venue to the next. Then, too, so had his age, compared to that of the new round of youthful partiers discovering the island for themselves.

The palms hadn't been there when Yianni was here last, but that was a few years back, and palm trees now were in fashion. So, too, were the high stacks of empty champagne bottles arranged pyramid-style around the bases of the trees bordering the entrance to the club. Most visitors took them as a sign of the *abbondanza* partying atmosphere awaiting them inside, but Yianni saw it as a cleverly improvised hide-in-plain-sight, bottle warehouse for champagne-counterfeiters.

Yianni headed for the entrance. Two of the club's bouncers stood waiting for him.

The bigger one said, "Can I help you?"

"Yeah, I'm here to see Angelos Karavakis."

"Is he expecting you?"

"No."

"Well, could you possibly move your car away from the entrance? It'll spook the customers. They'll think it's a raid or something."

Yianni gave him his best I'm-in-charge look. "Are you suggesting there are illegal activities taking place in this establishment?"

The bouncer raised his heavily tattooed arms. "No, not at all. Cops just make people nervous."

Yianni smiled, and patted the man's shoulder. "I know. And we like keeping it that way. Where's Karavakis?"

The bouncer stepped out of Yianni's way. "In the office, through the door in the light-gray wall out behind the bar."

Instead of heading directly into the club, Yianni circled around to the beachside entrance. Standing with his back to the sea, he had a panoramic, dollhouse view of everything going on inside the club. Well, *almost* everything.

He had to give credit to the entrepreneur owners behind clubs like this one. They knew how to create and sell the magic of the island to their audiences. It was more than simply the laser lights, deejays, nearly naked perfect bodies writhing all about you, and unrestricted booze and drugs...it was the irrepressible Greek ambience of the island.

Yeah, right. Yianni shook his head at the thought. Most of the kids in here probably couldn't find Mykonos on a map. Some likely didn't even know it was in Greece.

As he looked in, he couldn't help but feel like any other anonymous beach-going tourist fascinated by the wild-eyed action and actors at play inside the club. It wasn't yet packed but still crowded, noisy, and pumping. The deejay in his booth above the bar knew when to kick things into maximum party mode. With a three-hundred-sixty-degree view of the action in the club, and a panoramic view of what was happening on the beach, he was a master at managing the mob's mood through his music.

As Yianni took in the scantily clad sun worshippers wedged in along rows of sturdy wooden sunbeds and macramé umbrellas, he realized that—in his dark trousers, pale blue dress shirt and black street shoes—he stood out like what he was: a cop at a bikini contest.

Yianni pressed his way toward the bar through a mix of barely clothed dancers lost in the beat of the music. He made it to the door in the gray wall and knocked.

"It's open," came a shout from inside.

Yianni opened the door and walked in, closing it behind him.

"Who are you?" said the man sitting behind a tiny desk in an equally tiny office. All Yianni could think of was barrels. Barrel head, barrel neck, barrel chest, and barrel belly, topped off in unnaturally barrel-tar black hair.

"Detective Yianni Kouros, GADA Special Crimes." Yianni showed him his ID.

Yianni pointed at the wooden *taverna* chair in front of the desk. It looked purposely uncomfortable. "May I sit?"

"Of course." Karavakis leaned back in a plush leather armchair and waited for Yianni to speak.

"I'm here in connection with the investigation into the murder of Colonel Aktipis."

"A terrible tragedy."

"To get right to the point, sir, I understand you knew the man who was with the Colonel the night he was killed."

"Yes, Pepe. I've known him since we did our military service together, and later through the restaurant business. He's always wanted to open a place on Mykonos."

"Just like everyone else in Greece these days."

Karavakis smirked. "That's for sure."

"So, why help the competition?"

"You've got to understand the business. No workable space on this island remains vacant. Someone will move in and try to compete with you. So, if you're going to have competition, it's better to be up against someone you know and who knows you. Someone you can work with on common problems."

"Makes sense to me." Yianni paused. "I understand he asked you for a recommendation on security for his new place."

"Not exactly. I asked him how he planned to handle security and he told me he intended using his own people. I told him that wouldn't work here."

"Why did you say that?"

"Come on, Detective, don't play naive with me. We both know how big the protection business is on this island. No way to avoid it. It's pay or pray."

"Did you tell him that?"

"That and more."

"What more?"

Karavakis leaned across the desk. "I don't mean to speak ill of the dead, Detective, but I said, 'If you don't use the Colonel's goons, you're going to find your place shut down, burned down, or blown down.' And that's if you're lucky. The Colonel's attitude toward practically anyone doing any business on this island was, 'If you breathe, you pay.'"

"What did Pepe say to that?"

"He didn't believe me."

"You expressly told him to use the Colonel?"

"Of course I did. Even the dumbest souvlaki-seller on the island knew that."

"Why, then, did you suggest that Pepe speak to Mrs. Despotiko to get a recommendation from her husband?"

Karavakis shook his head and smiled. "Like I said, Pepe didn't believe me. He probably thought I was getting a kickback on business I steered to the Colonel. If I hadn't known Pepe for as long I did, I'd have told him to go fuck himself." He shook his head again. "Anyway, Despotiko's wife was at the next table, and when she asked my waiter who Pepe was, I saw a way to verify what I'd told him."

"Pepe knew of Despotiko?"

"Please. Who doesn't? Anyway, I told him, if he didn't believe me to ask Despotiko's wife for a recommendation from her husband. He did, and what happened after had nothing to do with me."

"Are you saying Mrs. Despotiko told Pepe that her husband recommended the Colonel?"

"No. A few days later Mrs. Despotiko was in the club and asked my son to tell me that Despotiko had recommended Pepe use the Colonel, just as I said he would. So, I passed the message on to Pepe."

"I assume he now trusted you to be telling him the truth?"

Karavakis seemed about to bristle, but didn't. "I guess so." He leaned forward in his chair. "To repeat, I had absolutely nothing to do with anything that went down after that."

"Do you have any idea of anyone who might have been involved in the Colonel's death?"

"Not a clue."

Yianni stood up and extended his hand across the desk toward Karavakis. "Thank you very much for your time, Mr. Karavakis."

Karavakis reached out to shake Yianni's hand but did not get up from his chair. "Glad to be of assistance."

Yianni turned toward the door.

"Detective."

Yianni looked back over his shoulder. "Yes?"

"Be careful around Despotiko's wife. She's a real tiger, and whether or not she shows you her claws…" he paused, as if considering whether to go on, "…while showing you everything else, those claws are always there and at the ready."

"Thanks for the advice."

He left the office, and pressed through the dancing throng toward the parking-lot exit, wondering how much of their conversation Karavakis had recorded. After all, performances like that were meant to be preserved.

"You didn't believe him?" said Andreas, tapping away on his desktop with a pencil in his right hand while holding his phone to his ear with his left.

Yianni sat in the police cruiser, engine and air conditioner running, at the far end of The Beach Club's parking lot. "Let's just say he was cagey. He tried to get me to bite on whether I'd interviewed Mrs. Despotiko."

"How would he know?"

"She or your buddy Telly could have told him."

"He might have assumed that since you were interviewing him you'd be interviewing her."

"Or some combination thereof. He's so used to lying to police, it's second nature to him not to cooperate. My guess is he wanted to tell us only what he thought we already knew."

Funny how cops and crooks so often think the same way, thought Andreas.

"So, where do I go from here, Chief?"

Andreas stared out the window at his building's reflection in the windows of the neighboring building. "Not sure, but tomorrow's Friday, and with any luck I'll make it to Mykonos with Lila and the kids on the afternoon ferry."

"Does that mean I'm on my own until then?"

Andreas smiled. "Try not to get into trouble."

"I'll remember that if I happen to run into any."

"You're not so bad at the cagey routine yourself."

"On that note, I think I'll say goodbye."

"See you tomorrow."

"Bye."

Andreas hung up the phone, but kept tapping away on the desktop with his pencil.

It was never the big things that tripped up a perp; the little details tended to be their undoing. Trouble was, they were often so small that even cops missed them. *Like now.*

Instead of backtracking the way he'd come to the beach, Yianni took a narrow, roughly paved road twisting up through the rural heart of the island. He planned to make his way to Lila's family's home through the farming community of Ano Mera, the island's only other town, five miles due east of the far-better-known harbor town that bore the island's name.

With roots tracing back to 4500 BCE, Ano Mera had a proud history, but like so many other island places, the tourist boom had decidedly changed the agrarian world of its residents. Though the road still offered breathtaking switchback views of deep-green farmland edged in hillsides strewn with massive gray-beige boulders, rapidly encroaching patches of new construction had infected the scene.

At the crest of a hill, the road narrowed to wind between old homes and businesses massed at the outskirts of the old town. A bit farther along, it passed by the village square to meet up with the main highway connecting Ano Mera and Mykonos town.

From there, it took Yianni fifteen minutes to drive to Lila's, most of it over one-time donkey trails with a hill on one side and a cliff on the other. As his police cruiser rocked and rolled along the washboard road, he wondered if Lila's family purposely kept it that way to discourage the curious from impinging on their privacy. Whether intentional or not, it must have worked, because he'd yet to see another soul on the road. As he reached the top of a particularly steep stretch of road, a panoramic view of a virtually unspoiled part of the island's north-central coast spread out before him. Below, at the very tip of a peninsula, sat his destination, a natural stone and stucco compound of gardens and broad terraces nestled up against the sea, with not a neighbor to be seen.

He wondered how long that would last.

Yianni stopped the cruiser, rolled down the windows, turned off the engine, and sat listening to the sound of the wind off the sea whipping up scents of wild rosemary and thyme over and around ancient stone walls lumbering up and across the rocky hillsides. This was a rare and peaceful moment, in a rare and peaceful place far removed from the craziness of the club he'd just left—and the life he led as a cop. He wondered if Andreas had similar thoughts when he came here. He must. How could he not?

Yianni started the engine. Enough daydreaming. Time to get back to reality. At least *his* reality.

Chapter Six

A maid showed Yianni to a guest room twice the size of his bedroom at home. It faced due east, overlooking a mat of pink and green oleander running down to the sea. He liked it here. But this was Mykonos, and with Andreas arriving tomorrow, this might be his last free night to enjoy the town. He took a quick nap, showered, shaved, changed, and left, hoping to catch the sunset at the bay in Little Venice, where six centuries-old windmills symbolized Mykonos itself.

He stopped by the police station to drop off the cruiser and asked a sergeant if he could borrow a motorcycle, a far more practical way to get around in traffic—and a much less intimidating way to offer a ride home to a newfound friend than in a police car. The sergeant handed him the keys to an impounded BMW motorbike, saying that its owner was locked up on Syros on drug charges and wasn't expected to need it any time soon.

Yianni turned right from the station onto the road connecting the airport to town. In five minutes, he'd weaved his way down through heavily backed-up traffic at its rotary with the new road, to a dead stop at its jammed intersection with the old road just before the bus station. In high season, and with a cop nowhere to be found, this was the most hectic intersection on the island, if not in all the Cyclades, but to get to the windmills' parking area you had to pass through the congestion.

Yianni abandoned his plan for parking by the windmills and squeezed his motorcycle into a sharp left turn, heading downhill toward the sandy cove of Megali Ammos. Eighty meters beyond the intersection, he turned right at a narrow lane and stopped by a large green trash container. He smiled. At least one thing hadn't changed in the years he'd been away. The secret parking space he'd discovered as a rookie cop still existed. He carefully worked the motorcycle up onto a rock ledge concealed between the container and a stucco wall separating the lane from the back of a hotel.

He stood for a moment to take in the view of Megali Ammos. He held many fond memories of that waning crescent moon beach, with its bamboo-capped, white stone shack of a taverna wedged onto the beach at its near end. He wondered if it was still as he remembered. For sure its view of the sea and sunset hadn't changed, each evening offering the romantically inclined shimmering combinations of gun-metal blue, silver, and gold against a backdrop of vermilion skies and shadowy, distant islands.

But he wasn't in the mood to be sitting alone watching a sunset. He wanted to be in the middle of the action. By now, every bar and taverna with a seaward view to the west would be packed with tourists. So, that's where he'd go, west along the one-time donkey path where he'd parked, toward the windmills and Little Venice. The path ran beside a ten-meter drop down to a rocky ribbon of sand bordering the sea. On the other side of the path sat the rear walls of a line of older hotels built back in the day when shielding guests from the fierce winds regularly whipping in off the sea seemed more important than offering a sea-view entrance.

The path meandered in the direction of a tiny, red-roofed white church atop a craggy promontory and a ridgeline dotted with windmills. He'd have no glimpse of the setting sun until he reached the church, but he still had plenty of time to make it there.

With practically everyone else already in place for the sunset, he had the path to himself, except for someone walking in the same direction a hundred meters ahead. From behind, he couldn't make out if the person was male or female, but whoever it was wore short blond hair, a white tee-shirt, and jeans.

Yianni smiled at the welcome moment of serenity before the coming night's likely disorienting madness. He heard only himself and the sound of water lapping up against the shore below.

That's when he heard the scream—a quick, muffled one, but undoubtedly a scream—coming from below.

He saw the person ahead of him run to the edge of the cliff and look down. Yianni did the same, expecting to see someone struggling against the sea. He saw no one in the water, but off to his right, on a bit of beach up by the entrance to a tiny cove near the church, he saw a man standing with his back to the sea.

"Hey, who's screaming?" he heard a woman shout in English. It was the stranger up ahead.

The man ignored her.

"*Malaka*," she yelled louder. "Who's screaming?" she yelled in Greek.

The man below darted a quick look up at her and then looked back into the cove. He said nothing.

The woman ran farther ahead to a place where she could see down into the cove. Yianni broke into a run to catch up with her.

"*Get the fuck away from her, asshole!*" the woman yelled in Greek, and then again in English.

Yianni ran faster. As he did, the woman began picking up rocks and whipping them over the ledge at the man down by the entrance to the cove. By the time Yianni reached the woman, her rock-tossing had sent the man running off along the shore away from the church.

Yianni looked over the edge into the cove. A second man wrestled with a woman on a beach towel, one hand gripped over her month, the other tearing at what remained of her bikini.

The quickest way down was to jump, but that would break a leg for sure. And he couldn't dare risk using his gun and hitting the victim. So, he yelled. "Stop! Police!"

The man looked up as the woman standing next to Yianni launched another rock, scoring a perfect bull's-eye on the attacker's forehead. His hands fell free of his victim, who screamed as she rolled away, jumped to her feet, and ran along the beach toward a set of rough-hewn stone steps leading up to the church.

The attacker didn't move. Yianni thought the rock might have killed him. Self-defense was a tricky subject in Greece. Especially in defense of a stranger. Even more so when you're a foreigner. He did not like the way this was shaping up. He'd have to arrest the Good Samaritan on a murder charge for doing the right thing. He needed to catch up with that victim to corroborate the rock-thrower's story.

But as Yianni was about to give chase, the attacker clawed to his feet. He fixed his eyes on the woman who'd thrown the rock. From his glare, Yianni didn't have to wonder what he had in mind for her. She responded with a new barrage of rocks aimed at the man's head. He ducked and ran away in the same direction as his accomplice.

"Lady, don't move from here. I'll be right back." Yianni raced off running parallel to the fleeing attacker. He knew where the man was headed. The only path up from the shoreline lay near where Yianni had parked his motorcycle. If the attacker made it there, he'd hit the main road and disappear into the crowds.

Yianni caught up with the man just as he staggered up onto the path from the shore.

"Stop right there," said Yianni.

The man froze, blood running down his face from a gash on his forehead. His eyes darted up the path toward the main road. He stood a bit taller and younger than Yianni, but lanky.

"Don't even think about it," said Yianni.

The man pulled a switchblade out of his pocket.

Yianni pulled a compact nine-millimeter pistol from a holster hidden inside the front of his pants. "You've got a knife, I've got a gun. You lose, asshole. Drop it or die. Five-four-three—"

The attacker dropped his knife.

"A wise decision." Yianni told him to turn around and stepped forward to handcuff him.

The man started to turn away, then suddenly whipped his arm around, aiming to strike Yianni in the throat with the flat of his hand.

Yianni blocked the attacker's move with his free hand, and with his gun hand cracked the pistol alongside the man's jaw, sending him sprawling back down the hill toward the water.

"Now, that was a dumb decision." Yianni edged down to where the man lay, yanked him over onto his belly, and pinned his arms behind him to cuff him.

"So, you really are a cop."

Yianni looked up to see the woman standing on the path.

"I thought I told you to stay where you were?" He jerked his head in the direction of the cove.

"You did."

"But you didn't listen."

"Right again."

The assailant cuffed, Yianni stood and looked at her. "I get it. You're the aggressive type."

"Type of what?"

"Rock-thrower." Yianni yanked the man to his feet and pushed him up the hillside.

"What else was I supposed to do?"

"I'm not saying you did anything wrong, but it's lucky for you I'm a cop. The law doesn't take kindly to what you did."

"To a pig like that? What about what he tried doing to the woman in the cove?"

"Agreed, but first we've got to find the victim. Without her, the most I can charge him with is assaulting a police officer."

"But we both saw what he was doing to her."

"Yes, and he'll say she was a tourist girl, willingly cooperating until some madwoman began tossing rocks and chased her off."

The woman stared at him. "You're serious."

"Just being realistic."

As the man stepped back up onto the path, Yianni pressed him into a sitting position on the ground. "Then again, a dirtbag like this has probably attacked other women, so there's a chance one of them is still on the island and could identify him as her attacker."

"Do you really think so?"

Yianni shrugged. "Who's to say? Most want to escape the memory and flee the island as quickly as they can, rather than endure the rigors and embarrassment of trying to prosecute a rape charge on a notorious party island."

"What if I find the woman from the cove?" she asked.

"And convince her to do what?"

"Press charges, or at least talk about how she feels."

"Don't let me discourage you, but my guess is you're the last person on earth she wants appearing on her doorstep. You'll remind her of what she's trying to forget."

"But she's had her Aegean vacation turn to horror. She's probably blaming herself for coming here alone, not the predatory bastards who attacked her. The experience could haunt her for the rest of her days."

Yianni wondered if she were speaking from experience.

"I agree. If you find her, hopefully she'll testify." Yianni yanked the attacker to his feet. "Time to get you into the welcoming arms of Mykonos' finest."

The woman stepped toward the man. He swung around to face her, his arms cuffed behind him, a sneer on his face.

She glared at him. "You think this is all fun and games?"

The man snickered and spat at the ground in front of her. The woman smiled, stepped forward with her left foot and let loose a World Cup-class soccer kick to the man's balls with her right.

Yianni grabbed the woman by her arm and pulled her away from the man, who was now writhing on the ground and screaming.

"That will be enough of that. Now sit down over there on that wall, or I'll have to arrest you too."

He called for backup and spent most of the ensuing fifteen minutes listening to the woman heap abuse on the attacker's every part, including the size of his manhood. One of the two cops who arrived immediately recognized the woman. He called her Toni. She gave her nationality as American, her place of residence as a hotel near where Yianni had parked his motorcycle, and her reason for being where she was that she was on her way to her job at a piano bar in Little Venice.

Yianni confirmed the details of Toni's statement, leaving out the part about the brief encounter between her right foot and the perp's balls and her fifteen-minute berating of the man.

By the time the cops finished taking statements and carted off the would-be rapist, the sun had long since set.

"So much for my leisurely Mykonos sunset stroll," said Yianni.

"Then take a walk with me," said Toni as she headed for the windmills. "I could use a big strong cop like you to protect me."

"Somehow I doubt that," he muttered but dutifully followed behind.

With sunset long past, they drifted with the flow of early evening strollers down to a bay on the backside of the old harbor. They stopped by the edge of the water, and stared out across a glassy silver sea toward a patchwork of lights on an island a dozen miles away.

"I've been to that island several times," said Yianni. "Each time thinking it nothing special. Just a regular place, filled with regular people, leading regular, everyday lives. "

"No one would ever say that about *this* place," said Toni.

"Here we cater to everything *but* the regular. We take great pride in being special, in having created a paradise for the very best, conveniently ignoring its parallel attraction for the very worst."

"You sound like a cop."

She shrugged. "It's a no-brainer what bad guys will select when offered the choice between hunting among regular folk in regular communities or the hordes of rich and beautiful party people uninhibitedly enjoying themselves in a no-boundaries community devoid of any meaningful police presence." She gestured all around them. "It's a paradise for everyone. Until you become a victim." Toni bent down and picked up a round flat stone. "On the other hand, victims are what keep cops like you employed."

"Are we back to rock-tossing?" deadpanned Yianni.

She smiled, leaned back, dropped her right shoulder, and whipped her arm forward, letting loose with the stone as she did. They watched the stone skip across the water three times before disappearing in a final splash. "Skimming stones reminds me of summers spent with my family on a lake."

"Where was that?"

"Different places, different times."

Before Yianni could ask another question, Toni turned and looked up at the windmills. "What do you think about asking shopkeepers and hotel employees up around the windmills if they saw the woman from the cove? After all, she was practically naked when she ran off."

"We could try, but shopkeepers generally avoid getting involved in matters that don't concern them. Afraid they'll step on the wrong officials' toes. And hotel workers are geared to protecting the privacy of their clients."

"Even from the police?"

"Especially from the police."

"I still think we should try."

"Frankly, from her choice of beaches my guess is she's staying in a rented room in a private home somewhere else in town."

Renting rooms in private homes was a longstanding tradition on the island, originally designed as a means of supplementing a meager wage-earner's income. But amid Greece's continuing economic crisis, the number of homeowners now engaged in the practice had increased dramatically across all economic classes. So much so that hotels at virtually every price point now viewed private home rentals as decidedly unfair competition against their heavily regulated tourist industry.

"So, you're saying it would be like looking for a needle in a haystack?"

"No, I'd say it's more like looking for an anonymous tourist who doesn't want to be found hiding somewhere amid twenty-five-thousand beds."

She turned away from the windmills. "Well, come on. It's time for me to go to work."

"Great, just what I was hoping to do on my free night on the island, watch you waiting tables."

She turned and began walking, not saying a word, just hooking a finger over her shoulder for him to follow. She led them toward a cluster of bars and restaurants by a dozen or so multi-colored, three-story, former pirate-captain homes lining the eastern side of the bay. It was those homes—unique in otherwise all-white, two-stories-maximum Mykonos—that gave the area its nickname of Little Venice.

Its unparalleled view of the island's iconic windmills and proximity to the most photographed church in the Cyclades, the fifteenth-century Paraportiani, had cruise-boat mobs flocking there by day, creating a paradise for taverna and tourist shop owners. But its nights belonged to all-night partiers who bounced from bar to bar in search of their island fantasies against the backdrop of a crystal bay ablaze with heavenly and man-made light.

Without wind, the walk along the concrete apron separating the seawall from the bars, offered a lovely view of the water; and with wind, a lovely view of the water dousing passersby. Tables were set up on the apron so snugly against the outside walls of the bars that only swizzle sticks could comfortably pass each other at the narrowest parts, but after midnight even its broadest stretches would be packed solid with revelers partying until dawn.

At the end of the apron, Toni turned right and took a quick left onto a lane running parallel to the sea on the land-based side of the captains' houses. A few steps farther, she stepped left through a doorway with a rainbow emblazoned atop its doorframe.

Yianni stood in the doorway, peering inside. It looked like an old English pub, with two young-looking men, one blond and one dark, standing behind a bar off to the right and talking across it to a stocky old man sitting on a bar stool.

Toni turned and stared at Yianni. "What's the matter, Detective, afraid of a gay bar?"

Yianni's face tightened. "I'm not sure if you're trying to test me, you're defensive, or both. But whatever it is, you're way out of line. First of all, the name is Yianni. Second, I happen to know the place. It's a favorite of a buddy of mine on the force who looks a little like the guy sitting at the bar. And, third, I'm reminiscing, not hesitating."

Toni waved for him to come inside. "Sorry, didn't mean to offend you, Detec—" She paused and smiled. "Yianni."

Yianni's expression relaxed and he stepped inside. "Apology accepted."

A well-worn, upright piano stood off to the left, just beyond the bar. It sat angled so the piano player could take in the action in the bar area while playing to a main room that opened onto a wide view of the bay through windows reminiscent of a massive sixteenth-century fighting galleon.

"Glad to see this is still a piano bar and not trying to be just another wannabe Las Vegas hotspot," said Yianni.

"I think you mean Miami wannabe."

Yianni shrugged. "I'll have to take your word on that. I've never been to Miami." He looked around the room. "Where's the piano player?"

Toni shook her head. "Artists…." She turned, waved to the folks at the bar, and said in English. "This is my friend Yianni. Make sure he doesn't get into any trouble." She walked over to the piano and sat down at its bench. "Because of the sort of music I perform, most conversations in here tend to take place in English."

"You're the piano player?" said Yianni.

"Yep, 'tis *moi*." She struck a deep chord on the keyboard with her left hand as she answered, then pulled a binder off the shelf behind her.

Yianni rested his forearms on top of the piano and glanced at a glass fishbowl with the word TIPS written across a piece of transparent tape stuck to one side. "I never would have guessed."

"Hopefully you won't say that after you've heard me play."

"Don't worry, I'll lie if necessary."

She stared at him. "Is that your effort at getting back at me for my bit of teasing at the doorway?"

"Could be." He smiled.

She smiled back. "I can handle it. Playing piano in a bar requires a certain mindset. We have to put up with all types."

The old man at the bar yelled, "Hey, piano player, play 'New York, New York.'"

Toni rolled her eyes. "See what I mean? Never fails. Every night I get that at least once, though in this bar they usually want the Lady Gaga or Liza Minnelli version. Damn if I understand the magic of that song to piano-bar crowds—and it's not only Americans who want it."

Toni smiled at the guy at the bar. "I'm not on yet for twenty minutes. I'll get to it in my first set, fella. Promise."

She whispered to Yianni, "They're all fellas if I don't know their names, and putting off requests into the next set gives them time to think about how much to tip me for playing their song. Tricks of the trade."

"Play it now and I'll double my tip," said the man, slurring his words.

Again she spoke to Yianni, but this time not in a whisper: "Am I correct that double nothing is still nothing?"

"I heard that," said the man.

"So, how much do you plan on tipping her?" asked Yianni.

"Who are you?" said the man.

"The piano player's accountant."

"Oh." The man paused. "Twenty euros."

At that, Toni dropped her binder back on the shelf and launched straight into his request. The man smiled and patted the bar in time with the music. When Toni finished, he slid off the bar stool, stumbled over to the piano and dropped fifty euros into the fishbowl.

"Sir, that's a fifty you put in the bowl. I agreed to play it for twenty."

The man shrugged. "I know, but I liked it so much I wanted to give you more."

"That's not necessary, sir."

He waved her off.

"Is there another song you'd like me to play?"

"No." As he walked back to his stool, Toni played the song again. The man waved his thanks without turning around.

When she'd finished, Yianni whispered. "I was very impressed."

"By my playing?"

"By the whole package. Especially the part where you pointed out you'd been over-tipped."

"Don't thank me for that; thank my parents for raising me that way."

"You're also obviously very patient."

"That's a risky assumption to make based on how I behave in here. Playing in a piano bar gives me very little choice other than to be patient. These aren't concert-goers. Bar patrons show up with a mix of interests and expectations regarding the music they want to hear." She waved to the guys behind the bar and made a drinking gesture.

"Friends come in celebrating, looking for upbeat tunes; businesspeople might ignore the music as long as they can hear each other talk; and, of course, any alcohol-fueled seduction requires a background of romantic music."

The blond from behind the bar walked over and handed Toni a bottle of water and napkin. "What would you like?" he asked Yianni in American-accented English.

"A Mythos. Please."

"So, you're a beer sort of guy," he said.

Yianni nodded. "This place makes me feel that way."

"I said *beer*," grinned the man, "not queer."

Yianni laughed.

"Jody, get away from him," said Toni.

"Killjoy," said Jody, walking back to the bar.

"I can see where you have a lot of fun in here."

"At times."

"What I've always wondered," said Yianni, "is how musicians who work in bars like this handle the constant background noise of rattling glassware and conversations?"

"If you work long enough in piano bars, you develop a mindset to cope with all of that. Or you go crazy." Toni took a sip of water, put down the bottle, and began waving one hand in the air as if conducting an orchestra. She spoke as if addressing Parliament.

"When I started out in the business, I'd shut my eyes when I played and sort of drift off into the sounds of the room. If I used my imagination, all the competing noise became part of the music. I was like the orchestra conductor, uniting all those different sounds into a unified, symphonic performance—ideally, drawing the audience into an appreciative, tip-giving state of mind in the process."

She dropped her conducting hand down onto the keyboard and returned to her normal tone of voice.

"Like I said, that was my thinking when I started out in the business. Over time, I've come to learn my actual job in a piano bar, and with that realization I've achieved a Zen-like understanding of the meaning of my life's work. It's so simple, so obvious, and so intrinsically calming to an artist's soul."

She waited.

"I get it," said Yianni. "That's my cue to ask what you learned."

She played the piano equivalent of a drum roll. "My job is to sell drinks. Period, end of story."

Yianni shook his head and grinned. "So, when did you start off on this career?"

"Ah, now we're into the personal questions. Sorry, Yianni, but they'll have to wait for another day. Now it's time for me to get to work."

"What time do you finish?"

"Three."

Yianni's face dropped. "That's a bit too late for me tonight. Tomorrow's Friday and a workday for me."

She picked up a pen from the shelf and scribbled a number on the napkin. "Here's my number. Call me when you have time. After all, I owe you at least a coffee as a commission on that fifty you got for me."

Yianni took the napkin and stared at the number.

"And one other thing," she said, standing. "Thanks for what you did before to help that woman in the cove. You're a good guy." She kissed him on both cheeks and sat down. "Now get out of here, before another good guy tries to pick you up."

Chapter Seven

Lila sat propped up in bed, reading. Andreas lay flat on his back, his head propped up slightly against the headboard, watching a football game on a muted TV.

"You do realize you're going to strain your neck lying like that," she said.

"I've done this all my life."

"You tell me that each time I warn you. Then, the next morning, I get to watch you twisting your neck every which way, trying to work out a kink."

"They're not related."

Lila rested her book on her chest. "And you wonder where Tassaki gets his stubborn streak."

"From the way this conversation is headed, I think he can thank us both for that trait."

Lila rolled over onto her side and poked Andreas in the chest with a finger. "And just what's *that* supposed to mean?"

"Can I just watch the match?"

"You started this."

"I did?"

"Yes, by lying with your head against the headboard."

Andreas pushed away from the headboard to lie flat on his back, eyes focused on the ceiling. He exhaled dramatically. "Okay, darling, what's on your mind?"

"Nothing."

He lay perfectly still, staring straight up.

"You're incorrigible."

He didn't move or make a sound.

"Speak to me."

Andreas turned his head to face her. "About what?"

"About what you know is bothering me."

Andreas blinked. "Any chance of a hint?"

"How can you be so out of touch?"

Andreas pushed himself up onto one elbow so that he faced her head-on. "Honestly, I have no idea what is on your mind, but if it's something I've done to upset you, I swear I didn't mean it."

"You just don't get it."

Andreas shut his eyes as he spoke. "The only thing I can think of that could be making you anxious is your plans for Mykonos."

"Why would I be anxious?" she snapped.

He opened his eyes. "You're all wound up to chart a new career path, based on what you hope to learn from strangers you hope to meet on Mykonos. That's a rather challenging goal you've set for yourself, and I think you're worried about coming up empty on the inspiration front."

She stared at him for a moment, then fell back onto her pillows, and stared at the ceiling. "You might be right."

"It's only natural." He paused. "Do you want a suggestion?"

She sighed. "Go for it."

"Follow the age-old waterskiing principle."

She turned to face him. "Meaning?"

"Don't battle to get up on the skis. Just let the boat pull you up. You've got the skills and ability, and when the water's right, you'll end up soaring."

"Did you just make that up?"

"Actually, Tassos told me something like that a few years back."

"I assume he was right."

"Let's put it this way: I didn't drown."

Tassos Stamatos and Andreas met when Tassos was chief homicide investigator for the Cyclades, and Andreas was Mykonos' police chief. They'd become fast friends, and through Andreas' unwitting introduction, Tassos and Maggie had become a couple. Though Tassos was well beyond retirement age, he possessed secrets and connections from both sides of the law that guaranteed him job security for as long as he wanted.

Lila took Andreas' hand in hers. "I'm glad you're coming with us tomorrow."

"Me too."

"Will Tassos be on Syros?"

"He should be. He's cut back on his fieldwork, and spends most of his time training young would-be homicide detectives."

"We should invite him to spend a few days with us on Mykonos. After all, Syros is only an hour away."

"Let's suggest he come over when Maggie's with him. That way he'll be easier to control."

"I assume there's a deeper meaning intended in that."

"We men need you women to keep us on our toes."

"It's our revenge for so many of you men wanting to keep us in stilettos."

"*Score!*"

"You agree?"

He pointed at the TV. "My team just scored a goal."

Lila let go of his hand, grabbed one of her pillows, and lightly beat him with it. "Men, you're all alike."

Andreas hugged her to him in a playful struggle to keep her from swinging the pillow. "Women, you're all so different."

Lila stopped swinging. "That's precisely what I'm hoping to discover on Mykonos."

"Amen."

• • ● • •

Toni lived in a hotel close by the cove where she'd met Yianni. It was more a big house with bedrooms than a hotel, but the Tourist Board allowed its owner to call it a hotel and gave it more stars than it deserved, entitling him to charge tourists higher room rates than Toni would ever pay if she didn't have a special deal as a year-round resident. Some might say the Tourist Board bent the rules for the owner because his cousin once was mayor, but to be fair, virtually every island local had a cousin who once was mayor.

On a normal day, Toni woke around one p.m., the perfect time to start your day when you lived in a hotel on a hard-partying tourist island. At that hour, the hassle of the noontime check-out crowd gathered at reception had passed, while the hordes arriving for a two p.m. check-in hadn't yet massed, and the rowdy, sun-worshipping crowd had long since left for the beaches.

Today, she felt, more than heard, the room phone on her bedside table ringing and grabbed for it without opening her eyes.

"Hello. What time is it?"

"Did I call too early?"

"If you have to ask, yes. And who is this?"

"Me, Yianni. I…ah…guess I should've waited later to call."

"Yep. But it must be important for you to have called at whatever ungodly hour it now is. Did you find the woman from the cove?"

"Uh, no, it's not about that."

Toni opened her eyes and grasped for her mobile phone. "Then what is it about?"

"I wanted to know if you'd like to go to the beach."

Her eyes fixed on the time on her phone. "It's ten o'clock in the f-ing morning!"

"I know, but—"

"I didn't get to bed until four."

"Is that a no on the beach?"

"I'm never up this early. I don't even know if there's sun on the beach at this hour."

"At least your sense of humor's awake."

"Don't bet on it."

"So, yes, or no?"

"Why so early? Besides, I thought today was a workday?"

"My boss arrives this evening, and I suspect I'll be pretty busy once he gets here, so I figured I should try to get in as much beach time as possible while I can."

"And I just happen to be the only person you know on the entire island with time to hang out with you on the beach."

"That sort of tells it like it is."

Toni swung her legs out over the edge of the bed and sat up. "So what time did you have in mind for picking me up?"

"Whatever works for you works for me."

"I doubt that, but let's compromise on an hour from now."

"See you then."

"Whoa, don't you want to know where I live?"

Yianni said the name of the hotel.

"How did you know that?"

"I'm a detective, remember?"

"Fine, I'll see you in an hour. Bye."

She waited until he'd said goodbye before hanging up the phone.

He seemed like a nice guy. But they all seemed that way when they were looking to get laid.

"Out of all the beaches on the island, why did you pick this one?" asked Toni as they walked through the main entrance to The Beach Club, headed toward the sea.

"I take it you're not impressed?"

"If I were looking for a beach filled with high expectations and low realization rates, this would be it. That is, of course, unless you're willing to pay for companionship."

"Don't worry, I'm springing for the sunbeds."

"Not on your cop's salary."

Yianni smiled. "So much of this place is illegal, I guarantee you we'll get the best seats on the beach at a special price for guys with badges."

Toni looked up and down the beach. "I haven't been here in years. That's a lot of people on the beach already."

"It's never too early for sun-worshippers anxious to start grilling themselves under the grand sunlamp in the sky."

Toni stared at him. "When are you going to tell me why you really dragged me out here so early in the morning?"

"Like I said, I wanted company."

"This is The Beach Club, and we both know it's owned by a guy who specializes in providing company to lonely guys, with, I imagine, 'special pricing for guys with badges,'" she said, using finger quotes for emphasis.

Yianni stared at her. "How do you know these things?"

She shrugged. "I've lived here a while, so I'm treated kind of like a local. Gossip is the lifeblood of an island this small, and island reality is much different from what you'll find in the news or likely hear from a local, unless you're also a local."

"Yes, but you seem particularly well-versed on the racy details about some prominent islanders."

"The cardinal rule of islanders is not to speak ill of their island to anyone but another islander, which leads to a natural corollary: 'Thou shalt complain long and often to thy neighbor.' Which means conversations are peppered with spicy bits of gossip about who's corrupt, who's more corrupt, who's most corrupt, who's fooling around on whom, who's getting away with ignoring the laws, and the island's various crimes and perpetrators."

She paused to take off her sandals. "Why am I telling you this? You must already know that once random crime works its way up to the status of somewhat organized, locals know who's committing it. The problem is getting anyone to do something about it."

"A big part of that problem," said Yianni, "is that as long as locals aren't the targets, far too many are willing to ignore it. It's like the weather, unavoidable. Plus, it makes plenty of them richer in the process."

"That's how they used to think, but now locals are coming to realize those days are past. It's not as seasonal as it used to be. Once tourists leave, the bad guys concentrate on the locals. Theft and robbery are a year-round plague. But like everything else that's out of whack on this island, locals keep it to themselves, fearing that to do otherwise might tarnish the island's image as a tourist paradise."

"The perfect attitude for losing control of their island to the predators." Yianni waved to a tan, fit, handsome young man in bright orange swim trunks standing by the club's beachside entrance.

The man jogged over to them. "May I help you?"

Before Yianni could answer, he heard an unfamiliar voice yell out, "*Toni, how* are *you?*"

Toni and Yianni swung around, looking for a body to go with the voice.

"We're over here," called a different voice.

Three rows of beach chairs closer to the sea from where they stood, and ten umbrellas farther down that row, a naked, well-toned and tanned man in Persol aviator sunglasses stood, waving madly at Toni. Beside him, a nude, tanned, and toned blonde jumped up and down, also waving wildly while the rest of her bounced in accompaniment.

It seemed that everyone on the beach had turned to watch them shout for Toni's attention. She looked at Yianni. "I have absolutely no idea who they are."

"Toni, come join us," came another shout from the woman.

Yianni turned to the young man in the orange swimsuit. "I guess we won't be needing your help after all."

Toni forced a weak smile, offered a brief wave, and together they squeezed toward the couple between snugly fitted rows of sunbeds and umbrellas. They kept apologizing as they jostled through the sunbathers.

"I still don't recognize them," muttered Toni.

"From this distance, don't bother focusing on their faces. You've got a better chance of recognizing them from all the work they've had done on their bodies."

The couple appeared to be surgically augmented in all the right places and dedicated to exhibiting the fruits of modern medical science—the kind of tourists who made the island a promotional paradise for plastic surgeons. The closer Yianni and Toni came, though, the more the couple aged, and Yianni pegged them for several decades older than he.

The instant Toni and Yianni reached the couple, bear-hug embraces locked them between greasy, sweaty, sandy, naked male and female bodies. After enduring what Yianni took to be a respectful period of time for a hugging reunion among siblings separated at birth, he twisted away.

"Enough already, guys," said Toni. "You're getting the whole beach excited." She dropped down onto one of the couple's sunbeds. Yianni remained standing, waiting to be introduced.

The woman plopped down and snuggled up next to Toni, while the man positioned himself on the bed directly across from her. Yianni made sure to keep his eyes focused on their faces.

"How long's it been, Toni?" said the man.

"Too long," said the woman, squeezing Toni's thigh.

Americans, thought Yianni from their accented English.

"Yeah, I know," said Toni, still with a blank expression on her face.

"Janet couldn't believe it was you. She said this was never your sort of place."

Toni gave a cautious nod and forced smile. "I'm glad to hear you know me so well."

The man dropped his head down so that Toni could see his eyes above his sunglasses. "You don't remember us, do you?"

"As a matter of fact, I am having a bit of trouble placing you."

Janet jumped up, hugged Toni, her breasts poking into Toni's eyes, and sat back down. "That's perfect!" Janet said, looking at the man for agreement. "See, dear, we really have changed."

The man crossed his legs in what Yianni took to be more a gesture of seriousness than modesty.

"We used to stay in your hotel, back when you first came to the island."

A look of recognition began to move across Toni's face. She stared at the woman. "Janet?" She turned to the man, "Larry?"

The woman clapped her hands and the man smiled broadly.

"My God," Toni said. "You each must have lost a hundred pounds, and...and—"

Larry raised his hand. "No need to search for a gracious way to put it, Toni. Yes, we've had a lot of work done."

Janet leaned in. "But only after we'd done all that we could to make our bodies better through diet and exercise."

"Whatever you did, you look terrific."

"We didn't like the direction our lives had taken," said Larry. "We'd made a lot of money but realized we'd enslaved our bodies and spirits to our Type A personalities. That's when we decided there had to be a better way. So, we sold our businesses and spent the next several years getting our bodies into the shapes we wanted. We're very proud of how it all turned out." Larry spread his arms. Janet did too.

"Trust me, I noticed. So has everyone else on the beach."

Larry laughed. "We always liked you, Toni. Are you still living in the same hotel, and playing in that same club?"

"Yes to both. No changes in my life."

Larry looked up at Yianni. "I wouldn't say that. You're here with this handsome young man."

Yianni smiled, extended his hand, and said in English. "Yianni Kouros. Pleasure to meet you, sir." He looked at Janet. "You, too, ma'am."

Larry shook his hand and Janet smiled.

"Say, why don't you join us on our boat for lunch? That's it out there." Larry pointed to a 118 WallyPower luxury yacht some two hundred meters from shore.

"I see that when you said you made a lot of money, you meant a *lot* of money," said Toni.

Larry shrugged. "We were lucky enough to be in the right high-tech spot at the right time."

"Obviously, I used a different GPS."

"Are you happy?" asked Janet.

"Relatively."

"Then you found the right spot for you."

"So, guys, are we on for lunch? I've got to let the chef know," said Larry.

Toni looked at Yianni.

He shrugged. "Why not?"

"Great," said Larry.

"Only one condition," said Toni.

"What's that?" said Janet.

"You'll dress for lunch."

• ● ⬤ ● •

"Quite a boat you have here," said Toni.

Janet grinned. "The sales brochure calls it a '118-foot carbon and fiberglass dream come true for lovers of luxurious seaworthy motor-yacht style.'"

"How fast can it go?" asked Yianni.

"Capable of 70 miles per hour. That's over 60 knots."

"I love the color," said Toni.

"It's a reflective dark-green metallic finish that changes with the light and landscape."

"Humble, but it's home," said Larry, motioning for them to move amidships to a dining table offering a three-hundred-sixty-degree view of all about them.

"Of all the possible words that come to mind for describing this floating palace, I can assure you humble isn't one of them," Toni said.

"It's all a matter of perspective. There's always a bigger boat out there waiting to anchor next to yours."

"I see," said Toni. "So, it's all tied into that male 'size-obsession' thing." She flashed finger quotes.

Janet glanced between Larry and Yianni. "Which of you boys is going to jump in here and defend your gender with something like, 'It's not the size that counts, but how you use it.'"

Yianni raised his hands. "Don't look at me. I'm only here for the food."

"A wise decision," said Larry. "These two will bait you to death if you allow them."

"Stop ruining our fun," said Janet. "How is Toni ever going to get to know her young man if we don't test him?"

Larry looked at Yianni. "I won't take it personally if you decide to dive overboard and escape back to shore. I've done that many times myself. It's probably why I'm such a good swimmer."

Janet stuck out her tongue. "But you always come back."

"Only for the last forty years."

Two Filipino women arrived, carrying serving bowls of salads and platters of grilled fish and chicken. They placed them in the center of the dining table.

"We tend to eat healthy. I hope that's okay with you," said Janet.

"Works for me," said Yianni.

"How many can you sleep here?" asked Toni.

"Six guests, six crew." Larry smiled. "And before you get the wrong idea, we don't own this baby, just chartered it for a couple of weeks."

"Whatever you pay, I'm sure it's a lot more than what I earn in a year," said Toni.

"Make that a few years," said Yianni. "Remember, I saw your tip jar."

"Ah, so the man can bite back," smiled Janet.

"We'll have to work on curbing that," grinned Toni.

"So, shall we eat?" Larry poured wine into his guests' glasses before serving his wife and himself.

"Help yourself to the food," said Janet. "It's easier that way."

Toni reached for the bowl of Greek salad, but instead of serving herself, served Yianni. Janet glanced at Larry and smiled.

They ate in silence at first, listening to the water lap up against the hull, while a soft breeze rolled over them.

"I just love it here," said Janet. "Don't you?"

"If you mean out here on the water doing what we're doing at this moment, absolutely," said Toni.

Janet waved her hand in the direction of the beach. "Oh, yes. Please spare me those pretentious places charging twenty euros to park and five to ten times that amount for a pair of sunbeds, employing restaurant staff that enjoys informing those they perceive as falling outside their preferred customer profile that a table is only available for an allotted period of time at an extravagant minimum amount per person." She flashed both hands toward the shore in a classic Greek curse.

"I see you speak Greek," said Yianni.

Larry laughed. "It's just their way of doing business, dear, intended to prod their clientele into competition with one another over how much they can afford to blow on a single meal."

"Speaking of blow," said Toni, "if you happened to be a coke head, all you need is a trip to the WC in many of those places, and a slow run of the side of your hand along any marble countertop, and voilà you have a quick little pick-me-up, gratis." She looked at Yianni. "Something I'm not into, FYI."

Larry jumped in. "But you have to admit, the food and service are terrific, and the prices aren't much more damaging than at other high-end places on the island. That is, as long as you avoid getting steered to inconceivably overpriced off-the-menu items." He paused to sip his wine. "If you approach it with that attitude, and of course, come prepared for a dousing in champagne spray from characters celebrating at surrounding tables, you'll have a great time."

Janet shook her head in disagreement and gulped a slug of wine. "You're just saying that because of that business deal you're considering."

"I'm not considering any deal," said Larry, matching his wife's gulp of wine.

"Yeah, sure," said Janet. She turned to face Toni. "Larry's on the phone with his investment people every day, hearing pitches from investment hustlers with the next deal of the century."

"I'm not in the habit of turning down deals I haven't been offered, my dear. It's why one *listens*."

"If all you did was listen, that would be fine, but you get so worked up you start cursing those people out afterward, and that sends your blood pressure off the charts." She turned to Toni. "Not to mention what it does to mine."

"That's a bit of an exaggeration, my love."

"It sure as hell isn't, considering what happened today."

Larry exhaled. "That was different." He looked at Yianni. "This guy was telling me to invest in a hotel project here that would 'revolutionize' the way the hotel business is done on the island. He has a plan to build a high-rise resort and casino complex on one of the island's last untouched coves. They have some connection through a guy on the mainland to a major marquee international hotel chain willing to add its name to the project. They haven't reached a deal on the land yet, but they're hopeful."

"That's not allowed," said Yianni.

"I said the same thing to him, and he said, 'Everything's possible if you have the money and the connections.'"

"But high-rises on Mykonos?" said Toni.

"His pitch covered that with a somewhat seductive logic. He said if you go to the island's most developed mountainside beaches, what you'll see are hotel rooms running from the base of the mountain all the way to the top. One unit piled behind and on top of another, making all of them effectively equivalent in height and room capacity to a single, stand-alone, high-rise hotel. If you go with that logic, building a high-rise hotel *avoids* destroying the mountain, therefore making it a major environmental improvement over business as usual."

"That's bullshit," said Yianni.

"Of course it is. That's why I want no part of it. But I can assure you what you've just heard is the PR line the city fathers will be espousing as justification for approving this project, and undoubtedly many more to follow."

Toni shook her head. "And I thought things couldn't get worse."

"They can always get worse."

"Who pitched you?" Yianni asked.

"The guy who owns that place," pointing to the beach. "Karavakis."

Chapter Eight

Most of what Andreas and Lila needed for spending the summer on Mykonos was already there. They'd packed their SUV with the children's things, including foods they liked that were too much of a hassle to find on the island at a reasonable price, and left with the children and Anna on the Friday afternoon ferry. Since Lila's parents kept a cook and maid at the Mykonos house all summer, and had a year-round caretaker, Marietta would stay behind in Athens, giving her a vacation of a different sort, away from attending to the family's needs.

They made it to the house in time for Andreas to catch his favorite part of the day. He loved watching the east-facing hillsides of ochre, gray, and black fade into shadow as the sun dropped behind the hilltops to the west. Lila, on the other hand, loved sitting on the beach in the morning as sunlight danced upon the water, blanketing the Aegean in hues of silver, rose, and gold.

Once, he'd discussed with Lila their different views on sunlight.

"No surprise, there," she said. "For the most part, my life's been one big, bright, sunshiny day. Whereas you, my love, are a cop through and through. For you, life's all about the shadows."

He wasn't sure she was right about that, but it sure as hell had sounded profound.

By the time Yianni got back to the house, sunset had turned the eastern sky into a pink and purplish dome, faintly pinpricked with starlight. He found Andreas and Lila sitting on the terrace by the pool, sipping wine.

"Nice sunburn. Looks like you had a busy day at the beach." Andreas smiled.

Yianni plopped into a chair beside Lila. He gestured with his head toward Andreas as he said to Lila, "You had to put up with that routine all the way from Athens?"

"I had the kids and Anna to distract him." Lila stood up. "Sorry to tell you this, but you two are on your own until dinnertime." She looked at her watch. "Which should be in about thirty minutes. I have to check to make sure the children are in bed. Tassaki's all wound up from the boat ride, and he knows how to manipulate Anna into allowing him to break the rules and stay up late."

"I wonder who he takes after?" said Yianni.

"Don't we all." Lila kissed Andreas on the forehead and walked into the house.

Andreas held up a bottle of wine and pointed at a glass on the small table in front of Yianni. "Would you like some?"

"No thanks. I've had enough booze this afternoon to qualify me for a detox program."

"I take that to mean you had a good time at the beach."

"And on a boat."

"Did it involve a young lady?"

"A very interesting one."

Andreas put down his wineglass. "We've got a half hour—tell me about her."

"What I'm sure is going to interest you more is what I learned from friends of hers with whom we had lunch."

Andreas shrugged. "It's your story, tell it your way."

Yianni described how he met Toni, where she worked, and how their day by the sea in front of Karavakis' club ended on her old acquaintances' yacht, with the husband revealing Karavakis' big plans for the island.

Andreas leaned in. "Karavakis is trying to build a casino and hotel resort on Mykonos?"

"That's what this guy Larry said."

Andreas shut his eyes. "Do you see a link between that and the Colonel's murder?"

"I see possibilities, but very few probabilities."

"Give me your best scenario."

Yianni drew in and let out a breath. "The Colonel wanted in on the deal and Karavakis said no."

"So, two big-time mobster businessmen, who've operated on the same island for years and who've likely worked together before, have a disagreement over a maybe-sometime-in-the-future mega-project, leading one to decide to resolve their differences by assassinating the other." Andreas shook his head. "That would be a hell of a change in the way mobsters do business in Greece."

"Maybe there was a warning we don't know about? A bomb blowing up some of the Colonel's property, like a car, a boat, a house, or maybe a beating delivered as the message part of a phony robbery. They're big on beatings here as warnings."

"I doubt anyone would be foolish enough to send a warning to someone as powerful as the Colonel. It risks him getting to you before you could get to him."

"Like I said, I'm talking possibilities, not probabilities."

"But how does dragging Despotiko into the mix tie in?" said Andreas.

"Maybe Despotiko wanted in on the deal, too, and whoever set up the hit on the Colonel thought tying in Despotiko might get him to back out. After all, if he and the Colonel were competitors for the same piece of Karavakis' deal, Despotiko had a motive for murder."

"The same logic that leads me to doubt that a warning was ever given to the Colonel has me doubting the killer was so unsophisticated as to think tying Despotiko into a hit would get him to walk away from a deal he wanted. Yes, I wouldn't be surprised if Despotiko wanted in, but he doesn't scare easily, if at all. Besides, he's used to being linked to deals involving murders. That's why he keeps so many lawyers, politicians, and media types happily busy working on his behalf."

Yianni sighed. "We need to come up with some other connection between Karavakis, the resort project, and the Colonel's assassination. Otherwise, all we have are coincidences."

"And we hate coincidences. Do we know who else is involved in Karavakis' deal?"

"So far, only Karavakis."

"What about the guy on the mainland with the hotel chain connection? What's his name?"

"I don't know."

"Does your naked friend Larry know it?"

"I didn't ask him."

"Can you reach him?"

"The only connection I have is through Toni."

"So, follow up with her."

Yianni smiled. "I was thinking of doing just that tonight."

"Why am I not surprised?"

"She starts playing at ten-thirty and works until three in the morning."

"Does she have a phone?"

"Of course."

"But the personal touch in such matters is so important." Andreas grinned.

Yianni looked at his watch. "Is it time for dinner yet?"

Andreas stood. "Okay, no more teasing." He waved for Yianni to follow him inside the house. "At least for now."

They passed through a large family room, complete with a

home-theater-size TV screen and a baby grand piano, into an outdoor courtyard the size of a tennis court. A weather-beaten, wooden plank dining table, set for three, sat under a decades-old olive tree. They'd no sooner sat than the maid, Tess, arrived with a pitcher of water and filled their glasses.

"Even my mother doesn't treat me this well," said Yianni, nodding toward Tess and saying, "Thank you."

"Coming from a Greek boy, that's what I call a true compliment," said Andreas.

"Wow," said Lila, walking into the courtyard from a passage leading to the children's rooms. "You must be hungry. I didn't have to call you for dinner even once."

Both men stood.

"I think our guest is more interested in fleeing further inquisition over his new lady friend than in whatever we might be having for dinner."

"Well, then he made a terrific blunder." Lila sat across from the men. "Because I want to hear it all, from first glimpse up to this very moment."

"What's to say?" said Yianni, as he and Andreas sat. "She's a very interesting person."

"That's precisely the sort I'm looking for," Lila in leaned toward Yianni. "What does she do?"

"She's a late-night piano player in a gender-bending bar in Little Venice."

Lila blinked. "Sounds fascinating."

Yianni cleared his throat. "And for fun, she throws rocks at the heads of would-be rapists, befriends naked mega-millionaires, and produces potential leads for detectives on their cases, while keeping her own past mysteriously cloaked behind disarming wordplay."

"As I said, fascinating. Tell me more."

Yianni sighed, and told his tale once more, leaving out details not directly related to Toni.

"I'd love to meet her."

"He's off to see her perform tonight," grinned Andreas.

"Really?"

"I figured to take a nap and leave in time to be there by midnight."

"Great," said Lila. "Let's plan on all going together."

The grin faded from Andreas' face. "We've had a long day, hon, and don't want to intrude on Yianni's time with his friend."

This time Yianni grinned. "No imposition at all. You can leave any time you want."

"Terrific," said Lila. "Let's eat, nap, and plan to shove off at eleven-thirty. This will be fun."

Andreas scowled at Yianni. "Yeah, sheer joy."

• • ● • •

They parked up by the six windmills, and walked down the ramp leading to the bay at Little Venice. The wind had picked up a bit, so rather than dodging waves along the shoreline walkway, they cut through a restaurant's outdoor seating area, past the island's only Catholic church, and onto the area's main street. Barely two meters wide in places, this street had once brimmed with shops attuned to the tastes and needs of locals and the more practically minded tourists. Today, though, much of it took aim at challenging the high-end glitz along Matogianni Street—Mykonos' Fifth Avenue—with its version of pricey fashion, jewelry, and pretentious clubbing experiences.

They waded through the crowds until Yianni stopped in front of a rainbow-framed doorway. "Here we are. Like nothing else in the Cyclades. A favorite of gays, straights, locals, and tourists."

The sound of a piano drifted out onto the street. "Is that her playing?" asked Lila.

Yianni peeked in. "Sure is."

Lila smiled. "This will be fun," she said and stepped inside.

Andreas followed. "Isn't this that place Tassos likes?"

"For years he had the hots for the singer, but she's long gone."

"Thank God, I'd hate to risk word getting back to Maggie that we're hanging out with Tassos' old flame."

"Yes, I can think of far less painful paths to suicide."

The moment Toni saw Yianni, her face lit up, and she shouted, "Welcome, handsome!" Then, stage-whispering at the bar, "Stay away from him, guys, this one's all mine."

Andreas swore he saw Yianni blush. He whispered in Lila's ear, "I think you're right. This will be fun."

They found a stool at the bar for Lila and stood next to her, listening to Toni play.

Within minutes the place was packed. The mysterious ebb and flow of partiers' moods had drawn a standing-room-only crowd to the bar, with the sing-along folks gathering around the tables closest to the piano, shouting out requests for "Defying Gravity" from the musical *Wicked*, "Mama Mia," and Neil Diamond's "Sweet Caroline."

"How can she stand all those interruptions?" said Lila.

"My guess is, it all depends on how well they treat her tip jar." Yianni pointed at the fishbowl on the piano.

"Does she sing too, or just play?" added Andreas.

Yianni leaned over. "If I were you, I wouldn't say, '*Do you just play?*' to her."

On a break, Toni hurried over to the bar, scooting past a bevy of suitors for her time. "Yianni, what a surprise. You actually can stay up past the pumpkin hour."

Yianni grinned. "Toni, this is my boss, Andreas Kaldis, and his wife, Lila."

Toni immediately extended her hand and smiled. "A pleasure to meet you both. Thanks for coming."

Lila shook her hand. "You're terrific. I'm amazed at how well you maintain your composure amid all the interruptions."

Toni shrugged. "Tonight was a little wild. It's usually not that rambunctious a crowd. But my attitude is always the same. As long as the crowd's having fun, I'm okay with it."

"But with so many yelling out different requests, how do you decide what to play?"

"You have to read the crowd, even a wild one like this. For some, it's their first night on the island, and they're up for hell-raising. For others, it's their last night, and it's all about nostalgia. My job is to adjust on the fly and try to make sure everyone has a good time."

"And buys more drinks, right?" said Yianni.

Toni winked at him, then leaned in toward Lila to say in a mock conspiratorial tone, "In all honesty, if left to make my own playlist, I'd turn the room into one big rock 'n' roll party."

"Why rock 'n' roll?"

Toni leaned back. "It just speaks to me, always has. I love the sounds and cadences of great trains rolling down the rails, and I hear that in classic rock's combination of country and rhythm and blues." Toni paused. "Sorry to ramble on. I must be boring you to death, but I tend to get wound up when I talk shop."

Lila reached out and patted Toni's hand. "Absolutely not. I'm fascinated."

"Really? You're very kind."

"I'm serious. I'd like to hear more about your career."

"I'm not sure I'd call it a career."

"How long have you been doing this?"

"Okay, it's a career."

Andreas turned his head so only Yianni could hear him. "I see what you mean about your friend keeping her past mysteriously cloaked behind disarming wordplay."

Before Yianni could answer, Larry and Janet burst through the front door and headed straight into the middle of their conversation.

"Toni and Yianni! Our old lunch crew, back together again." Larry patted Yianni on the back and kissed Toni on both cheeks.

"This is Lila and Andreas Kaldis," said Toni. "Yianni works with Andreas."

"He's my boss," said Yianni.

"Only in name," smiled Andreas, extending his hand to shake Larry's hand.

"Larry and Janet kindly hosted Toni and me for lunch today on their magnificent yacht."

"Remember, it's chartered," said Larry.

"Sorry, guys, but I've got to get back to work," interrupted Toni. "I can feel the owner's scowl on the back of my neck."

"Can you join us after for a bite to eat?" said Larry.

Toni looked at Yianni.

"It's up to my ride," he said, nodding toward Lila.

"Sounds like fun," she said.

Andreas closed his eyes for an instant before smiling. "Sure, why not?"

"Terrific," said Toni. "Fasten your seatbelts, folks, a new Toni's in town." For the remaining sets, Toni sang as well as played, and shut down the crazies in the crowd with humor and musical jabs. She played the crowd's favorites: Michael, Amy, Aretha, Adele, Barbra, Liza, and Frank, but mixed in homages to Chuck Berry, Jerry Lee Lewis, Buddy Holly, Jerry Garcia, and Freddie Mercury. It was a wild evening at the piano bar.

The wildness continued as the "bite to eat" with Larry and Janet turned into an all-night pub crawl down the couple's memory lane. They recalled their early days on the island, wandering lost through the then-empty back streets of the old town and stopping to ask a black-clad grandmother sitting in her doorway for directions back to the harbor. They spoke no Greek back then, and the old woman spoke no English, and when she hurried into her house they thought they'd frightened her. They'd started to walk away when she came out carrying a plate of cookies and two glasses of water, and together they spent half an hour conversing in the international language of smiles, nods, and charades. Every year thereafter, Larry and Janet made a point of stopping by to pay their respects to their cookie-serving friend.

She'd passed away a decade ago, and today her home was a

bar run by a grandson. The crew visited that bar, followed by at least a dozen more, but no matter how much a venue might have changed over the years, Larry and Janet had a story to tell about it. They spoke of a more innocent era, when drugs, booze, and sex were casual accessories enjoyed by visitors rather than targeted profit centers of modern business plans.

Between their stories, Lila spent much of the evening huddled together with Toni and Janet, talking out of earshot of the men. The men did the same among themselves. It was the traditional Greek arrangement for mixed couples out for a night on the town.

Yianni had lost count of the number of places they'd been to, not to mention the amount of drinks consumed, when he remembered to ask Larry for the name of the guy with the big-time hotel chain connection tied into the Karavakis deal.

"Why do you want to know?" asked Larry.

"Chalk it up to natural cop curiosity."

"That's how I raised him," said Andreas, lifting his beer and toasting, "*Yamas.*"

The three men clinked drinks then turned to the women to do the same.

Lila waved them off. "Not a chance, guys. As it is, I'm going to have to drive us home."

"At least your drive home will be in daylight," yawned Janet, "because unless my cataracts are back, I think that's the sun struggling to come up over there." She nodded east. "I hate to be a party pooper, but I've got to get some shut-eye."

"Me, too, my love. Just let me get the bill," said Larry. He looked at Yianni. "I don't remember the guy's name, but I have it marked down somewhere. I'll call you with it tomorrow." He paused. "I mean today."

"Thanks," said Yianni. "Now the two of you just head on home. I'll take care of the bill."

"No, I'll get it," said Andreas.

"No, you're our guests," said Larry.

"You men can stop battling over the check," said Toni. "I can handle this one." She smiled. "Besides, I know the owner. He won't charge me."

Larry laughed and patted Toni on the back. Janet leaned down to hug and kiss her goodbye. And everyone got into the act.

"Thanks for a great night," waved Larry as they wobbled out the front door.

Toni smiled at the waiter. "Check, please."

"There's no check," said the waiter.

"That can't be," said Toni. She looked at Yianni. "I'd lied about the owner. He counts every penny."

"A lady at the bar paid it," said the waiter.

Everyone's head turned to look for her, but whoever she was, she had gone.

"She left right after paying. She told me to tell you it's a thank-you for something you and he did for her." He nodded at Yianni.

"Who was she?"

"Never saw her before. A tourist."

"Did she say what we did for her?" asked Toni.

"It made no sense."

"Just tell me what she said."

He sighed and addressed Toni. "She said to thank you for being such a good rock-tosser."

Yianni woke with his eyes tightly shut. He opened one eye and looked for the clock. It was gone. Someone must have stolen it. He shut his eyes, and remembered the clock was on the other side of the bed. He turned his head slowly, and paused while the pulsing in his temples slowed, before opening both eyes. Sure enough, the clock was where it should be, glowing twelve-fifteen p.m. in a highly accusatory manner.

Twelve-fifteen? He couldn't believe he'd been asleep for six hours. His head felt as if it had rested for six minutes. Had he been slipped *bomba*? The counterfeit booze that plagued Greece's tourist towns had gotten its name from the bomb that went off in your head when you drank it. No, he'd have known if he were drinking that garbage.

He stared at the bathroom door, contemplating how best to bring himself back to life from one of those wild island nights he'd years ago promised himself never to repeat.

He twisted himself up and around to sit on the edge of the bed closest to the bathroom as his mind calculated the number of steps to the shower. He felt sure he could make it. Twenty seconds later, he did, pausing only long enough midway to shed the clothes he'd slept in.

In his experience, cold water was an overrated method of shocking the system into sobriety. Nevertheless, he tried it. Five minutes into cringing through his icy water-dance routine, he heard his mobile ringing.

Dripping, he made it to the bedside table and grabbed the phone, more desperate to stop the ringing than caring who called.

"Yianni, are you awake?"

He only faintly recognized the voice. "Who's this?"

"Larry, from yesterday, last night, and early this morning."

"Oh, Larry. Sorry. Didn't recognize you. A bad connection."

"No problem. I thought I might be calling too early."

"Not at all." Yianni contorted his face, trying to bring himself closer to the edge of sobriety necessary to carry on a conversation. "Thanks again for everything. It was a great night. At least the parts I can remember."

Larry laughed. "We enjoyed it too. Anyway, you asked me about that guy with the hotel connection to Karavakis."

Yianni concentrated. "Did you find the name?"

"I'm honestly not sure."

"I don't understand."

"Karavakis kept telling me that he had a rock-solid in with the hotel chain, but he refused to give me the name. He said it wasn't relevant. I kept pressing him, saying it was very relevant. Finally, he blew up at me and shouted out a name, but only a first name."

"So, you have it?"

"Well, I marked it down, but it's not a Greek name. I figure he made it up just to shut me up."

Yianni dropped onto the edge of the bed. He felt like going back to sleep. "Oh, well, thanks for trying."

"Don't you want to hear it?"

Damn. I'd better sober up fast. "Of course, I do."

"Pepe."

Yianni jerked himself back up onto his feet. "Did you say, Pepe?"

"Yes, P-E-P-E."

"And that's who Karavakis told you was his connection to the hotel chain?"

"Yes."

"Thanks, Larry. Much appreciated."

"Anything for a friend of Toni's. She has only the best people for friends."

"You and Janet are proof of that."

"Thanks. I'll let you go. We're sailing off to Naxos this morning but hope to see you and Toni again soon."

Yianni wished them safe travels, put down his phone, and stared at the bathroom door. He couldn't believe what he'd just heard. It was the link they'd been looking for between the Colonel's assassination and Karavakis' hotel project.

Yianni wondered if Andreas' hangover was as bad as his own. If, so Yianni now had a far more effective shock cure for chasing away the cobwebs than an ice-cold shower.

But first he had to get dressed.

• • ● • •

Yianni found Andreas and Lila sitting in the family room watching cartoons on TV with Tassaki. "I never thought you guys were into this sort of television."

"We're not." Lila smiled. "And we generally never let Tassaki watch them either. But this morning is special."

"What my bride is trying to say, is we're desperately trying to keep the kids calm and quiet while we recover from last night."

"Amen," said Lila, clutching her forehead. "And I thought I was the sober one."

"You were," said Yianni. He plopped down on the sofa next to Andreas and slapped him on the thigh. "Man, do I have some news for you, Chief."

Andreas shut his eyes. "Do I have to hear it now?"

Yianni smiled. "Nope."

Andreas kept his eyes shut. Twenty seconds passed. "Okay, you win, tell me the news."

"Larry called me with the name of the guy who was Karavakis' connection to the hotel chain." He paused. "Pepe."

Andreas blinked his eyes open. "Pepe, as in that restaurant owner with the Colonel when he was murdered?"

"He didn't have anything more than a first name, but how many Pepes could Karavakis know?"

"I think we should ask him."

"Not until after breakfast," said Lila. "I mean lunch." She looked at her watch. "Oh, no. It's after one. I'd promised Toni I'd meet her in town for coffee around noon."

"Well, it still is 'around noon,'" said Andreas.

"She's American, not Greek."

"But she's lived here long enough to have adopted our ways."

"A half-dozen years on this island, she told me," said Lila.

"Ah," said Yianni, "that explains why I never met her when the Chief and I were stationed here. She arrived after we left."

Lila stared at Yianni. "You mean you didn't know that about her?"

"I told you, she doesn't like to talk about herself."

"More likely, you didn't ask. Men can be that way. Self-absorbed." Andreas smiled.

"Are you trying to be a wise guy?" said Lila, staring at Andreas.

"Nope, just anticipating an appropriate response."

"What else did she tell you about herself?" said Yianni. "I mean things you feel comfortable telling me."

Lila smiled. "Very well put, Detective. Get me to share confidences I might otherwise be unwilling to broach."

"It's just that I know nothing about her past."

Lila drew in and let out a breath. "Okay, here's what I feel I can tell you without betraying a sister:

"Her father was a lawyer in New York City when she was born. A couple of years later he gave it up and went to work for the U.S. State Department, something he said he always wanted to do. She spent her post–New York City childhood bouncing with her mother and father from one foreign capital to another and attending an endless string of American schools for diplomats' children. She said music was her only constant during those years, something her mother kept pressing her to study and perform.

"From what she told me, I'd say her mother was the free spirit in the family. She traced her roots back to the original settlers coming to America on the *Mayflower* and all that. But Toni said that whenever anyone asked about her origins, she always said, 'My roots are firmly planted in the harshest lessons of British prisons and asylums.'"

"Sure sounds like Toni," smiled Yianni.

"Sadly, her mother passed away a couple years ago. My guess is she takes more after her mother than her father, though he always told her she had a gift for solving problems that would make her a terrific lawyer."

"How did she end up here?" asked Yianni.

"Straight out of high school she skipped college and took off on her own, bumming around Europe, dreaming of setting the world on fire with her music. A decade or so later, here she is, her roots now firmly planted in the island's sand, tip jar on the piano."

Andreas leaned in. "How can she possibly support herself year-round on tips she makes off summer tourists?"

"Spoken like a true cop," said Lila. "Which is particularly apropos, considering what she calls her day job."

"Day job?" said Yianni with a bit of anxiety in his voice.

"It relies on what she calls her 'non-musical talents.'" Lila paused for dramatic effect. "I'd call them somewhat unique skills, though you two most likely would describe them differently. She helps folks with problems they can't trust to the local authorities. Apparently, sometimes that means pursuing politically sensitive matters involving those same authorities, but most often people come to her because the official bureaucratic channels simply aren't doing them any good."

Andreas spoke up. "Just what sort of *matters* are you talking about?"

"She said that a significant portion of her work owed its existence to lowlifes burglarizing hotel rooms and vacation homes."

"She's a private detective?" said Andreas.

"I don't think she'd call herself that. 'Recovery expeditor of stolen goods,' would seem more accurate. The police's usual approach is to add a robbery victim's name to a very long list, and by the time the authorities get around to investigating the claim, both the victim and the victim's former property are long gone from the island."

Yianni shrugged. "She's got a point."

"And a market. Which reminds me. As I said, I'm supposed to be meeting Toni for coffee." She stood. "Excuse me, I've got to tell her I'll be late."

She called out to Tassaki, "Time for lunch." She picked up the remote and turned off the television.

"Can I go with you to town to meet your friend?" said Tassaki.

"I thought he was watching television," said Yianni.

"Five-year-olds are the original multitaskers," said Lila, taking her son's hand and walking out of the room.

After Lila had left the room, Andreas stared at Yianni. "*Recovery expeditor*, my ass. If your girlfriend gets Lila involved in her private cop/fixer bullshit..." He waved a hand in the air.

"Hey, don't blame me. I'm as surprised as you are."

"I know. Which doesn't make me feel any better. Here we are, two experienced cops, who spent a considerable amount of time with a piano player living full-time on a part-time tourist island, and neither of us thought to ask how she supported herself during the rest of the year. I wonder if we'd have acted the same way if *she* were a *he*?"

"I know I wouldn't have," smiled Yianni.

"Sexist." Andreas shot him the Greek open palm equivalent of the middle finger. "Right after lunch we're going to pay a visit to Karavakis. I need to get back to thinking like a cop. Make that, *we* need to."

Chapter Nine

As usual, Karavakis' club was crowded, noisy, and pumping. The security guy at the entrance said he had no idea where Karavakis was, and to ask at the bar. Andreas and Yianni pressed their way through the usual sweaty mix of salt- and suntan lotion-coated dancers grinding away in bikinis, Speedos, and less. They'd made it to a miraculously open bar stool when a shirtless young man, all tan, fit, and smiling, popped up in front of them from behind the bar.

"Hi, Chief Inspector."

It took Andreas an instant to recognize him. "Jason, what are you doing here?"

"Bartending, to make money while the sun shines. Like everyone else on the island."

Jason was the son of one of the island's most famous ex-pat beauties, and his father perhaps the greatest island athlete of his generation. Andreas and the father had played soccer together casually during Andreas' stint on the island, and clearly the son had inherited the finer traits of his parents.

"My Lord, I haven't seen you since you were this high." He dropped his hand to the level of the bar. "Last I heard from your dad, you were playing football for a feeder team into the pros."

Jason pulled two beers out of a cooler, opened them, and set them down on the bar in front of Andreas and Yianni. "The beer's on me. I have to make it look like I'm actually working."

"You didn't answer my question." Andreas took a sip from the bottle.

"This job pays a lot better. I'll get back to football later."

So, Jason had succumbed to the common curse of far too many island kids. They made so much money from tips in clubs in the summers that they put the rest of their lives on hold, often missing out on those ever-so-briefly-open windows of opportunity for a far more sustainable and financially rewarding career. But a lecture on the subject wouldn't mean a thing to him. No more than it ever had to most kids Jason's age.

"How's your mother?"

"She's great. Thanks for asking." He reached out and extended his hand toward Yianni. "I guess I should introduce myself since you're becoming a regular here."

Yianni smiled as they shook hands. "I didn't think anyone would notice, what with everything else going on in this place." Yianni pointed toward the beach, where a man wearing nothing but an elephant-trunk-shaped sock over his genitals stood on a table shaking his hips to the delight of the crowd of bikini-clad young women surrounding him.

"To me it's all background noise. I keep sane by focusing on new and interesting faces like yours. One day you're in here to see the big boss, and the next day you show up with one of my favorite people on the island, Toni. Now *that's* interesting."

"I see you inherited your parents' wit and charm," said Andreas.

"Thank you," said Jason. "I try."

"By the way, where's your boss?" said Andreas.

"If you mean old man Karavakis, he won't be in until after midnight."

"You mean you're on your own with a cash register?"

"Not exactly." He jerked his head in the direction of a basketball-court-sized restaurant next to the bar. "His son's in there."

Andreas peered into the restaurant at a table for twelve flanked by five males of about the same age and three pretty young girls. On the table were twin, jeroboam-size champagne buckets filled with Cristal, a fifth of vodka, assorted mixers, platters of lobster pasta, chateaubriand, and some sort of green.

"He's the one with his back to the bar. He looks sort of like that North Korean leader, Kim something or other, but with longer hair."

"Sounds like you don't consider him one of your best buddies."

"What's there to say? He won the gene pool lottery."

"You didn't do so badly."

"Thanks, but he hit the money part."

"Don't worry, I'll tip you well."

"Your money's no good in here."

A flash of neon behind the bar caught Andreas' attention. A young female had walked in wearing skintight Lycra leggings patterned in screaming neon flames that locked eyes up and down the bar onto her butt. Above a tanned and toned bare midriff, she wore a multi-colored, checkerboard- and helix-patterned sports bra several sizes too small to conceal most of what lay beneath. As a final attraction, her sneakers matched the electric rainbow scarf tying her dark brown hair back from a brightly made-up caramel-color skin. She walked directly to the son's table and sat next to him.

Jason turned his head to see what had caught Andreas' attention. "Do you know her?"

"No. I was wondering how many different patterns and colors could fit on a single body."

"How old is she?" said Yianni.

"Not sure, but something like fifteen."

"He likes them young," said Andreas.

"What can I say? He and I are the same age."

"Which makes it hard to imagine why, with all this around him," Andreas waved his hand at the room, "he'd stick to one girl."

"I didn't say he did."

"Meaning?"

"When she's with him, she's his girl, and when she's not, it's a whole different story."

Andreas stared. "I still don't get you."

Jason leaned across the bar. "You know the song, 'Love the One You're With?' That's how it works here. Every girl at the table is one of *his* girls. Until he tells them to love the ones they're with."

"Like father like son," said Yianni.

Jason shrugged. "We don't talk about that in here."

Andreas shook his head. "Really, man. What are you doing working in a place like this? The father runs the biggest prostitution ring on the island and now you're saying he's turned his son into a pimp."

"Like I said, making money. We all know that if you want to live on this island you can't fight the devil or city hall. Especially when they team up together."

"I never heard it put that way before," said Yianni.

Jason grinned. "Well, out here on the beach it's the motto." He glanced around the bar. "Time to get back to kissing up to the paying customers. Good seeing you."

"My best to your mom and dad," said Andreas.

Jason nodded and moved on.

Andreas and Yianni did the same.

Lila had agreed to meet Toni at her "office," a trestle table nestled up against the stucco front wall of a tiny taverna, tucked under a weather-beaten blue-striped awning on the southwestern edge of the old town harbor. The taverna stood directly across a flagstone road running between the taverna and a narrow bit of beach. Each morning farmers sold their fresh produce from the backs of tiny vans and trucks parked along the road, and fishermen offered their fresh catch from a marble stall permanently mounted on the sand.

Here, too, each morning, the island's fine-feathered symbol, Petros the pelican, strutted about, hard at work creating the island's emblematic symbiotic tourism experience. His routine had him using his bill to prod tourists into buying him fish, and then posing with his benefactors for souvenir photographs of them feeding him their purchases. He'd created a win-win proposition for the fishermen, tourists, and himself. If only some of the other businesses along the harbor had such intuitive marketers as that pelican, when it came to capitalizing on the island's storied history.

The taverna owner had been a friend and fan of Toni's music since she first started playing on the island, and according to Toni, they had an arrangement: Toni could use the table whenever she wanted, without charge, as long as her clients paid for what they ordered and Toni pushed them to tip well.

How long that arrangement would continue was anybody's guess. In summer, the island was awash with monied foreign investors eager to capitalize on its popularity. Any day now, the owner would probably decide it was time to cash in, while things were hot, before the big crash that everyone expected to come. Until then, though, it was business as usual at the office.

Lila parked in a private lot up by the bus station. She usually parked there, and normally it took ten minutes of brisk walking along narrow, twisting, uneven flagstone paths, through a maze of sun-bleached shops and homes, to reach the harbor. Today, it took fifteen because she had to weave her way through throngs of cruise-ship tourists.

When Lila reached the port, she saw Toni sitting with a woman wearing oversized sunglasses perched, hairband style, atop straight dark hair framing a round expressionless face. She thought that must be Toni's friend Stella, who'd married a local boy she'd met here on holiday. In their long night of huddled conversation, Toni had described fellow expat Stella as her best friend on the island but her polar opposite when it came to such things as punctuality. A difference Toni attributed to Stella growing up in a prim and proper Manhattan household.

Lila arrived at the table in what she took to be the midst of a heated argument. "Hi, Toni. Sorry, I'm late."

"No problem. Stella and I were just engaged in our normal back and forth over how much she hates her husband." Toni turned to Stella. "This is Lila, the very nice lady I was telling you about."

Lila stuck out her hand. "Hi."

Stella nodded and shook hands but said nothing.

"Uh, perhaps I should come back at a later time," said Lila.

"No, please sit. Right, Stella?"

Stella nodded.

Lila sat on the side of Toni farthest from Stella. Toni poured Lila a cup of coffee from the pot in front of her. "Milk? Sugar?"

"Today, I think I'll stick to black."

Toni looked at Stella. "Do you have anything to say to our guest?"

"I hate my husband."

"How about something original?"

"He didn't come home again last night."

"Does he have a girlfriend?" said Toni.

"Does the sky have stars?"

"I meant, does he have a *steady* girlfriend?"

Stella looked down at an untouched glass of orange juice. "For him, every tourist girl on the island's a potential score." She touched the glass with the fingertips of her right hand.

Lila said nothing, but appreciated how upset the woman must be. She wondered how she'd react if her husband cheated on her. No, she *knew*. It would be done, over, finished. None of this bullshit about staying together for the kids.

Stella ran her fingers up and down the glass. "I guess I should be thankful that he doesn't embarrass me by going after local girls."

Toni picked up her coffee cup. "Stella, my love, you have one very screwed-up relationship. You are married to a *kamaki* who considers seducing women a national sport. Rationalize it any way you like, and as long as it works for you, it works for me. But don't seek out my opinion again. I've been down this conversation road with you way too many times. You know where I come down on it."

"Cutting his balls off is not a viable alternative."

"But it will work." Toni took a sip of coffee. "And if you use a rusty butter knife, you might even enjoy it."

Stella sighed. "Thanks for your understanding."

"You're welcome."

Stella sighed again, picked up the glass and took a sip of the juice. The waiter placed a toasted cheese sandwich in front of Toni, and Stella promptly picked up half of it.

"Hey, that's my breakfast," said Toni.

"I'll pay for it."

"Dimitri doesn't charge me."

Stella batted her eyelashes, took a bite of the toast, and offered the other half to Lila. "I'm sorry for being so rude before. It's just that my husband is such an asshole."

Lila gestured no to Stella's offer. "So it appears."

Stella smiled. "I can assure you that I'm not insane, though it may seem that way at times."

"At times?" said Toni snatching the remaining half of the toast from the plate. "Any time you get on the subject of your husband, the folks with the straitjackets start hovering around."

"There are a lot more toxic relationships on this island than mine."

"Considering the island we're on, I wouldn't take that as encouraging."

Lila sat with her eyes bouncing from one face to the other. She couldn't recall witnessing an exchange quite like this before. At least not since college.

"Okay, Stella, you've piqued my curiosity, possibly even Lila's, so why don't you tell us whatever bit of 'toxic relationship' gossip's on your mind."

"Fine," muttered Stella, turning to face Toni. "You were late getting here again this morning, and I saw this young woman walk in, sit at the table next to me, and start sobbing."

"And you, being the soft-hearted sucker that you are, asked what was wrong."

Stella ignored Toni's comment. "It took an hour for her to unload her truly sad *and* unbelievably naive experiences with men on this island."

"Coming from you, it must have been a doozy of a story." Toni raised her hands in a sign of supplication. "But okay, I'm hooked. Let's hear the story, abridged version, please."

Stella exhaled. "She's a self-described 'free spirit' from California. She came alone on holiday to sort out her feelings over whether to accept a marriage proposal from a stockbroker suitor."

"Ah, the quintessential California romantic dilemma. Free spirit versus free market."

"It's not funny, Toni."

"I'm sure. Sorry, go on."

"Anyway, she got here three days ago and immediately took off to our most notorious party beach, where she met a beach waiter who came across as the nicest guy in the world."

"Plus great pecs, I'm sure."

Stella frowned a smile. "Anyway, they got to talking and she told him why she'd come to the island. He asked her what she wanted in a man, and she told him in precise detail. Which, from the way she droned on, likely described her dream man down to the length of his toenails."

"Let me guess what happened next."

Stella continued. "The kindly waiter suggested that they meet up later that night at a club in town."

Toni picked up the thread of the story. "And when she got

there, the waiter hadn't shown, but a buddy of his was there to offer the waiter's apologies."

Stella rolled her eyes. "What can I say? They talked and, lo and behold, the waiter's friend miraculously possessed all the mystical qualities of her ideal man."

Toni waved for more coffee as she recited the next line in Stella's story. "Precisely as she had described to the waiter earlier that same day on the beach."

"You got it."

Toni shook her head. "I assume she got it too."

"Yep, she brought him back to her hotel room and they went at it as if there were no tomorrow."

The waiter set the coffee down in front of Lila on his way to another customer.

"And since that blessed evening, her ideal man hasn't called, written, sent flowers, et cetera. But you, being an ever-optimistic soul, pointed out that it's only been two days."

Stella sighed. "As a matter of fact, I did."

"Come on, Stella, It's the oldest hustle on the beach. One guy approaches the woman, acts as the innocent interrogator of her desires, and passes the details on to a buddy, who later just happens to bump into the woman at a place where she's supposed to meet up with the original guy. New guy turns out to be the ship owner, brain surgeon, or cowboy of her dreams, and in rejoicing at their miraculous fate in finding each other, they're off to bed practicing for her honeymoon night."

"I know all of that."

Lila sat transfixed by what she was hearing. *How do these women* know *these things? I must have been raised in a bubble.*

"So," said Toni, "did you encourage her by saying he might return, or did you decide to tell her the truth?"

Stella nibbled at her lip. "I didn't have the chance to do either."

"Why?"

"Because there's more to her story. Last night she went back to the place where they met, hoping to find him."

"And?"

"He was talking to another girl. She went over to him and he told her to fuck off."

"Ouch."

"It gets worse."

"How?"

"This morning she was sitting in a taverna a couple of places down from here, sobbing to herself, when the waiter who'd set it all up in the first place walked by. He saw her and came over to ask what was wrong."

"You're kidding me."

Stella continued. "She told him about his shit of a friend, and the waiter agreed. He said he had no idea his friend was so insensitive. He spent fifteen minutes consoling her, then she excused her herself to go to the bathroom."

Toni raised her eyebrows.

Stella swallowed. "A minute later he followed her into the stall, and they had consensual sex with her leaning over the toilet."

"This can't be true," blurted out Lila. "I mean I'm not a prude, but this can't be true."

"I'm sorry to say that it is," said Stella. "And it's a rather benign story compared to tales of what other men on this island have done to tourist girls."

Lila shook her head in disbelief. "What did you tell her when she told you what she'd just done in the bathroom?"

Stella peered over the tops of her sunglasses. "'Go home. Straight home. Marry your boyfriend and never come back here.'"

Toni clapped. "Bravo, Stella, the perfect advice."

Stella stared at Lila. "I know, I should have followed it myself."

Lila raised her hands in a sign of peace. "It's not for me to judge."

"But I will, because Lila doesn't know you as well as I do. It's never too late to deal head-on with an asshole."

"On that note, I'm out of here." Stella stood up and grabbed her bag. With her other hand she reached out to shake Lila's hand. "A pleasure to meet you. I promise to be in better spirits the next time we see each other."

Lila stood and hugged her. "No need to apologize, your reaction is fully understandable."

"Thank you," said Stella. "As for you," she turned to face Toni, "take some lessons from your friend on compassion."

"I call it enabling."

"Asshole."

"Me or your husband?"

Stella stormed away, calling back over her shoulder, "Both of you."

Lila and Toni sat quietly for a moment, watching Stella tear across the harborfront.

"I may have sounded a bit rough on her, but early on I realized that I'm about the only person on this island with whom she feels comfortable unloading the details of her lousy marriage. That makes me feel responsible for reinforcing that she's the one being wronged."

"You mean she doesn't see it that way?"

"As a foreigner married to a local, Stella's complaints about her husband to another local are generally met with some form of lecture on how it serves her right. After all, they'd say, she voluntarily decided to marry one of the island's sons without appreciating the wandering-male side of their culture. On the other hand, if she complained to another ex-pat married to a local, all she'd hear would be how much worse that person's life was compared to Stella's."

Lila wondered whether her jaw was hanging open. "How do you know these things?"

"That's an interesting question. Probably a combination of watching my father the diplomat in action, listening to my mother the crusader, and far too many late-night gigs learning when to charm and when to roughhouse a boisterous bar crowd."

"Sounds stressful."

Toni shrugged. "What isn't? Take my work…" She picked up a document from the table. "This is a list of items stolen over the last few days from my clients. It's up to me to figure out ways to recover them."

"I'm married to a cop, so I understand all that, but is it really what you want to do for the rest of your life?"

"I guess it's the challenge, but I love what I'm doing. Otherwise, I wouldn't be doing it. Plus, I haven't thought that far ahead. I'm not married, don't have children, and don't plan on changing any of that in the foreseeable future."

"I used to think much the same way when I was working at a job that I liked," said Lila, biting at her lip.

"I take it you're not happy with what you're doing now?"

"That's just it, I'm not doing a thing. I'm looking to find something to do that makes me feel relevant and involved in the world."

"You're raising children."

Lila waved her hand. "That's the traditional cop-out for a lot of women. I'm not knocking those who think that way, it's just not how I wish to pass my life."

"Understood, but for what it's worth, I'm having fun living my life, and for me that's enough for now."

"I know a lot of women who would envy you," said Lila. "They live desperate lives, some quietly, others aggressively, but all driven to avoid confronting deep-rooted insecurities that haunt them, often through frenetic lifestyles filled with endless social events, whirlwind affairs, and extravagant expenditures."

"First-world problems, as they say. It's hard to image women with so much, feeling so empty."

"It's sad but true. There's a lot of angst out there among people you'd never suspect."

"Well, come with me tonight and see how the other half lives. Not to say their mental health is any better."

"Don't you have to play tonight?"

"Nope, an old friend's sitting in for me, so I get to take off and catch up on my friends performing elsewhere." Toni smiled at Lila. "Are you up for a girls' night out on the town?"

Lila rolled her eyes. "Partying two nights in a row? I'm too old for that."

"You're not much older than I am. Besides, we won't start before midnight. That gives you plenty of time to take a siesta."

Lila moved her head as if to gesture no, but paused. "You're right. Why not? A girls' night out it is."

Chapter Ten

Andreas was in a foul mood. He hadn't taken kindly to Lila's announced plans for a night on the town excluding him. It wasn't jealousy or envy, but concern. He pressed her at least to allow Yianni to join them, but his warnings only earned him a curt response: "I won't be unaccompanied. I'll be with Toni." His chances of changing his wife's mind fell precipitously from there.

He did convince her, though, to take their SUV and park in her usual lot, since late-night taxi and limo services were notoriously unreliable. Then he added, "And, if you drink too much, just call me and I'll arrange to have you driven home." His offer generated precisely the sort of response he'd hoped for: a scowl on Lila's face, making clear she'd rather walk home than call Andreas for a rescue.

His intention hadn't been to aggravate Lila, but to enlist her likely preference for sober independence over tipsy helplessness in charting her evening. In that respect, it was mission accomplished, but his minor success at navigating spousal relations came at a price.

Giving Lila the SUV had left Andreas and Yianni with Yianni's borrowed motorcycle as their only means of work transportation that night. They would have borrowed the cook's little pickup truck, but a run-in with a pothole had sidelined it for at least a few more days until a part completed its journey from the U.S.

Nor would they take the caretaker's car and risk leaving the children and help without transportation in case of an emergency. That meant a two-man, midnight motorcycle ride along narrow, uneven, unlit roads, dodging drivers under the influence coming at them from every which way, an experience that did nothing to improve Andreas' disposition when they arrived at Karavakis' club.

They parked by the front entrance and headed straight for the bar, just as crowded as it had been at the height of its afternoon madness. Things hadn't always been this profitable for beach bars. In the old days, they closed around sunset and customers headed back to their rooms to rest up and prepare for a riotous night in town. But no longer. These days the beaches competed head-to-head with the town for late-night partiers' cash, and between the town's horrific traffic and parking situation, and the growing late-night presence of hookers and their keepers, both domestic and foreign, the beach bars were winning.

As they walked toward the entrance Andreas clenched his teeth. "This guy is a real scum bucket. Everything about him is dirty."

Yianni stopped at the bar to ask if Karavakis was in, but Andreas kept right on walking toward the door to Karavakis' office. He banged on it twice. "Open up, Angelos, it's Andreas Kaldis."

"I'm busy."

Andreas opened the door and stepped inside.

"What the fuck do you think you're doing?" said Karavakis, standing next to two men around a table piled with euro notes.

"Coming in to bust your balls for busting mine."

"Get the hell out of here."

Andreas grabbed a chair from in front of Karavakis' desk, spun it around, and sat facing the men at the table.

The much smaller of the two men stepped toward Andreas.

"Don't even think of it," said Andreas to the man coming at him.

The bigger man stepped in behind the smaller just as Yianni came through the door.

Karavakis waved his arm for his two men to stop. "What is this, a cop convention?" He looked at the smaller man. "I thought I told you to lock the door."

"The others haven't made their drops yet."

"The way it works is this, *malaka*. When there's a knock, you ask who is it, you unlock door, you take cash, you close door, you lock door, and you repeat until finished. It's not that complicated." Karavakis shook his head and looked at Andreas. "Do cops have to put up with this sort of shit when they bring their kids into the business?"

"Why don't you ask your colleagues here to leave so we can get down to business?"

Karavakis grinned. "What is this, a shakedown?" He pointed at the cash on the tabletop.

Andreas leaned forward. "As a matter of fact, why don't you let them stay, so they can learn firsthand what a lousy liar you are?"

Karavakis squeezed his hands into fists. "No one calls me a liar in front of my son."

Andreas crossed his left leg over his right. "Then tell him to get the hell out of here before he hears a lot worse."

Karavakis charged around the table toward Andreas.

Andreas casually pulled a nine-millimeter semi-automatic from the ankle holster inside his left pant leg, and waved it in Karavakis' direction. "Do you really want to go there?"

The son lunged for Andreas' gun, but before he could reach him, Yianni delivered a hard, sharp thrust of the heel of his hand to the son's solar plexus, dropping him to the ground gasping for breath. Karavakis stopped moving toward the cops and bent to aid his son. The other man crouched to help.

"I'll take care of this," Karavakis said to the other man as they raised the son to his feet. "Get him out of here, and stay away until I call for you."

Karavakis clenched and unclenched his fists until the men had left. Andreas motioned with his hand toward the door, and Yianni locked it. Andreas holstered his gun. "Now, why don't you sit down behind your desk so we can have a civilized, non-theatrical talk?"

Karavakis stormed around his desk and fell into his chair. Yianni remained standing by the door.

"Just in case you're wondering, I'm not here about the cash. I'm sure you have receipts running every euro through your business. After all, that's the way laundries work, don't they?"

Karavakis said nothing.

"I'm here because of what you told my detective. Or rather what you didn't tell him."

"I don't know what you're talking about."

"It's about your buddy Pepe. The one with whom you arranged for the Colonel to have his last meal."

"What about Pepe?" He pointed at Yianni. "I already told him how I was trying to help Pepe set up a place here on the island. That was it."

Andreas tutted. "Angelos, Angelos, what am I going to do with you? You're a pathological liar."

Karvakis' face turned red. "That's the third time you've called me a liar."

"Then stop lying. Or perhaps you're so wasted on whatever you're taking that you've forgotten Pepe is your connection to your casino-hotel dream?"

The bright red in Karavakis' face blanched to chalk.

Andreas waited for a response. "Well?"

"How did you know that?"

"We're cops, we know everything. Now tell me what the Colonel's death had to do with your resort deal."

"Nothing, I swear."

Andreas smiled. "With all due respect, Angelos, do you really expect me to take you at your word? Try convincing me with the real facts."

"I don't have to tell you a damned thing."

"You're right, but taking that road will lead me to impound all that cash as evidence, send every tax agent on this island plowing through your businesses for black money, and of course exposing those point-of-sale credit-card machines you undoubtedly have steering a certain percentage of your take directly into a Swiss bank account. Plus, you'll have earned my relentless dedication to making your life as miserable as humanly possible."

Karavakis clenched his jaws and pounded his fists on the table. "*Gamoto, gamoto, gamoto.* Damn you, Kaldis."

"I'll take that as your damning way of saying you're going to tell me what I want to know. Please, feel free to proceed."

Karavakis pounded on his desktop twice more. "Pepe's brother is a senior guy in one of the world's top hotel chains, and in exchange for my helping Pepe get his place opened on the island, he's arranging for his brother to bless my deal with his company."

"Now, tell me the real reason he met with the Colonel."

"Like I said, to sign a security contract. The Colonel had his hooks into virtually every sizable business on the island. For some he just provided security, with others a bit more. There was no way for Pepe to get around using him."

"What do you mean by 'a bit more'?"

"If it was a place involved in on-premises drug dealing, he'd muscle in on that. When he could, he'd extort a piece of a legitimate bar, restaurant, hotel or shop business. If you want to talk about point-of-sale machines, he'd put his own into places where he'd extorted an interest so that his percentage of credit card sales went directly into his own bank accounts. Sometimes, he'd take over an entire business by making the owner an offer he couldn't refuse, to '*rent*' him the place." He sneered on the word "rent."

"In other words, he wasn't a universally loved guy."

"No shit, Sherlock. Stop busting my chops. You already know all this. His 'security business' was just the cover for a major protection and extortion racket."

"What was he demanding of you?"

"I'm not in the drug business."

It didn't matter whether Karavakis was telling the truth on that point. On an island as much into partying as this one, clubbing and drug dealing went hand in hand. While the clubs weren't necessarily directly involved in the dealing—though some undoubtedly got a piece—they also didn't interfere with it. Who got to sell in a specific club was another story, a territorial thing worked out by competing mobs.

"Spare me the holier-than-thou routine, Angelos. We all know the business you're into. I just want to know if the Colonel wanted a piece of your resort deal?"

Karavakis paused as if studying his desktop. He looked up. "Of course he wanted a piece. Who wouldn't? But he wouldn't dare try to muscle me. We've known each other too long." He clenched his teeth. "I kick back." He swallowed. "He knew I'd only bring him into the deal if he added value to the project."

"What kind of value?"

"Like I said, I'm not in the drug business, but the way things work around Mykonos, you know as well as I do that tourists spending big bucks want access to that shit when paying five-star luxury resort prices. That would be his slot in the deal. He knew it and I knew it. Sooner or later we'd be doing business together. We were just doing the negotiation dance until then."

"Pepe knew this?"

"Pepe had no idea of what role the Colonel might have in my project. It never came up. Honest, I fixed them up for the reason I said, a security contract for the club Pepe wanted to open. That had nothing to do with me."

Andreas leaned in. "Then let me ask you a final question. If everything is as simple and straightforward as you say, why didn't you come clean before?"

Karavakis leaned in toward Andreas. "Because I'm not in the business of telling cops that I'm being shaken down by one of their distinguished alumni to use his services as a drug dealer."

Andreas sat up straight. "Good answer." He stood. "Let's go, Yianni. Thanks for your time, Angelos."

Karavakis grunted. Yianni unlocked and opened the door. Four giants stood on the other side, blocking their exit.

Andreas turned and smiled at Karavakis, waiting.

Karavakis bellowed at the giants, "What the fuck are you doing blocking my doorway?"

The one closest to the door answered. "Your son told us not to move from here in case you needed us."

"Oh, yeah? And where's my son?"

"He took off into town. He said he had to meet some people."

Karavakis waved his arm at them. "Well, get the hell out of my guests' way." He looked at Andreas. "Sorry about that. My son tends to be overprotective of me at times."

"You must be very proud to have raised a son who cares," said Andreas, turning to leave with Yianni.

Karavakis looked unsure whether to glare or nod at the comment.

"I think it's time to head home," said Andreas as Yianni and he walked toward the parking lot.

"Or maybe to town," said Yianni. "Just in case the ladies have reconsidered the value of our company."

Andreas looked at his watch. "Good idea."

Lila met up with Toni, who was waiting for her in front of the only remaining bank in the bus station area. The others had moved farther out of town, to more convenient locations for their local customers. It wasn't actually a bus station, just an area big enough for five buses and a half-dozen taxis to park fifty meters into the old town.

Here, public buses and private vans of all sizes discharged their passengers into a relentless stream of cars, SUVs, ATVs, and motorbikes funneling back and forth along a narrow two-lane link to the hopelessly overloaded public parking area down by the windmills. Without a single cop to control the bedlam, and no sidewalks on the island's narrow roads, often clogged narrower still by double-parked vehicles, pedestrians had no choice but to dodge and weave among the madness.

Together, Toni and Lila passed through a bazaar of bus station businesses catering to tourists' holiday needs and fantasies: food shops for a fast meal and booze; kiosks selling cigarettes, postcards, phone cards, candy, gum, ice cream, condoms, and more; tattoo parlors offering indelible memories that seemed such a good idea at the time; stands hawking last-minute souvenirs; motorbike and car rentals; and, conveniently, ATMs.

Once safely within the old town's maze of crowded lanes, Toni told Lila they were headed to a tiny bar burrowed away on the other side of town amid a tangled warren of streets alongside the harbor. This place drew a different crowd than the piano bar—a mix of aging ex-pats, longtime visitors, and fresh-faced local kids, all united in a quest for memories of the island's bygone "hippie" days. Some were there to relive them, others to discover them.

For those who simply stumbled upon the place and stopped long enough to stare in through the front door, the scene must have seemed surreal. Tucked away in a far corner in front of a stone slab wall hung with a variety of local artists' paintings, four guys in their fifties, sixties, and seventies played music for an appreciative crowd. One played a West African djembe drum, another a guitar, the third a harmonica, and the eldest a tambourine.

Tonight, a crowd—eclectic in age, gender, and dress—filled every bar stool and table in the place, while more packed in along the bar, each finding a way of keeping beat with the music. Some with a head bob or finger tap; most with a steady beat of their feet on the scarred concrete floor, shiny in places from decades of similar toe-tappers.

Toni pointed out the musicians. The djembe player stood

out as the youngest, clean-shaven and short-haired but carefully dressed in the genre's traditional uniform of tee-shirt, blue jeans, and low-top Converse sneakers. He did the Ringo Starr thing, lagging the beat just enough behind the others to keep the train on the tracks.

Tambourine Man was the oldest. Now retired from his long tenure as the island's original rock 'n' roll singer, he still took care to jazz up his standard-issue apparel with a flashy velvet vest.

But, according to Toni, the main attractions tonight were the guitar player and Harmonica Man. For islanders, it was the equivalent of Jerry Garcia and Bob Dylan hooking up for a concert in their local bar. They played together a couple of times a year, whenever the guitar player visited from the States, and diehard fans packed every performance.

Guitar Player's variation on the dress code was a tan linen jacket, sleeves rolled up, and a black Kangol cap worn backwards. Harmonica Man filled the role of sartorial nonconformist in the band, dressed all in black, from his pointy-toed cowboy boots to his gambler-style, feather-in-the-hatband cowboy hat.

Younger fans stood around trying very hard to look different from all but each other. They strove to be cool, but Lila wondered if they realized that in this room at this moment, they were moving to precisely the same beat as their elders, caught up in the essential, bottom-line magic of music: *all within its reach are ageless.*

Lila noticed one significant difference between the gathered generations. Most of the young were stoned, while the older showed signs of the daily battles they now waged with the consequences of too many earlier trips down that same road.

"Hey, Toni, welcome! Glad to see you got away long enough to catch us." It was the guitar player calling her out from the stage in the middle of a song. No higher accolade than that could come from one musician to another. Toni nodded a smile and waved as he went on playing.

Lila studied two dark-haired Roma girls in their early teens, but looking closer to twenty, standing close to the improvised stage, offering roses for sale to the customers. They had to know this crowd of locals would yield few buyers, which meant they were here for the same thing as everyone else: the music.

Such a charade could prove tricky for them if their clan leader saw through it. In Athens, some Romas had unforgiving reputations for punishing those of their flock who did not fully dedicate themselves to his single-minded purpose of selling whatever could be sold to anyone willing to pay the price. Lila wondered if the same held true here.

Toni waved to one of the girls. "I've known her since I arrived on the island." The girl danced more than walked toward her, holding out a rose. Toni took it and offered her two euros, but she refused to take the money. Toni insisted, and she took it only after giving Lila a second rose.

A man reached around Lila and tapped Toni on the shoulder. "You're Toni?" he said in English.

Toni turned and gave a tentative smile. "Yep, that's me, the one and only."

"I've heard you've helped many people. I'd like to talk to you." The man spoke broken English with a heavy accent, likely Albanian.

Toni switched to Greek. "Sorry, but I'm here to catch my friends' performance. We can talk tomorrow."

The man's expression turned grave. "I'm sorry, but I need to talk to you now. It's a matter of life and death."

Toni hesitated. "I really can't talk in here, sir. It's rude to the performers."

"Then let's talk outside."

Lila could tell the guy was starting to annoy Toni.

"Sorry, no can do. See me tomorrow."

He raised a fist to Toni's face, and both women braced for things to turn physical. But he opened his hand, revealing a hundred-euro note. "Five minutes. It's all I ask."

Toni looked over at Lila and shrugged. "Hmm…if I stood just outside the front door, I still could hear the music, so it wouldn't be as if I were walking out on my friends. Besides, for a hundred euros, they'd understand."

"I'm not letting you leave with him alone."

The two women followed the man toward the door. He wore a laborer's jeans, work boots, and faded tee-shirt. He looked to be in his mid-thirties, about Toni's height, and possessed the wiry build that so many of his countrymen gain through years of hard manual labor at jobs no native-born islander would ever willingly do again.

Lila made Toni stop two paces outside the door. No reason to get too far away from the crowd, just in case he had another motive for getting Toni outside.

"So, what can I do to help you, sir?"

"Who's she?" He pointed at Lila.

"My associate. We work together."

He paused. "It's my daughter." He looked down at the ground. "She's in with bad people and won't listen to me."

"Sorry to hear that."

He looked Toni in the eyes. "She's only fifteen. We live on the island. She met a boy she knew from school. An older boy, a local boy from an important family."

By "local" he likely meant one born to a family of Greek heritage linked to the island. Even if this man lived on the island for a lifetime, raising generations of family members in the process, he and his family would never be considered Mykonian by the locals, but categorized instead according to their place of ethnic origin, and identified as such. The Albanian. The Bulgarian. The Roma. The Pakistani. That was the most immigrants could likely hope to be called. And, unless a local happened to do business with one of them—or they attended school together—one might never get to know the other, for many immigrants went about their lives in virtual anonymity away from most locals, preferring to keep to their own communities.

The man told Toni and Lila how his daughter had felt special for being singled out by the boy. Both he and his wife had warned their child that a local boy would only hurt her, and that she risked turning herself into an outcast among "her own kind." But to no avail.

Lila was thinking his story had begun to sound like a Mykonian variation on a *Romeo and Juliet* theme when Toni spoke up. "Sir, I feel for your situation, but I'm not sure what I can do. Affairs of the heart are not the sort of thing I handle."

"The problem is much worse. He's hooked her on drugs."

The women's faces tightened.

He bit at his lower lip and looked away. "And he gives her clothes. Clothes to attract men."

Poor kid...she's been hooked by a pimp. Lila spoke up. "Have you gone to the police?"

"The police?" He laughed. "The boy is from a prominent family. The police will not touch him."

"What about your friends in the Albanian community?" asked Toni. "Have you considered asking them for help?"

He made a hopeless gesture. "You mean the Mafia? Even if they could help, if I went to them, they'd own me forever. They might do even worse things to my daughter."

"I can't argue with you on that, but, frankly, sir, I still don't see what I can do for you."

"Get her away from him, get him to leave her alone."

"On such a small island, that's a hard thing to do. Unless she leaves the island."

He shook his head. "We have no place to go. My family's life and work are here, and if I send my daughter to live elsewhere, who knows what might happen to her...away from family." He pressed the hundred euros into Toni's hand. "Please, take this, save my daughter. I will pay you more."

"The money's not it, sir. I just don't think I can do anything for you. These sorts of problems are better handled by the clergy or professional counselors."

The father looked at Toni as if she were an innocent kinder-gartener. "My daughter...she's *trapped* by this boy. He controls her." He dropped his head. "My family is doomed."

Lila forced a smile. "I'm sure that's not so."

"Yes, it is." He stared at Toni. "Because if you can't help, my only choice is to kill the boy."

Whoa, thought Lila.

Toni simply nodded. "Yep, that will destroy your family for sure. I've another choice for you. Spend the money you want to pay me on professional help for your daughter, and some for yourself, too."

"It is too late." He inclined his head toward the bar. "The boy's inside with two others. I followed him here tonight to kill him." He pulled a switchblade far enough out of his pocket for Toni and Lila to see it, then slid it back inside. "When the man playing the guitar called out your name, I took it as a sign that you had come to help me. I know about you. People say you help them."

"That's very nice of you to say. But you have to give me a day or so to think about what I might be able to do for you. Who's the boy?"

"Bright-green tee-shirt, at the table closest to the front door."

Toni peeked inside and turned around visibly shaken. "I see your problem."

"Will you help me?"

"Permit me to consult with my colleague." Toni pulled Lila aside. "I better humor this guy, just in case he's serious. You should leave now."

"Not a chance. I'll call Andreas to get the police here."

"No way. This is a real mess. For the past five minutes we've been talking in public with a man describing in detail how he's prepared to kill the son of one of the biggest players on the island. If I walk away from him and he kills the boy, I'll never be able to convince the father I had nothing to do with his son's murder."

Toni glanced back toward the bar. "On the other hand, if I warn the boy or his father, this guy, his daughter, and the rest of their family will likely disappear off the face of the earth."

"You mean he's *that kind* of player."

"The worst." Toni shook her head. "I'll take this as a lesson for the next time I consider leaving my piano-playing fantasy world for a night wandering among the crazies out here."

"What are you going to do?"

"Something you shouldn't be any part of."

"I'm not leaving you alone with this man."

"He's not the one I'm worried about. But he's left me no choice but to say I'll try to help him." Toni looked down at her feet. "What I have to figure out is how the hell to get his daughter away from the bad guys."

Toni motioned for the man to come over to her. She looked him straight in the eye. "First of all, what's your name and where do you live?"

He gave his name and address.

"And your daughter's name?"

"Adina."

"Before I agree to do what you asked, let's get something straight. I didn't get your daughter in this situation, and you're the one who won't accept the obvious solution and send her off the island. So don't try making me feel responsible for the mess she's in. And by the way, don't blame me if you and your wife can't keep your fifteen-year-old daughter home at night."

He leaned back slightly and glared at her.

"And don't give me that look. Save it for your mirror. If you want to go ahead and wreck your life with your switchblade, be my guest. But if you want me to try to help, you'll have to do it my way and be patient."

He dropped his head.

"I appreciate what your family is going through, but this is a nasty situation. Now, I'm willing to try to find some way to end it without putting you and your family at risk. Or me." She paused. "Understand?"

The glare had gone from his eyes, replaced by welling tears. He nodded. "Yes."

"Meet me at the harbor tomorrow at two." She gave him the name of the taverna that served as her office.

He hugged her, saying, "Thank you. May God be with you," and hurried off.

Lila stared at Toni. "I'm truly impressed at how you handled that. So was he. He even blessed you."

"I think a more appropriate blessing for the situation he's put me in would be, *God help you.*"

Lila took Toni's arm and steered her back into the bar. "It's time to return to having fun. Things can only go uphill from here."

"That, my dear optimist, is what I call true prayer."

Chapter Eleven

Yianni drove the motorcycle, with Andreas doubled up behind him, a now-common practice among Athens police. But they were not in uniform, not on a police bike, and not in Athens. Motorcycles and ATVs streamed passed them, blindly cutting tightly into sand-strewn corners at high speed, weaving in and out of the oncoming lane of traffic, and performing any number of other fate-tempting maneuvers, all accompanied by the sounds of horn-honking and sing-song shouts of "MY-KON-OS."

Yianni had been carefully avoiding all the partying drivers passing by on a winding road barely wide enough for two small jeeps to pass one another, when a motorcycle charged up behind them. Yianni glanced back in his left mirror but couldn't make out the driver in the glare of the trailing bike's headlight.

To give the motorcyclist enough room to pass without having to move into the oncoming lane, Yianni moved over to the right, close by a low stone wall separating the road from a steep hillside drop.

The motorcycle roared up beside them but didn't pass, instead mimicked their pace, revving its engine, and cruising beside them, leaving no more than a meter between the two bikes. Yianni glanced to his left and didn't recognize the driver beneath his helmet. Out of the corner of his eye, Yianni saw him lift up his right foot. He immediately knew what the man had in mind, a technique used by beach peddlers of massages and counterfeit goods for persuading potential competitors to stay away from beaches they'd claimed as their own. A quick kick would send Andreas and him crashing into the stone wall or over it. Just another road accident for their local police brethren to clean up.

As the driver swerved in toward their bike, Yianni hit his brakes hard, skidding in the process, but he avoided the boot and managed to keep his overloaded bike upright. The driver hadn't expected Yianni's move and lost his balance when his foot kicked nothing but air.

While the driver struggled to regain control, Yianni sped up on the left side of the driver. Andreas delivered a kick of his own to the driver's center of gravity, sending him and his bike to the ground and skidding into the wall.

Yianni jerked to a stop, and Andreas and he ran back to the driver, who lay perfectly still. Yianni gently removed the driver's helmet. The man underneath looked like many of the island's heavily tattooed, muscled, private-security types: a beard and shaved head, military camouflage shorts, a tight black tee-shirt bearing some ambiguous but macho symbol over the heart, and black leather high-tops. Were it daytime, he'd undoubtedly have worn Ray-Ban Wayfarers rather than a helmet.

Andreas felt for a pulse. "Still ticking. Call for an ambulance."

Yianni called on his mobile. "Lucky he wore a helmet."

"The bastard wore it so we couldn't recognize him if we somehow survived."

"I meant lucky for us. Now we can get him to tell us who sent him."

Andreas knelt and shone the flashlight from his mobile phone on the man's face. "I can guess at his answer. Take a look at him."

Yianni crouched down. "Son of a bitch. He was in the office with Karavakis and his kid."

Andreas stood. "Looks like Karavakis has decided to play hardball."

Yianni clenched his fists as he stood. "Let's go back and show him how to do it right."

"I'd love to, but there's no chance of hanging this on him unless, and until, our unconscious witness talks."

Gawkers from ATVs, cars, vans, and bikes stood scattered all across the road. Andreas yanked his police ID out from under his shirt and yelled at them, "Get moving. You're blocking access to a crime scene."

He looked at Yianni. "As much as I'd like to take this guy's bike and shove it sideways up Karavakis' ass, I'll get much greater joy nailing him for murder."

A siren wailed in the near distance. "It must be the ambulance coming for this guy," said Yianni.

"Good. But when we come for Karavakis, the only sound I want him hearing is a cell door slamming shut behind him."

"I can live with that."

Yianni and Andreas followed the ambulance to the medical clinic, which wasn't equipped to handle the sort of trauma their attacker had sustained, and so he was airlifted to Athens. Andreas notified GADA and the Athens hospital that the patient was under arrest for the attempted murder of two police officers and should be treated accordingly. In describing to the Mykonos police chief what had happened, Yianni and he offered no opinion on the man's identity, why he attacked them, or if anyone else might be involved.

"I can't believe you have no idea, not even a guess, at why a complete stranger would want to kill you," said Telly.

"Why are you surprised?" said Andreas. "It's crazy season on the island. With so many nuts concentrated and high in one place, it's only a matter of probability until something bad happens to you."

"You must think I'm an idiot."

"No, I think you're a cop just trying to do his job, which includes never believing the first story you're told by someone involved in an altercation."

"Fine, stick to your story. Just tell me why you were on the road coming back from Karavakis' club?"

"My wife had plans with a girlfriend in town, and we thought it would be a good chance to check out the action at the hottest place on the island."

"Yeah," said Yianni. "Great idea, Chief. Next time why don't we enter a tag-team cage-fighting competition? It's less risky."

Telly waved them both off. "Enough already. I still don't believe you. But just in case you're not feeding me a bullshit story, and you come up with something to explain what happened tonight, you will let me know, won't you?"

"Of course," said Andreas.

Telly sighed as he walked out of the medical center.

"What now?" said Yianni.

Andreas looked at his watch. "It's half-past three. I'd say home."

"What about Lila and Toni?"

Andreas took out his phone. "No message from Lila." He put the phone back in his pocket. "And if they're still out on the town, I don't want to know about it."

Yianni looked at his phone. "No message for me either."

Andreas patted Yianni on the back. "Then I guess home it is."

Lila and Toni left the bar around three. The main streets were filled with partiers, so they took the back streets to an all-night sandwich place just off the harbor. They grabbed two beers, split one sandwich, borrowed two chairs from a shuttered harborside taverna, and lugged everything down onto the narrow strip of beach separating the harborfront road from the sea. They now had front-row seats on a nearly full moon lighting up the sea, and of the harbor clubs doing much the same thing to their customers.

Toni took a bite of the sandwich. "That was quite a night we had."

"For sure. Are they always like that?"

"They don't usually involve guys with switchblades."

Lila took a sip of beer. "Do you mind if I ask you a question? I think you might be able to help me with a problem I'm wrestling with."

Toni took a sip of her beer. "If I can, sure."

"I'm sure it's no secret to you that I'm experiencing a young-mother-out-of-the-workforce quandary. I'm trying to figure out how to go about finding a meaningful focus for the rest of my life."

"You think I can help you answer that?" Toni rested her beer on the sand. "I'm flattered, but not only am I childless, younger, and without a college education, to be perfectly blunt I'm a pauper compared to you. Make that compared to practically everyone on this island."

"But you know how to *live*. You found your dream and seized it."

"I've always found the need for food, clothing, and shelter to be a great motivator."

"Stop with the jokes," said Lila. "I'm serious. You have true gifts. I've seen you perform at the piano bar and how you handled that distraught father. You mastered your crafts, and did so without a college education. That's inspirational in and of itself."

Toni paused. "How do you expect me to respond to that without a joke?"

Lila smiled. "See, you can even handle the awkward situations I create." She tipped her beer toward Toni in a toast, then took a sip. "Is it instinctive or did you learn how to think that way?"

Toni shrugged.

"Please, at least try to describe how you do what you do. There's no telling how it might help launch me in the right direction."

Toni stared at her. "And you expect me to tell you all this at three in the morning, on my second consecutive night of too much drinking." She raised her hand holding the sandwich. "I know, no more jokes." She sighed. "Okay, here goes." She took a small bite and chewed it slowly, as if taking the time to think. "Forget about my gig at the piano bar. That's driven by inner demons I can't explain. Music is more an addiction to me than a career. I can't shake it and don't want to. Whatever it takes to get a fix, I do it. Almost without limits. But that's another story. A very long one. So, let me focus on my day job as a finder of stolen goods."

Toni took a sip of beer.

"So, the thefts I follow typically involve a heavy concentration of what I call *the four C's*: cash, computers, cameras, and cell phones. In my experience, victims tend to be least upset about the loss of cash. It's fungible and replaceable. But the computer often holds a lifetime of records in need of a backup; the lost camera means bye-bye to a lot of meaningful memories; and the missing cell phone is a royal pain in the ass, whether backed up to the Cloud, or not."

She took another sip of beer and put it down on the sand. "Of course, there are also credit cards and passports. Some thieves take a shot at using the cards before their victims have time to notify the credit card companies, and others can even sell the passports, but most thieves discard them. Not worth the effort."

Lila didn't budge from her chair, move to sip her beer, or taste her sandwich.

"The first thing I do when a client is burglarized is conduct a thorough search of the area surrounding the scene of the theft, including every nearby trash container. That bit of effort often turns up the missing credit cards and passports, yielding me an easy fee and satisfied clients.

"It's the stolen jewelry and watches that get tricky. First, I accompany my clients to the police and assist them with the paperwork they need in order to file insurance claims back home."

"Hmm," said Lila. "Did you ever think that could be the tourist's way of cashing in back home?"

Toni picked up her beer from the sand and took a sip. "I see you are a cop's wife. Yes, thoughts of insurance fraud have crossed my mind, especially after I've located the thief and—in negotiating the return of my client's property—the thief swears he never took certain items my clients claim were stolen. That's not to say I trust the word of a thief over that of my clients, but then again, the concept of a burglary victim adding a few extra items to a list of stolen valuables does reinforce my take on the basic larcenous nature of our species."

"How do you find the thief?"

"Ah, now you're trying to get at my trade secrets." Toni smiled. "If my clients come to me straightaway, I've a good track record at getting their stuff back. In part, because I know most of the lowlife thieves on the island, and they know that I won't turn them in if they cooperate. I've even been known on occasion to split a client's fee with the bad guys, assuming they return the property. It's not a perfect world, but it's a living."

Lila sat back in her chair. "Amazing. And you figured out how to do all of this on your own?"

"If you're asking whether there's a Fagin to my Oliver Twist, the answer's no. It's just little old me. My mentor is human nature."

"Meaning?"

"Human nature explains many things, such as why our civilized society tolerates so much criminality. As I see it, too many folks whom we like to think of as upstanding members of society share a primal kinship with those baser types who look to take criminal advantage of the system at every opportunity." She leaned closer to Lila. "Let me give you an example drawn from my experience with what could be called 'the fifth C,' the most popular item in the stolen-goods trade: clothing. There's a thriving bazaar-like market in Athens—in Piraeus port, to be precise—for high-end secondhand clothing, especially shoes. If my clients are interested enough in recovering their stolen clothing, I'll take them there. On occasion we've been lucky enough to find the missing items. Rather than threatening to call the police, I get them a good price—so good, in fact, that many clients often buy other items without so much as a passing thought about the provenance of their new purchases."

Lila shook her head. "It's the world we live in, I guess."

Toni tapped Lila on the knee. "Speaking of the world we live in, I think we should move along. Our little sisterly chat on the beach is about to be crashed by a crew of drunken tourist guys headed our way."

Lila turned toward around to see five men staggering toward them, yelling, "It's time to party."

"No, boys," said Toni loudly, "it's time to go home." Toni pulled Lila up onto her feet. "Leave the chairs. It'll give our newfound friends hope that the sort of ladies of the evening they're looking for might stop by to fill them."

"Human nature?"

"You got it."

Andreas beat Lila home in time to claim the moral high ground, but just barely. He feigned sleep until she'd crawled into bed. "Everything go okay?"

"Yes. And with you?"

Andreas paused. "Just the usual night-out-on-the-town sort of excitement."

"Me too. We'll talk in the morning."

"About what?" asked Andreas.

Lila didn't answer. She'd faded off to sleep.

"I said 'about what'?"

Still no answer.

About what? kept Andreas tossing and turning for nearly a

half-hour, but nothing he did roused her from her sleep. Finally, he drifted off…and missed the broad smile on his wife's face once he had.

● ● ● ● ●

Andreas woke to the sound of Tassaki running around the house imitating a police siren. He patted the bed next to him for Lila, but she was gone. He looked at the clock. Ten a.m. Not bad. A lot later than the kids usually allowed them to sleep. In this case, allowed *him* to sleep. He wondered what time Lila had gotten out of bed. Which brought him back to thinking of his unanswered question to her on the subject of the night before.

He went to the bathroom, pulled on a pair of shorts and a tee-shirt, and followed the scent of the coffee. Yianni and Lila sat on the terrace, Sofia between them in a high chair as Tassaki terrorized the nanny by the pool. A picture-perfect scene of domestic tranquility.

Andreas kissed Sofia on the forehead, poured himself a cup of coffee, and sat down across from Lila and Yianni. "Morning, my fellow revelers."

"Morning, my love."

"Ditto," said Yianni.

"What time did you get up?" asked Andreas.

"About nine," said Lila.

"A half-hour ago," said Yianni.

"Thank you for letting me sleep in."

"Me, too," said Yianni.

"After what happened last night, you two needed it."

Andreas glanced at Yianni. "What did you tell her?"

"I told her we went to The Beach Club, and had a bang-up time bumping into old and new friends."

"Now, dear husband, why don't you tell me what really happened?"

"It's like Yianni said." Andreas took a sip of coffee. "So how was your evening?"

"Not much. A man showed us what he had in his pants, and we decided to do what he asked."

Andreas stared at her. "Stop putting me on."

"It's precisely as I said." She forced a smile and poured herself some orange juice. "Amazing, the sorts of people you run into on a Mykonos late night."

Andreas glanced at Yianni. "What did you really tell her?"

"Chief, you're about the most guilt-ridden innocent I've ever seen. I told her N-O-T-H-I-N-G."

Lila sipped her orange juice. "If you want to hear about my evening, you better tell me the truth about yours."

Andreas fluttered his lips. "We went to a club on the beach to question a witness in a murder investigation. On the way back, we had an accident with another motorcycle. The other guy was seriously injured and had to be airlifted to Athens."

"That's terrible. How is he doing?"

"I don't know," said Andreas.

"I checked," said Yianni. "He's still unconscious, but they expect him to live."

"What's his name?" she asked.

"I don't know."

"Me either," said Yianni. "But the local police said he's not Greek."

"Your turn," said Andreas, looking at Lila.

Lila leaned forward and her face lit up. "It was fascinating. Toni is an extraordinary young woman. Her outlook on life is spot-on. She reminds me of my college roommate, a true free spirit with a big heart, who was always there for you when you needed her." Lila swallowed and looked at Yianni. "She passed away a few years after graduation, long before Andreas and I met."

Andreas gave a quick look at Yianni before catching Lila's eye. "I'm not sure I'm going to say this right, because I do like Toni, but, darling, you sound like you're using the memories of your roommate to vouch for the virtues of a new acquaintance."

Lila paused. "Could be that you're right, but I've always gone with my first instincts on meeting someone new—"

"And look where that's landed you," interrupted Yianni, pointing at Andreas.

"Okay, guys, I get it," said Andreas, waving his hands in surrender. "Forget what I said." He looked at Lila. "So, tell me about the guy with the thing in his pants?"

Lila smiled. "Oh, that little old thing. Hardly worth talking about."

Andreas turned his look into a stare.

Lila picked up her coffee cup. "Some worker on the island wanted Toni to get his daughter away from the bad influences of a local boy. He showed us the knife he was planning to use on the boy if she didn't agree to help."

"I knew you shouldn't have gone out alone."

Lila shrugged. "What are you talking about? We had a great time, and no one we bumped into ended up in the hospital."

"*Touché*," said Yianni, picking up his coffee cup.

"You know what I mean," said Andreas.

"Of course I do. In your world, we little women need the protection of you big, strong men. If you look at things honestly, I think in most situations you need more protection from each other than we do from you."

Andreas shut his eyes. "This conversation is going nowhere. Let's go to the beach."

"Which one?" she asked.

"You pick it."

Lila looked at the sea. "With this wind, the best beach is one you don't like."

Andreas sighed. "I don't like it because of the clientele, but I agree it's the best beach for today." He slapped his thighs. "Okay, your choice it is, and we'll eat there, too. Just to show you I'm a good sport."

Lila stood. "More like to show you have a guilty conscience."

She picked Sofia up out of her high chair and sing-songed over her shoulder as she carried their daughter inside, "But don't we all?"

● ● ● ● ●

Lila stood in the nursery changing Sofia's diaper. Andreas was right about why she felt so strangely close to this complete stranger. In Toni she saw the spirit of her old friend. That was the only logical explanation for feeling as if she'd known Toni all her life.

But that's a good thing. Isn't it?

Both possessed a contagious zest for life. Lila did things with her friend she'd never imagine having done on her own. Crazy, wild things; but never hurtful, and always with a good motive—even if authorities didn't sometimes agree. Lila smiled at the memories.

Her friend had glorious plans for living a life doing all that she could to better her world, but in her way. Yes, glorious plans.

Tears welled up in Lila's eyes.

But then she died.

Not in some dramatic fashion. Not on some glorious quest, not tending to the injured on some far off battlefield, not as a victim to a heinous crime, or even an accident. She died with a whimper alongside her daughter.

In childbirth.

Tears streamed down Lila's cheeks.

If Toni is but half as dear to me as you were, she will be a glory to your memory, my beloved friend Sofia.

Chapter Twelve

Andreas drove the SUV up to the beach entrance servicing both the nearby restaurant and the beach. He handed the keys to the parking valet, who immediately requested twenty euros in advance.

Andreas handed him a twenty. "And so the fun begins," he muttered to no one in particular.

Lila, holding Tassaki's hand, and Anna, carrying Sofia, led the way onto the beach. Andreas and Yianni followed behind, both with a beach bag in each hand.

A body-builder-sized beach attendant in black shorts, white tee-shirt, Ray-Ban Wayfarers, and a black baseball cap, asked Lila if he could help her. She asked for four sunbeds and two umbrellas.

"That will be four hundred euros."

"*What?*" shouted Lila.

"I said four hundred euros. It's two hundred euros for two beds and one umbrella. Those are the only beds available."

"That's preposterous."

"I'm sorry, madam, but after all, this is the most desirable beach on Mykonos and it is high season."

On that, Andreas stepped in between the attendant and Lila. "That's okay, my dear, we'll just spread our towels on the open sand next to this high-rent district."

The attendant wiggled a finger at Andreas. "You can't do that here."

Andreas forced a grin. "Of course we can. All beaches are open to the public in Greece."

"Not here."

Andreas gave him a knowing smile. "Son, I know that's how beach businesses with seasonal leases from the town to rent sunbeds would like the law to be. After all, clients of yours who pay exorbitant sums for a prime spot don't want just anyone dropping down beside them on a towel." He shook his head, "But Greek law holds that all beaches are open to anyone, and you need not rent a sunbed if you don't want one. Beds also may not go up to the water's edge, though I suspect those concepts are politely ignored by your municipal officials charged with enforcing the laws. I shall not guess why that is."

The attendant crossed his arms. "I repeat. You can't put a towel down here."

Andreas motioned for Lila to lead the way to an open bit of beach just beyond the sunbeds.

The attendant waved for two burly fellows dressed all in black standing by the beach entrance to the restaurant.

"Andreas, please don't start anything. We can find another beach," said Lila.

"Don't worry. Yianni and I will be right along."

"You ought to listen to your wife, sir," said the attendant.

Lila turned to Anna. "Quick, let's get the children away from here." They headed off toward the open area.

The beach attendant and his fellow no-necks took up a position blocking Andreas and Yianni from following Lila.

"Boys, I've taken great pains to explain the law to you. May I suggest you reconsider taking a course of action that will soon bring great personal pain to each of you? Not to mention the potential need for extensive rehabilitative physical therapy."

"Enough with the fancy tough talk, asshole," said the attendant, assuming a karate stance.

"Ah, so much for the sirs," said Andreas. "Last chance to walk away."

Yianni tossed the beach bags he'd been carrying to the side and motioned with his hand for the two no-necks to come at him. "I'll try to leave you two in good enough condition to carry your numb-nuts buddy to the ambulance. But no promises."

The rapidly escalating confrontation had generated excitement among the sunbed crowd—a bit of a break in their roast-until-you're-toast sun-worshipping routine. Rent-a-cop sorts like these guys, with the encouragement of their employers, enjoyed putting on a rough house show for the paying clientele when someone protested their bosses' fees and rules too strongly. After all, there was big money to be made in sunbed rentals. Some restaurants made more off the rentals than they did from their food operations. Pricey places like this might even make more from *one day's* rentals in high season than the *total annual* fee they paid to the government for the right to rent their beds.

Andreas stood still, one beach bag in each hand, and facing the attendant, waited for him to make the first move. The man lunged, and Andreas stepped back, swinging the bag in his right hand up to catch the man hard under his chin, immediately followed by a wide overhead arc crashing the bag in his left down on the back of the man's head, dropping him to the sand.

"Never underestimate the striking power of a baby formula thermos bag."

The two men facing Yianni hesitated. Andreas angled his stance toward them while keeping his eyes on the man on the ground. "Wise decision, gentlemen. You're about to assault a detective and chief inspector of the Hellenic Police."

The two men stared at each other for a few seconds before turning away from Yianni, and moving in to help the attendant to his feet and away from the scene. None said a word.

Andreas and Yianni turned to follow Lila but stopped when Andreas heard his name shouted from up on the restaurant's terrace. "Andreas, stay there. I'll be right down."

A small, deeply tanned man dressed in white linen with tasteful gold chains draped around his unbuttoned neck scurried over. He owned the restaurant and held the license for the exorbitant beach-chair rentals. "I'm so sorry. I had no idea what was going on until one of my staff told me there was a fight on the beach."

"I wouldn't exactly call it a fight," said Andreas. "More like a civics-lesson disagreement over whether you or the Greek people own the beach."

The owner offered a nervous smile. "You know I'd never have allowed this to happen if I knew it involved you and your family, Chief."

"Yes, I do, especially when I see how very well you've done for yourself in my absence."

The owner gave a nervous laugh. "Please, allow me to attempt to make up for this unpleasant experience by having you and your family as my guests for the day."

Andreas hesitated. "We have four adults and two children."

"No problem."

"Okay," said Andreas. "I'll accept your kindness on the beds and umbrella, but I insist you let me pay for lunch in the restaurant."

The owner smiled. "A smart offer. It will likely be cheaper paying for the food than the sunbeds."

"But not by much."

The man grinned and patted Andreas on the shoulder. "Again, I'm very sorry for the misunderstanding." He waved to a different beach attendant. "Four sunbeds and two umbrellas in the front row for my friends."

"But, sir, they're all reserved."

The owner glared at his employee. "Not anymore." He looked at Andreas. "Please, follow him."

Yianni started off behind the attendant. "I'll catch up with Lila and the rest of the crew and bring them back to the sunbeds."

"Not sure I'll want the lecture I'm likely to get from her when you do."

"Don't worry. She's used to you by now."

Andreas paused as Yianni kept walking. He wondered if that might be an underlying cause of Lila's discontent. *She's used to him.* Did she see her life as too predictable and fixed?

I thought only men went through that sort of crisis, and much later in our lives.

He carried the two beach bags over to the four unoccupied sunbeds. Everyone around him had witnessed what just happened, and he knew they'd be eyeing him suspiciously. He couldn't blame them. He stared down the rows of beds. Amazing how many people had so much money, or at least acted as if they did. Once, Americans, Brits, and other Europeans made up the professional and business types who could afford to play like this on holiday. These days, Middle Eastern, Indian, and Russian spenders dropped truly big bucks. So, too, did another sort: well-heeled criminals from around the world. After all, this was their party island too.

He dropped the bags on one of the sunbeds, tipped the attendant, stripped down to his bathing suit, and headed straight for the sea. He waded in up to his knees before diving into the water. He loved the Aegean. It had perfect clarity, temperature, and buoyancy—at least for his body.

Andreas swam to the line of blaze-orange buoys running parallel to the shore and separating the swimming area from boat traffic. He turned at the buoys and began a slow, steady crawl stroke, swimming parallel to the beach toward the cliffs bordering the bay. The first ten minutes were always the most difficult for him, his muscles not yet in sync with his will. Things smoothed out after that, and the next twenty minutes breezed by, drawing him into a nearly meditative state.

At forty minutes, he decided to call it quits and swam back to the beach. As he skipped onto shore, he looked for Lila and the kids. Sofia lay shielded from the sun with Anna under an umbrella while Yianni and Tassaki built a sand castle together atop the slice of sand between the sunbeds and the sea.

"Have a good swim?" asked Yianni.

"Terrific. There's nothing like the Aegean." Andreas looked around. "Where's Lila?"

"Some Athenian friends dragged her off to a new shop that just opened next door."

"Maybe that will get her mind off of playing detective with Toni."

"I doubt it," said Yianni, using a bright yellow bulldozer to plow a new driveway for Tassaki's castle. "She called Toni and asked her to join us for lunch."

"That's nice."

"But Toni said she can't make it. Something about a meeting with a client."

Andreas crouched down next to Yianni, and whispered. "I'm worried about Lila playing private detective, even as a bystander. This isn't a kid's game. Guys who flash knives actually use them." He leaned in. "What do you think I should do to get her to listen to me?"

Yianni looked at Andreas. "You're asking me? Have you noticed the amount of influence I have with Toni?"

"But that's to be expected. You two hardly know each other."

"Yes, and you and Lila know each other about as well as two people possibly could."

Andreas picked up a tiny shell. "Hmm, you might have just answered my question."

Yianni stared at him. "I have no idea what you're talking about, but I'm glad to have helped out."

"I think my best chance at impacting Lila's decisions, and vice versa, was in the period between our first meeting, and when we became truly in tune with one another. Now that we know each other so well, whichever one of us is agonizing over a decision has likely already processed the other's anticipated opinion into the decision, leaving little chance for a change of mind."

"Daddy, daddy," Tassaki yelled, pointing at a series of huge waves generated by the wake of a mega-yacht passing by too quickly and close to shore.

"It's going to hit our castle," he cried.

Andreas and Yianni quickly gathered up the toys. "We can't fight Mother Nature, son. Let's just get out of its way, and stay safe until the crisis passes. We'll come back to rebuild later."

Yianni smiled. "Sounds like pretty good relationship advice to me, Chief."

● ● ● ● ●

To Andreas, lunch at this beach always seemed more about the social scene than the food. He had hoped for one of the tables off to the side, away from the action, but no such luck. The owner had held open one of his prime tables, set squarely in the middle of the action, high chair for Sofia and all. Champagne spray already filled the air, launched by celebrants at adjacent tables. Lila took care to seat Sofia as far away from them as possible.

Andreas asked Lila if he should request a different table.

"This'll be fine. She's a Greek girl. Sooner or later she'll have to get used to men making fools of themselves in public to attract attention."

Yianni chuckled, sitting down next to Anna and across from Lila and Andreas.

"I hope much later," said Andreas. He glanced around the room. As expected, the curious eyes of the couture-bedecked patrons studied every detail of what Andreas' crew wore, undoubtedly searching for a clue to the identity of the woefully underdressed folk sitting at one of the "you must spend a minimum of five thousand euros to sit here" tables. He shrugged to himself. Maybe they'd convince themselves that the Kaldis party was so badly dressed as to be chic.

The owner hurried over to Lila. She stood and he kissed her on both cheeks. "So happy to see you again, my dear Lila."

"Careful," warned Lila. "My hair is still wet from the sea."

"Thankfully, the sea didn't ruin your makeup."

"Don't be silly. I'm not wearing makeup."

The owner's jaw dropped. "You must be kidding me. You look simply radiant."

Lila rolled her eyes. "You don't have to lay it on so thick."

"For sure," said Andreas, "we're paying for lunch, whether or not you're charming."

The owner winked at Lila. "Let me know if you ever tire of this troublemaker." He patted Andreas on the back, and walked away.

"I take it you know him," said Yianni as Lila resumed her seat.

"He's an old friend of my mother and father. We knew him when this place was nothing but a shack on the beach."

"All I know," said Yianni, "is that if I had to pay what he charges for this table, I'd be washing dishes for a year."

Lila smiled. "He's not going bill us like tourists."

"I still couldn't handle this on my paycheck," said Yianni.

Lila looked around the room. "I understand. But you have to give him credit. He's a businessman who has a unique gift for anticipating big spenders' wants and getting them to pay him extraordinary amounts to satisfy their desires."

Yianni nodded toward a table of scantily clad young women interspersed between much older men. "I see what you mean."

Andreas jumped in. "Would you two mind changing the subject? Can we just enjoy the scene and avoid a deep and meaningful cultural analysis of our times?"

The waiter dropped off menus and a wine list. Without opening them, Lila ordered a half-dozen appetizers from memory. Andreas ordered a bottle of white wine.

"I hope you don't mind my being so bold as to order the appetizers," she said to Yianni. "I'm sure you'll like them."

"It all sounds great to me."

"Same apology from me on the wine," said Andreas.

"No problem. I'm just glad you didn't order champagne. It might have been taken as a sign of aggression by one of our adjoining tables."

A young man at the next table with a shaved head and week-old black beard was making a big deal of shaking up a bottle of Dom Perignon White Gold. He aimed it in the direction of a smiling, blued-eyed blonde, clearly unconcerned about her fate.

Andreas shook his head. "That bottle costs almost as much as a car. And he's going to spray it?"

"Remember your rule: no cultural commentary," said Lila.

The young man let loose with the spray at the girl.

"What an idiot," said Yianni.

"It's My-kon-os," said Andreas, mimicking the ATVers sing-song chant.

"Why, Lila, darling, what a pleasant surprise. How are you?" A couture-styled, svelte blonde in Chanel sunglasses bent down behind Lila and kissed her cheeks.

Andreas and Yianni immediately stood. Lila made it to her feet a few seconds later, looking a bit surprised. "Oh, my, so nice to see you. You know my husband, Andreas."

Andreas smiled.

"And this is our friend, Yianni—"

"Nice to see you again, Mrs. Despotiko."

The woman smiled. "Likewise, Detective." She turned back to Lila. "We must get together while you're here. We simply must."

"Certainly," smiled Lila.

"I've interrupted your lovely family lunch long enough, but when I noticed you sitting behind us, I just had to come over and say hello." She nodded to Andreas, gave a smile to Yianni, squeezed Lila's arm, and went back to a long table behind Andreas and Lila.

"That was a surprise," said Lila, sitting.

"There's more surprises to come," said Yianni, looking at Andreas. "Guess who's with her at that table." He paused. "Our dear old friend Angelos Karavakis."

Lila swung her head around and stared straight at the table. "So that's the famous Angelos Karavakis."

"Infamous," said Andreas, clenching his jaw.

"Who else is at the table?" she asked.

"Their backs are to me," said Yianni.

Just then a bald, stocky, middle-aged man walked through the doorway shook hands with the others at the table and sat down.

"Correction, I know another one." said Yianni. "The island's illustrious mayor just joined their party."

"Just birds of a feather flocking together," said Andreas.

"Songbirds or vultures?" said Lila

"Definite meat-eaters," answered Andreas.

"Sort of makes you wonder," said Lila.

"Wonder about what?"

"What's worse? Drug dealers and sex-traffickers destroying lives, or supposedly legitimate business and government types doing the same thing to entire communities? I mean, can you really separate them out for me? Which ones are dealing in drugs and sex, and which are destroying the essence of the island?"

"I get your point," said Andreas, "but let's not forget that most of the people in here are on holiday. Back home, they're likely just plain folk. Yes, some may be celebrities, others possibly criminals, but there's no way of telling what they do in their everyday lives just from looking at them."

"I wonder what the big meeting's all about," said Lila.

"Me too," said Andreas. "I'd love to know what Mrs. Despotiko is doing there. Her husband's not among the group."

"But from the way everyone at the table is deferring to her," said Yianni, "you'd think *she* was the Godfather, not her husband."

"Respect must be paid," said Andreas turning to take a better look at the table. His move caught the eye of the mayor, who promptly raised a wineglass to him and smiled.

"We've been outed, folks. Glasses up, smiles on, and toast away."

Everyone at their table except for Sofia exchanged smiles and air-toasts with the other table.

"Well done, Tassaki," said Andreas, smiling at his son, and turning to put down his glass. "Glad that bit of hypocrisy is over and done with."

Lila sat staring across their table into the middle distance.

"Are you okay?" said Andreas, touching her hand.

"Not sure."

"What's wrong?"

"Remember that man who told Toni he planned to kill someone for corrupting his daughter?"

"Yes," said Andreas.

"Well," she said, voice lowered, "his intended victim is sitting to the left of Angelos Karavakis. I recognized him when they toasted us."

Andreas and Yianni abruptly turned to look at the table.

"Jeez," said Yianni. "That's Karavakis' son."

Andreas looked at Yianni. "I think it's time we have a serious chat with your friend Toni."

"That's *our* friend," said Lila abruptly.

Two waiters arrived with the appetizers.

"Time to eat," said Yianni. "We can return to puzzle-solving later."

Right, thought Andreas. *Solving would be nice.*

Toni was quite proud of herself at having made it to her office precisely at four, just as she'd promised her client.

The waiter handed her an envelope. "An Albanian left it for you about an hour ago."

She opened it and found a note.

I'm afraid to be seen with you in harbor. Please come to house.

He obviously had a better appreciation of the risks involved than she did.

She did not recognize the address he'd given for his home. Thankfully, he'd also drawn a map showing its location. That, she recognized: an alleyway between Little Venice and the bus station.

She dropped a couple euros on the table and wandered out into a crush of tourists and sidewalk hawkers busily culling prospective patrons into their tavernas. At her first opportunity, she escaped the harbor and plunged into the old town's confusing maze of narrow alleyways and lanes.

Things always seemed calmer in here, even when the town was packed with tourists. Perhaps because when you're wandering inside a labyrinth you're never quite sure what might lie around the next twist or turn. It gave rise to hope that you'd run into something better than the mess you were caught up in at the moment.

No wonder her father called her an optimist. *I really do need to call him.*

When Toni first moved to the island, children played in the old town maze while black-clad grandmothers sat in doorways and on geranium-filled balconies, chatting with one another as they kept watch over their grandchildren.

These days, the only grandmothers you'd likely find here were stylishly dressed and keeping watch over the goods in their shops. The buildings were now far too valuable to serve as residences, and most had been leased to strangers or used as businesses for the buildings' owners. As for the grandchildren and their games, today you'd mostly find them tucked away indoors like the rest of their digital generation.

She followed the sound of the birds. They congregated in the part of town where she was headed, high among the sturdy eucalyptus trees lining the wall encircling the town's grade school. During the school year, these same birds sang backup to the sounds of children at play, but in summer they headlined the show.

Toni watched four boys of no more than twelve scoot over the schoolyard wall and head for the playground, basketballs in hand. Their chatter interrupted the birds, scattering some. Toni shook her head at how, even as young as twelve, they'd mastered the many uses for the word *malaka* in male company.

At a lane that once housed the post office, she turned. Now the building stood vacant, hung up for years in intra-governmental and family feuding over whom had the right to determine its future. The old town seemed to be aging rapidly, though you couldn't tell that in tourist season. Much like an aging film star who's neglected her underlying health, she could still fool the masses when outfitted in her finest party clothes and makeup.

But in off-season, or even during tourist season, if you wandered down neglected back streets away from the glitz and shopping areas, you'd notice distinct differences. Sewer smells, leaking pipes, uncollected garbage, unenforced building regulations, and cosmetic neglect were what had sent locals fleeing to out-of-town residences, with foreign workers moving in to fill the void.

Or perhaps it was the other way around: Because locals had left the old town, their elected officials no longer cared what happened in the out-of-sight/out-of-mind parts of the old town.

Whatever the reason, this was where Toni was headed.

The front door to the home she sought stood two steps up and back from the street. To get to it, she had to duck under a clothesline tied to a hook to the right of the front door. The line stretched across the door, past an adjacent casement window, to a hook above another door in a wall running perpendicular to the front of the house.

She knocked. No answer. She knocked again. The door could have used a paint job. So could the building. She doubted the owner cared, and certainly not the renters. They likely were happy to have an affordable place to live, and an improved property would increase the chance of them being booted out in favor of tourists.

She rapped her fist hard against the door twice more, and before she'd finished with her third knock, the door swung inward.

"Sorry," said her client, wearing a wife-beater tee-shirt and boxer shorts. "I fell asleep. I don't sleep much at night."

"Get dressed, and then I'll come inside." She stood without budging. "You don't want to be seen with me in the harbor, and I don't want to be seen with you with your pants off."

He hurried back inside and returned a moment later wearing pants and a shirt but no shoes. Toni stepped inside without being asked. A tiny kitchen sat beyond and to the left and a tiny bedroom off to the right. The toilet was likely outside behind that second door. She stood in the main room of the home.

A neatly made cot ran along the left wall, a small square dining table and three chairs sat below the room's single window, and a well-worn couch lay along the right wall with a wide-screen TV hanging above the cot. Two floor lamps stood unlit, one by the couch, one between the table and cot. Religious relics and pictures dominated the walls, along with a single photograph in the middle of the dining table of a young schoolgirl marching in a parade.

"Nice place." Toni pointed at the photograph. "Is that your daughter?"

"Yes, Adina."

It wasn't hard to imagine how a child living amid these stark surroundings could be tempted by a fast-talker into doing anything to escape.

"Please sit." He pointed to the couch, and pulled up a chair from the table to sit across from her. "Have you found a way to save my daughter?"

"Where is she?"

"She's not here."

Toni waved a hand around the room. "I guessed that. So, where is she?"

"She should be home within an hour. But she'll change clothes and go right out again." He squirmed in his chair. "She avoids being home when her mother is here. She says her mother lectures her too much."

"Where's her mother?"

"She works in the laundry of one of the big hotels."

"Hard work."

He shut his eyes. "I know. We all know." Tears appeared in his eyes and began to run down his cheek. He clumsily wiped them away. "We wanted to protect her, to give her a better life than we had. It's why we work like this. For our daughter. And now…" he waved his hands in a gesture of hopelessness.

Toni leaned in. "What I need from you is a schedule of when and where you think your daughter is going to be over the next forty-eight hours, and with whom. Be as precise as you can, but if necessary, a good guess will have to do."

"How can I get that?"

"I don't know, be creative. She's your daughter. Who would she tell? Where would she write it down? Can you access her phone? Does she have a job? Where do her friends work or hang out? Like I said, do your best."

His eyes darted around the room as if searching for answers.

"And I'll need a current photograph of her."

He paused, then stood and walked into the bedroom. Toni heard a drawer open. A moment passed, and she heard a drawer close. The father returned, holding a poster in one hand.

"I'm not proud of this, but I have no reason to hide it. Everyone has seen it posted around town." He handed her an advertisement for Karavakis' club featuring the image of a scantily clad Las Vegas-type showgirl in a deliberately enticing position.

"This is your daughter?"

His head drooped. "Yes."

Toni stared at the poster. *Your kid's in serious trouble.* All she could think of to say was, "Get me that list right away."

What she'd be able to do with it, however, she had not a clue.

Chapter Thirteen

Toni's hotel-room line rang four times before Yianni heard a fumbling, "Hello?"

"I've been trying to reach you on your mobile for a half hour."

"There's a simple and obvious explanation for that," said Toni. "I turn off my mobile when I want to sleep, and turn it back on when I don't. Why do people have such trouble remembering that basic principle?"

"The receptionist at your hotel wouldn't put me through to you on the house phone."

"Thank you for reminding me to tip her."

"I had to find the owner to get him to ring you."

"So much for his tip," she yawned. "Okay, my love, now that you have me, why don't you get to your earth-shattering news."

"We have to meet."

"Is it passion or professional?"

"Professional."

"Oh."

"Not that I'm averse to the former."

"I guess that's some consolation. What's it about?"

"I'll tell you when we see you."

"We?"

"Yes, Andreas and I."

"Hey, if this is about last night with his wife—"

Yianni cut her off. "Let's not talk about this over the phone. We'll see you at your place in the harbor in thirty minutes. Okay?"

"No, everyone on the island will see me meeting with you. My crook contacts might get the crazy idea I'm actually chummy with the police."

"Well, we have to meet."

"Okay, I get that. Let's do it at the *cafenion* next to the police station. There's an upstairs no one ever uses. We should have it to ourselves."

"Fine, see you there in thirty minutes. Bye."

Yianni waited for her to say something. All he heard was a click.

Toni was waiting upstairs when Andreas arrived at the *cafenion*.

"You're prompt for a Greek," smiled Andreas.

"That's because I'm Greek in spirit, not genetically."

He chuckled. "We do seem to lack that punctuality bit of DNA."

"Where's Yianni?"

"Downstairs getting us coffee. Would you like one?"

She held up a cup. "Already set, thanks." She bit at her lip. "I hope I didn't somehow create a problem for you and your wife last night. She's really a great lady and we had a good but wholly innocent time."

Andreas smiled. "I know. She feels the same way about you. I practically had to handcuff her to keep her from following us here, but I told her it was official police business and she couldn't be involved."

"That sounds ominous."

Yianni stepped into the room from the stairs. "Are you talking about me?"

"No," said Toni, "then I'd have said *obvious*."

Yianni feigned a smile as he handed Andreas a coffee. "I see you and I are back to our normal routine."

"Yes, you try being cute, and me burying you."

"Okay, kids, playtime's over." Andreas sat across from Toni at a four-top hardwood table, and Yianni sat between them.

Andreas leaned in toward Toni. "You guessed right. This is about last night, but not about anything you or Lila did. It's about the man with the knife."

"You're not going to arrest him, are you? He's just distraught."

"I seriously doubt that either you or I are competent to make that determination, but this isn't about arresting him. It's about your helping us with an investigation, one that potentially may help resolve your client's problem with his daughter."

"I don't understand," said Toni.

"I don't know if there's anything more to what the girl's father told you than what he said, but since the kid he threatened to take out is Karavakis' son, and we all know how involved Karavakis is in the dark side of things on this island, I want to know if there's anything more going on here than a personal grudge with the son." Andreas took a sip of coffee. "What I'm about to tell you is confidential, so keep it to yourself. Karavakis is putting together a huge hotel-casino project on the island, and if there's a gang war brewing over it, I want to know. If organized-crime types ever start thinking it's worth the risk to eliminate their competition and bodies begin turning up, it'll be lights out for the island."

Toni shook her head. "I get the bit about the risk to the island's tourist-paradise image, Chief, but I don't get the *we* part of your point."

He smiled. "You have access to the other side of the street. You asking questions in your normal gossipy manner could pick up things that we'll never hear as cops."

"I think you just called me a gossip."

"Okay, let's call it folksy or chatty. Whatever the word, we both know that you're good at getting people to tell you things."

"Come on, now. Be real. No one's going to tell me that sort of stuff."

"Maybe not in so many words, but people like to talk as if they know the inside story on what's happening on the island. So, while you're out looking for a way to help the daughter get away from Karavakis Junior, we'd appreciate your keeping your ears open for anything that might help us with Karavakis Senior and his crowd. All we're asking is that you keep your ears open and let us know if you hear anything."

She looked at Yianni. "Are you on board with this?"

"Absolutely." He paused. "But I don't want you taking any risks. Just let us know if you hear something."

She stared at him. "I hope you stop by the bar tonight."

Yianni smiled. "I'd hoped you say that."

She stood. "Is that it?"

Andreas nodded. "Lila wanted me to say hi and ask if you're free for lunch tomorrow at the house."

"Depends."

"On what?"

"On what sort of leads I might come up with on that little project you just gave me."

"For the record, and because some of the people tied into this can be very dangerous, I agree with what Yianni said. Don't take chances."

She smiled at Yianni. "Then maybe you shouldn't stop by the bar tonight, handsome." With that, she scooted to the stairs and down.

Andreas smiled. "The lady certainly knows how to make an exit."

"Yes, she does," said Yianni, glancing toward the empty stairs.

"I think she likes you."

"That's why I feel bad not telling her about a possible Karavakis tie-in to the Colonel's murder."

"We warned her to be careful, and that dangerous people are involved. If we get her thinking there's a possible link to a murder, she might panic, and that would endanger her more. Ignorance is bliss in this instance."

"I wonder if you'd feel the same way if Toni were a man?"

"Are you suggesting I'm sexist?"

"No, just possibly overprotective because a woman is involved. I do have a question, though."

"What is it?"

"Would you have asked Lila to do what you just asked of Toni, without at least warning her what she might be getting into?"

"Hey, we both told Toni not to take risks."

"You haven't answered my question."

"I know." Andreas stood. "And don't think it hasn't crossed my mind that the two of them might go out there playing Nancy Drew together." He gulped down what remained of his coffee. "But I still think an ignorance-is-bliss approach is best for them both. At least for now."

Yianni said nothing.

Andreas drummed his fingers on the table. "Any change in the condition of our hospitalized motorcycle hit man?"

"He's still in a coma, but his vital signs are improving, and he's expected to come around soon."

"Let's hope so. He's our best chance at nailing Karavakis."

Yianni looked down at the tabletop. "I don't get it, Chief. If you think Karavakis was willing to risk ordering a hit on you and me simply for asking him questions, why don't you see Toni facing the same sort of danger if she's out there snooping around?"

"We're cops, and when we ask questions we get noticed. Toni isn't one of us, and people on the island expect her to be nosing around about bad guys as part of her business. They won't regard her snooping in the same light as they would ours."

Yianni looked up at Andreas. "It sounds to me as if you're taking a hell of a risk with Toni's safety."

"It's a judgment call."

"Influenced by the fact she's a woman?"

"Yes, sexist thinking is involved." He pointed at his chest. "But I'm not the sexist. I'm relying on sexist thinking to give

Toni the cover she needs. The bad guys tied into this are classic misogynists, and because of that, the last person they'll suspect of informing on them is someone like Toni."

Yianni kept up his stare. "I still think you should tell her of the potential link to the Colonel's murder."

"And I still disagree."

Yianni drew in and blew out a breath. "I hope you're right."

Andreas looked at the ceiling. "I pray that I am."

Toni made it back to her hotel with the intention of taking a nap before preparing to head off to the piano bar. But when she saw the hotel owner, Niko, sitting alone on the terrace with bottles of ouzo and water, glasses, a bucket of ice, and a plate of *spanakopita*, she dropped into the chair next to him.

"How are you doing, my friend?" Niko asked.

"I could be better."

"I figured when you didn't head straight inside for your nap there must be something important on your mind."

"Am I that obvious?"

"Yep."

Toni frowned but reached for a *spanakopita* and took a bite. She spoke while chewing. "I need to know who you think is best informed about gritty, nasty, secret things happening on the dark side of the island."

"Are you talking about politics or something else?"

"Something else." She kept chewing.

"Why would you want to get mixed up with that crowd? They don't like the curious."

"I don't want to get involved. I just have some questions I need answered, and my connections into the island's criminal side are confined to thievery and burglary. I'm a babe in the woods when it comes to knowing the truly nasty folks. Present company excluded, of course."

"Of course," Niko yawned. "I doubt you *need* them answered, you just want them answered. Which brings me back to emphasizing what happens to the curious."

"I'll be careful."

Niko scowled. Then his face lit up. "I know who you can talk to. And he's someone you already know. He's close enough to the island's underbelly to know what you want to know, but not so close as to feel the need to eliminate you for asking questions. Or at least I don't think he will."

"That's comforting. So, who do you have in mind?"

"Like I said, someone you already know."

"So, tell me already."

"Christos."

Christos Kleftis, Lucifer's main man on the island. In any organized thievery, you could bet Christos had a hand in it. Toni and Christos did a lot of business together, and that encouraged her to stay on his good side, despite her natural aversion to men sporting multiple thick gold chains, jewel-studded rings, and bracelets.

"I didn't think Christos was into the violent end of things. I thought his gig was burglarizing houses and hotel rooms."

"It is," said Niko, "but he has eyes and ears all over the island, looking for ripe places and rich visitors to hit. His network picks up a lot of information on a lot of things beyond what he needs for his business, making him perhaps the best-informed bad guy on the island."

"What time is it?"

"Nearly sunset," said Niko looking at the sky rather than his watch or phone.

"That means Christos is likely down in the harbor."

"Why do you say that?"

"He'll be checking out potential scores parading back and forth in their finery." She jumped up. "Gotta run if I want to catch him."

She hurried off into town and reached the port in what felt like record time. She found Christos sitting alone, bedecked in gold, at the front table of the most expensive taverna on the waterfront. She commandeered the seat next to him.

"Don't you ever worry that someday one of the folk passing by will recognize something you're wearing as one of their long-lost heirlooms?"

He kept studying the crowd. "Why do I sense you didn't stop by to warn me of the errors of my ways?"

"Because you're so smart, clever, handsome, and a judge of good liquor."

"In other words, my dear Toni, you want something from me."

"Like I said, you're brilliant."

"So, what sort of things did your clients misplace that you think I might be lucky enough to find for you sitting alongside the road?"

"That's…ah…not the sort of assistance I need."

"Okay, you've got my attention. What's up?" He kept his eyes on the passersby.

"This is highly confidential."

"You know you can trust me."

"Since I know you wouldn't dare go after the guy I'm about to ask you about, I do."

He looked at her. "Where's this headed?"

"To be honest, I don't know. That's why I'm asking you." She leaned in conspiratorially. "An old family friend from the United States has been approached regarding a potential investment here and asked me if I knew anything about the players involved in the deal."

"I don't do legitimate."

"If anyone knows that, it's me, Christos. But I have no one else to turn to."

"Okay, shoot." His eyes returned to the passing tourists.

Toni swallowed. *Screw subtlety.* If the cops wanted info, they'd just have to do it her way. "What do you know about a big-time hotel-casino project being put together by Angelos Karavakis?"

Christos' eyes jerked back to fix on Toni's. "That's not the sort of thing you talk about if you want to keep on breathing."

"Come on, I didn't ask you if he murdered anyone, I just want to know what you know about his new project."

Christos looked around furtively before fixing again on Toni's eyes. "Toni, I like you, so I'm going to tell you this. Don't go poking around in this guy's business. You just might find a body, and the next one could be yours."

The *next* one. "What are you telling me?"

"Karavakis is lining up all the players he needs for his new project. Even has a guy tied into a big-name foreign hotel family willing to brand and operate it as one of its own."

"That's going to upset a lot of local hotel families who have big money at risk if he succeeds."

"Already has. Up until now, the local families have been able to do whatever they wanted, wherever they wanted. That doesn't exactly give them the moral high ground for objecting to Karavakis' play."

"Interesting to hear you use the phrase 'moral high ground.'"

Christos smiled. "Knowing the words doesn't mean I accept the concept."

"So, you're saying the other locals can't out-influence Karavakis' move into the hotel business?"

He shook his head. "Not with money or political influence. And the guy's smart, because he's also made a deal with Despotiko."

Toni's face went blank at the name. "Who's that?"

Christos lowered his voice. "Despotiko is probably the most dangerous guy in Greece. That means strong-arm tactics also won't work against Karavakis, so long as Despotiko's on his side."

"Why's Despotiko involved? What's in it for him?"

"It's an investment. The casino's meant to be action central for all the big-time vices that draw high-rollers to the island. That'll make it one of the most profitable operations in Greece. At least that's what I've heard. But if you ask me it's more likely his wife is pushing him into it. She likes being a big shot on Mykonos, and being part of this will certainly make her that. Whatever his reason, Despotiko wants to keep his fingerprints as far away as possible, so Karavakis has agreed to front the whole thing with Despotiko's contribution characterized as a passive investment, like a bank would make."

Toni stared at him. "I'm truly impressed. How do you know all this stuff?"

Christos smiled. "It's simple. I've got inconspicuous friends all over the island. Taxi drivers, maids, waiters, plumbers, gardeners, beach attendants. You get the picture. Sometimes they bring me information I can use in my operations, and I pay them for it. Other times, it's just to have a drink with me and I listen to them gossip about things they overheard at work. For reasons I'll never understand, big shots talk freely in front of them, almost like they're furniture and can't understand the secrets being discussed."

Toni crossed herself.

Christos pointed at her chest. "I didn't know you were Greek Orthodox."

"I'm not. Just scared shitless at how close I'd have come to getting killed if I hadn't spoken to you."

He laughed, and patted her arm. "Just buy me a drink the next time I stop by the bar."

"For sure." Toni started to stand, but sat back down. "One last question, if I may. It's also about the Karavakis family."

"What are you, an amateur genealogist? What the hell do you want to know now?"

"It's about the son. Someone asked me if he could be trusted with a girl's virtue."

Christos burst out laughing. "That's easy: No. Fucking. Way."

"Why is that?"

His laughter tightened, then ceased. "You have to understand, I'm not about to risk having my name tied to an answer that implies Angelos' son is a pimp. Got it?"

In his special way, Christos had answered her question.

"Yes."

"Be careful."

"That seems to be the conventional wisdom on the subject."

"I suggest you follow it." Christos stood up. "It's time for me to move on. This seat's getting a little too hot." He patted her shoulder. "And for my answer to your last question, my bill is now yours."

She watched him walk away, glancing as he did at the wrists of three flashy men at a nearby table. Gold Rolexes, all around. He looked back at Toni over his shoulder with a wry smile and mouthed, "*Fakes.*"

The man certainly knew his business.

The question is, do I know enough to stick to my own?

On his way to the piano bar, Yianni was reminded of a book he read back when he'd been assigned to Mykonos. It was a novel by Mary Renault called *The King Must Die*. It was a variation on the myth of Theseus slaying the Cretan Minotaur and escaping the labyrinth with the help of Ariadne. The book puts the escaping Theseus and Ariadne on the neighboring Cycladic island of Naxos during a festival night of wild celebration filled with drinking, sexual revelry, and bloody sacrifices, yielding stark revelations come the dawn. Yianni had no doubt that if the gods had chosen to set their myth in modern times, they'd have picked Mykonos on a full-moon night as their party venue.

There was something about a full moon that yanked the inhibitions out of otherwise sedate souls and instinctively sent the prudent off in search of safe shelter until the dawn.

Aided by drink and drugs, and emboldened by the irresistible romantic draw of silver moonlight, many tossed sexual caution to the wind, while others sacrificed their youth to crippling, bloody road accidents.

In town, they howled past bars in packs, having entered the streets already drunk on cheap vodka or drugs consumed in their rooms to avoid paying the fortunes necessary to get equally intoxicated in town.

Arriving at the piano bar, Yianni saw its owner by the door telling all arrivals to leave cans and bottles outside. Some were turned away, others entered after gulping down whatever they held in their hands, some argued, some cursed, but none chose to start a fight. Which was good, because the owner kept at hand a half-meter length of lead pipe that he would not hesitate to use. Hard to imagine who'd want to fight a gorilla with a tree limb in his hand, but the night was still young.

Yianni walked in and scanned the crowded bar. The waiters were hysterically busy, practically jogging to meet, greet, seat, and treat new customers. That meant the place was making money, and Toni was meeting her prime directive of seeing to it that the place did exactly that.

From the piano, Toni smiled at him, and he smiled back. He stood patiently sipping a beer waiting for his turn for a seat at the bar, and when it came, he stepped up to take it. As he did, one of two black-clad, tree-trunk-sized security guards grabbed Yianni's arm and motioned for their client to take the seat instead. One of the guards aimed his best dead-man, eye-to-eye stare at Yianni.

Yianni looked down at the man's hand on his arm, and kept his stare fixed there until the guard released his grip. That's when Yianni looked up, locked eyes on the guard's eyes, smiled, and turned away from the bar to relinquish the seat.

A war had just been avoided.

Toni abruptly announced a break in her set. "I'll be right back, folks."

She hurried up to the bar and tapped the client on the shoulder. "Sorry, sir, but in here you wait your turn for a seat at the bar."

The client stared at Toni before turning to say something in a foreign language to the guard who'd grabbed Yianni's arm. The guard stepped forward and paused for a second before whipping his hand up to deliver a hard slap across Toni's face.

Toni's surprise at what hit her wasn't nearly as great as the guard's at what hit him, and kept hitting him all the way to the floor and then some. The second guard jumped on Yianni from behind as Yianni pounded away on the first guard, but the second guard's rescue effort ended with a hard rap to the back of his head from the owner's lead pipe.

It all was over in less than ten seconds, so quickly that the crowd gathered at the bar hardly had time enough to instinctively jump back from the fray, let alone flee in panic.

"It's all over folks," shouted Toni. "Just a little full-moon floorshow at the piano bar."

She leaned in and said something to the security guards' client as Yianni and the owner dragged the bodies of his two muscle men out the front door.

The client nodded frantically at Toni.

She stood up straight and yelled, "As a thank you to all of you who've stayed through the show, this fine gentleman has offered to buy everyone in the place a drink! That's any kind of drink you want!"

The client tossed a mound of euros on the bar and hurried out the door.

A few minutes later, Yianni and the owner walked back inside, smiling and nudging each other with fist bumps like triumphant comrades-in-arms.

As soon as Yianni saw Toni, he started shaking his head. "Why'd you do that?"

"Sometimes a girl's gotta do what a girl's gotta do."

"You didn't have to. I know how to take care of myself."

"I know. I also know you didn't want to make a scene where I work, which is why you let that asshole security guy push you into giving up your seat. That really pissed me off."

"So I noticed. You've got to get a better handle on your temper. It could get you seriously hurt someday. Guys like the ones we tossed won't cut you any slack just because you're a woman."

"It's not a temper. I'm just impetuous." She paused. "But, I have to admit, I didn't expect him to hit me."

"And I'm sure the asshole didn't expect what happened to him either," said Yianni.

"Yes, you can be quite impetuous yourself. Good thing the owner was here for backup with his lead pipe."

"You mean good thing for the guards," said Yianni flatly. "If your boss hadn't ended it with his pipe, things would have ended far worse for them both."

"Uh, huh. Good to know that."

Yianni couldn't help but smile. "Your boss actually thanked me. Said he'd been waiting a long time for a good excuse to use his pipe on that sort. He thinks black-shirt protection types like those two are taking over the island, acting like an occupying army, and at times bringing more crime to the island than they prevent."

"Isn't he worried they might take revenge on him or the bar?"

Yianni shook his head. "Nope. We explained the consequences of that sort of thinking to them outside when we lifted their IDs."

Toni's expression showed she didn't quite know what to make of what he'd just said.

"So, what did you say to their client to get him to spring for a round of drinks for the bar?"

"Not much. Just that with his playmates indisposed at the moment, it might not be safe for him to be wandering around the island unprotected. After all, he'd offended a lot of people with the ruckus he'd caused. Perhaps he should consider buying a round to make amends."

Yianni shook his head and said, "You're pretty good at handling ruckuses yourself."

Toni's boss waved at her from the door and pointed to the piano.

"My master calls. Time for me to get back to work."

"Don't you want to ask me if I have a musical request?"

"No need to. I already know it."

She strolled over to the piano, sat down, and launched into the theme from *Rocky*.

Toni and Yianni left right after her last set, a fringe benefit of being a musician in a bar. You didn't have to clean up. They found an all-night crepes and ice cream place along the street leading to the bus station.

"Thank God, no more booze," she said.

Yianni nodded. "It's been too many late nights. I have no energy left."

"For what?" smiled Toni.

Yianni laughed. "No comment."

She patted his hand. "Patience."

"Now I get to ask, 'For what?'"

"No comment."

Yianni waved off the subject. "What kind of ice cream would you like?"

"Vanilla, two scoops."

"I'll be right back."

When he returned, Toni thanked him and started in on her ice cream. She didn't speak.

"Is everything okay?" he asked.

"Uh-huh." She looked up. "Why do you ask?"

"You just seem unusually quiet."

She took another taste of her ice cream. "I have a question for you."

"Sure."

Without looking at him, she asked, "Was someone murdered in connection with that hotel project you're interested in?"

Yianni froze. "Who told you that?"

"First, answer my question." She still didn't look at him.

"There was a murder, but we had no indication it was related to the hotel project."

"Don't you think it would have been nice to let me know that before sending me out to ask questions?"

"We told you not to take any risks."

"When you send someone out to swim alone there's always risk, especially when you don't warn them that there might be crocodiles."

"Since you put it that way, you're right."

"Is there any other way to put it?"

"Yes. We didn't want to panic you."

"I see...you decided to leave that up to others."

"Okay, you're right. I'm sorry." He sat silently for a moment. "Who told you there'd been a murder?"

"You just did." She paused. "Though my contact did drop me a hint." She picked at her ice cream with her spoon. "Considering the size of the project, and how worried you and Andreas are over a potential gang war, I guess I shouldn't be surprised that a body's involved."

She looked up and stared him in the eye. "How many so far?"

He bit at his lip. "One."

"Do you have any idea how big this project is?"

"Obviously not."

She shook her head. "The people behind it are the most dangerous on the island, and the island's major hotel families are worried the project will cost them their control over the island's tourist business. A lot of people feel threatened, but they're even more afraid of a guy named Despotiko who's involved with his wife in the deal through Karavakis."

Yianni blinked. "They're right to be scared. And again, I'm very sorry. I don't want you asking any more questions about Karavakis or Despotiko. It's too dangerous."

"Now you tell me. So, what am I supposed to tell my client?"

"What client?"

"The father with the knife who wants to use it on Karavakis' son for pimping out his daughter."

"You really want my advice?"

"No."

"Well, you're going to get it anyway. You didn't create this mess for the father or the girl. There's a simple way out that they won't take. *Get her off the island.* What you don't do is screw around with Karavakis or his son. They're too dangerous. And Despotiko, even more so. This is not like throwing a temper tantrum in a bar when I'm there to protect you. Messing with these guys could get you killed."

She stood up. "Thanks for the ice cream. And the advice. I've got to get home and crash."

"I'll walk you home."

"No, thanks. I know the way. Catch you later." She hurried off.

Yianni sat, watching her leave.

He couldn't blame her for being aggrieved. He hoped she'd forgive him for his role in her unexpected swim among the crocodiles.

Thanks, Chief.

Yianni took out his mobile and sent a text message to Andreas: JUST LEARNED DESPOTIKO IS PART OF HOTEL DEAL.

He didn't care if it woke him up.

Toni headed home through a less-traveled part of town where families still lived, though few of them were native Mykonians. She skirted the still-open bars along the way to the bus station, crowded with foreign workers and Greek *kamakis* plying tourist girls with two-euro shots as a prelude to a cheap sexual encounter down some dark alleyway or in the girls' rooms.

She thought to call her father and looked at her phone. It was still early back in the U.S., but that would inevitably lead to a conversation about what she was doing with her life. And from the way things were going at the moment, she wasn't sure she had an answer that would please him. On that downer of a thought, she put her phone away.

As she moved through the neighborhood, she cursed herself for having walked out on Yianni as she had. It hadn't been his intention to put her at risk. The opposite, in fact. That's how Greek men thought. At least the good ones. Women need to be shielded, protected.

Lord, give me the strength.

Toni sighed. It was going to be quite a lift, getting men to change their mindset.

As she walked up the steps to her hotel, she smiled.

I think I'll start with Yianni.

Chapter Fourteen

Toni woke up early enough to make it to breakfast by ten, an appearance that earned a burst of applause from Niko.

She dropped into a chair at his table.

"This is for you," he said, handing her an envelope. "An Albanian left it with the night man."

Toni took it.

"Aren't you going to open it?" he said.

"No."

"Aren't you curious?"

"Not as curious as you."

"Fine. I know when I'm not wanted." He stood up and walked into the kitchen, leaving his coffee cup and burning cigarette on the table.

Toni opened the envelope. As she'd suspected, it was the daughter's schedule. It had her starting work at eleven that morning at a bike- and car-rental kiosk just off the harbor at the intersection by the entrance to town. The father described Adina's job as attracting tourists onto the lot so her boss could close rental deals.

Toni made it to the kiosk fifteen minutes early. She bought a cup of coffee from the mini-mart behind the kiosk and found an empty bench across the intersection. The bench had been installed by the town to accommodate those waiting for municipal buses, but when the town decided to move the bus stop, it had neglected to bring along the bench.

Toni leaned back to sip her coffee and watch the procession of cruise-ship visitors shuffling off to sightsee or shop in town, tourists looking for transportation to the beaches, and stragglers wandering home after a hard night of partying. She was sur- rounded by a sea of barely coordinated blouses, tank tops, and tee-shirts, shorts and swimsuits, rubber flip-flops and sneakers, topped by all manner of unappealing sun hats and ball caps cocked every which way. She felt trapped in a fashion parade made up of marchers outfitted from the laundry baskets of the world's most unsuccessful secondhand thrift shops.

The eclectic array of body types in this world had always amazed her, but not nearly as much as how utterly oblivious the possessors of many of those bodies were to the images they conjured up in dressing as they did. Then again, her night job had accustomed Toni to club crowds, which tended to dress better and took pains to ensure they showcased their bodies in the most attractive possible manner. But those folks were likely in some bed somewhere at this hour, still sleeping off their night on the town.

The whining roar of an engine jerked Toni out of her trance long before she saw the motorcycle. It swerved off the road with- out slowing down, aimed straight for the kiosk, and abruptly stopped just short of four college-aged female tourists engaged in animated rental negotiations with the owner. Their backs were to the road, so they never saw how close the driver came to hitting them. The owner did, though, and Toni braced for the inevitable demonstration of the many glorious uses of the word *malaka*.

But the owner said nothing. He simply nodded to the driver and kept talking to the girls.

The helmet-less driver fit the island's muscled private-security image perfectly, and his young female passenger possessed the sort of buxom, hard-bodied physique that her neon-green and black second-skin Lycra body suit was created for.

Adina swung off the bike, and the driver immediately sped away, leaving her standing at the kiosk. The owner waved for her to move to the edge of the road, close to the flow of tourists passing by the kiosk. She lowered her head and walked to where he'd pointed.

Toni watched her smile as she engaged passersby, mostly groups of young men, steering them toward the kiosk. She targeted the testosterone-driven types, who matched perfectly the rental agency's macho dirt bikes, quads, beach buggies, and other exotic toys.

Toni doubted the girl's customers had any idea how young she was, or would care if they did. For sure, the owner wasn't bothered. She wondered if he paid her on commission or an hourly rate, or for that matter, if he paid her at all. The likely scenario was that he paid her boss directly.

After watching for a half-hour, Toni decided there was no reason to sit on the bench any longer. She wouldn't learn more than she already had. The daughter was an attractive young woman with a charming way about her, caught up with some bad guys. So far, nothing she'd seen suggested the girl's virtue had been compromised, though she'd definitely developed advanced skills as a tease.

Toni headed off to the harbor to surprise Stella with a prompt arrival at her friend's usual coffee time. She'd resume with Adina at five, when her father's schedule had her moving on to her next job, at Karavakis' club.

It wasn't yet noon when Toni came looking for Stella, but she wasn't there, and on seeing Toni, the owner feigned a heart attack. The waiter playfully delivered a champagne flute and ice bucket to the table, which held a bottle of water instead of bubbly.

He followed it up with a pot of coffee.

The harbor had come alive with tourists crowding into tavernas and cafés from three giant cruise boats. Many of those she'd watched walk by her at the kiosk had now joined in the island's most popular pastime, people-watching.

That got her to thinking of a conversation she'd had in this very taverna with a former mayor shortly after she'd come to the island. She'd asked him about the sort of tourists the island liked to attract. The first words out of his mouth came with a smile: "Fashion victims."

Toni'd thought for sure that she'd misunderstood what he said, so she explained what fashion victim meant and that he must have meant something different.

His reply was the first of many lessons she'd learned from islanders, all running to the same proof: when it came to knowing their customers, island locals were anything but yokels. "We *want* fashion victims on our island. People love to sit in our tavernas and *cafenions*, laughing and pointing as they watch the fashion victims walk by. It makes them feel good, thinking how superior they are to the masses. Even if they're not."

That's when it hit Toni that her stroll along the harbor from the kiosk, dressed as the proverbial example of "what the cat dragged in," must have put a lot of smiles on a lot of gawking faces. Folks she'd been poking fun at just a few moments before. Payback's a bitch.

Toni tried calling Stella, but her phone was off. With nothing of importance to do that morning, Toni hung around the taverna, chatting with locals while she waited for Stella to call back. By the time Stella did, it was a little after one. She said she was in Athens, having left early that morning to accompany her mother-in-law to a doctor's appointment. She'd be back on Mykonos tomorrow. Toni asked why she hadn't mentioned the appointment to her earlier. Was everything okay? Stella said her husband was supposed to take his mother, but out of the blue that morning he'd said he couldn't, leaving Stella to deal with her.

That sounded like Stella's husband.

"Besides, I knew you wouldn't be awake until two," Stella added.

"As a matter of fact, I've been here waiting for you since before noon."

"Yeah, right."

"Honest."

"Got to run, the doctor just called us in. Bye."

Toni stared at her phone. How did she come to develop this reputation that she couldn't function before mid-afternoon? That's when she remembered Lila's invitation to join her at her house for lunch. She'd forgotten all about it.

"Damn," she muttered as she slammed her hand on the table.

"My, oh my, having a fit of temper, are we?" said Christos, lowering his bejeweled and bangled body into the chair across from her.

"I just remembered an appointment I forgot."

"Don't worry, what I have to say won't keep you long. It will only take a minute."

"Always with the drama?"

"It comes with the lifestyle." Christos looked around to see who might be listening, then leaned in. "I suggest you keep your nose out of Karavakis' business."

"What makes you think I'm interested in him?"

"Okay, maybe not him, but his son."

"Same question."

Christos smiled. "Perhaps you forget that you asked me the other day about trusting the virtue of a girl to Karavakis' son. But aside from that, do you think you don't get noticed sitting for almost an hour on a deserted bench across from one of the places where Karavakis' girls work on hustling tricks?"

Toni hoped he didn't see her blanch. "Tricks?"

"Tricks, johns, clients, whatever you want to call them, they don't turn them there, but part of the girl's hustle for enticing guys into renting bikes and quads is to send them over to party with her and her friends at Karavakis' club."

Toni couldn't believe she'd been so naive as to have missed that angle.

"Just take my advice and don't get involved. It isn't worth it." He paused. "She isn't worth it."

Tell that to the girl's father.

Christos sighed dramatically. "Be realistic, Toni. Times are different. It used to be that strong-arm tactics were rare on the island, but life's different here today." He shook his head. "You might think you're close to the police chief, but do you think for a moment you'll get more than his sincerest sympathies if anything bad happens to you at the hands of Karavakis? Cops and city hall don't give a damn what private muscle does, as long as it doesn't embarrass them. The deal is simple. They protect private security, so private security can protect the money-making businesses that make all of them rich."

Toni glanced in the direction of city hall. She hadn't directly said or done anything to stir up Karavakis, and Christos had no reason to spread a rumor about her that would. Up until now she'd thought she'd remained under the radar on this, but if anyone other than Christos had suspicions, she didn't dare do anything that might turn them into opinions. That meant no more hanging out around the kiosk where the daughter worked. That also meant no trip to Karavakis' club. At least not today.

Christos stood. "Toni, did you hear what I just said?"

She struggled to maintain an innocent expression. "Yes, but I'm not doing any of the things you're suggesting."

"Good, then stop acting in a way that might get people who could do you harm thinking that you are." He patted her shoulder and walked away.

Toni watched Christos strut off along the harbor. The day had developed a pattern. First, she unintentionally blew off lunch with Lila. Now, she learned she'd spent her morning unwittingly putting a target on her back. Since tradition had bad things coming in threes, all she could think of doing next was heading straight home to bed for a nap.

And pulling the covers up over her head.

• • ● • •

The afternoon had drifted lazily along, with Tassaki and Anna playing in the pool, Andreas and Yianni spearfishing in the cove, and Lila reading a book in the shade while Sofia slept peacefully next to her in a stroller. Toni's apologetic call canceling their lunch date had disappointed Lila, but not nearly as much as she sensed it would Yianni. Lila had never seen Yianni so drawn to a woman. Then again, everyone seemed drawn to Toni, including Lila.

Andreas and Yianni came up onto the terrace each waving their fishing bags in one hand and an octopus in the other.

"We're going to feast today," said Andreas, feining a toss of his octopus into the pool. The maneuver got a giggle out of Tassaki and a scream out of Anna.

"Stop that this instant!" shouted Lila.

"You're no fun," grinned Andreas.

"Take them straight into the kitchen so Dama can prepare them."

"No way. We caught them, we prepare them. Right, Yianni?"

Yianni looked around the terrace as he answered. "Yeah, anything you say, Chief." He looked at Lila. "Where's Toni? Shouldn't she be here by now?"

"She called to cancel. Something about a meeting with a client she'd forgotten about."

Yianni bit at his lip. "Oh."

"That leaves more fish for us," quipped Andreas.

"Just take it into the kitchen, *please.*"

The sound of a phone went off inside the house. "Sounds like my ring," said Andreas.

"It's been going off like that for over an hour."

"And you never answered it?"

"I figured if you'd wanted to be disturbed you'd have taken it with you, or at least told me to answer it. Absent that, I had no intention of disturbing this perfect afternoon of domestic bliss."

Andreas shook his head, exhaled deeply, and moved into the house. He dropped his fish on the kitchen counter and headed

for his phone. Yianni followed, leaving his fish next to Andreas'
catch.

"What am I supposed to do with all that?" said Dama, nodding at the fish as she carried two twelve-liter jugs of water into
the kitchen, one under each arm.

Yianni hurried toward her. "Here, let me help you with those."

"No need, Mr. Yianni. I'm very strong. I just need a man for
other things." Dama grinned.

Dama was Lila's parents' cook, and had been with the family
since immigrating to Greece in her teens. During the summer,
she lived on Mykonos, keeping an eye on the house. Filipino,
fortyish, wiry, and not quite five feet tall, her presence reminded
Yianni of his tough, no-nonsense Navy SEAL buddies.

"There's no man good enough for you," he said.

Dama put the water down next to a refrigerator. "What about
the fish?"

Yianni glanced to see where Andreas had gone in search of his
phone, then whispered, "Just prepare them the way you usually
do." He pointed in the direction of Andreas. "But let's not tell
him I said that."

"For you, Mr. Yianni, anything." Dama smiled.

Yianni hurried off.

Andreas found his mobile sitting on his bedroom nightstand.
He studied it for a moment before turning to Yianni standing
in the doorway. "There's a load of calls from a number I don't
recognize. But no message. As if someone doesn't want a voice
record." He pressed the screen to call the number and waited
for an answer.

"Hello?"

"This is Chief Inspector Andreas Kaldis returning your call.
Who's this?"

"I've been calling you for over an hour from the hospital."

Andreas' heart skipped a beat, as his mind flashed to thoughts of possible bad news about family or friends. "Who is this and what are you calling about?"

"I'm Sergeant Rallis, in charge of the detail assigned to keep an eye on the prisoner who attacked you and your detective on Mykonos."

Somewhat relieved, Andreas braced for a different sort of bad news. "And?"

"We've been keeping an eye on him to make sure he didn't escape, and—"

"You're not going to tell me the prisoner escaped, are you?"

"No."

"Good," said Andreas.

"He died."

Andreas blinked, looked at the phone, and hit the speaker button. "Would you please repeat that, Sergeant, for Detective Kouros?"

A noticeable swallow could be heard on the other end of the phone. "The prisoner's dead."

"*What?*" said Yianni. "I spoke to his doctor this morning and he told me everything was fine. What the hell happened?"

"We won't know for sure until after the autopsy."

"Sergeant—did you say your name's Rallis?"

"Yes, Chief."

"Sergeant Rallis, I don't have time for officialese answers. All I want to know is this: *What the hell happened to the prisoner you were supposed to be guarding?*"

"W-w-we thought we were here to make sure he didn't escape. No one ever told us someone might try to kill him."

"Is that what happened? Someone killed him?"

"We're not sure."

"But *you* think that's what happened, don't you?"

Pause.

Andreas spoke in a calm, level voice. "Sergeant, I want answers, and I can assure you that you do not want to aggravate me any more than you already have."

"It wasn't on my watch. I got called in after all hell broke loose. My chief told me to keep a lid on things and speak to no one, but your number was on the file as the arresting officer, so I figured you'd want to know."

"Okay, Sergeant, I get it, and you're slowly crawling back into my good graces. Now tell me what you know."

"According to the officer on duty, twenty minutes or so before alarms started ringing on the medical equipment, a nurse was in to adjust his IV."

"Did the guard on duty recognize her?" asked Yianni.

"No. But he said she was very friendly."

"And pretty too, I bet," said Yianni.

They heard another swallow. "Yes. And before you ask, we have video of her on the security cameras, but no one on the hospital staff can identify her; they never saw her on the prisoner's floor. The video shows her coming onto and leaving the floor through a stairwell between the nurses' station and the prisoner's room. That's how she avoided being noticed by the other nurses."

Yianni and Andreas locked eyes. "Sergeant, I want to see every-thing any camera caught of her, inside or outside the hospital, and every other piece of information you have on this cluster-fuck. And I want it now. Send it to my email address in the case file."

"Yes, sir."

"Is there anything else you think you should tell me?"

"Honest, we had no idea the prisoner might be a target."

"You've said that before."

"If anyone thought it was a possibility, I can't imagine my chief assigning that rookie to my detail."

"What rookie?"

"The one on duty when that nurse showed up in the prisoner's room. My chief got a sick call-in at the last minute from the cop scheduled for the next shift. So, he sent the rookie over to cover the shift. The kid was fresh out of the academy and hadn't been to the hospital before today. He had no idea who worked there and who didn't. All the other guys assigned to my detail were vets and knew the nursing staff. A new face, no matter how pretty, would have set off alarms."

"So, why the rookie?" said Yianni.

"My chief said he needed his experienced personnel out in the field, not babysitting a comatose suspect."

Andreas drew in and let out a breath. "I suggest we keep this conversation just between us, Sergeant."

"I was hoping you'd say that."

Andreas heard someone yelling at the sergeant from the background, telling him to get off the phone.

"Sorry. I've got to run if you want me to get that information to you while I still can get my hands on it."

"Don't let me hold you up. And, by the way, thanks." Andreas ended the call and looked at Yianni. "What do you make of that?"

"Same as you. A well-planned hit. And unless coincidence has once again reared its ugly head, someone set the stage for that phony nurse to pull it off."

"I'm surprised we didn't hear from the doctor or the sergeant's chief."

"Me too," said Yianni.

"Someone's pulling some mighty powerful strings." Andreas pointed at his phone. "And that sergeant knows it." He paused. "On the other hand, as head of the guard detail, it's his ass on the line for what happened."

"Unless he can shift blame to someone else."

"You've got that right."

"So, you don't buy the story about his chief?"

"At this point, I'm not believing or disbelieving anything. The more we learn, the more we realize everything is possible."

Yianni nodded but didn't speak.

"What's on your mind?" asked Andreas.

"We now have two organized hits tied to Karavakis, and gossip has Desptiko somehow involved in the hotel project. Don't you think now we should tell Toni to back off on the snooping?"

"Why don't you take a ride into town and bring her back here, where we can have that conversation in private."

Yianni sighed. "My last meeting with her did not end well. She might not come."

"Persuade her, man. Use your charm. She still thinks you're good-looking."

Toni made it back to her hotel from the harbor with the intention of going straight to bed. But then she ran into Niko sitting on the veranda with a group of guests. Most looked to be old-timers who'd been coming to the island since Niko's father had run the hotel. Niko had once told her, in what Toni took as jest, that the best possible option for his business would be to turn it into an old-folks home. No rowdiness, no late nights, no worries about getting paid. He called it his plan for "a more peaceful life."

From the cast of characters gathered around him on the veranda, he seemed to be putting his plan into action. The youngest looked to be about fifty, a striking woman with curly, dark brown hair and green eyes sitting next to him on a bench.

"Toni, come over here, I want you to meet some old friends of mine," said Niko.

"*Old* being the operative word," said a handlebar-mustached, silver-haired fellow in a lilting Scottish accent.

"Don't mind Ricky," said Niko with a wave of his hand. "He's still working on developing a sense of humor. Come, join us." The green-eyed woman next to him moved over to make room, and Niko patted the spot where she'd been sitting.

That was the curse of being a performer indebted to your landlord—always on call to serve as entertainment. "Just for a bit. I've got to prepare for tonight."

"What's to get ready for?" said a tanned, nattily dressed woman with shoulder-length blond hair next to Ricky. "By now you must know all your songs by heart." She spoke in a distinctly Midwestern American non-accent.

Toni forced a smile. "There are always new ones to learn."

"Well, I haven't heard any, and I've been going to that bar where you play since it opened."

Toni shrugged. "I try to play new music all the time. It's just that customers keep asking to hear their old favorites."

The woman practically scowled. "It's your piano. Take charge of your own life."

Before Toni could respond, Ricky waved his hand at the woman. "Don't let Margo get to you. She's just grumpy that all her plastic surgery hasn't made her feel any younger inside."

Margo shot him the middle finger. "What would you know about how I feel inside? Go to hell, limp-dick." Then she turned and scowled directly at Toni.

Toni stared at her. "I'm sorry, but have I somehow offended you?"

Ricky laughed. "Yeah, by being forty years younger and a hell of a lot prettier."

Margo's face flushed and she jumped up to storm off, but Niko grabbed her by the arm. "Margo, sit down. And Ricky, shut the hell up."

"That's like asking a toilet not to flush," said Margo.

"Then stop pulling on my handle," quipped Ricky.

A distinguished, fair-skinned fellow sitting next to a similarly elegant, dark-skinned, younger man on a love seat, cleared his throat. "Ah, we've finally reached the crux of the battle between these two. For over forty years, Ricky's been desperately trying to get into Margo's pants, but now that she's willing, he can't deliver the goods."

This time Ricky jumped up and started for the fair-skinned fellow, but Niko used his free hand to grab him. He held on to Ricky and Margo as the two of them, and everyone else on the veranda, erupted into a shouting match until Niko finally worked out a truce among his warring guests and let go of the two main combatants' arms.

Toni looked at Niko. "Does there ever come an age when conversations don't always tie back into sex?"

The woman next to Toni leaned in. "I hope not." She held out her hand and smiled. "My name is Eugénie. I caught your performance the other night, and I loved it."

Toni smiled. "Thank you," and shook her hand.

"Our beautiful Eugénie used to be a regular on the island," said Niko. "But she hasn't been back in years. She was an actress in Paris."

Eugénie laughed. "Thanks for the compliment. I prefer that romanticized description to the life I actually lived."

Niko smiled. "What can I say, you're an unforgettable lady."

She laughed. "It's my nature."

"After you, they threw away the mold."

"No need to lay it on so thick, old friend. We both know the truth." She waved her hand at the group. "In fact, everyone here does."

No one spoke.

Toni perked up. "I don't."

Still no one spoke.

Eugénie patted Toni on the hand. "They're all being gracious in my presence, but once I'm gone, they'll tell you all about me."

"No we won't," said Ricky.

"Of course you will," said Eugénie. "How could you resist telling such a juicy story? I know I couldn't." She looked at Toni. "So I'll tell you my story in my own words, quickly and to the point."

Eugénie drew in and let out a deep breath. "Bottom line, I was what was called back then euphemistically a high-class call girl. But hooker or whore works too."

"You're kidding," said Toni.

"I was quite a looker back then."

"That's not what I meant."

"I know." She patted Toni's hand. "But it was the best way I had to make the kind of living it afforded me. No education, no skills, just my looks and a personality."

"You worked as a hooker on Mykonos?"

"Mostly I came here on holiday." She smiled. "Yes, even hookers go on vacation." Her gaze seemed to drift off into the middle distance. "But on occasion I did entertain a few clients. In fact, that's how I met the man who turned out to be my husband, right here on the island. We married and had a family. Two boys."

"Great kids," said Niko. "They've stayed here with me.

"Thank you, Niko." She looked at Toni. "Yes, my husband knew my past before we married." She looked down at her hands. "He passed away last year."

"So sorry," said Toni.

"He was the joy of my life." She smiled. "And just to rob my friends here of the punchline to my story…he was very, very rich, so this Cinderella found her true Prince Charming."

"What a tale. Bravo for you," said Toni.

"Believe it or not," said Niko, "that sort of thing happens around here more often than you might imagine. This island's a regular fairy-tale production center."

"Complete with hookers everywhere," snapped Margo.

"It's cheaper to pay than marry," added Ricky.

"If anyone would know about that, it would be cheap-o you," chimed in Margo.

"Now, folks, play nice," said Niko.

"I do doubt, though, whether Ricky could afford the top tier," said the distinguished-looking fellow. "Last I heard, the price is twenty thousand euros a day, ten thousand a night, or fifteen hundred an hour."

"You must be joking," laughed Eugénie. "That's almost enough to lure me out of retirement."

Niko nodded. "Yep, I've heard those prices, too, but they're not the norm. The pimps set prices based upon how they size up their customers. Twenty thousand euros is what they charge a mega-rich client. One who wants his couture-draped celebrity fantasy helicoptered in for twenty-four hours of escort service to the island's priciest clubs and restaurants. If you're an average sort of hotel guest, you're charged between three hundred to a thousand euros for a round of sex, but in the big villas, where the wildest partying goes on, it's between one and three thousand. On yachts, I've heard it's between five and ten thousand for a half-day. Those are Mykonos prices, double what you'd pay in Athens or Thessaloniki. Then there are special prices for '*special arrangements*.'" He shook his head. "Any way you look at it, that's why there are so many hookers on the island."

"And pimps," said Ricky.

"And money laundries," said the distinguished fellow.

"Is Angelos still in business?" asked Eugénie.

"Karavakis?" asked Niko.

"Yes."

"Bigger than ever."

"I'm not surprised. He knew how to ingratiate himself to the right people," said Eugénie.

"What do you mean?" said Toni.

"I know there's a lot of bad things to be said about him, but I'll always have a soft spot in my heart for him."

"Why's that?"

"He introduced me to my husband."

The only response Toni could think of to say to that was "Oh."

At that moment a motorcycle roared up onto the hotel terrace. It stopped close by their bench. Toni turned to see who'd broken the trance she'd established with Eugénie.

Yianni smiled at her.

Great. Now what?

Chapter Fifteen

Yianni didn't have the difficult time he'd expected in convincing Toni to come with him. She initially resisted, saying she was exhausted and needed a nap, but a green-eyed woman next to her said, "Darling, as the adage goes, you'll have plenty of time to sleep when you're dead." Then she whispered something in Toni's ear that had both women laughing.

Whatever she said, and Yianni wasn't sure he wanted to know, the next thing he knew Toni had mounted his bike, snuggled in tight behind him, and wrapped her arms around his waist.

"Hast thou come to rescue me from these dour and dreary times?" she said.

"Hun?" said Yianni, pushing off with his feet to turn the bike around.

"Just drive, Prince Charming, just drive."

On the twenty-minute ride back to the house, Yianni tried concentrating on the road, but his mind kept wandering to other thoughts brought on by the press of Toni's tight body up hard against his own, her face nestled against his neck, and the BMW humming rhythmically between their legs.

When they reached the house, Yianni pulled to a stop and turned off the motor. Toni stayed as she was for a moment, her arms still tight around Yianni's waist.

"Thanks for the ride."

"My pleasure."

"And I'm sorry if I snapped at you last night. I know you wouldn't intentionally have tried to deceive me."

"Or knowingly put you in harm's way."

She dropped her arms, and swung her leg off the bike. "Which I assume brings us to why you brought me out here to meet with you and Andreas."

"And don't forget about me," said Lila coming out of the house. "I'm so happy you finally were able to make it, no matter what reason Yianni and my husband concocted to get you here."

The women took each other's hands and exchanged cheek kisses.

"I'm glad, too," said Toni, giving Lila's hands a squeeze before letting go.

"Come, let's sit on the terrace. Andreas is waiting. We held off lunch until you got here. He's famished."

"I know the feeling," said Yianni.

A breeze had picked up on the terrace, steadily ruffling the branches of the oleanders and olive trees. Lila brushed her fingers through her hair in an effort to control the strands tussled by the wind. She looked at Toni. "We're used to this, but if you'd prefer to eat away from the wind, we can move inside."

"No, I love the wind. It gives me an excuse for not keeping a napkin on my lap. Something that used to drive my mother crazy when I was a kid."

"Hi, Toni. Welcome." Andreas kissed her on both cheeks. "I appreciate your coming out to join us."

"I wish it were purely for social reasons, but from the little I've gleaned from Yianni, it's not."

"Sadly, you're right."

"Excuse me," said Lila looking at Andreas. "I don't mean to sound like some ditzy sit-com wife, oblivious to all the important things you professionals do, but would you mind waiting until our guest at least has a plate of food in front of her before turning the screws?"

"And a glass of wine," added Toni.

"Point made," said Andreas swooping his hand in the direction of a buffet spread out atop a table overlooking the sea and shaded from the sun by the house.

Green salad with figs, avocado, and *prosciutto*, Greek salad, *tabouleh*, *spanakopita*, *keftedes*—meatballs made from beef, some from chicken—grilled octopus, and a basket of breads alongside *tzatziki* and *taramasalata* dips, all sat surrounding a gigantic platter filled with different types of freshly grilled fish.

"Where's the rest of the army coming for lunch?" said Toni.

"We do tend to get carried away with things out here," said Lila.

"I'll say. You must have a heck of a compost heap."

"You'd be surprised how rapidly this disappears, what with guests popping in unexpectedly, and these two guys getting hunger urges at all hours," pointing one hand at Yianni, the other at Andreas.

Toni filled her plate and walked to the spot at the table with the lone filled wineglass.

"I take it this is my place?"

"Sit wherever you'd like," said Andreas.

"I just wanted to make sure I didn't take the prosecutor's chair."

"I'll take that as a sign you're ready for my lecture." Andreas and Lila sat across from Toni, and Yianni sat next to her.

"Ready as ever," said Toni, picking up and taking a bite of spinach pie. "Mm, delicious."

"Okay," said Andreas. "I asked you to pick up local gossip on Karavakis' project because I thought you could gather it without risk to yourself. But that's all changed. It's too dangerous. I'm calling you off, and telling you to stop whatever snooping you're doing into his affairs."

"I assume by *telling*, you mean suggesting."

Andreas didn't respond.

"But, to be fair, that seems to be the order of the day for me. I just got a similar warning from someone else."

"What kind of warning?"

"Not a threat, a friend looking out for me. Well, not actually a friend, more like a business acquaintance who told me my clandestine sleuthing was about as subtle as a polar bear at a dance recital."

"Nice visual," said Lila.

"Trouble is, I don't see how I can just walk away from a fifteen-year-old girl who's been, or soon will be, turned into a prostitute by Karavakis' son." Toni told them of her morning watching the daughter at work at the kiosk, and her subsequent conversation with the unnamed Christos.

"Who warned you?"

"Can't say. Professional confidences forbid it. Just take my word for it that he's not the bad guy. At least not in this instance."

Andreas looked at her sternly. "Toni, two men are already dead. Murdered. Both directly tied into this island and Karavakis. The most recent murder victim tried to kill Yianni and me, and now he's dead. Our current best guess is that whoever's behind this was afraid the killer would talk. Bad guys are in panic mode, and you don't want to be out there giving them ideas about what you know or might learn. You may only be trying to rescue the girl, but they won't see it that way."

Toni took a sip of wine. "I've had those same thoughts."

"When?" said Yianni.

"After my conversation with my sometimes bad-guy friend." She caught Yianni's eye. "And while we were riding out here." She looked away. "I don't know why I feel compelled to take such a big risk for someone I don't know. If I knew Adina, I might not even like her." She shook her head. "Then I hear a story like the one I just did from Eugénie," Toni turned to Yianni, "the woman sitting next to me at the hotel when you picked me up." She focused back on Andreas. "I guess I think I'm the one person on earth who could steer this young girl away from a life of prostitution and toward something fulfilling."

Andreas patted the table gently. "That's all good and admirable thinking, and the thought of being able to rescue some poor soul from a life filled with demons is an extraordinary motivator. But let's be honest with ourselves. Pressing ahead in this instance is not likely to lead to a storybook ending. Here we're talking about crossing a mega-bad guy…and possibly someone worse."

Toni, chuckled. "Funny you should say that. You're not going to believe who played fairy godmother to Eugénie, the one-time hooker."

Blank stares.

"Karavakis. The very same mega-bad guy you're worried about."

Lila reached for the wine. "I don't know about you two, but I sure could use a drink. I must say, one does learn the most interesting things at lunches on Mykonos."

Through the rest of lunch, Yianni and Andreas pressed Toni for details on her conversations with Eugénie and Christos. After extracting a promise from Toni that she'd not do anything further with respect to the Albanian father or his daughter that might aggravate Karavakis without first clearing it with them, Andreas and Yianni went inside to watch a football match.

Andreas sat on the sofa in front of the TV, and Tassaki immediately jumped onto his lap.

"I want to watch the game with you, Dad."

"I see you're teaching him early."

"Never too young to bring another fan on board." Andreas tussled his son's hair.

The three sat silently watching the game.

"Hard to imagine Karavakis caring about what happened to one of his girls," said Andreas.

"I don't think Eugénie was one of his girls. That would explain why he fixed her up with her husband. If she worked for someone else or was a freelancer, getting her married eliminated a high-priced competitor from his marketplace."

"That's cynical thinking worthy of Machiavelli," said Andreas.

"Or a whoremaster."

Andreas rolled his eyes in the direction of Tassaki.

"Whoops, sorry," winced Yianni.

They waited for a *"Daddy, what's a _____?"* question that never came.

"So, where do we go from here?" asked Yianni.

"I'm still waiting on that information from the sergeant, but my guess is it won't yield much. The woman who tampered with the IV was probably expendable. She might not even be alive anymore."

"Great, a case with all dead ends."

Andreas rubbed his son's arm. "I think we've got to go back to the beginning. As far as we know, everything started with that restaurant owner. What's his name?"

"Pepe."

"We have to press him on his story. We know it doesn't match up with the deformed shell casing. Find out where he is, and tell him we want to see him tomorrow."

"Where?"

"Mykonos. After all, he's building a club here, so it shouldn't be a big inconvenience. Let him pick the place on the island where he wants to meet."

"What if he objects?"

"Tell him GADA has some very uncomfortable interrogation rooms. His choice."

"Fine. And what will you be doing while I'm making our witness happy?"

"Calling our buddy, Tassos, to see how he and Maggie are doing on Syros. Lila invited them over for next weekend, but he's been on my mind since that surprise call from the sergeant made me think something bad had happened to a friend."

"I had the same thoughts. I hear he's been following his doctor's advice."

"I think Maggie's threats have had more impact."

"Don't they always?"

The two men nodded and went off to make their calls.

• ● ● ● •

It took Tassos six rings to make it to the phone. He cursed it after the third ring, gave up tending to his tomato plants after the fifth ring, and made it from his garden to the phone just before the seventh. "Whoever this is, you better have a damn good reason for disturbing me in the middle of doing what gives me the most pleasure in my life."

"Now that's about as terrific a straight line as I've ever heard. Give me a moment to come up with a comeback worthy of it."

"Asshole."

"Why don't you get a phone with caller ID? That way you can avoid calls you don't want."

"I like living dangerously."

"You're one screwed-up cop."

"There are more of us than there are of you," chuckled Tassos.

"For sure. Which brings me around to the reason for my call." Andreas paused. "But first, how are you doing?"

"Honestly, I think great. Maggie may not agree, but I've dropped twenty kilos and cut out the drinking. My cardiologist is proud, my girlfriend is unimpressed. She wants me to drop another twenty."

"I'd go with Maggie."

"As if I have a choice. She controls the cooking and has told every taverna on Syros that if they dare serve me anything other than salad, chicken or fish, she'll personally burn down their place. I don't dare imagine what she's told the bakeries. They won't even let me through the door."

Andreas laughed. "Are you guys going to make it over here next weekend?"

"We're planning on it."

"Great."

"So, what's on your mind?"

"We've got a serious mob mess developing on Mykonos, and my instincts see it as tied into the assassination of Colonel Aktipis."

"How so?"

Andreas described what he knew about the Colonel's murder, and the roles played by Karavakis and Despotiko in setting up the meeting with Pepe.

"Quite a cast of bad guys you've got there."

"There's more." Andreas described Karavakis' hotel-casino project, Despotiko's financing role, and the club Pepe planned to open on Mykonos in exchange for getting his brother to bring the hotel chain on board.

"Let me guess, you think the Colonel got killed for trying to extort a piece of the deal?"

"I see you knew the Colonel."

"We go back to when he was in charge of police in the Southeast Aegean Region and I ran homicide out of Syros. I never liked the guy, but we maintained a simple truce. He never screwed around in my backyard, and in turn I never went digging up holes in other folks' yards looking for one to bury him in."

"Sounds like classic local police work."

"Don't be such a cynic. It worked. After he left the force, I lost interest in following his shenanigans, but frankly, I'm surprised it took this long for someone to knock him off."

"Do you think Karavakis would do it?"

"Anything's possible, but it must have been a hell of a dispute for that to happen after so many years of them working together."

"That's sort of what Karavakis told us." Andreas paused. "What about Despotiko arranging the hit?"

"Same answer. Same question. Why now? And don't forget the possibility of a hotel owner who felt threated by the project setting it up."

"Maybe it's something personal, not business."

"Like what?" said Tassos.

"I don't know. You're my link to the dark side. What have you heard?"

"On this, nothing. But I haven't asked. Which I assume is the purpose of this call."

"Mind reader."

"I'll get on it right after I've finished battling the aphids on my tomato plants."

Andreas laughed. "I so envy the excitement in your life."

"No, my sarcastic friend, in truth you envy my newfound calm."

Tassos' remark caught Andreas off-guard. He glanced out onto the terrace at Lila and Toni chatting. "You know, you just might be right about that."

"Bye."

Yianni had changed into his bathing suit and begun swimming laps in the pool when Andreas walked out onto the terrace. Toni and Lila still sat at the dinner table, engrossed in what looked to be serious conversation.

"May I join you, or is this private?"

"The good stuff's already been covered, so it's okay with me," said Lila.

"Me too," said Toni.

"She doesn't mean 'me-too,' the movement," Lila said with a smile at Toni, "although that was one of the subjects of our conversation."

"Uh, clue me in, please," said Andreas, "I'm joining this movie a bit late."

"The *me*-too movement against sexual assault and harassment?"

"Gotcha." Andreas smiled. "May I ask what got you started on that subject?"

"One way or another, any serious conversation among women about moving forward in a career has to take that into account," said Toni.

"Especially here," added Lila.

"Why do you say that?" asked Andreas.

"How many women are in your unit?" said Toni.

"That sort of information is highly confidential."

Toni looked at Lila. "See, more official obfuscation of facts showing how women are held back from equal opportunities."

"Why do I sense I should join Yianni in the pool?"

"At least he obfuscates in a charming way," said Lila.

"Yeah, I'll give him that," said Toni.

"Give him what?" said Yianni, drying himself with a towel as he approached the table.

"A hard time," said Andreas. "If I were you, I'd jump back in the pool."

"Oh, it's one of those conversations."

"And just what does *that* mean?" said Toni.

"Nothing, I promise. So, what were you actually talking about?" said Yianni, sitting down.

"Before Andreas showed up, I'd been telling Lila more about that interesting woman I met at my hotel. The one who'd been a prostitute but met her Prince Charming, thanks to Karavakis, and lived happily ever after?"

"A modern-day Cinderella story," quipped Yianni.

"She's far from the only woman with that story line," said Lila.

"How do *you* know?" said Andreas.

"I don't *know* it, but there are society women in Athens rumored to have once been of—shall we say—negotiable virtue, who ended up marrying their clients."

"Any of them tied into Karavakis?" asked Andreas.

"I'd never even heard of Karavakis before this week. But I can tell you that the most prominent subjects of that fallen woman-meets-Prince Charming rumor mill are your dear friends, Mr. and Mrs. Marcos Despotiko."

Andreas and Yianni lurched forward.

"You're kidding," said Andreas.

"It's been a rumor for so long that no one bothers to bring it up anymore. The gossip mill prefers grinding fresh meat."

Andreas looked at Yianni. "I wonder how that plays into their relationship?"

"Whether it's true or not, the whole world knows about it," said Lila, "So, I can't imagine why either of them would care anymore."

"I meant between Karavakis and Despotiko, if it was Karavakis who made the introduction."

"My guess," said Toni, leaning forward to pick up her wine-glass, "is that on Facebook you'll find all of those relationships listed as, 'it's complicated.'"

Lila sighed. "I actually feel sorry for the wife. Think what her life must be like knowing everyone she meets has heard or likely will hear the rumor that she was a prostitute. I can't imagine the demons that must haunt her."

Yianni looked at Andreas. "Sort of makes you wonder what Mrs. Despotiko might be willing to do to prove to the world that she's more than just the ex-hooker wife of a powerful man."

"Like orchestrate the killing of someone she perceives as a threat to her husband's interests?" Andreas fell back into his chair. "This just keeps getting more curious by the moment."

"It's the life we chose to lead."

"Thanks for reminding me of that in front of my wife," said Andreas, winking at Yianni. "So, what did Pepe have to say about our request to meet?"

"He never answered his phone. I called three times, and left two messages. He might know it's me from caller ID."

"Or he's just busy. Whatever. If he doesn't get back to you in an hour, leave him a message that if he doesn't call you back immediately, you're going to reach out to him through Karavakis."

"Why drop Karavakis' name?"

"I think it's time to stir the pot, even add a bit of spice to the mix. If Karavakis has anything to do with these murders, and Pepe knows it, the last thing he wants is Karavakis thinking he might be cooperating with the police."

Just then a phone on the table beeped. "What's that?" said Andreas.

Yianni reached for the phone. "It's an SMS for me." He looked at his phone. "Well, we won't have to employ your nuclear option, Chief. It's Pepe saying he'll be *happy* to meet with us tomorrow at ten in the morning. He suggests a taverna in Ano Mera."

"Tell him okay."

Lila watched Yianni type the message and put down his phone. "Now that business is done," she said, "I guess we can start having fun."

Toni reached over for Yianni's phone and looked at the time. "Wow. I can't believe how late it is. I hate to run but I've got to get back and take at least a bit of a nap if I'm going to make it through until three tonight."

"I understand," said Lila. "Yianni, drive her back in the SUV. No need to subject her to that motorcycle."

"Oh, no," piped up Toni. "The motorcycle's fine. It actually energizes me."

"Me too," said Yianni.

"Suit yourselves," said Lila. "Though I can't imagine why you'd want to bump along on a bike when you could comfortably ride in a car."

Toni and Yianni exchanged awkward glances.

Andreas turned away to hide a smile, and mumbled to himself, "Methinks the game's afoot." He wondered if that sort of thinking made him a sexist. He couldn't imagine how it did, what with both parties obviously interested in playing.

●　●　●　●　●

The narrow road of dirt and random patches of concrete wove west toward the sunset, though by now the sun had dropped behind a line of rocky, barren hillsides. For centuries, only goat herders roamed among the steep hillsides crisscrossed with old stone walls. Too far out of town, too much wind, and too little—if any—water, had spared this region from development. Yianni wondered how much longer until elegant homes sprouted on these seemingly unbuildable sites. It was amazing what people with money could do when they wanted something.

Yianni stopped the motorcycle at a break in a stone wall running along the right side of the road and turned off the engine.

"What are you doing?" asked Toni, withdrawing her arms from around Yianni's waist.

"Shh."

A moment passed. "I hear nothing but birds."

"That's the point. That and the view."

Each shade-of-brown hill faded into the next slightly darker rise until only a haze of retreating, graceful curves remained to vanish into the horizon.

"And the scents."

Salt-wind-driven fragrances of wild rosemary, savory, and thyme seasoned the air.

A small lizard, as brown as the dirt, scurried out from the base of the wall, past their feet, and across the road into the shade of a wild thistle.

Toni pointed to the break in the wall. "Is that a road?"

"More like a path. It leads down to that goat herder's shed two hundred or so meters away."

"Can we drive there?"

"We can try," said Yianni, restarting the engine.

He carefully negotiated the motorbike along a true goat path through endless gray-green and browning brush and dirt mixed with wild-goat and donkey crap.

When they reached the hut, Yianni looked up at the road. "I sure hope we can make it back up there."

"Who cares?" said Toni swinging off the bike and waiting for Yianni to lead the way into the shed. It was a one-room stone hut with a woefully neglected bamboo roof. Open to the west, it had been built with the same sort of stone as the walls separating the fields, and was likely equally old.

"The goat herders stayed here?" she asked.

"With their goats," he smiled.

"Good, then this won't shock the spirits of the place."

"What won't?"

She stepped forward, wrapped her arms around him, and kissed him hard on the lips. He drew away. But she kissed him again. Harder. And forced her tongue into his mouth.

This time he kissed her back, running his hands along her sides, down to her butt, to squeeze and pull her hard up against him.

She pushed away, pulled off her top and undid her bra.

He stood as if not sure what to do.

"Well?" she said.

He kicked off his shoes and yanked off his jeans and the rest of his clothes, all the while watching her strip bare before pressing herself back into his arms. Each ran their hands along the other's body, from butt to breast to between the other's legs, moaning and kissing as they did.

He felt her wet, and she felt him hard. He turned to pick up his jeans, then spread them on the ground, pulling a condom from a pocket as he did. She grabbed it from him, dropped to her knees, rolled it onto him, and lay back on his jeans.

He dropped to between her legs and gently moved to find his way inside her.

She jerked. "Uh."

"Am I hurting you?"

"No, not at all." She slid her hands down onto his butt, gently drawing him into a rhythm punctuated by another "uh" with each thrust.

The louder Toni moaned, the faster Yianni moved. Between her voice and touch and warmth, Yianni knew he couldn't hold off much longer. That's when he heard and felt her release, and let himself do the same.

Neither moved for several moments, until Toni slowly stroked her hands along his back.

"That was nice," she said.

"Very nice."

"I'm glad we did it."

"Me too."

"I don't think either of us could stand holding off much longer."

"Obviously," he said, kissing her neck.

"Isn't it nice being adults?"

Yianni laughed. "I never thought of it that way."

"Of course you did. You thoughtfully had a condom."

"I always carry one."

"Doesn't everyone?" Toni smiled.

Yianni raised up off her chest to look in her eyes. "Why do I have this feeling you're not like any other woman I've dated?"

"Or screwed." Toni patted him on the butt. "This one's got to get back to town and prepare for work."

"What? We've only just begun."

"Just how many condoms do you have?"

Yianni smiled. "Enough.

Chapter Sixteen

Toni made it to work without a nap but only after a long, hot shower. As she walked into her familiar bar space, she couldn't remember the last time she'd felt this way.

Content was the word. Yes, she felt content.

Yianni struck her as a really nice guy. He'd wanted to stay with her when he dropped her off at the hotel, but she insisted he return home. It would be tough enough finding a way to survive at her piano until three, and impossible if she spent the intervening time with Yianni in bed.

She had no idea where this was headed, and though she knew it was way too early to contemplate more than a physical relationship, broader thoughts kept creeping into her mind. She wondered whether some universal, innate feminine instinct triggered "is-he-the-one?" thoughts about every man a woman slept with.

She tried putting those thoughts out of her mind, because reading a piano-bar crowd required a skill akin to gaining your balance on a surfboard...while playing a piano. Tonight, it took longer than usual for her to find her footing, what with random thoughts of her afternoon with Yianni popping up in her head, but she finally caught her second wind, and the room responded by steadily filling her tip jar.

"Hey, Toni, play us some Barry Manilow," shouted a guy at the bar.

Her fingers cringed. It would kill the room's party-hardy mood. "Barry Manilow? I don't do Barry Manilow."

"Of course you do," said another.

"Not on Thursday nights," she said.

"It's Monday."

"Close enough." She smiled.

The guy stumbled off his stool headed straight for her. He had the dark black curly hair, deep blue eyes, broad practiced smile, and athletic figure that would set many a woman's heart instantly aflutter. And many a man's, too, she suspected.

"I'd like to buy you a drink."

"That's very kind, thank you."

"Not here, back at my hotel." He named the favorite hotel of big-spenders looking to impress one another with their pricey couture clothes and jewelry.

He was hitting on her more directly than most. That sometimes came with the territory of working in a bar. But in light of her recent pondering over female instincts, she wondered if there might also be a male instinct that sensed when a woman had just been laid.

"No, thank you. I find I do my best work in a goat herder's hut."

As soon as her last set was over, Toni put her stuff away and headed out the door, aimed straight home to bed.

At three in the morning you'd think that would be easy to accomplish. But the island's party scene was only gaining momentum. It didn't matter which way she walked, the crowds were the same, and so with little wind tonight, she took the route next to the seawall.

She made it to where the walkway narrowed down to single-file passage between the sea on one side and café tables on the other. As she waited patiently for her turn to pass through the pinch point, she realized she was standing next to Karavakis' son. He and another local of about his age sat at one of the café tables, commenting in Greek on everyone passing by.

She'd never actually met Karavakis' son. Yes, she'd heard a lot of bad things about him from a lot of people, but she'd never had the chance to sit down and talk with him. Or even listen to him.

A young woman at the table next to his jumped up and squeezed past Toni, immediately followed by the guy who'd been sitting with her, calling out in English for her to wait for him. Toni took the unexpected drama as a sign from the Fates, and grabbed the empty chair closest to young Karavakis.

A waiter yelled to her in Greek, "What do you want?"

That caught the son's attention. He turned to see who'd gained the waiter's interest.

Toni said in English, "Please speak English, I don't speak Greek."

"What do you want?"

She ordered a beer, taking great care to mispronounce its Greek name.

The son shook his head and sneered, "*Xenos*," to the waiter, dissing the foreigner, then continued his conversation with his tablemate.

The subject of their conversation, Toni quickly learned, was neither interesting nor unexpected. It focused on the female bodies passing by...more specifically, on one part.

He pointed at a woman passing by in skin-tight gold lamé shorts and matching halter top and commented on the tightness of her ass. "You ever notice how tight a girl's butt cheek gets when she steps with the opposite foot?" He squeezed one hand tightly closed, then sprung it open. "Then it releases. I love that moment."

"I think the same thing happens to a man's ass," his companion said.

The son leaned across the table. "I'm not interested in a man's ass."

"I didn't say that you were. Just pointing out a fact."

"All I want to know from you is how to make more money from the business. If you can tell me that, then I'll be interested in your *facts*."

"I thought things were working pretty good."

"Not good enough. If we want to grow, we've got to be bold, think big, modernize."

"Like what?"

He held up his phone. "I want you to make us an app."

"What kind of app?"

"One that draws in the customers."

"That sounds risky. Might make it too easy to trace you."

"You think collecting face-to-face from johns and janes is any safer?"

His associate had no response.

"Let me show you what a competitor out of Athens is running right here on our island. They actually have the balls to call it consumer-friendly." He tinkered with his phone. "Once you download the app, you take a selfie and send it off to the site." He held up his phone and snapped his friend's picture. "That way the woman knows who you are. Then you describe the body type and whatever else you're looking for, and the site sends you photos of women in your area who meet your specs. You pick the one you want, and she shows up." He fiddled with the keys on his phone.

"Bullshit. I don't believe it."

Junior smiled as he worked his phone. "Just wait. Like every other Athenian business, they realize the only real money to be made during tourist season is on Mykonos."

"It's too crazy to be true."

"Which is precisely the sort of thinking that keeps us operating in the Stone Age."

Just then, the waiter showed up with Toni's beer. The bill was three times what it should be for a local. As Toni fumbled through her tip money, two breathtaking blondes—at least breathtaking at close to three-thirty in the morning—stopped in front of the son's table.

"We understand you boys want to party."

The son gave his colleague a wink. "Welcome to the future, my friend. Hassle-free hooker service."

Toni handed her money to the waiter, stood, motioned for the two women to take her table, and walked away with her beer. She'd heard enough. No reason to worry about misjudging the lad. He'd most definitely earned the "like-father-like-son" title of *Boy-pimp*.

Andreas and Yianni spent much of their morning studying the hospital's videos and the local police's slim file on the now-dead motorcyclist. The videos showed a confident young woman dressed as a nurse entering the hospital through its main entrance, going directly to the staircase leading to the victim's floor, entering his room, injecting his IV, and leaving the same way she'd come; all as if this were something she did every day.

They stared at a paused close-up of the killer's face.

"Not a hint of anxiety," said Yianni.

"She could be on drugs." Andreas leaned in closer to the image. "I think she's wearing a dark, short hair wig to cover up much lighter, longer hair."

"That could be face putty here and here to disguise her features." Yianni pointed at her cheekbones and nose.

"It'll be a guaranteed zero on fingerprints from the IV." Andreas turned off the video. "In keeping with hospital procedures, she wore hospital-issue gloves in the room. She probably wore them coming into the hospital, too."

Andreas picked up the file. "Not much more in here on the victim than we already knew. A twenty-five-year-old Bulgarian immigrant, received residency permission to work on Mykonos, despite a checkered criminal background. No record of criminal activity since coming to the island two years ago."

"Extraordinary, isn't it," said Yianni, "how when authorities in their wisdom grant an immigrant with his sort of background the chance to work as muscle for a truly bad guy, he undergoes a miraculous transformation and no longer does bad things."

"Someone's been protecting his arrest record from expanding, because for sure we're not the first ones on the island to experience his kick-the-bike routine."

Yianni smiled. "But we are his last."

Andreas stared at Yianni. "You sound like Tassos. The guy's dead. At least try to show some respect."

"You mean like the respect he'd have shown to us at our funerals? Or do you mean like the respect whoever ordered him to kill us would have shown Lila and the kids with a huge bouquet of flowers?"

Andreas kept up his stare. "Like I said, you sound like Tassos. Which reminds me, I ought to check in later with Maggie to see what sort of luck she's having with the other hospital video footage."

"What do you expect her to find?"

"No idea, but if anyone can find something, it's Maggie." Andreas slapped his thighs and stood up. "Let's get going. It's time to head off to Ano Mera and our visit with Mr. Pepe."

Yianni and Andreas sat on the outdoor terrace of a virtually empty one-story taverna facing Ano Mera's architectural highlight, the fortress-like monastery of Tourliani. The taverna sat amid a slew of other one-story buildings, mostly tavernas, surrounding the flagstone town square.

"So, where's our guest of honor?" said Yianni, looking at his phone.

"Give him time, he's only twenty minutes late."

"It shows no respect. Do you think he'd be late for a meeting with Karavakis?"

Andreas gave him a long look. "What the hell has you so ornery?"

"I'm not ornery," said Yianni.

"Yeah, sure. Considering your mood, I'll play bad cop with Pepe."

"Okay, it's Toni. I don't know what to make of her. I know she likes me. At least I think she does, but she doesn't want to be with me as much as I want to be with her."

Andreas shook his head. "My friend, you sound smitten."

"Bitten?"

"Either word works. It's none of my business, but I think you ought to step back, give her room to figure out her own way into a relationship."

"Relationship? Who said anything about a relationship?"

Andreas smiled. "Frightened as you may be by the word, I'd say that's where you're headed."

Yianni pressed his lips together. "She's not like any other woman I've ever known."

"That can be good." Andreas paused. "It can also be a dangerous novelty. One kind wears well, one kind wears off."

Yianni stared at Andreas. "Since when did you become a relationship counselor?"

"Since the day I got married." He nodded across the square. "Looks like there's our guy."

A pudgy man in a blue-and-white-checked shirt stood at the entrance to the square from the parking area.

"He seems to be looking around for where he's supposed to be," said Yianni.

"I thought he picked this place," said Andreas.

"He did," said Yianni.

They left Pepe to find them on his own.

"Ah, there you are," said Pepe finally, giving them his finest restaurateur smile.

Yianni stood, shook hands, and introduced Pepe to Andreas. Andreas did not stand.

"Pleased to meet you," smiled Pepe, extending his hand as he sat in a chair directly across from Andreas, facing into the taverna.

"You're late," said Andreas.

"Sorry."

"Half an hour late."

Pepe's smile faded as he withdrew his hand. "You dragged me all the way here from the mainland. You should be happy I came at all."

Andreas leaned in. "Be happy I'm not poring over every millimeter of every place you have an interest in, to see how dirty you really are. Because once I do, I can assure you that your businesses will be shut down tighter than a gnat's ass. As for your new place on this island," he waved his hand in the air, "never happen."

"Fuck you."

Andreas smiled. "Many have tried, but even your buddy who told you to pick this spot to meet with us knows better than to try that. It's why he uses expendable numb-nuts like you to do his dirty work and take his falls." Andreas leaned in across the table. "Let me put it to you this way. Either follow us out of here, or lawyer up for what I'm sure you and your partners will find to be years of joyful investigations, plus inevitable long-term accommodations provided by the state, all coming to you and them courtesy of *you*."

Andreas stood, motioned for Yianni to do the same, tossed ten euros on the table and walked away, turning only long enough to toss a kiss at a waiter standing in the doorway between the terrace and the building—and wearing an earpiece.

As they walked across the square toward the parking lot, Yianni said, "Tighter than a gnat's ass. What the hell does that mean?"

"*Gamoto*. It's the only thing I could come up with at the moment. Is he following us?"

Yianni glanced back. "Yep."

"Then at least *he* knows what I meant."

Back in the parking lot, Andreas told Pepe to leave his car and ride with them. Yianni drove with Pepe next to him, Andreas in the backseat.

"Head to Fokos," said Andreas. "Ever been there, Pepe?"

"N-no."

"Relax, you'll enjoy it. It's a trip back to old Mykonos, or at least to what's left of its spirit."

They turned left out of the parking lot onto the main road, and took an immediate right at a tiny square. A paved road soon narrowed down to barely a lane and a half as it wove between borders of old and new stone walls. Beyond the walls, beige-brown fields and pastures ran off toward hills of different shades of brown, all heavily peppered in new construction threatening to overrun the tiny white churches and classic farm buildings of another era.

After about a mile, the road widened to two lanes and turned to dirt. It ran north alongside a mile-long rainwater reservoir nestled between pristine desert hillsides veined in old stone walls and speckled with wild rosemary, savory, thyme, and goats.

"The reservoir looks pretty low," said Yianni.

"The one in Marathi's even lower," said Andreas. "It's a brewing catastrophe, brought on by years of drought, phenomenal growth, and woefully inadequate desalinization facilities."

Yianni glanced over at Pepe. "I guess he's saying, 'Pray for rain.'"

Pepe sat looking out the window, saying nothing.

"Isn't the natural beauty of this island extraordinary?" said Andreas.

Pepe still said nothing.

The road alternated between broad arcs to the left and right, before a sharp swing to the left brought the far end of the reservoir into view.

Hovering above the end of the reservoir, as if devouring the hillsides around it, loomed a mass of white villas.

"Talking about catastrophes," said Andreas. "Last I heard not a single one's been sold, and the asking price keeps falling every year."

"The builder must owe a fortune to the banks," said Yianni.

"A lot of people owe fortunes to the banks, but the savvy debtors know the banks won't push to collect. If they did, they'd have to report the defaulted loans to the EU as non-performing, and that would dramatically affect the banks' financial health requirements. So, big debtors owing millions just ignore the banks and go on living as if debt-free."

"If it's that obvious, how do the banks get away with it?" asked Yianni.

Andreas smiled. "Makes you wonder, doesn't it?" He stared at a bright white egret standing on the muddy edge of the reservoir. "On top of that, you've got bank-loan portfolios filled with dead loans—ones where no one knows what's owed, how to locate the debtors, or where to find written proof that there's a loan at all. Some of those portfolios have been sold off to foreign speculators who are in for a big surprise."

Yianni glanced over at Pepe. "What do you think, Pepe? Is it too risky for you to be opening a new place in this treacherous economy?"

Pepe gave him a quizzical look but didn't speak.

"I get it," said Yianni. "Your business plan is simple: There will always be a big demand for booze, sex, and drugs."

"Not to mention the black-money part of the business," added Andreas.

Beyond the end of the reservoir, the road dropped steeply down toward a wide, sandy cove edged in black- and rust-colored stone. A taverna of natural stone sat in the middle of the cove, fifty meters back from the sea. It was a postcard vision that magazines and moviemakers often used to present the paradise known as Mykonos to the world. *Sans* villas. Locals and longtime fans of Mykonos escaped here to remember how very beautiful their island once was.

Yianni parked by the taverna's entrance. They'd barely made it up the steps when the owner, a grizzled Mykonian the size of a bear, recognized Andreas and tried dragging the three of them over to his table. Andreas begged off, promising to return with his family soon. He asked for a table in the back of the taverna—and that no one be seated near them.

The owner took a long, hard look at Pepe and nodded. "I understand." He showed them to a table virtually invisible to other patrons yet still offering an uncluttered view of the sea.

No sooner had they sat down than a waiter delivered octopus, calamari, and the owner's wife's famous broccoli salad. *Tsipouro*, ice, and water arrived next.

Andreas leaned back in his chair. "So, Pepe, isn't this a more comfortable place for our chat?"

Pepe didn't speak.

"I respect your desire to remain silent. That's usually the smart play. Trouble is, in this case not talking is all downside for you."

Andreas reached for the liquor. "*Tsipouro?*"

Pepe nervously nodded yes.

Andreas poured a large slug into a glass. "I'll leave it to you to add ice and water as you choose." He tasted a bit of the octopus. "Try this, it's delicious."

Pepe took a gulp of his drink but declined the food.

Andreas patted the table. "Here's your problem. We know you were lying about what you saw in that parking lot the night the Colonel was murdered. The only question is whether you were involved in the planning or just the cover-up."

"That's ridiculous. I had nothing to do with either."

Andreas shook his head. "How stupid do you think we are?

Shots are fired in the middle of a small town on a lovely summer evening and you think no one turns around or looks out their windows to see what's going on? This isn't the U.S.; gunshots are rare here."

"No one saw a thing."

"How do you know that? From your buddies on the local police force? Sorry, Pepe, but this case is mine now, and my people are working it."

Pepe took another gulp of his drink.

"Besides, we don't have to identify the killer. We have you to do that."

"I saw nothing."

"Yeah, I know your story. No one drove out of the parking lot from the time you heard the shots." Andreas shook his head. "Why, then, do we have three witnesses who say someone did drive out?"

"They're lying."

"All three?"

Pepe stared at his drink.

"Your ass is in a sling. How do you want to play it?" said Andreas.

Pepe rubbed at his face with his free hand, holding his drink in the other. "Okay, just as I came out of the restaurant, this guy came roaring past on a motorcycle. At least I think it was a guy. The driver wore a helmet."

"And you didn't tell us this before because you were...?" Andreas rolled his hand for Pepe to finish the sentence.

"Afraid. I knew it was a hit. I didn't want my name associated in any way with something as big as this. No way." He shook his head. "If they were prepared to kill someone as important as the Colonel, I was as good as dead if they thought I saw something."

"Who's they?"

"Not a clue."

"Good story, Pepe." Andreas picked up the *tsipouro* bottle

and poured Pepe a larger slug. "Now tell me what you've left out. Like the part about you being able to identify the killer."

"What are you talking about?"

"You saw the hit take place. That's how you knew where to walk so to avoid the shell casings. You saw them hit the ground."

"No, that's not what happened."

"Pepe, Pepe…Don't you see how by admitting you saw the hit actually helps you? If you knew it was going down, you'd have put yourself as far away from that door as possible, and let someone else find the body. Only an idiot would admit to standing by the door to watch a hit that he knew was about to happen."

Pepe seemed to ponder the thought. "Okay…I saw it. I saw it all."

Andreas raised his hands. "Whoa, there. You're changing your story again? You better convince me why we should believe this version."

"Because, you're right, I know who killed the Colonel."

"You do?" said Andreas,

"The guy you two had a run-in with a couple of nights ago."

Andreas raised his eyebrows.

"How convenient," said Yianni.

Andreas reached for a glass and poured himself a shot of *tsipouro*. "You know, I actually believe you." He added three ice cubes, and a small measure of water. "How did you recognize him in his helmet?"

"I'd seen him wear it many times at Karavakis' club."

"How did you know about our incident with him?"

"I told Karavakis I'd be on the island today. He asked why, and I said because you wanted to see me. That's when he told me what happened."

"Why didn't you tell us this sooner?

"The killer was my friend's employee. The last thing I wanted to do was involve my friend in this mess."

"You mean the same friend who would eliminate you if he thought you'd noticed something?" said Yianni.

Pepe scowled. "He didn't tell me not to come to see you today. And I'm still breathing. That should answer your question."

"Did Karavakis pick the place for today's meeting?" asked Andreas.

"It belongs to his nephew."

"Well," said Andreas leaning back in his chair, "now that you've gotten that off your chest, do you care to tell us who killed our motorcyclist friend in his hospital room?"

"What? He's dead?"

"You didn't know?"

"How would I know?"

"Karavakis, perhaps? Or maybe one of your *friends* on the police force in charge of protecting him?"

"Look, I've told you everything. What more can I say?"

"Not sure, but I'm looking forward to the day when you do." Andreas picked up his glass and toasted. "To truth. May we hear it all soon."

Pepe did not lift his glass. "Do you mind if we leave now? I have to catch a boat."

"No problem."

Andreas called for the bill, but the owner said there was none, as long as Andreas followed through on his promise to come back with his family.

Pepe said not a word on the ride back to his car, and once they'd dropped him off, Andreas moved to the front seat for the ride home.

The first words out of Yianni's mouth were, "What three witnesses?"

"I bluffed. But we knew he was lying."

"Do you think he knew the motorcyclist was dead?"

"For sure. Karavakis would know by now, whether or not he was behind the murder. He'd have told Pepe before sending him off to his nephew's place. By the way, thanks for the heads-up on Pepe looking lost as he headed into the Ano Mera square. It's what made me think the table was wired."

The Mykonos Mob   221

"As you always say, it's the little things that make the difference in police work."

"And in romance," smiled Andreas.

"So, now we're back on that subject, are we?"

"Well, I thought I should at least give you a warning."

"Of what?"

"Unless I'm mistaken, that motorbike down by the house is likely Toni's."

Chapter Seventeen

Syros lay forty-five minutes due west of Mykonos by fast boat. Capital of the Cycladic Islands, and home to the Cyclades' central police headquarters, its architecture differed substantially from traditional Cycladic forms. Stunning neo-Classical buildings, streets paved in marble, and an opera house said to be the first in Greece, all stood in faded testament to Syros' last great aristocratic run as Greece's nineteenth-century shipbuilding and refitting center. Today, it served primarily as the political center of the Cyclades.

Just off the harbor in Syros' capital port town of Ermoupoli, and tucked in behind a line of potted oleanders and tamarind, Tassos sat at the same rear table, in the same snug taverna, as he did most days. He'd stuck to that routine since becoming Chief Homicide Investigator for the Cyclades, more decades ago than he cared to remember.

He sat with another man of about his age. The man held a Greek coffee in his right hand and looked puzzled. "I don't understand why you want to visit Mykonos in high season. You're way too old and poor for that island's craziness."

"Speak for yourself, Vassili. As long as I'm not dead, I'm never too old for Mykonos."

"And as long as you're a cop, never too poor."

Tassos waved him off.

Vassili ignored him. "So, why the big rush to see me today?"

"Because no one knows Mykonos better than you."

"I haven't lived there in years. You know that. I prefer life here. I've no idea what's hot and what's not back over there." He waved in the general direction of Mykonos.

"I'm not looking for restaurant recommendations." Tassos leaned in. "Nor do I mean to intrude upon your newfound serenity, but with your vast portfolio of Mykonos rental properties tossing off all the income they do for you, I can't think of anyone who's kept his claws closer to the jugulars of every Mykonos mayor in the past fifty years than you."

"*Claws to the jugulars.* You've always had a flair for colorful phrasing. Just like back on Gyaros. You always made me laugh."

"What choice did you have but to laugh at my jokes?" said Tassos. "You were a political prisoner on an isolated prison island, and I was your keeper."

Vassili laughed. "There you go again. But you were always one of the good guys." He jiggled a finger at Tassos. "Even then you knew there'd be a change in political fortunes, that someday the Junta would be gone and your inmates would be back in power." He stared off into no place in particular. "And that we'd remember how we were treated, and by whom." He looked at Tassos and smiled.

Tassos shrugged. "Who would have guessed that my simple Golden Rule approach to treating enemies of the state would yield such an unexpected benefit as your friendship?"

"Stop blowing smoke up my ass. We've known each other far too long for that."

"But it's true. Our friendship is worth a lot more to me than even my pension."

"Is that meant to be a compliment or another joke?" Vassili grinned and leaned back in his chair. "Let's see, after fifty years of service you should be entitled to a monthly pension of just about what it'll cost you to rent a pair of beach chairs for the day, plus lunch for two, at one of those chic Mykonos beach clubs."

Tassos spread his arms. "What's with this sudden hard-on you have for Mykonos?"

"It's my way of mourning."

"For what?"

"For all that the island has lost forever."

"Are you running for office?"

"Me? Again? Never. The place has lost its way. I give it no more than five years until maximum burnout. At best, it becomes Europe's Las Vegas. At worst…" He let his words drift off. "I've thrown in the towel. "

"I hear that a lot," said Tassos. "But people always complain about change, no matter where they live in this world. Besides, if you don't like the new ways of Mykonos, there are a lot of islands still offering the old ways."

"Yes, but Mykonos was special. At least to me. Sure, we did drugs. And sex. A joint on the beach, maybe some LSD. But these days, drugs and sex *are* the island's image. Some tourists arrive actually expecting drugs and hookers as part of their holiday package. Worse still, today's dealers don't care if they kill you with what they're selling."

"You make it sound like the place is run by mobsters."

"Your words, not mine. Have you heard about the poor money-launderers who opened businesses on Mykonos looking to clean black money generated from drugs, prostitution, and human trafficking, only to find themselves making so much in their new legitimate businesses that they can't justify running their black money in on top of it?"

"Like I said, no one knows Mykonos better than you. Which brings me to what's on my mind."

"I thought we'd never get there." Vassili took a sip of coffee.

"It's about Aktipis."

"The Colonel?"

"Yes. I want to know what you've heard about his death."

"A lot more than I'd be willing to talk about if he were still alive." He put down his coffee cup. "The guy was dirtier than the rumors about him, which is a pretty hard thing to achieve in Greece. He was also ruthless. He'd do just about anything to get what he wanted or to keep someone else from getting what he couldn't have."

"That sounds like a perfect combination of personality traits for making friends and influencing people."

"I think he was about as friendless as anyone I've ever known."

"I take that to mean a lot of people didn't mind what happened to him."

"No doubt about it."

"Can you give me some names?"

Vassili picked up his coffee cup, took a sip, and put it down. "It would be much easier giving you a list of those who conceivably might miss him."

"And those names would be?"

He paused. "People who looked to him to keep things running smoothly on Mykonos. His job was to maintain order among the different mobs looking to cut in on the island's action."

"What mobs?"

"Greek, Albanian, Roma, Italian, Bulgarian, Russian," Vassili shrugged. "Plus, who knows how many other gangsters from the former Soviet satellites who've found Mykonos was a new Nirvana for their style of doing business. With all the free-flowing tourist money, vice, and inadequate police, the island's irresistible for their sort."

"Sounds like you're saying the Colonel was Mykonos' boss of bosses."

"I guess you could put it that way, if you're into American mob movies."

Tassos waved to a waiter. "Two more coffees, please." He looked at Vassili. "What other way is there to put it?"

"The Colonel didn't control criminal activity on Mykonos. He just kept those who wanted in on the action from killing the golden goose of those running it."

"Do you think that's what got him whacked?"

"Hard to say. I always thought he had a gift for knowing how to spread enough money-making opportunities around to the mob chiefs without upsetting his government patrons—and that he did it in a way that had all sides seeing a benefit in keeping him alive. I guess I thought wrong."

"So, who do you think *didn't* want him eliminated?"

Vassili shut his eyes and opened them again. "At the top of that list I'd put Marcos Despotiko and Angelos Karavakis."

Andreas' top two suspects. "Why them?"

"Each in his own way is much like the Colonel. Despotiko portrays himself as above the hunt, charming his prey rather than stalking it. He keeps local and national officials happy and onboard through whatever means necessary. Karavakis is more of an operations guy, legendary for screwing his friends, even family, and embracing his enemies. For both men, it's all about what you can do for them at the moment. Power is all that matters."

"Anyone else?"

"You want more? Nosing around those two is where you're most likely to find your answers. But, take care, because you could lose your pension."

Tassos gave a puzzled look.

"By loss of pension, I meant surviving to collect it."

Tassos forced a smile. "You said Karavakis screws his friends."

"Actually, I think he's a sicko who takes great joy in sabotaging those closest to him. He wants no one but himself to succeed." Vassili took a sip of coffee. "There's a phrase I've heard him use that says it all: 'If you see someone drowning, push and hold the head under.'"

Tassos lifted his eyebrows. "But I understood he's been helping an old friend of his set up a competing hotel-casino resort on Mykonos."

"News to me. And I thought I was supposed to be your source of info on Mykonos."

Tassos paused. "I trust you not to repeat this, so I won't even ask for your word on what I'm about to tell you, but I heard the guy Karavakis is helping is an old friend of his named Pepe."

Vassili stared at him. "You mean the Pepe who owned the restaurant where the Colonel was killed?"

"Yep."

"Son of a bitch." Vassili shook his head. "That sure makes it look like Karavakis was involved in the hit."

"Why do you say that?"

"Because Pepe has an abused-spouse-like compulsion to do Karavakis' bidding, no matter how much crap Karavakis heaps on him. For years, Pepe tried getting permits to open a place on Mykonos, relying on his *friend's* promises to help him, yet at every juncture Karavakis worked behind the scenes to block him."

"Did Pepe know that?"

Vassili shrugged. "I sure as hell didn't tell him, but you'd think he'd have figured it out after all those years of trying and failing. I mean, let's be real, his buddy had mega-juice on the island, yet Pepe never got the licenses or permits he needed, even though he always made sure to offer the necessary officials their customary gratuities."

"You're absolutely certain about this?" said Tassos.

"I personally witnessed some of the permitting deliberations. It was an open joke. One year, I even heard an official say, 'It's time to screw Karavakis' buddy again.'"

Tassos shook his head. "This guy Pepe must be a real *malaka*, but is he enough of one to have set up the hit on the Colonel for Karavakis?"

"That's up to you to figure out. But I must say, even if he was conned into playing a part in the hit, I don't have much sympathy for him, considering his bad choices in friends."

"Unlike us," smiled Tassos.

"Yes, unlike us." Vassili downed the rest of his coffee. "Anything else I can help you with?"

"Nope, you've been great. Thanks."

Vassili stood. "Only one favor I ask."

"Sure, anything."

"Please, don't ever tie me into this conversation. I enjoy being around to collect *my* pension."

Tassos smiled. "Deal."

• ● ⬤ ● •

Toni wasn't sure what possessed her to decide to drop in unannounced on Yianni.

No way she'd catch him at Lila and Andreas' with another woman. Nor could she figure out why even the thought of such a possibility had passed through her mind. But it had. Was it some innate insecurity or something else?

Whatever the reason, first thing that morning she'd stopped by the motorbike rental shop next to her hotel and, in keeping with her longstanding arrangement with the owner, taken the worst bike on the lot for half its normal day rate. At this time of the year, it saved her a lot of money. On the other hand, what she had left to choose from made the expression "runt of the litter" a compliment by comparison.

By the time she'd reached Lila's place, Toni wished she'd rented a Jeep, but it wasn't the bumps, potholes, and crazy drivers that had her feeling a bit insecure riding alone on a bike. It was the motorcycle that had followed her all the way from town to within a few hundred meters of Lila's gate before turning off by the entrance to a modern windmill facility.

She sat on Lila's terrace telling herself it was Yianni and Christos' warnings playing with her imagination that had made her anxious. Then her thoughts drifted to what it would be like riding again on Yianni's bike, hugging him tightly.

She would have loved to do some more of that, but Yianni wasn't there to hug.

She shook her head. *Why am I thinking this way?*

"Is something wrong?" asked Lila.

"Huh, no. Why?"

"Since you arrived, your mind's been elsewhere. Now you're sitting quietly, staring out to sea, and shaking your head."

Toni blew breath out between her lips. "I'm worried about Adina," she lied. "The fifteen-year-old girl Karavakis' son is trying to, or already has, turned into a prostitute."

"Yes, I've thought about her, too. It's a shame there's nothing we can do for her."

"By sheer coincidence, I ran into the son last night. He's disgusting." Toni told Lila about the overheard conversation.

"Great. He's going to bring the family business into the digital age."

"If only I could convince Adina's father to send her off the island."

"I don't know the girl or her situation, but I doubt that alone would help."

"Why do you say that?"

Lila shrugged. "My guess is, assuming she's not hooked on drugs, she has horridly low self-esteem, and your 'boy-pimp's' exploiting it. Some men are very good at finding a woman's greatest insecurity and homing in on it."

"Lucky for us, we're both perfectly well-adjusted."

Lila laughed. "Yeah, sure. More like we're lucky to have well-adjusted men in our lives who don't take that route."

We, thought Toni.

"Though I guess it's presumptuous of me to have already coupled you up in my mind with Yianni."

Toni shrugged. "No problem, but Adina is doomed if I can't come up with something. I've seen where she lives. She must be desperate to escape her life."

"Fifteen's an impressionable age. Especially on this island. Every day she's exposed to pretentious grandeur and extravagant living. It's no surprise that a girl of her age and humble family background wants to be part of that other sort of life. She doesn't realize yet that appearances aren't what matter most."

"Right. She can only imagine bettering her life by attracting the attention of men."

"What she needs is a mentor who inspires her to think independently." Lila paused and smiled. "Sounds to me as if she and I are looking for the same thing."

An instant passed in which neither Toni nor Lila said a word. Then Toni caught Lila's eye. "Are you thinking what I'm thinking?"

"Nah, it's too crazy," said Lila. "Too crazy."

"She needs you," said Toni pointing at Lila. "You're the perfect role model to mentor her."

"Not a chance. Let's be realistic. What do I have in common with her? I was born to all of this." She waved her hand at the pool and house.

"And Boy-pimp was born to his life. It's your personality, your experience, your offer of friendship that can make all the difference."

Lila stared at Toni. "You really are serious."

"Absolutely. It will be great for both of you."

Lila shut her eyes for a moment and opened them. "If this foolishness is going any further, you better start speaking in terms of '*We.*'"

"Fine, it will be great for both of us."

"But how do we go about it? We can't just show up and say, 'Hi, we're your new best friends who've come to change your life and save you from hell and damnation.'"

Toni grinned. "That sort of approach has worked rather well for generations of missionaries, but I agree it won't work in this case." Toni bit at her lip. "Larry and Janet have a lot of connections around the world, and they're generous souls. Maybe they'd be interested in helping her find a career?"

"Come to think of it, I know some people who might be

willing to sponsor a girl like her in need of a fresh start." Lila began rocking back and forth in her chair. "Mm. I have to admit, I'm getting a bit excited at the idea."

"That's good to hear, because I can't think of anything more natural and meaningful for you to do than this." Toni smiled, then quickly added, "I mean for *us* to do."

"Let's not forget what Andreas said. 'Rescue can be enticing.'"

"Yes, I know. I also realize there are life-threatening risks for those foolish enough to try separating prostitutes from their pimps, but the upside offers such extraordinary life-changing potential on so many levels that it boggles my mind."

"Okay, no reason to get overly psyched." Lila smiled. "At least not until after we figure out how to deal with the risks."

"We also have to figure out how best to go about getting Adina to listen to us."

Lila looked toward the house. "I hear a car. The men must be back." She turned to Toni. "Until we've thought this through, let's keep this just between us."

"Yep, just between us girls."

• ● ● ● •

"What a pleasant surprise," said Andreas walking out onto the terrace and crossing over to Toni to kiss her on both cheeks.

Yianni stood back, as if unsure what to do.

"See what happens once you're married with two kids?" said Lila. "Your husband always kisses the prettier younger women first."

"That's just to warm me up for the main event," grinned Andreas, stooping down to kiss Lila on her lips, forehead, and cheeks.

She shooed him away with her hands. "Not sure that was the right answer, but I get your drift. Yianni, would you please not allow him to drink so early in the day?"

"Wrong, my love, only coffee."

"Then stick to milk."

Toni walked to Yianni and whispered, "Do I always have to make the first move?"

He smiled. "No," and lightly kissed her on the lips.

She paused for a moment before putting her arms around him and kissing him hard.

"Bravo, Toni," said Lila. "Greek men are so shy about showing romantic affection around other men."

"Not just Greek men." Toni quickly added with a smile, "At least so far as I can tell from my observer status at the piano bar."

"How did your meeting go?" asked Lila.

"Pepe's quite a character," said Andreas taking a chair across from the women. "He couldn't keep his story straight long enough to keep his lies in order."

"Is that your way of saying you learned nothing?"

He smiled. "As a matter of fact, we learned a lot. Whether it proves true or helpful, we'll see."

Yianni sat next to Andreas. "Pepe identified the Colonel's killer as a now-also-dead guy who worked for Karavakis."

"So you've solved the case?" said Toni.

"Not by a long shot."

"Too many potential villains," said Yianni.

"Too many *actual* villains. We just need to separate out the ones responsible for the mess we're trying to figure out."

Lila stood and looked at Toni. "Let's leave them to their crime-solving. We can go inside and knit, or bake a cake, or something."

"Sounds like a plan," said Andreas with a smirk.

"I think that just might count as strike two," said Toni, earning three blank stares.

"Strike two?" she repeated. More stares. "Whoops, sorry. American baseball. Three strikes and you're out."

"I like that phrase," said Lila.

"But what does 'you're out' mean?" said Yianni.

Lila motioned for Toni to follow her inside. "In this case, sleeping on the couch."

"Thanks for obtaining that clarification, Yianni."

"Any time, Chief."

They watched the women walk inside.

"I like Toni," said Andreas.

"I do, too."

"It's good they like each other."

"Makes it easier for them to team up on us."

"So…" Andreas reached for two empty glasses on the table next to him and filled them with water. He handed one glass to Yianni. "Where are we?"

Yianni took a sip. "Damned if I know. We've got practically everyone who knew the Colonel wanting him dead. That is, except our suspects."

"I've got an idea. Instead of focusing on who wanted him dead, let's think about who knew where he'd be the night he was murdered. No matter how much you wanted him dead, if you didn't know where he'd be, you couldn't kill him."

"I count four probables, not including the Colonel. That's Despotiko, his wife, Karavakis, and Pepe. Plus those they might have told. For sure someone told the killer, but given where the meeting was held, I think the participants wanted to keep it secret. Otherwise, the most logical place to meet was on Mykonos."

Andreas took a gulp of water. "As far as others knowing goes, if Karavakis and Despotiko knew, I see no reason for them to be talking about it unless they were arranging or encouraging an assassination. The other two, Pepe and Mrs. Despotiko, are unguided missiles. No telling whom they might have told, or why."

"Or if they had their own agendas." Yianni shook his head. "I don't see much progress here."

"Well, we've reduced it to five likely sources for the info that got the Colonel whacked. We'll just have to press the survivors about who they passed the info to."

"Please don't tell me I have to talk to Despotiko's wife again."

Andreas smiled. "If it comes to that, we'll do it together."

A phone rang inside the house. "Could you get that, please?" Andreas shouted toward the house.

After two more rings, Tess stood in the doorway. "It's Mr. Tassos."

"Thank you." Andreas motioned for her to bring him the phone.

He took the phone and hit speaker. "Hi, Tassos, I'm here with your clone, Yianni."

"Always liked the kid; he made you a better cop."

Yianni smiled. "I like you too."

"So, to what do we owe the honor of this call?"

"Actually, it's Maggie who wanted to talk to you, but I had a conversation earlier today with an old friend who gave me some information that might be helpful to you on that Colonel's assassination business."

"Great," said Andreas.

"According to my friend, Pepe and Karavakis go way back together."

"We knew that."

"Yes, but did you know that Karavakis always did everything he could to hurt Pepe's chances of opening a place on Mykonos?"

"Did you say hurt or help?" asked Yianni.

"*Hurt*. As in kicked him in the balls at every opportunity."

"That sounds mighty painful."

"And a source for one hell of a lot of resentment."

"You got that right."

"But why would he take it from Karavakis for so long?" said Yianni.

"I asked the same question."

"What was the answer?"

"Abused-victim syndrome. Like a pet or spouse so desperate for acceptance by their abuser that they take the abuse in exchange for an occasional crumb of recognition or kindness."

"Jesus," said Yianni.

"He sounds like a mesmerized puppet of Karavakis."

"But wait, there's more."

Andreas shook his head at the phone. "Tassos, your theatrics are going to be the death of me yet."

"Hey, we old guys have to get our thrills some way. Besides, it's not my part of the story to tell. It's Maggie's. Here, darling, the show's all yours."

Andreas and Yianni heard a shuffling of the phone from one person to another.

"Hi," said Maggie.

"How do you put up with him?" said Andreas.

"You've trained me to accept virtually anything."

Yianni laughed. "When are you going to give up trading quips with her?"

"When I'm dead."

"From the people you're chasing, you might not have to wait much longer."

Yianni laughed again.

"So, what do you have to tell us?"

"It's about those hospital videos. I've gone through enough of them to find what I think you're looking for."

"How could you have gone through them so quickly?"

"Do you think I'm lying?"

"No, just curious."

"There's such a thing as fast-forward, and if you concentrate on the screen you can cover a lot of ground quickly. I also started with the videos of the most likely place for action, the hallway outside his room."

"Okay, my curiosity is satisfied. What did you find?"

"The day after your prisoner was admitted, a guy walked back and forth in front of his room about twenty times."

"Pacing the halls of a hospital is not unusual. People do it all the time," said Yianni.

"Yes, but not just twenty times and never again. Anyway, I ran through videos from other parts of the hospital recorded at about the same time, and lo and behold, caught one of him entering the lobby stairway leading up to the very door used by the motorcyclist's assassin."

Andreas leaned in. "I love you."

"I know."

"Who is he?"

"Are you going to take back the love?"

"*Maggie.*"

"I don't know who he is. But check your email. As we speak, I'm sending you a full facial shot from the video."

"Just a minute." Andreas ran inside, grabbed his laptop, and ran back onto the terrace. He and Yianni stared at the screen waiting for the email to come through."

"Damn Internet," said Andreas. "You'd think an island so popular with the world's movers and shakers would have better service."

"Patience," said Maggie. "By the way, aren't you one of those folk always complaining about missing the island's good old days?"

The email came up, and Andreas clicked to open the photo. Another delay. "No one ever said I wasn't a hypocrite."

"Not that I've heard."

The photo came up on the screen.

"*Son of a bitch,*" said Yianni.

"Holy hell."

"I take it you guys recognize him."

"It's Pepe."

"My Tassos' Pepe?"

"One and the same."

"He must be the dumbest idiot on the face of the earth," said Maggie. "Doing recon for a hit in full view of cameras."

Andreas leaned back in his chair. "Yes, the dumbest idiot on earth." He looked at Yianni. "Or perhaps the sacrificial lamb of one of its cagiest plotters."

Chapter Eighteen

Lila and Toni sat in the den, far away from the men on the terrace but close by the children's rooms.

"We're in luck, the kids are still napping."

"They're adorable."

"Especially when they're napping," joked Lila, adjusting her position on the couch to face Toni sitting at the other end.

Toni lowered her voice. "I think I have a way of getting to Adina that doesn't violate my agreement with Yianni and Andreas not to aggravate Karavakis, and actually gives us official cover for counseling her."

Lila's eyes widened. "That sounds like quite a plan."

"It's tricky and will require some help from the Mykonos police chief, but I think it might work. And if the police won't go along, we'll just drop it."

"So, what do you have in mind?"

"Simple. Adina's only fifteen. She's too young to be drinking. If I can convince the police to arrest her for underage drinking and offer her the choice between the consequences of an arrest record and going to us for counseling, we might have a chance."

"Do you think it will work?"

"If the police bless us as counselors, I think it has a shot at getting Adina's attention. It also gives us cover from her pimp, because we're officially designated, not some bleeding heart inter-lopers."

"Like we actually are," smiled Lila.

Toni waved off Lila's comment. "We'll just have to find a place for the arrest that's not tied to Karavakis. Besides, I doubt Telly would go along with an arrest at any place related to Karavakis."

"Telly?"

"The police chief. I'll try selling it to him as a favor to the girl's hardworking parents. That sort of approach is more likely to appeal to a macho man's sensitive side."

Lila laughed. "So, how are things going with Yianni?"

"I was wondering when you'd get around to asking about that."

"I've been resisting since that moment on the terrace when you said your mind was on Adina. I knew it had to be on Yianni."

"So, my fibbing didn't sell you?"

"Not for a minute," Lila said, smiling. "Been there, done that. After all, you're not the first woman to fall for a man and been utterly lost over how best to let him know your feelings."

"No, but I had hoped I wasn't the most obvious." Toni looked at her phone. "I'd better take off if I want a shot at catching Telly at the police station. It's not the sort of conversation I want to have with him over the phone."

"I'll walk you out." Lila stood. "And, by the way, when you say goodbye to Yianni, don't hesitate to ask him when he plans on seeing you again."

"Is this a rehearsal for your mentoring gig?" said Toni.

"Nah, just plain old meddling by a married lady into the affairs of her single friend."

Toni gave a thumbs-up, and they marched out together onto the terrace.

The weather had suddenly turned, and the Island of the Winds was earning its name with a vengeance. So much so that Yianni insisted it was too dangerous for Toni to drive back to town on her jalopy of a motorbike.

"On that piece of crap, one good gust will send you flying off the road."

"But I have to get back."

"Too risky."

Toni bristled. "I don't need a savior. I've spent more time riding bikes on this island than you have. I know what I'm doing."

"Yianni, throw her bike in the back of the SUV and drive her into town," said Andreas. "Will that work for you?"

Toni started to speak, but Lila interrupted. "It would be a bit safer, don't you think?" She smiled. "And certainly much more comfortable."

Toni drew in and let out a breath. "Yes, thank you, it will be." She kissed Lila and Andreas goodbye, thanked them for their hospitality, and turned away from Yianni to walk to where she'd parked her bike. "I'll meet you at the bike," she said without looking at him.

Yianni glanced at Andreas and followed after Toni.

They'd been on the road for five minutes without a word passing between them.

Toni had thought to say something when she saw the motorcycle that had followed her from town still parked by the windmill. But the driver was nowhere to be seen, so she said nothing.

"Okay, why are you so angry at me?"

Toni kept her eyes glued straight ahead.

Another minute passed.

"I said—"

"I heard what you said. I just didn't want to answer. Or rather I didn't think an answer was necessary."

"What does that mean?"

"It means exactly what I told you back at the house. I don't need a savior."

"I'm not trying to be your savior. I'd have said the same thing to anyone intending to ride a bike like that in wind like this."

She said nothing.

"Let me modify that. I'd say that to anyone I cared about."

Toni bit at her lip. "Now we're getting to the nitty-gritty of your reason for all this BS about the bike and agreeing to drive me into town."

"Huh?"

"You're just hoping to get laid again."

Yianni's face burned red. "You have a real knack for saying the wrong thing at precisely the right time." He slammed his fists on the steering wheel, sending the SUV veering off toward the cliffside.

"Watch out," screamed Toni as Yianni pulled the SUV back into line.

"I don't know what kind of guy you think I am, but I'm sure as hell beginning to get an idea of the kind of woman you are."

"And just what exactly is *that* supposed to mean?"

"Someone burned so many times you're afraid to get close to the flame again."

"How poetic, but I'm not sure I like the point."

"I didn't expect you to, but it's how you behave."

"Truth is, that's not the reason. In fact, it's virtually the opposite. I've avoided flames all my life. My music generates all the heat I've ever wanted. Solitude and song work for me. Flames threaten all that."

"But what about what happened in the hut? That wasn't what I'd call an icy performance."

"I didn't say I was icy. I just avoid flames. What happened was pure unadulterated lust. That, I can handle. It's the long-term stuff that frightens me." She turned to look out the passenger-side window. "I can't believe I just said that."

"Because it's not true?"

"No, because it is true. Though I've never acknowledged it openly before."

"Well, that's a start."

"Toward what?"

"Toward learning to love the flame."

She smiled. "Persistent, aren't you?"

"At times."

She looked out the windshield. "Is there a place where we can pull over around here?"

"It's still not safe for you to drive the bike. Wait until we get closer to town."

"That's not why I want to stop."

He turned his head.

She smiled. "Yep, I think it's time baby learned to burn, baby, burn."

"I don't understand."

"Just find a place where we can be alone."

He did.

Yianni dropped Toni off at a mini-mall, close by the rotary connecting to the airport.

He dragged her bike out of the SUV and promised to stop by the piano bar that night.

"That would be nice," she said, kissing him on the lips.

"Sorry about before. I didn't mean to be so pushy."

"Like I said, it ended up that I'm happy you were. Besides, if anyone is owed an apology, it's you."

"Not necessary." He kissed her goodbye.

Toni watched him drive off before starting her bike and heading for the police station.

She'd always gotten along well with Telly, and not just because she arranged for his drinks to be comped any time he stopped by the bar. That sort of treatment was standard operating procedure on the island. A good relationship with the police was a necessary part of her business.

In her investigative work, when she thought her clients' stolen items remained on the island, often the only way to get the loot

back was to split her fee with the thieves. But persuading the
police to do their duty and recover stolen items for her clients
was a far more lucrative alternative. Good relations with the
police meant money in her pocket. A concept many on the island
followed, whatever their business pursuits.

She told the sergeant at the desk she wanted to see the chief
and stood just inside the station's front door, waiting to be called
up to his office.

A female officer waved for her to go upstairs. "Turn right at
the top of the stairs. The door's open, but wait for him to call
you in."

Toni did as she'd been told and waited patiently outside Telly's
door.

Funny thing about being in a police station, even if you've
done nothing wrong, there's always the sense of being a stranger in
a strange land, where the rules followed by its inhabitants shadow
your own, yet are different. Rules that meant, if you gave the
police cause, your life could become very difficult, very quickly.

Telly looked up from reading something on his desk and
pointed to a wooden chair across from him. He said nothing,
only kept reading.

The office was bright and sunny, and faced away from the
road, but the view was not in keeping with the sunshine. It once
overlooked the backyards of the island's working class—people who no longer could afford to live there. Gone were their
scratched-out gardens and scraggly goats, replaced by commercial
operations seeking to take advantage of the area's close proximity
to the airport and tourists.

Toni sat quietly while Telly kept reading, slowly swiveling his
chair from side to side as he did. After a minute he looked up.

"Do you know what this is?" He waved the paper he'd been
reading.

"If I did, you'd probably arrest me for spying on you."

He didn't smile. "This isn't funny, Toni. It's a memorandum

from my boss back in Athens about a request for an inquiry filed with Interpol to look into the possible link between the assassination of a police colonel on the mainland and a proposed hotel-construction deal on Mykonos."

Toni hoped the bright sunlight covered the drain of color from her face. "Oh."

"That's all you have to say?"

"Why would I have anything to say about a memo to you from your boss?"

"Because, according to this memo, Interpol's informant claims to have learned '*from reliable sources on the island,*' that the Colonel was assassinated over a threat he posed to a major casino-hotel construction project involving '*powerful interests*' on the island, and that '*local authorities*' are involved in a cover-up." He leaned across his desk and stared at her. "Do you have any idea who or what sources he's talking about?"

Toni leaned back and struggled to keep meeting his glare. "How would I know anything about any of that? I stopped by to see if you'd recovered any of my clients' stolen things."

He slammed his hand on the desk. "Screw your clients. With all your contacts on the island, if anyone would have heard something about this, it would be you."

She shrugged, still playing ignorant.

He pushed back from his desk. "How is it that Interpol has an informant who claims to know all about this assassination link, and neither you nor I have heard a thing about it?"

Toni struggle to maintain her expression. "I don't know."

He swore and went back to looking at the document.

"But perhaps there is another way to look at this," she said.

"And what would that be?" Telly's eyes fixed on hers.

"Let's suppose there *is* something to the informant's story."

Telly's jaw tightened. "This project is huge and involves some of the most powerful families on the island. We're talking a mega-scandal."

Toni took that to mean Telly didn't relish the risk of angering his hotel and contractor friends by sticking his official nose into their mega-deal.

"I understand, but even if the killer was somehow tied into the project, that doesn't mean the motive had anything to *do* with the project. You know better than I, these sorts of things are generally personal, not business."

Telly looked back at the document. "The Colonel certainly had a lot of enemies."

"The most likely outcome is that there's nothing here to affect the project or reflect badly on you." Toni leaned forward in her chair. "We both know how bureaucratic your police superiors can be, so if they don't at least make a show of convincing Interpol that their concerns are being pursued, the heat will only intensify, perhaps to the point where Athens feels compelled to send someone here to take over the investigation."

That had Telly fixing his eyes on Toni. She met his stare and held it until he looked away. He spun around to face the window. "That would explain why Kaldis is here," he muttered to himself, then swung back to face her. "So, how can I help you with your clients today?"

Toni exhaled slowly. "Actually, I have another reason for coming as well. I'm here to ask for a favor for a friend."

"Oh, one of those kinds of requests."

She wasn't sure what he meant, but kept on talking. "A hard-working Albanian mother and father are very worried about their fifteen-year-old daughter. She's hanging out with a bad crowd."

"That's easy enough to do here."

"They asked me to come up with a way to help her, and I have an idea, but it needs your assistance." She paused until he nodded for her to continue. "She drinks a lot, this kid, and since she's underage, I thought if you arrested her and gave her the choice between an arrest record and seeking counseling, she'd take the counseling and maybe that would straighten her out."

He bit at his lip. "I get the idea, but arresting a fifteen-year-old for drinking on this island is about as low on our priority list as busting litterbugs."

"I wouldn't want you doing anything to the bar owner, just scare the girl enough for her to agree to go the counseling route. We'll take it from there."

"Who are we?"

She froze at the thought of introducing Andreas' wife into the conversation. "My friend Lila."

Telly thought for a moment. "This counseling-at-risk-children concept sounds like a good idea to me." He smacked his hands on his desktop. "Fine. You and your friend are now my official counselors. I won't even pretend it's because I owe you one for listening to me rant about the mess this Pepe guy's causing me."

Toni swallowed. "Pepe?"

"That's the name of Interpol's informant. He had dinner with the Colonel on the night of his assassination."

Toni couldn't breathe.

"Are you okay?"

"Yes, just overwhelmed at how nice it is of you to agree to help that poor hardworking family."

"I'll take that as a genuine compliment." He smiled. "Just let me know where and when the girl will be doing something we can arrest her for. I'll take it from there." He stood. "You're a pretty good kid too." He extended his hand. "Stop by anytime."

Toni prayed she'd recovered enough lost strength from the Pepe bombshell to stand. She literally willed herself to her feet. "I will, and thanks." She shook Telly's hand and left the office. From there she walked across the street to a supermarket parking lot, sat on a stone wall separating the lot from the road, and wondered what in the world to do next.

She called Yianni.

●●●●●

"This can't be happening," said Andreas, standing in the kitchen holding a cup of coffee in one hand and shaking a fist in the air. "Pepe actually went to Interpol!"

"I checked, and it's true. He filed a report claiming local authorities were trying to cover up a connection between the Colonel's murder and 'international business interests seeking to take over effective control of the island of Mykonos.'"

"The man is crazy, mad, or insane. More likely all three." He slammed his free hand on the countertop, jarring some coffee out of the cup held in his other.

"I'm surprised the press hasn't picked up on it," said Yianni.

Andreas dumped his coffee in the sink, grabbed a paper towel, and wiped up his spill. "Because part of their job is to bury bad news about the island." He shook his head. "It makes no sense. Bad press coverage could kill the casino deal, and benefit none of our suspects."

"But it would benefit other hotel and club owners."

"That's just what we need. More suspects."

"What do you want to do about Pepe?"

"Grab his ass and sweat him for the truth. If we can find a prosecutor willing to charge him as an accessory to the motor-cyclist's murder based on what we have, that might shake him up enough to give us better answers than he has so far. But, first, we need to find him."

"He said he had to catch a boat."

"Check with his restaurant back on the mainland, and if they don't know where he is, roust his buddy Karavakis. Somebody must know." Andreas rested his hands on the top of the counter. "*Son of a bitch*," he shouted, slapping the countertop again.

Lila came running into the kitchen. "Is everything all right?"

"Yeah, great."

"Then stop swearing so loudly. The children can hear you. You're frightening them."

Andreas drew in a breath. "Sorry about that." He exhaled.

"Our only witness to the Colonel's murder is broadcasting a theory to the world that local authorities are engaged in a cover-up."

"That's terrible. When did you learn that?"

"Toni called Yianni while he was driving back to the house. She'd gone to see the local police chief on the status of her clients' stolen property, and he unloaded on her about how a guy named Pepe had gotten him in hot water with Athens by complaining to Interpol."

"Why in the world would Pepe do that?"

"That, my love, is the very first question I intend to ask the *malaka* the moment we find him."

Lila looked at Yianni. "How's Toni?"

"She's fine. She said it shook her up hearing the chief of police talking about the same people we'd just been talking about, but she didn't mention any of that to him."

"I'll give her a call." Lila left.

"I'll go run down Pepe." Yianni left.

And I'll pray for a break that makes some sense of this madness.

● ● ● ● ●

"Toni, it's Lila. Are you all right?"

"Yes, I'm lying on my bed, dodging arctic blasts from the clanking air conditioner mounted in the wall above my head."

"Why don't you open a window?"

"The partiers outside my window make it sound like a war zone. I need the AC's white noise to keep my sanity."

"As long as you're okay. I just heard about what happened in your meeting with the police chief."

"It was surreal. When he said Pepe's name, I thought he somehow knew everything about what I'd been doing. At that instant, I felt as if I had no secrets from the police."

Lila laughed. "I know what you mean. Andreas knows how to make me feel that way at times. But he's confessed his trick to me."

"Tell, please."

"The guilty always think police know more than they do, and so they talk to the cops as if it's old news to them. Savvy cops listen encouragingly until the guilty inevitably incriminate themselves."

"Good thing I was too speechless to utter a word."

"Luck is good."

"Speaking of luck, I've got good news on our project." Toni told her about Telly's offer to help and designating them as his official counselors. "I'll speak to Adina's father and ask him to find the best place to set her up for an arrest."

"Sounds unfair when you put it that way."

"Don't get sentimental on me, now. Screw fair play. We're trying to save a fifteen-year-old girl from a pimp."

Lila sighed. "You're right, of course. Chalk that remark up to my shielded upbringing."

"From what I hear, Athens high-society disputes aren't exactly settled in pillow fights."

Lila laughed. "More like beaks and claws to the death."

"Just keep thinking that way, and all will go well. Assuming all goes as planned on my end, I'll let you know when they've picked her up. By the way, where shall we hold the *counseling* session?"

Lila paused. "I guess here."

"At your home?"

"Sure. It should help make your point to her."

"What point?"

"That I'm a successful woman who cares enough about her to want to help her find the right road to a better life."

"Works for me. But what will Andreas say?"

"There's no reason to tell him. If he asks, we're just playing mentor to a local youngster."

"Are you sure?"

"It's the truth, isn't it?"

"Yes, but there are a few additional relevant details I think he'd be interested in knowing."

"Maybe, but I see no reason to go out of my way to tell him."

"If you say so."

"Don't worry. I'll find the right time to let him know and it'll all work out fine. It's our fate."

Toni thought to tell her about the motorcycle that had followed her to Lila's. She'd seen it again when leaving the police station on her way to returning the bike. At least she thought it was the same motorcycle. *But why risk frightening her with what's likely an innocent coincidence?*

"Yeah, it's our fate."

"We'll speak later. Bye."

"Bye." Toni dropped the phone into its cradle and lay on her back staring up at the ceiling. She wondered about that mysterious motorcycle and, more importantly, who might be having her followed. The obvious choice was Karavakis or his son. But how would either of them know about her interest in the son? Unless Christos had told them. But why would he? She shut her eyes and let her imagination sift through all sorts of random thoughts in the hope that something might crystalize.

Her eyes bolted open. "Oh, my God. What have I done?" *If anyone had a strong motive for getting rid of the Colonel, it was Christos.* And she'd told him precisely what Andreas had warned her to keep to herself.

Christos' business was theft by stealth. He considered private security of the sort run by mobsters like the Colonel unfair competition. "Like foxes guarding the henhouse," he called them. If Christos could trigger a war among the Colonel's competitors for control of the island's security operations, he'd be free to do his thing while they battled each other.

At least that's what Toni's imagination was telling her.

"Okay, imagination, you're working overtime," she told herself aloud. "We both know Christos doesn't do violence."

Or so I hope.

Chapter Nineteen

Yianni walked into the living room clean-shaven and dressed for town.

"Can I borrow the car, Dad? I don't want to mess up my hair on the bike."

Andreas looked at his watch. "It's nearly midnight."

"That's why I asked to borrow the car. I figured this is way past your bedtime and Lila wouldn't dare leave you home alone in your dotage."

"Nicely handled not to lump me in with the old guy," smiled Lila.

"Off to see Toni?"

"I should get there just about the time things start jumping."

"Don't be out too late, because we've got to follow up on Pepe first thing in the morning."

"I know. I just checked in with his restaurant people. No one knows anything more than what they told me before. He called to tell them he'd missed the fast boat to Rafina and hoped to catch a ride with a friend. They can't reach him on his mobile, but that's not unusual. If he decided to go fishing with his buddy, he could have ended up doing God-knows-what after. Their best guess is he'll turn up tomorrow around noon."

"Well, that fits in nicely with your plans for this evening."

"One can't challenge the Fates." Yianni smiled.

"Hear, hear to that," added Lila.

"The car keys are on the table."

"Thanks, guys. See you in the morning."

After Yianni left, Andreas said, "We really should rent another car, at least until Dama's truck is repaired. I think that qualifies under the emergency-preparedness exception to your commitment not to contribute unnecessarily to vehicle congestion on the island."

"Let's talk about it tomorrow."

"I'll take that as a maybe, leaning to yes."

They went back to watching a movie from the sofa. Two minutes passed.

"I think they make a great couple," said Lila.

"Uh-huh."

"I really like Toni."

"Uh-huh."

"Their personalities really work well together."

"Uh-huh."

"Do you think she's a lesbian?"

"Nope."

"So, you are listening."

"Your every word is my command."

Lila smacked Andreas with a pillow.

He turned to face her. "Do *you* think she's a lesbian?"

"No, absolutely not. I was just seeing if you were listening."

"There are many other things you could have said to tease me. Why did you pick that?"

Lila leaned back on the couch. "I guess because, in my experience, when most men meet a bright, assertive, independent, confident young woman, all traits men consider masculine, they often assume she wants to be more like a man, as opposed to somehow possessing those qualities independent of gender. And should the woman not care about makeup or clothes, it adds to the stereotype. As if being gay means the woman isn't threatening their masculinity, but rather wishes to emulate it."

"And you came up with all of that on the spur of the moment, sitting here watching *The African Queen*?"

"I guess because I'm preparing myself to act as a counselor to at-risk children."

"And I fit into that category?"

"No, dear. At least not at the moment."

"When do you plan to start? I assume you'll need some training."

"Yes, I'm sure I will. But I've volunteered to help out here if the need arises."

"That's nice."

"I'm sure it will be a worthwhile experience."

"Uh-huh."

"You're back into the movie?"

"Uh-huh."

Lila patted Andreas' hand and smiled. "Good."

Toni was playing her next-to-last set when she felt her phone vibrating. *Who would be calling at this hour?* Perhaps something had happened to her father? Well, whoever it was would have to wait for her break.

Yianni sat at the bar, trying to listen to Toni play, but her boss had taken a shine to him, and kept bending his ear with stories of his old days working on merchant ships. Or rather, the many fights he'd been in. He had typecast Yianni as a tough guy, making him a comrade-in-arms.

The bartender handed his boss the phone from behind the bar, perennially set to blink, not ring. It was blinking. The boss answered, looking concerned. As he listened, his look turned angry and he waved at Toni to come to him.

"I'm in the middle of a set," she yelled.

"Hell with the set, get over here."

Toni cut the song short, apologized to the room for the interruption, and hurried over to the bar, convinced something bad had happened.

She took the phone. "Yes?"

"Toni, it's Telly."

"Thank God. I thought something had happened to my father."

"This is about *a* father, but not yours. That girl we had an understanding about…"

"Yes?"

"We picked her up right where you said she'd be."

"Good."

"We picked up her friend, too."

"Friend? Why the friend?"

"They're both fifteen-year-old girls and totally shit-faced. We couldn't arrest one and not the other without raising suspicion."

"Since when do you worry about attracting suspicion?"

"Since learning something you neglected to tell me."

Toni swallowed. "What's that?"

"That your friend's daughter is one of Karavakis' girls."

"She is?"

"Yes. From the moment my guys approached them in the bar and asked for IDs they started screaming his name, like he's their get-out-of-jail-free card."

"Is he?"

"Not this time." He paused and lowered his voice. "But only because I have a young daughter of my own."

"I don't follow."

"These girls are into a lot more than underage drinking. Wait until you see how they're dressed and made-up. Toss in Karavakis as their savior and I don't have to tell you what that means."

"No, you don't."

"So, when can you pick them up?"

"Pick them up?"

"If you want to help them, you better get right over here. I gave them the choice of being formally arrested and held until a parent shows up to claim them, or agreeing to accept your counseling. If they spend the rest of the night in here, when they sober up they'll likely tell me to screw off and wait for one of Karavakis' crew to get them out."

"Hold on a second, Chief." She looked at Yianni and said, "I've got a bit of a problem."

"Anything I can help you with?"

"As a matter of fact, you can. I don't use van services. Do you happen to know one that will drive out to Lila's at this time of night?"

● ● ● ● ●

By the time Toni and Yianni left the bar, Lila had called Toni to say the girls had arrived, looking the picture of innocence asleep in the van, high heels, skimpy outfits and all.

In the parking lot, Toni jumped into the front passenger seat and leaned over to give Yianni a kiss.

"How did things work out with the van service?" he asked.

"The girls arrived safely and are crashing in the small guest room for the rest of the night. You get to keep the big room, but there's a catch. You'll have to share."

"With whom?"

"Do you want me to draw straws with the other female guests?"

He laughed. "Andreas must be annoyed at you for waking them up in the middle of the night."

"Not according to Lila. She said it happens all the time, though usually the calls are for him."

"Fair point."

He swerved to swing around an accident scene. Two bikes down on the road. Four victims. Police and ambulance on the scene.

Toni shook her head. "More driving-madness victims."

"Never seems to end, especially at night." He coughed. "By the way, speaking of madness, do you mind telling me how you got into this counseling gig?"

"It's Lila's project. She wants to help at-risk kids get back on track."

He cocked his head. "That's admirable. I just hope she's up to it."

Me too.

It was nearly midday when the girls first stirred. They woke to find their faces scrubbed clean of makeup and all but their underwear gone, replaced by two sets of sweatpants, oversized tee-shirts, and flip-flops stacked neatly at the foot of the bed they'd shared.

Following the scent of coffee, they stormed out into a court-yard where a small boy pedaled a bicycle around an olive tree, under which two women sat at a table drinking coffee.

"Morning, ladies," said Lila.

"Where are we and who are you?" said the taller, dark-haired girl.

"My name is Lila."

"I'm Toni."

"And this is my home," said Lila.

"Do we know you?" said the dark-haired girl.

"What's your name?"

"Adina."

"Nice to meet you," said Lila. "I think Toni knows your father."

"And what's your name?" said Toni to the other girl.

The girl whipped her head around in an attempt to order her tangled mass of blond hair. "Fuck you. When my boyfriend finds out about this, you'll both be in a shit pile of trouble."

Lila laughed. "What a lovely name, but if you don't mind I'll call you Ino. That's the name the police said you gave them when you were arrested."

"Like I said, fuck you."

Lila shook her head. "Ino, look around you. This is where I live on this island. It's my home. I own it and all the property surrounding it. Do you think it matters to me if you curse me? I know you're afraid. I'd be, too, if I were you. But it's not me you're afraid of. Your bad mouth and bad attitude only reflect your genuine fear at the life you're leading. I'm simply trying to help you find a different and better road."

"Are you some kind of missionary?" asked Adina.

"No," Lila said smiling. "I see two young women with great potential, who need only a bit of direction to get back on track toward a rewarding life. But, if you don't want my help, I'll give you back your clothes and send you on your way to wherever your current life is taking you."

"Yeah, I want my—"

Adina interrupted Ino. "What kind of help?"

"We don't need them," Ino spat. "Our boss gives us all the help we need."

Toni laughed. "Karavakis? And how's that working out for you? Fifteen years old and already busted. Has he put you on the street yet? Or is he going to use you in one of his notorious houses branded on the outside with his trademark blue light shining twenty-four/seven above the door?"

Lila picked up on Toni playing the bad-cop role. "That will be enough of that, Toni. The past is the past. We're talking about the future. About giving these girls a fresh start. They're only fifteen. In ten years they'll only be twenty-five. Think how very different their lives can be then if they take control today. And in twenty years they'll only be thirty-five. They could own the world by then!"

Adina looked at Ino. "I think we should stay. At least for coffee."

Ino took a long, hard look at Toni and then at Lila. "Okay. But is there anything to eat?"

"Of course." Lila called out and two women appeared with platters of food and fresh coffee.

"Would you prefer eating here or on the terrace?"

"You mean this place is bigger?" said Ino.

"Yes." Lila stood. "Come, let's eat on the terrace."

The women with the platters led the way, followed by the two girls and Toni and Lila trailing behind.

"Wow," said Adina as she stepped out into a panoramic view of the sea. "Is that Ikaria?" She pointed east.

"You have good eyes. Ikaria's hard to make out from here, but yes, it is."

Adina smiled.

"Please, help yourselves to the food."

The girls filled their plates and sat, making sure to find seats facing the sea. They ate quietly.

Lila broke the silence. "Any questions?"

"How did we get here? I don't remember seeing you before," said Adina.

"You haven't. A van service drove you here from the police station. You were both out cold when you arrived. The cook and I carried you into the bedroom. We cleaned off your makeup and tucked you into bed."

"Thanks," said Adina.

The thanks surprised Lila, as she'd been expecting a somewhat belligerent response.

Ino hesitated. "Yeah, thanks."

That really surprised Lila.

The conversation shifted to less personal, more general matters, like music and fashion. On those topics, the four spoke as equals, with Lila and Toni deferring to the girls' better knowledge of the subject, and complimenting them on their insights. After lunch came dessert. The girls first resisted, saying they had to watch their figures, but when Dama brought chocolate cake out from the kitchen, their reservations disappeared, along with most of the cake.

"So, ladies," said Lila, sipping her coffee, "would you like to continue with these counseling sessions?" She smiled on the word *counseling*. "Perhaps next time down there." She pointed to a private cove sprinkled with sunbeds, sailing paraphernalia, and snorkeling equipment.

"That's yours too?" said Ino.

"Yes."

"I'd love to come back," said Adina.

"Me too," said Ino.

"Great. Only one condition."

"Here goes," sighed Ino.

Lila ignored the remark. "You must promise me that you'll take an honest look at how you're living your lives, where you see yourselves headed, and whether that's where you want to end up. Though I'd like you to think that you want to take a different path—one filled with education and efforts at establishing a lifelong career for yourselves—if you come back to me and truthfully say that you like the way your life is headed, we'll still be friends and you'll always be welcome in my home. I just want honesty from you."

Adina bit at her lip. "But how can girls like us possibly hope to get an education or a career? The Greek economy sucks, and as non-Greeks, we're treated as second-class citizens, even though we were born here."

Lila's face turned stern. "Because I'll have your back. If you're honest with me and try your best, I'll do my very best to support you. That gives you a hell of a lot better chance than going at it alone."

Adina looked at Ino. "Maybe she can help us with Flora?"

"Who's Flora?" said Toni.

"We can't talk about that," said Ino. "You know how he feels about us talking about other girls with outsiders."

"But she's our friend, and no one else seems to care."

"I'm sure she'll turn up sooner or later," said Ino.

Adina shrugged. "It's been days."

"Okay, what's going on?" said Toni.

"We lost touch with a friend," said Ino.

"She's more than a friend," said Adina. "She's like our big sister. Always trying to protect us."

"She's nineteen."

"When we asked where she was, we were told it's none of our business."

"Where is Flora's home?" asked Lila.

"Thessaloniki."

"Maybe she went there?"

"Not without telling us," said Adina. "She said she'd been told to do a favor for a friend of Karavakis."

"Who was the friend?" said Lila.

"She didn't know."

"Who told her to do the favor?" asked Toni.

Ino snickered. "Who do you think?"

"Karavakis?" asked Toni.

The girls nodded.

"What kind of favor?" asked Toni.

Adina tensed. "She didn't say, but she got hooked on drugs in nursing school, and now does whatever she's told to support her habit."

"Anything else you can tell us about her?" said Toni.

"What good will that do? How could you help?" said Ino.

"We have connections," said Lila.

"I have a photo in my bag of the three of us," said Adina.

"Let me see it. I'll make a copy," said Lila.

"You shouldn't do that," said Ino. "If word gets back that we're talking to outsiders…" Her voice trailed off.

"No one's going to know," said Adina.

"We never showed up at the club last night. How do we explain where we were?"

"Tell the truth," said Lila.

"What do you mean?" said Ino.

Toni answered. "You were arrested for underage drinking and released into our custody for counseling."

"I don't think you want to be messing around with these people," said Ino.

Lila smiled. "No, I don't think they want to be messing around with us."

"Karavakis won't be impressed by this." Ino waved her hands around her.

"No, but he will by this." Lila cleared her throat. "Tell him you've been enrolled in a program called—" she looked at Toni.

Toni said, "Fresh Start."

"Yes," said Lila. "Fresh Start. Run by Lila Vardi, wife of Chief Inspector Andreas Kaldis, head of GADA Special Crimes. I think that will shut him up."

"Your husband's a cop?" said Ino.

Lila nodded.

"Is he here now?" said Adina.

"No, he left this morning before we got up. When he gets back, I'll get him to start working on finding your friend."

"That would be great," said Adina.

"So," said Lila, "do we have a deal? Your honesty in exchange for my support?"

The girls looked at each other before turning back to Lila. "Okay," they said in unison.

Toni smiled. "To quote the last line of my favorite movie, 'I think this is the beginning of a beautiful friendship.'"

"I know that movie," said Ino. "*Casablanca!*"

Adina smiled. "Of all the gin joints, in all the towns, in all the world, we walked into yours."

Lila called for a taxi to pick up the girls and take them to town. Lila told them to keep the sweats, tee-shirts, and flip-flops to wear the next time they visited. Both girls promised to call her tomorrow and make arrangements to come back ASAP.

"What do you think?" Lila asked Toni.

"You're a natural at this."

"Thanks, but I meant about the girls."

"I think you nailed it. They're afraid. Afraid of Karavakis, afraid of where their lives are headed. That last part alone draws a lot of kids into drugs. Toss in the prostitution angle, and drugs are almost a sure thing."

"Your plan to use the police chief as cover seems to have worked, but I'm happy the girls were out cold when they arrived last night, and sound asleep when the men left this morning. I don't think Andreas and Yianni would have appreciated the nuances of your plan once the girls started talking about their ties to Karavakis."

"I think that's what's called an understatement."

"It's the protective nature of men."

Some women, too, thought Toni. After all, she still hadn't mentioned anything to Lila about the motorcycle that might be following her. With everything going so smoothly, she'd seen no reason to create unnecessary alarm.

Lila picked up the copy of the photograph of the girls with their friend Flora. "I wonder what happened to her?"

Toni shrugged. "She's nineteen. Maybe she ran off with one of her clients. I'm more interested in what happened to Yianni and your husband. Yianni crept out like a cat burglar."

"Andreas wasn't quite as thoughtful. I guess those sorts of romantic kindnesses wear off over time."

"I'll take your word on that. Time has never played a part in my romances."

Lila laughed. "Are you looking for counseling?"

"No, just for my boyfriend." Toni paused. "Wow, I can't believe I just called him my boyfriend."

"If he doesn't mind, why should you or anyone else?"

"But I've never called him that before. Certainly not to his face." Toni waved her hand. "Whatever. Where are they?"

"I don't know. All Andreas said was that the local police chief called to ask for his help on something a fisherman found."

"Is your life always this mysterious?"

"Not nearly as much as my husband's," she paused, then smiled. "Or your boyfriend's."

Chapter Twenty

The call from Telly came with an apology for its timing, but Andreas had no quarrel with the reason. The primary focus of most police stationed on Mykonos fell to the enforcement of traffic laws, building codes, and the licensing of business operations, including bars, shops, and hotels. Solving serious crimes was not part of their training or duties. That fell to other police, such as Andreas' unit.

In fact, Andreas appreciated Telly's request for help. Too many local police chiefs jealously guarded their turf, often botching investigations they never should have undertaken. That said, he couldn't blame Yianni for not sharing his enthusiasm at their early-morning motorcycle jaunt across the island.

Yianni'd had only two hours sleep, and in light of that, and for both their sakes, Andreas did the driving. He'd thought to take the SUV, but with a houseful of problematic guests, decided it best to leave it with Lila.

When they met up with the main road in Ano Mera, Andreas turned left and followed it toward its terminus on the southeast shore at Kalifatis Beach. Just before Kalifatis, he turned right onto a dirt road, crossing over an isolated peninsula toward two hills at the end that locals called the "Mounds of Aphrodite."

The road turned east at the base of the first mound and ran between a gauntlet of one-story buildings, mainly private homes, rooms to rent, and a taverna. Just past the taverna, he turned left down to a cove behind the building. Tied up at a tiny concrete pier, with its far end and west side open to the sea, sat a maritime police Zodiac and a small fishing boat.

Telly and two of his cops stood on the pier by the fishing boat, surrounded by three maritime police and an old man with a broad, steel-gray mustache, Greek fisherman's hat, denim work shirt, and jeans.

"Looks like an early-morning police prayer meeting," said Andreas shaking hands with Telly and nodding to everyone else.

"Thanks, for coming, Andreas."

"No problem, glad to help out. So, what do we have here?"

"As I told you when I woke you—sorry again for that—our friend Petros here," he pointed to the fisherman, "was reeling in his nets and found a body tangled up in one. No identification on the victim."

"Must have been quite a shock," said Andreas, looking at Petros.

"Not really," said Petros with a shrug. "This was a fresh one. Not floating yet." He sounded clinical, detached from what he'd witnessed. "When they drown, they sink to the bottom. Don't float for eleven or twelve days in the summer. This one was still down there. That's how it got tangled in my nets. If it hadn't, it would likely have ended up in Naxos."

Andreas looked at Telly. "Sounds like he has a lot of experience finding bodies in the sea."

"I'm sad to say he does. But not here. He's spent a lot of time as a volunteer on Lesvos, trying to save refugees crossing over from Turkey to Greece. He's pulled a ton of bodies out of the sea. Alive and dead."

Andreas shook his head. "That's a true tragedy. One seemingly without end."

"Let me show you the body," said Telly. "Petros hauled it on board rather than dragging it behind his boat. It's laid out at the stern."

Yianni and Andreas followed Telly to the edge of the pier but stopped short when the body came into view.

"*Panagia mou!* This can't be happening," said Yianni, in the Greek's traditional plea to the Virgin Mary.

"Can't be," repeated Andreas.

The body lay belly up, face obliterated by an apparent shotgun blast. The victim's pants gone, likely stripped away to remove any identification in the pockets. Only the shirt remained, covering the rest of the torso in a blue-and-white check pattern.

"Do you know the guy?" said Telly.

Andreas ran his hand though his hair, drew in and let out a breath. "Telly, let's take a walk to where we can talk privately."

Andreas led Telly and Yianni twenty meters or so away from the others.

"We've known each other for a long time, and you know I like you."

Telly bristled. "Stop with the bullshit—what's on your mind?"

"Okay, I'll put it to you straight. I don't know, and at this point I don't even care, what action you're involved in on this island."

Telly tried to speak, but Andreas raised his hand. "*Just listen.* Like I said, I don't care. What I do care about is this is likely the third murder connected to at least one of your big players on this island. And God knows how many more there'll be if he gets away with it. He's going down, so help me God. And I'd like to think you're with me on this."

"Is that a threat?" said Telly.

Andreas fixed his eyes on Telly's. "Absolutely."

Telly clenched and unclenched his fists. "What makes you think the murders are connected?"

"Because the Colonel, the guy who killed the Colonel, and the dead guy on the boat are all tied into Karavakis. More specifically, likely Karavakis *and* Despotiko's hotel and casino project."

Telly ran his hand across his hairless scalp. "Shit. That project has Interpol and Athens breathing down my neck."

Andreas pointed at the boat. "And the guy in the boat is the one who put them there."

Telly's jaw dropped. "That's Pepe?"

Andreas nodded.

Telly stomped his foot on the ground. "*Gamoto.* They'll be all over me now."

"So, are you with us or not?"

Telly shook his head and sighed. "Of course, I'm with you."

"What do you have to do with the hotel project?"

"Nothing. I just know about it. To tell you the truth, this makes no sense to me."

"Why's that?" asked Andreas.

"Because Karavakis told me—in so many words—that he was working on a project that he saw as his chance to go legitimate. At least legitimate, to his way of thinking."

"What's that supposed to mean?"

"He knows better than anyone what's happening on the island. It's become a magnet for a very dangerous crowd of international bad guys. He knows it's only a matter of time before they move in on his operations. That means a war, and he feels too old for that. So, he came up with this hotel project and teamed up with Despotiko. He knew the bad guys wouldn't dare take them both on."

"I thought it was up to the Colonel to protect them?" said Andreas.

Telly shrugged. "With all the crazy money being made here off drugs, hookers, and protection, Karavakis knew that couldn't last. He decided the safest course in his old age was to build his big resort, concentrate all his businesses there, and leave the rest of the island for the others to fight over."

"In other words, only deal with hookers and drugs on his own property?" said Andreas.

"Like I said, legitimate, to his way of thinking."

"I guess he's had a change of heart," said Yianni. "Because in killing the Colonel he's sped up the timetable on an all-out war among competing mobs."

Andreas kicked a pebble across the dirt. "That's true, but what makes even less sense is what's lying dead in the boat."

"I don't understand," said Yianni. "Killing Pepe gets rid of a witness who could tie Karavakis into two murders."

"But this murder likely killed something very precious to Karavakis," said Andreas.

"What's that?" said Telly.

"Pepe's the brother of Karavakis' only link to the international hotel chain he's depending on to make his deal work. If the brother somehow sees Karavakis as tied into this murder, his project and all his future plans are likely as dead as Pepe."

"Where do we go from here?" said Yianni.

"As far as I can tell, there's only one witness left."

"Who's that?" said Telly.

"If I knew I'd have her in custody."

"Like I said, who's that?"

"The woman who killed the Colonel's assassin."

"Considering the number of bodies turning up, what do you think the chances are of her being alive?"

Andreas sighed. "I'd say between slim and none."

"With the way things have been going for us so far," said Yianni, "those sound like pretty good odds."

Telly looked at his watch. "Forensics should be here from Syros within the hour. Maybe they'll give us something to go on."

"What I could use to go on right now is some breakfast," said Andreas.

"I'd rather take a nap in the back of Telly's cruiser," said Yianni.

"To each his own," said Andreas. "Come on, Telly, jump on the back of the bike, and we'll head off to breakfast to tell each other lies about how our grand service to the nation has made Greece a better place for all its people."

Telly smiled. "I see you still believe in myths."

• • ● • •

Andreas parked in front of a modern-looking taverna a hundred meters or so to the left of where the dirt road to the Mounds of Aphrodite met the main road. It drew more of a dinner crowd, and at this time of day tended to be quiet. The owner knew to leave his customers alone when they wanted privacy, so after making the obligatory fuss at hosting both the current chief and an ex-chief, he sent over a platter of assorted pastries, courtesy of the house, and retreated to a table in a far corner.

Andreas picked out his favorite, the Mykonian treat *kalathakia*, named after its shape, which resembled a little basket. Made of walnuts, eggs, sugar, butter, flour, and a dab of marmalade at the bottom, they had been forbidden from entering their house by Lila.

"So, how's the family?" said Andreas, taking a bite.

"My daughter's almost fourteen, and the boy is a terror at twelve."

Andreas grinned. "You mean it gets tougher than battling wits with a five-year-old boy who knows it all?"

"Yep, brace yourself."

"I have a seven-month-old daughter, too."

"The boy will seem an angel compared to what's coming down that road."

"Sounds a bit sexist to me."

"Call me in fourteen years and tell me if you still think that way."

Andreas smiled and took a second bite of the *kalathakia*. "This is a messy one."

"Why do I sense you're not talking about the pastry?"

"Three murders, all execution-style, and all signs point to one of the baddest guys on the island, but the S-O-B has no apparent motive for setting things in motion. It makes no sense."

"It could be worse. The signs could be pointing at Karavakis *and* Despotiko."

"That duo's still a possibility. Despotiko's wife was tangentially involved in putting together the meeting that got the Colonel killed, and she did so in a way that gave both her husband and Karavakis plausible deniability of any substantive part in setting it up."

"A wonderful piece of work she is."

"You know her?"

"Know her? We're practically her official babysitters. I cannot tell you the number of times we've had to haul her drunken, drugged-up ass home or out of trouble." Telly shook his head. "I'm not complaining, mind you. In return, her husband takes very good care of us." He shot a glance at Andreas. "I mean legitimately so. He buys us a lot of police equipment we can't get through Athens."

Andreas shrugged. "Every little bit helps. So, what can you tell me about her? I've heard there's a story out there about her being a working girl and that's how she met her husband."

"I've heard the same story. One version even has them introduced by Karavakis, but you'll never hear a word on that topic from his lips. Honestly, I don't think she was a hooker, and certainly not one of Karavakis' girls. She was more like an attractive woman on the make who liked to party and chose her lovers wisely."

"Aiming to land a rich husband?"

"I think our town hall lists that as an official summertime sport. These days, though, they come *from* Athens looking to land a rich Mykonian."

"Good for her."

Telly grimaced. "Not so sure about that. My instincts tell me she was a relatively innocent, nice person who sold herself to the devil and now is a prisoner of her deal."

"Meaning?" said Andreas.

"She may not have been a hooker when she met him, but Despotiko sure as hell uses her like one now."

"He passes her around?"

"No, not directly. She's more his mercenary. His personal representative when he needs one."

Andreas wondered if that explained why they'd bumped into her having lunch with Karavakis and the mayor. It would also explain why they'd treated her with such deference.

"She's also his eyes and ears on what's happening on the Athens-Mykonos party scene, and she does whatever he tells her to do, whenever he tells her to do it. In exchange, he lets her have her flings."

"What a wonderful life she's made for herself." *The kind that builds resentment.*

"That's why we end up driving her home so often." He leaned in and whispered, "More times than I care to mention from rented villas, filled with hard partiers so hyped-up and loud we've no choice but to bust them."

"Now that's saying something. There must be some serious shit going down to be busting Mykonos tourists in their high-priced villas."

"You wouldn't believe the half of it." Telly sipped his coffee. "Though we never busted her, of course."

"Of course."

"But it's not all bad. Sometimes we babysitters do get to do a mission of mercy or two."

"It's what keeps us coming to work." Andreas finished off the pastry.

"I did one yesterday.

"You rescued a treed cat?"

"No, a bird," said Telly, shooting him the middle finger. "A woman came to me asking for my help at getting some immigrant's fifteen-year-old daughter into counseling for too much boozing."

"There must be a well-established program for that on the island."

"Not that I know of."

"My wife's participating in something like that. In fact, two girls are at our house right now. At least they were there when I left."

"Two girls? Wait. They must be the ones we turned over for counseling overnight." Telly paused. "Do you know a woman named Toni?"

"As in the piano player Toni?"

Telly raised an eyebrow. "By chance, is your wife's name Lila?"

Andreas stared at him. "You can't be serious."

"Son of a bitch. What a coincidence."

Andreas struggled to keep a poker face. "What can you tell me about the girls? I heard they have drinking problems."

"They have bigger problems than drinking." Telly leaned in across the table. "They call themselves Karavakis' girls."

Andreas shut his eyes. "Tell me you're pulling my leg."

"Nope. My sense of humor is not that dark."

Andreas opened his eyes. "I can't wait to get home."

"I bet," said Telly waving for the check. "But that'll have to wait. The forensics guys just drove by. We better get back to Mr. Pepe."

The owner waved back. "No check!"

Andreas left a tip for the waiter, and as they headed to the door, Andreas asked, "What do you know about Toni?"

"I like and trust her, but she has a way of doing things her own way that can test my patience at times."

"Sounds like someone else I know."

"Who?"

"My wife."

• ● ● ● •

Ino had run away from her Balkan home when she was twelve, and she'd learned early on how to survive off the kindness of strangers. She shared a tiny, beaten-down two-room stucco home wedged in behind a gas station on the new ring road with a friend she'd made in Athens. She considered herself blessed to have it, and only had it because her friend happened to be a favorite cousin of the home's owner.

She'd found a way to beat the Mykonos summer worker's biggest challenge: earn enough to pay for food and shelter and still end your summer season with sufficient funds left over to survive the winter. The work she did wasn't something she was proud of, but she'd done worse, and the money beat waitressing.

She thought about the two women who'd taken her and Adina away from the cops. Ino had been arrested many times before. This was Adina's first. Maybe that's why she was so ready to believe those do-gooders. If there was one rule Ino had learned, it's that you have to take care of yourself in this world.

Before taking Adina home, the taxi dropped Ino off at her dilapidated little house. True, this life was far from what Ino wanted, and it certainly wasn't anything like the life that Lila led. But it was the only life she had, and she intended to protect it. As soon as the taxi carried Adina out of sight, Ino pulled out her phone and called her boss. He'd want to know where she'd been. And what she'd been doing.

Riding double on a motorcycle does not encourage conversation, which was probably a good thing. It allowed Andreas and Yianni time to cool down rather than dwell on how pissed they were at Lila and Toni. Their hearts may have been in the right place, but as far as these two cops were concerned, their heads were someplace quite different.

Andreas used the drive time back to the house to think about what the forensics team from Syros had said. Other than confirming Pepe was dead, they wouldn't venture a professional opinion on anything until they'd had the opportunity to examine the body back in their lab.

They were prepared, though, to engage in a few off-the-record theories. They put Pepe's time of death at several hours after Andreas and Yianni had dropped him off in Ano Mera; and from the angle of the wound, the victim had been standing, the shooter sitting.

Obviously, Pepe never took the boat he said he would. Instead, he went to meet someone. They left together on a different boat and, planned or unplanned, the killer shot Pepe. Either the shotgun blast sent Pepe overboard or the killer disposed of him in the sea.

What didn't make sense was an experienced island mobster like Karavakis allowing a body to drift around freely in the sea, what with all the chains, rocks, and cement readily available back on land. That suggested the murder was unplanned, but regardless, all he'd had to do was fish the body out, bring it back to shore, and pack it with sufficient weight to permanently bury it at the bottom of the sea far from shore.

Unless the killer lacked the necessary physical strength. The only suspect likely fitting that potential scenario was Mrs. Despotiko. Then again, killing someone unexpectedly face-to-face, as opposed to ordering someone to do it for you, has been known to induce panic and foggy thinking in even the strongest of killers.

Whatever the exact circumstances, the more Andreas thought about it, the more he believed that, after leaving them in Ano Mera, Pepe'd met with whoever was behind all three executions, including his own. Andreas wondered if their meeting with Pepe had triggered his death. If so, that didn't bother him, for he didn't see the killing in any way as his fault. He was just doing his job, and that job now included finding Pepe's killer.

Virtually all signs still pointed directly at Karavakis, but without a shred of real evidence behind them.

At least not yet.

Andreas and Yianni found Lila and Toni sitting in the den.

"So, how did your early morning gallivanting turn out?" smiled Lila.

"Where are the two girls?" Andreas asked coldly.

"We sent them home by taxi," said Lila.

"Do you know who they are?"

"Two girls in trouble I believe we can help."

"I checked. One has a record as long as your arm; the other is just getting started in the business."

"What's that supposed to mean? Are you suggesting we abandon them, simply write them off?"

"No, but didn't you think to tell your husband that your new projects happened to work for the subject of a murder investigation? An investigation, I must point out that, as of this morning, has a body count of three."

"Three?" said Toni.

"We just fished Pepe's body out of the sea off Kalifatis."

"Oh, my God."

Andreas sat down next to her. "You've got to be careful who you bring into our home. Girls like Adina and Ino have all kinds of connections to all kinds of bad actors. Even if the girls don't intend you any harm, they could easily tell others who do. This is serious stuff."

Lila shut her eyes, thinking. "We were assigned the children by the police as official counselors, and I'm sure we didn't say or do anything that would get us in trouble."

"Really? The girls know where you and our children live, and they work under duress for a local crime lord who's also probably behind three vicious murders. If they tell Karavakis, do you think he's going to thank you for your intervention or give a damn about your titles?"

Lila glanced in the direction of the children's rooms. "How could I have been so naive?"

"Your heart's in the right place, and I'm sure you're good at counseling, but going forward please find a neutral place to do your thing. Or better yet, run it by Yianni and me first."

Toni looked to Yianni. "Why are you so quiet?"

Yianni avoided looking at her. "I've decided to allow the more experienced man in such matters express my feelings."

"To be fair, there was only supposed to be one girl," said Toni. "And she came from a family that lives on Mykonos. The second one just happened to be swept up by accident."

"It might have been worse," said Lila.

"How's that?" said Yianni.

"They have a close girlfriend who works with them," said Toni. "We could have had three of them here."

"Actually, their friend's missing and I promised the girls you'd see what you could do to find her."

Andreas tightened his jaw. "You're the one into counseling. I'm the one investigating homicides. I don't have time for missing-persons work now."

"How about you?" Toni picked up a photograph of three young women from the coffee table and handed it to Yianni.

"He doesn't have time either," snapped Andreas.

"Curb your tone, please," said Lila.

"My tone—"

"Chief, I think you'd better take a look at this. Those girls might have given us a break in the case."

Yianni handed the picture to Andreas. He looked at Toni. "Who is this girl?"

"They called her Flora. She's nineteen and also works for Karavakis. They speak of her like she's a mentor, of sorts."

"What else do you know about her?"

Lila spoke. "She's been addicted to drugs since nursing school. To support her habit, she left to do a favor for Karavakis and she hasn't been heard from since."

Andreas shut his eyes, leaned back, and exhaled. "This 'mentor' figure executed the Colonel's assassin with the help of Pepe."

He opened his eyes. "If the pattern continues, she's either dead already or soon will be."

"You can't be serious," said Toni.

Andreas looked at Yianni. "We've got to get those two girls into protective custody ASAP. Slim as it is, they're the only witnesses we have who can testify to a link between Karavakis, Pepe, and their friend who killed the biker."

"I'll get Telly on it right away." Yianni reached for his mobile.

Andreas held up his hand to stop him. "Come to think of it, tell him to meet us at Karavakis' club, and to bring the girls with him."

"You're going to bring our only witnesses along to make an arrest?" said Yianni.

"Who said anything about an arrest?"

"Isn't he our number-one suspect?"

"Yeah, but we've got no proof. The girls can try to testify to a link, but his defense lawyers'll shred their testimony. We need something that puts him at the heart of the killings. To do that, we have to shake his tree. Try to make him panic."

"How are you going to do that?" said Yianni.

"I'll let you know when I figure it out. But for now, all I'm certain of is that we've got to do something."

"Yeah," said Yianni. "If only to slow down the body count."

Andreas looked at Lila and Toni. "The first thing we need to do is get everyone out of here, to a place where Karavakis can't find you, and keep you there until after we have him in custody," said Andreas.

"Why?" said Lila.

"To protect my family from a killer."

"I understand, but you're forgetting that this place is built like a fortress. It stands overlooking the sea with only one road in, and we can see someone coming from more than a kilometer away. It can withstand earthquakes and typhoon-force winds. It has its own generators, fire-fighting equipment, and steel shutters on every window designed to keep out burglars. Do you really think there's a more secure place on the island?"

"But Yianni and I can't leave you alone here."

Toni raised a hand. "If you two plan on going after Karavakis, you'll be leaving us alone no matter where you move us."

"But we'll take you to where cops can protect you," said Yianni.

"Then send them to protect us here."

Andreas sighed with frustration.

"Look," said Lila. "You just admitted you don't have enough proof to arrest Karavakis. Do you plan to keep us cooped up in whatever place you have in mind until you do?" She shook her head. "I appreciate your concern, but I think the most secure place on the island is here—just send us whatever number of cops with guns you think we'll need to protect us."

Toni jumped in. "If you want to get in Karavakis' face ASAP, you can get cops out here a lot faster than you can pack us all up and move us to some as-yet-determined secure location."

Andreas took a long breath and turned to Yianni. "When you speak to Telly, tell him to send a heavily armed protective detail of whatever number of cops he can spare out here right away." To Lila he said, "I see why you two are getting into this counseling game. You make a pretty good team when it comes to convincing folk to modify their thinking."

Yianni reached for his phone. "Hopefully for the wiser."

Chapter Twenty-one

This time, Andreas and Yianni took the SUV. Between the care-taker's car and the motorcycle, everyone at the house could flee using them, if necessary. They stopped to wait for the police about two miles from the house, at the juncture of the dirt road leading back to the house and a paved road running to Ano Mera. The only vehicle they'd seen since leaving the house was a massive cement-mixer truck, prompting Yianni to quip, "These days, cement mixers are more the symbol of Mykonos than windmills or Petros the pelican."

Andreas bit at his lip. "Do you think we're doing the right thing leaving them alone?"

"We're not leaving them alone. Police will be with them."

Andreas drew in and let out a breath.

"Besides, we're heading off to go face-to-face with the bad guy you're worried about, looking to take him into custody for three murders. Once we do that, the last thing on his mind will be taking revenge on Lila and Toni for counseling some of his girls on bad life choices. He'll be too busy worrying about his own."

Andreas turned on the engine. "Here comes the cavalry." A four-door police pickup truck packed with three officers dressed in SWAT gear turned onto the dirt road. Andreas gave them a thumbs-up and they returned the gesture. He smacked Yianni on the thigh. "Thanks for the pep talk, but seeing those guys headed for the house makes me feel a lot better."

"Good," said Yianni. "Now, we can concentrate on making Karavakis' day miserable."

• ● ● ● •

When they arrived at The Beach Club, two blue-and-whites sat parked by the entrance. Two uniformed cops sat in one car with Adina and Ion in the back. Telly and another uniform waited in the other cruiser.

Telly stepped out of his cruiser when Andreas pulled in behind him.

"I see you brought backup," said Andreas.

"Just in case."

"Ever wonder why the thought of that never makes you feel more comfortable?" said Andreas with a rueful smile.

"Experience," said Telly, handing him an envelope. "Here's what you asked for. If it's okay with you, I'll leave my guys here with the girls."

"That makes sense. Let's see how it goes." Andreas checked his phone for messages, and shut it off. Yianni and Telly did the same. "Maybe we can avoid putting the girls through a face-to-face with their tormentor-in-chief."

Telly led the way into the bar and headed straight for Karavakis' office. No one tried to stop them. Telly knocked on the door, but opened it without waiting for an answer.

"Howdy, Angelos."

"What the hell are you doing here?"

"I've brought company." Telly nodded at Andreas and Yianni as they walked in, then he shut the door behind them.

"So I see. I assume you're not here to solicit a donation for the police-welfare fund."

Andreas dropped into one of two chairs in front of Karavakis' desk. "Where were you from yesterday morning up until, let's say, four in the afternoon?"

"Why should I answer that question?"

"You shouldn't if you were taking a boat ride."

"Boat ride?"

"Yes."

"Well, if that's all you want to know, I can assure you I was firmly on land."

"Can you prove it?"

"Why should I have to?"

"Let's say because your life may depend upon it."

Karavakis leaned back in his chair. "Intriguing, Kaldis, but I won't take the bait. Yes, I can prove it, but until the time comes that I know what's behind it, I'm not about to compromise the good name of my companion during those hours by drawing her into whatever this is."

Andreas opened the envelope Telly had given him and pulled out a photograph. "Here's a photo of someone you know." He handed it to Karavakis.

Karavakis appeared unsure of what he was looking at, then his eyes widened. "Is this Pepe?"

"Recognize the shirt? I'll admit, the face is hard to make out. A twelve-gauge blast of buckshot at close range tends to do that."

"I've never seen the shirt, but the cross around the neck is his. He's worn it every day I've known him." Karavakis kept staring at the photo. "When did this happen?"

"Sometime yesterday. Before four in the afternoon."

"And you think I did this to my longtime friend?"

"Spare me the violins. We've got a serious problem here, Angelos. A very serious one."

"I'm sure we can work it out."

"It's not that kind of problem," said Telly from behind Andreas.

"It's about the murder of three people." Andreas leaned forward and tapped an index finger on the photograph. "All tied together through this guy."

"I don't see how any of that involves me."

"For starters, everybody involved either worked for you or was tied into your new hotel project with Despotiko."

"Bullshit."

"No, fact."

"Prove it."

"You will concede that Pepe's brother was your link to hooking you up with the hotel chain?"

"Yeah, sure. But why would I kill him?"

"What about the Colonel? He wanted a piece of your deal, didn't he?"

"Yes, but as I already told you and your sidekick over there, that was no problem."

"So you say," said Yianni.

"And then there's this guy." Andreas drew another photo out of the envelope. "He killed the Colonel. And he worked for you."

Andreas caught a twitch in Karavakis' eye as he looked at the photo.

"What else do you have?"

"Isn't that enough?"

"What? Three dead guys with tenuous ties to me?"

"Why do you call the ties tenuous?"

Karavakis shrugged.

"But, yes, Angelos, there's more. Witnesses who can tie you directly into all of this."

"You're bluffing. And I say that because I had absolutely nothing to do with any of this. Period. End of story." He banged his fists on the table, though the rage seemed more staged than real.

"One last thing to show you." Andreas handed him a photo of three girls.

"Do you recognize the girls in the picture?"

He looked at the photo. Another twitch before he tossed it back at Andreas. "What if I do? What does it prove?"

"Well, we happen to have another photo of the girl in the middle. Her name is Flora, and she works for you. We have her in a photo from a hospital security camera, catching her in the act of murdering this guy." Andreas slammed his fist on of the photo of the motorcyclist. "Another of your employees."

"I don't know anything about any of this, nor do I have anything to do with any alleged illegal activities on the part of any of my alleged employees."

"You sound like a lawyer. Sorry to tell you, but we have witnesses who disagree with you."

"Screw your witnesses. They're lying."

"Why would they lie? If anything, they'd be afraid of you."

"Because they're trying to frame me."

"For what purpose?"

"To take over my operations."

Andreas laughed. "Poor boy…are you telling me that you're being extorted?"

Karavakis jumped up and thrust his fist in the direction of the door. "Get the hell out of here and take your cop buddies with you."

No one moved. "Perhaps you didn't hear me correctly," said Andreas. "I'm here to tell you that we have witnesses who can identify you as the person who sent your employee, Flora, off as an assassin. Aren't you even slightly interested in what they have to say?"

Karavakis drew in and let out a deep breath before dropping back into his chair. "Fine, so tell me."

"That's better," said Andreas. He repeated the two girls' story about how their friend had been sent to do a favor for a friend of Karavakis. The favor being the assassination of the motorcyclist.

"The storytellers are two miserable pieces of shit. Like I said before, someone put them up to it." Karavakis started to stand.

"Hold it right there," said Telly. "We're actually here to help you."

"Help me? Some bitches are accusing me of murder!"

"Think about it: we're trying to find out what you know, so that *if* you're innocent, we have proof to debunk their story before it circulates. Who knows what someone as violent as Despotiko might do if he wrongly thinks you've been running rogue on a project involving him?"

Nicely put, Telly.

Andreas let Telly's thought sink in. "So what is it, Angelos? Why did you send the girl off to meet Pepe? More importantly, where is she now?"

Karavakis fixed his eyes on Andreas. "I repeat. I had nothing to do with any of this. I never told that girl to do or meet anyone, and I have no idea where she is."

"So, you're calling the witnesses liars?"

"Absolutely."

Andreas looked at Yianni. "Bring them in."

He hadn't wanted things to go this way, but if Karavakis were involved, then Adina and Ino's best chance at surviving the next twenty-four hours was to confront Karavakis now, in the presence of police.

Or so Andreas hoped.

Adina and Ino balked when Yianni told them they had to meet with Karavakis. Yianni understood; anyone with any sense would be afraid. That's why he told them the truth: "The police want to protect you, but there's nothing we can do other than let Karavakis go if you won't cooperate. Then you'll face the worst of all possible worlds. He'll know who you are, that you've spoken to the police, and that you're afraid to confront him. That gives him every reason to keep you fearing him for the rest of your lives—however long or short that might be."

Pale and nervous, the girls agreed to come with Yianni.

When they reached the closed office door, Yianni put a hand on each girl's shoulder. "Just tell the truth when you're asked a question, and everything will be fine. Okay?" He didn't say to trust him on that, because deep down in his heart he wasn't sure it was true.

Both girls nodded, and Ino shut her eyes. Perhaps to say a prayer.

The moment the girls entered his office, Karavakis leaped up and shouted, "You miserable Balkan sluts. How dare you tell such lies about me? I'll have your tongues cut out!"

Andreas jumped up, shoved Karavakis back down into his chair, and with a finger pointed dead-center at Karavakis' forehead: "That's called intimidating witnesses. If you open your mouth like that again, I'll drag you out of here in handcuffs."

Telly rattled the handcuffs on his belt. "And I'm not about to have this island turned into a war zone because of your macho bullshit temper. Shut up and do as you're told."

Nice performance, Telly.

Andreas turned to the girls standing by the door. "So, young ladies, is this the man who asked your friend, Flora, to do a favor for one of his friends?"

The girls stood trembling uncontrollably, looking down at the floor.

"No," said one, then the other.

"*What?*" said Andreas.

"They said no!" shouted Karavakis.

"You intimidated them," Yianni said.

"Fuck you. They're telling the truth."

"What the hell's going on here?" asked Telly.

Andreas raised a hand. "Just a minute." He faced Adina and gently lifted her chin up with his hand to look in her eyes. "I understand you're afraid, but the only thing that will help you is telling the truth."

"I told the truth," she said.

"See, I told you so," said Karavakis.

Andreas shook his head and let go of Adina's chin. She refocused on the floor.

"I don't understand. You told two witnesses that Flora said she was ordered by Karavakis to do a favor for a friend of his. Why are you saying now that this is not the man who told her to do that? *This is Karavakis.*" Andreas pointed across the desk.

Adina looked up at Andreas. "This is the father. Flora was told to do the favor by the son."

"Yes," said Ino quietly. "It was the son."

Boy-pimp.

For an instant, you could hear a pin drop in the room. Then the father started calling the girls names again in what Andreas took to be the knee-jerk reaction of a father defending his son.

Andreas let him vent for a bit before raising his hand. "Okay, now that most of that is out of your system, let's get down to where we stand." He looked at the girls. "I don't think we need you in here any longer. Why don't you go back and wait in the car."

Ino hesitated. "I didn't do anything wrong, Mr. Karavakis. Honest."

Karavakis looked away.

But Ino wasn't finished. "I didn't tell them anything about you or your son, and as soon as I got back I called and told him everything that had happened."

Andreas swung around to face her. "Told who? And got back from where?"

Ino looked back and forth between Karavakis and Andreas.

"Hey," said Andreas, "I'm the one you better worry about."

Karavakis ignored her.

"When I got back from your house, I called Mr. Karavakis' son and told him everything."

"What did he say?"

"Nothing. He just listened and hung up."

"Nothing?" said Telly.

"That's not good. Sounds psychotic," said Yianni.

Karavakis glanced up at Yianni but said nothing.

"Okay, girls, please go back to the police car and wait for us there. Yianni, make sure they don't lose their way." Andreas waited until they'd left. "So, Angelos, what can you tell us about your son? Does this sound like the sort of thing he'd do? Murder three people?"

Karavakis sat quietly.

"Come on," said Telly. "The whole island knows your kid's a screw-up. He's also a braggart. If he had anything to do with the murders, sooner or later he'll tell somebody…assuming he hasn't already. That means word will get back to Despotiko, and we both know how displeased he'll be with your son's efforts to link him to the hit on the Colonel. Next thing you know, your son's involved in a terrible crash or boating accident and you're getting flowers and sincere condolences from the Despotikos."

Karavakis spoke flatly, without emotion. "My son had nothing to do with any of that. He had no reason to be involved."

Andreas shook his head. "You sound like you're trying to convince yourself more than us."

"Do you have a son?"

Andreas nodded.

"Then how would you feel if all your life you watched him make one stupid decision after another, never learning, always doubling down?"

"I hope that won't be my fate."

"For your sake, I hope so too."

"What are you telling us?" said Telly.

Karavakis placed his massive forearms on the desk and dropped his forehead onto them. "I can't believe he'd be so goddamned stupid." He sat like that for half a minute before lifting his head, his eyes glazed with tears. "He's my only son, and…" His words ran off into a sigh, and he wiped at his eyes. "You might have heard that I'd decided to get out of the club business, leave this sort of thing to others, and concentrate on my new project."

He reached for a bottle of water on his desk and took a gulp. "My son didn't like my idea. He thought we should do just the opposite, and move aggressively toward wiping out our competitors in the club business. On top of all that, he said that instead of giving in to the Colonel's demand for a piece of our operation, we should take over *his* operation and become the island's true boss of bosses. I told him he'd been watching too many American gangster movies. He exploded, told me I'd lost my nerve, and stormed out. He never raised the subject with me again."

"Now we know why," said Andreas. "He's been busy setting you up to appear responsible for the Colonel's assassination. Neat plan. Your son gets you and Despotiko fighting each other while he slides into taking over the Colonel's business on his way to becoming the island's 'boss of bosses.'"

"But what about Pepe?" said Yianni. "Why would he turn on you?"

Karavakis rubbed his hand across his forehead. "Pepe was my son's godfather. They were very close. I'm sure my son told him things about how I'd not been the best of friends to Pepe over the years, and that got him on my son's side."

"But enough to be party to murder?" asked Telly.

"Pepe was no angel. He'd done that sort of thing before. We all—" he caught himself in the midst of a confessional moment and sighed deeply instead. "So, where do we go from here?"

"From what I'm hearing," said Andreas, "this is one of those father-son rivalry situations gone terribly wrong. Despotiko will likely see it the same way and not hold you to blame for your son's actions. That is, if you act immediately. On the other hand, if you let things drag into a trial, there's more than enough evidence for Despotiko to consider your son *and* you guilty, regardless of the verdict."

"Are you suggesting I have my son plead guilty to murder?"

"If he did it, yes. This isn't going away, and if he confesses, things will go easier for him."

Telly added, "We also know from the way our beloved system works, he'll likely be out of prison in a few years."

Sad but true.

"On the other hand, if he fights and is convicted, he'll have a much longer and harder time in prison."

Andreas raised his hand. "And let's not forget that if you come to Despotiko now with what you've learned and promise your son will go to jail, you're behaving reasonably. For him not to accept that proposal means he's the one destroying your joint project and potentially starting a war between your families. On the other hand, if you persist in protecting your son, despite knowing he's guilty, you'll be the one creating the mess and dooming the project. Care to guess how Despotiko might react to that?"

"Like arranging for your son to be shanked in prison?" added Telly.

Karavakis rubbed and squeezed at his cheeks with the fingers and thumb of his right hand. "I'll talk to my son and see where we go from here. If I think he did it, I'll make him turn himself in. But if he didn't, I'll die defending him." He stared at Andreas. "And woe be unto those who try to harm my family."

"I'm completely on board with that concept," said Andreas. "So, now that we're agreed, where can we find your son?"

"Out on his boat. With some of his friends."

"What friends?" said Telly.

"Some of his 'Special Forces.' That's what he calls the crew he hires for security around here. I've been letting him take care of that sort of thing. He seems to have a knack for operational planning and detail."

"I suspect three dead guys would agree," said Telly.

Andreas' mind jumped to his family and Toni. *Thank God for those SWAT guys.*

"We'll wait around and keep you company until he returns," said Andreas. "And please don't screw things up by trying to warn your son. We want this to go down without anyone else getting hurt."

Karavakis shut his eyes. "Understood."

● ● ● ● ●

Andreas left Karavakis in his office with Telly and went out to tell Yianni to keep an eye on Adina and Ino until the son was in custody. No reason to risk one of them warning him in a moment of misplaced loyalty. It always amazed him how often victims of longstanding abuse felt compelled to protect their abusers. Mostly out of fear, of course. And in the case of the son, these girls had legitimate concerns. He was likely sociopathic, if not psychopathic, which meant there was no telling what he might do next to protect his fantasy of becoming Mykonos' boss of bosses.

After speaking to Yianni, Andreas turned on his phone and walked back toward the office. A half-dozen missed call alerts from Lila popped onto the screen, plus a voicemail message from her. He stopped just short of Karavakis' office door, his mind racing with nightmare scenarios. He checked the time of the message. About five minutes ago.

He hit play.

"*Where are you? You're not answering. A boat sailed into the cove about a half-hour ago, and a couple swam to shore and are lying on the beach.*"

She couldn't be calling about that. That happened all the time. The cove appeared private, but under Greek law anyone could sail into it and use the beach. Most who stopped, though, felt uncomfortable once they realized it served a private home and left. But some didn't.

"*A few moments ago a Zodiac roared into the cove with six men aboard. They ran their boat up onto the beach, and five got off dressed like security guards. They're just standing around doing nothing. Toni's looking at them through binoculars, but doesn't recognize any of them. The man still on the boat is behind a canopy. She can't see his face.*

"*I don't think the men are with the couple. The couple looks uneasy around them. I think the men are waiting for the couple to leave. Andreas, I'm worried. Toni is too. We've told Anna to lock herself and the children in our bedroom and shutter down the windows. Toni's trying to make out the name on the men's shoulder patches. Uh-oh, the couple's swimming back to their boat.*

"Where are the police who are supposed to be here?"

A chill ran up Andreas' spine. No police? How could that be? They'd passed him and Yianni on the road headed toward the house.

"What's the name on the patch?" he muttered aloud, even though he knew she couldn't hear him.

Andreas opened the door to Karavakis' office as a text message alert sounded on his phone.

"Telly, I've got to get home. There could be some trouble at the house. Uninvited security guys have shown up on the beach, and your cops are nowhere to be found."

"That can't be. They must be there. The last message I had from them was that they'd passed you on the road headed to your house and expected to be there in five minutes." Telly turned on his phone.

Andreas read his message from Lila, hoping it said that SWAT had arrived. As he read the message, his face blanched and jaw tightened.

"THE PATCHES SAY SPECIAL FORCES."

He fixed a stare of unambiguous meaning on Karavakis. "Your son's gone after my family. Pray for them. Pray very hard."

Chapter Twenty-two

Lila put down her phone. She'd tried her husband a half-dozen times, and left a voice message. Now she'd texted him, and still no answer. Toni'd had no better luck at reaching Yianni. They must be in a serious meeting. Her heart skipped a beat at the thought they, too, might be in trouble with whoever sent the men in the cove. And where were the police Andreas had said were on their way? Her hands were trembling now. *Stop*, she ordered herself. *Think*.

She had to protect her family.

"We've got to assume the worst," she told Toni.

Toni kept watching the men in the cove through the binoculars. "The couple from the beach is back on their boat and lifting anchor. The one on the Zodiac looks about to come ashore." She paused. "Oh, my God, it's Boy-pimp!"

"Karavakis' son?" Lila felt as if she'd thrown up. "Okay. I need you and Anna to take Tassaki and Sofia to the caretaker's house, and use his car to get away from here. Dama and Tess can take the motorcycle."

"And leave you alone to deal with those Neanderthals?" said Toni. "Not a chance."

Lila shouted, "But I have to protect my babies!"

"Let's get the caretaker to help us."

"He won't be a help," said Lila. "He's into flowers, not fighting."

"Don't worry, we'll do whatever has to be done. We just have to hold them off until the police get here. Do you have any guns in the house?"

"My father has a shotgun somewhere."

"But where?"

"I don't know."

"Mrs. Lila," came a voice from the kitchen doorway.

Lila turned. "Not now, Dama."

"Mrs. Lila, I know where your father keeps his shotgun. It is in a cupboard in the kitchen."

"Show me," said Toni, running for the kitchen. She emerged seconds later with the shotgun. "All I could find were four shells."

"It's better than nothing," said Lila.

"But not by much." Toni looked around the room. "We've got to prepare some other surprises."

"Like what?"

"Like I don't know." Toni tapped her foot. "Do you have bleach, ammonia, that sort of stuff?"

"Yes, I'd think so."

"Well, get it. What about pitchforks, gardening tools?"

"How do you expect us to use them against these sorts of men?"

"These rent-a-cop types aren't going to risk getting shot, stabbed, or scarred to prove a point for Boy-pimp. He doesn't pay them enough. It's human nature. We just have to do enough to discourage them. This isn't a TV show, and they're not TV bad-guys."

"And you're no MacGyver TV hero, capable of turning duct tape into a parachute."

"Do me a favor, Lila. Unless you have a better idea, please just do what I'm saying."

"I have a better idea! Take the children and let me deal with these men on my own terms!"

Toni shook her head. "No can do. I'd never forgive myself."

"Mrs. Lila, they're coming up from the beach." Dama pointed out the window.

Lila motioned Dama back into the kitchen. "Quick, gather up anything you can think of to hurt them. Lye, bleach, ammonia, whatever you can find." She turned to Toni. "Hurry, and bring the shotgun."

Lila headed for the door opening onto the path that the men were following up from the beach.

"What are you doing?" said Toni.

"Just follow my lead."

Lila stood at the top of the hill, Toni at her side, watching the men head toward her. "*Okay!*" she shouted. "That's far enough! You're now trespassing on private property! The police have been called and are on their way!"

The men ignored her and kept coming. Lila reached for the shotgun. "In case you didn't understand me...*stop!*" She racked a shell into the chamber.

That unmistakable sound stopped the two men in the front of the pack. Boy-pimp yelled at them from the rear, "Keep marching."

They started moving. Lila took aim and pulled the trigger. The dirt in front of the lead men kicked up. "That's where I was aiming. The next shot is at your heads."

The men stopped and began backing up.

"That's a much wiser decision," said Lila.

"Up the hill, you assholes! Up!" shouted Boy-pimp. But they didn't move.

He pulled a pistol out of his waistband, leveled it at Lila, and pulled the trigger, barely missing her. Toni grabbed Lila to pull her back into the safety of the house. A second shot rang out, striking Toni in the head and dropping her to the ground just outside the doorway. Lila froze for an instant before stooping down to her friend. Another bullet whizzed by her head, and a grip of steel grabbed her arm, yanking her inside the house.

"Mrs. Lila, stay here," said Dama. "If I cannot stop the man with the gun, you must kill him when he comes inside or he will kill us all."

"Dama, how can you—?"

"Just watch the man from here. Do not let him inside the house."

Lila peeked around the doorframe. Boy-pimp was nearing the top of the hill, but he'd lost three of his crew. They'd hurried back down the hill toward the boat, apparently unwilling to play any further part in the young man's madness.

Three men coming, three shells left in her gun. She remembered what Toni had said. *He doesn't pay them enough to take a bullet for him. It's human nature.*

She'd use all three shells on Boy-pimp if she had to, and take her chances with the other two.

She peeked around the doorframe at Toni. *Oh, Lord. She's not moving.*

"Hello there, Lila," shouted Boy-pimp as he reached the top of the hill. "Or do you prefer to be called savior of whores?"

He's a psychopath.

"You had to meddle in my affairs." He paused as if to catch a breath. "For what purpose? To prove some righteous point? All you've accomplished is to ruin me in the eyes of my father."

He fired at the doorway and kept firing until he'd emptied his magazine.

"Don't breathe," he called out. "I have more magazines."

Lila peered around the doorway, hoping to get a shot off at him while he reloaded.

That's when she heard a water-pump motor roar to life somewhere off to her left and saw Dama dragging fifteen meters of fire hose toward the men. The hose jerked her to a stop, and Dama shouted something in Tagalog to Tess. Dama dropped down onto the hose and aimed its nozzle in the direction of the approaching men. Tess ran to join Dama, knelt behind her, and grabbed hold of the bucking hose. Together, they directed a torrent of water at the men, pounding at them with the blasting force of an enraged bear beating on their chests.

One of the two gorilla-sized men still with Boy-pimp caught the full thrust of the water square on his chin, jerking his head straight back and knocking him out cold. The second man reached for a gun in his belly pack, but the water hit him mid-chest, knocking him off his feet, and the women kept the water directed at his face until he threw up his hands screaming for them to stop.

Boy-pimp seemed lost in a video game as he watched the water mow down his men, but when the women turned the hose on him, he turned to run down the hill, tripping on the uneven wet stone steps, and dropping his gun as he tumbled head over heels to a jarring stop against a boulder. There he lay, caught on his back, hands trying to protect his face, while the women kept the full force of the water ricocheting off the boulder and onto him.

Lila ran out of the house carrying the shotgun. She yanked the waist-packs off the two bodyguards, collected Boy-pimp's gun, and stopped beside him, aiming the shotgun at his head. She signaled for the women to turn off the water.

Boy-pimp didn't budge—just kept his hands in front of his face, his eyes glued to the open end of the shotgun barrel.

Lila stared at him, saying nothing. She handed the shotgun to Dama and ran to Toni's fallen body. She knelt and felt for a pulse, shut her eyes, and prayed. A moment passed.

Lila turned to Dama. "Keep him there." She pointed at Boy-pimp. "But don't hurt him unless you have to. Leave that to my husband, Yianni, and me."

• • ● • •

Andreas drove, oblivious to the dangers of the road. Deep, unguarded cliffside drops to the sea, bordering a narrow, undulating loose-dirt road, left little room for errant driving. More than once the SUV slid into a curve close enough to skim a wheel over the edge. But Andreas didn't slow, and Yianni urged him to go even faster.

"Do you hear that?" said Andreas, struggling to avoid skidding through a sharp turn.

"Sounds like sirens." Yianni turned to look out the rear window. "They're pretty far behind us, but it looks like blue-and-whites and an ambulance."

"Telly must have sent them. What the hell happened to those SWAT guys?"

"How could they have just disappeared?"

The road narrowed to a series of sharp switchbacks with steep hillside drops, leading into a blind uphill curve to the left.

"*Theos filaxi*," said Yianni staring out his passenger-side window.

"What has you asking God to save us?" shouted Andreas, his eyes glued to the road ahead of him.

"The SWAT team's truck is down there."

Andreas skidded to a stop, and looked down into the bottom of a valley several hundred meters away. The pickup lay on its side, with no sign of anyone outside the truck. Andreas crossed himself three times. "We can't stop," he said. "Call Telly and tell him what happened."

"But what *did* happen?"

Andreas pointed ahead to the road's curve near a break in a low stone wall on the right side of the roadway. "They must have missed the turn and taken out that part of the wall."

"How the hell could they have missed the turn?"

"I don't know," said Andreas as he drove into the same turn, "but they—"

"Watch out," screamed Yianni as they slid head-on toward a cement-mixer truck blocking their way.

Andreas brought them to a stop a meter before the front bumper of the mixer.

"That was close," said Yianni.

"What the hell?" said Andreas, hitting his horn. The mixer had started toward them, catching the SUV's front end head-on and pushing it backwards toward the edge of the road. Andreas threw the SUV into reverse and hit the gas, steering it away from the edge. "That's the bastard who pushed the SWAT guys off the road."

Yianni pulled out his gun and leaned out the window, aiming at the mixer's windshield. The driver ducked back out of sight, but the mixer bore ahead at them.

Andreas drove backwards, his body turned sideways to see out the rear window as he steered frantically with his left hand.

"I can't get a clear shot at him from this angle."

"Shoot for his front tire!"

Yianni dropped his aim from the windshield to the driver-side front wheel and emptied his magazine into the tire.

By the time the driver reacted to Yianni's gunshots, the blown-out tire had pulled the mixer far enough to catch the edge of the road. In apparent panic, the driver braked hard and jerked the steering wheel sharply away from the edge. In so doing, he successfully transferred the momentum of his behemoth load precisely opposite to where he wished to go, and sent the mixer tumbling down into the valley.

Andreas braked to a stop, pausing only long enough to draw in and let out a quick deep breath before throwing the SUV into a forward gear, stepping on the gas and continuing toward home. "*Panagia mou.* I hope it missed the pickup."

Yianni stared out his side window. "The mixer's in pieces, but none of it looks to have hit our guys." He paused. "Assuming they're still alive."

"The cops behind us will see to them. We've got to get to the house."

Yianni looked solemnly down into the valley. "I know."

As they came over the last ridgeline before the house, they saw the Zodiac craft still in the cove.

"*God help me*! If they've hurt anyone…" Andreas let his words tail off. "Brace yourself. I'm going to drive straight through the parking area, across the vegetable garden, and onto the terrace. Let's hope they're not expecting us to come at them from that side."

"I don't care if they are." Yianni jammed a new magazine into his nine-millimeter and racked a cartridge into the chamber. He drew in a deep breath, held it for several seconds and let it out. He pressed his free hand against the dashboard and focused straight ahead. "Bring it on."

The SUV entered the parking area doing twenty miles an hour, took out a low stone wall at the far end, and bounced through lettuce, tomatoes, cucumbers, onions, and herbs, before crashing through another low wall bordering the pool area. Yianni was out of the SUV before it jerked to a stop, Andreas followed seconds later, and they raced toward the house's pool entrance.

They came in through the door, guns out in front of them. They saw no one, and paused to listen for a sound.

"We're out here!" shouted Lila.

They followed her voice, guns drawn and trained ahead.

Lila sat with tears streaming down her cheeks, cradling Toni's head in her lap. "The miserable bastard shot her. He wanted to kill me and shot her as she tried to save me."

Yianni squeezed the butt of his gun. "Which one did it?"

"The Karavakis kid."

Yianni spotted him cowering at Dama's feet and stepped toward him.

"Yianni, not now!" shouted Andreas. "See to Toni first."

Yianni hesitated.

Andreas spoke in a softer tone. "Yianni, please."

Yianni exhaled, turned, and hurried to Lila. "How is she?"

"I thought he'd killed her, but I feel a pulse and she's breathing."

Yianni crouched down and leaned in to take a closer look.

He separated Toni's blood-matted hair with his fingers. "There doesn't seem to be a puncture. It looks like the bullet grazed her." He looked up toward heaven. "Thank you."

"But what about her forehead?" said Lila. "Look at all the blood."

Yianni pointed to a rough stone step covered in blood next to her. "Head wounds bleed a lot. She must have hit her forehead on the step when the shot took her down."

"That's still serious; she might have a concussion," said Andreas.

Yianni stood and glared at Boy-pimp. "You'd better pray she's okay."

A couple of minutes later the ambulance pulled up to the house. Andreas told the EMS techs to get Toni to the medical clinic ASAP.

An attendant pointed to the two men Dama and Tess had taken down, both now awake and moaning in agony. "What about them?"

"We'll get them to the clinic in police cars."

"The police won't be here for a while," said the attendant. "They're all down in that valley trying to get their buddies out of the pickup truck. More ambulances are on the way."

"Are they okay?" asked Andreas.

"They're pretty badly beaten up, but the driver somehow managed to keep the truck on four wheels most of the way down, and they were all wearing helmets and ballistic protection when they went off the road. The cement mixer guy wasn't so lucky."

"I'll follow Toni on the motorcycle," said Yianni.

"First, let's straighten out the mess we have here." Andreas looked at Lila. "What happened?"

She told the story as if reliving it in a trance.

As she finished, Telly and another cop showed up.

"How are your men?" asked Andreas.

"They're all alive and the ambulances found a goat path to follow down to them. I thought I'd come by to see how things are going here, and to make sure you're taking good care of the bastard who tried to kill my guys." He pointed at Boy-pimp.

The instant Boy-pimp saw Telly, his demeanor changed from cowering to cocky. As if his rescuer had arrived.

"Chief, thank God you're here. I wish to file a complaint against these self-entitled rich Athenians who think they can do whatever they please on our island. My friends and I came to spend the afternoon in this lovely cove, where your good friend my father and his father used to swim and fish, but they tried to scare us away, claiming it's private property. *Their* private property." Warming to his performance, he added, "When we refused to leave, they sent a crazy woman to assault us with deadly force, and I had no choice but to defend my friends and myself with my licensed firearm."

Telly turned to Andreas. "Well, you've heard his defense."

Andreas' eyes narrowed. He looked at Lila. "You ought to check on the children." He turned to Telly. "Why don't you, your officer, and I step inside the house to discuss the situation? Detective Kouros will stay out here to keep an eye on the prisoners." He stared at Yianni. "*Understand?*"

Yianni nodded.

Andreas led them to a room far away from the scene of the attack. They stood around talking football, while, outside, Yianni gave an up-close-and-personal demonstration to Boy-pimp of some of the finer points of the kicking and penalty-card aspects of the sport.

"Do you hear screaming?" said the cop with Telly.

Telly held his hand to his ear. "Nope, sounds like the wind to me."

"The winds can get downright nasty out here," said Andreas.

A few minutes later, Lila walked into the room. "The children are fine, thank God. Yianni's left for the hospital. He said to tell you the Karavakis kid is really clumsy. He tripped and bounced down our rocky hillside all the way to the beach."

Telly shook his head. "Accidents do happen." He stood. "Don't worry, we'll collect him and his buddies and deliver them to where they belong." He smiled at Lila. "Good work."

"Thank you."

"And thank you," said Andreas, turning to hug Telly goodbye.

After Telly left, Lila put her arms around Andreas and rested her head against his chest. "I hope Toni's okay."

"We all do." Andreas kissed her on the forehead.

"If not for Toni, Dama, and Tess, I don't know what would have happened to us. To the children…" She held back a sob.

"From what I heard, you and your shotgun made half of the attackers back off. I'd say that was a pretty good contribution to the war effort."

"But that was only because of Toni."

"Whatever the reason, I agree with Telly that it was very good work. I'm proud of you." He smiled and kissed Lila again on the forehead. "I couldn't have done better myself."

"For sure."

"What's that supposed to mean?"

Lila forced a smile. "We did it without taking out two walls, the garden, and our only means of family transportation."

Andreas had to laugh. "True enough."

Chapter Twenty-three

"How's the patient doing?" asked Andreas.

"Terrific." Lila moved the phone away from her ear to glance at Toni lying on the sunbed next to her. "She's still complaining about my insisting she recuperate here, but I told her it's only been a week since the attack, and no way I'm letting her out on her own until she's a hundred percent."

"Hmm, some women can be hard-headed. In her case, it saved her life."

She sighed at his humor. "So, how are things back in Athens?"

"Same messes, same people, same aggravations."

"Sounds like you're ready to return to Mykonos."

"Yianni and I are coming on Friday, God and criminals willing."

"An interesting mix."

"But sadly true."

"Maybe Tassos and Maggie can make it, too," said Lila. "I felt badly about cancelling our plans last weekend with them."

"They understood. Hell, you were on TV. It's not every day that 'the Magnificent Quartet' repels a marauding horde."

"Well, I'm here to tell you, it wasn't as magnificent as the media portrayed it."

"I very much doubt that," said Andreas.

"In any case…I just had the strangest call from Mrs. Despotiko. It's why I called you."

"What did she have to say?"

"That she'd been meaning to call me since first hearing what had happened but was too embarrassed. She couldn't believe her husband was in business with people like the Karavakises."

"How sweet."

"No need for sarcasm, dear, I understood where she was coming from. She feared I'd turn Athens society against her. And to be honest, she sounded as if she'd been drinking." Lila paused. "Wait a minute, let me put this on speakerphone so Toni can hear."

"Hi, Andreas."

"Hi, Toni, happy to hear you're doing so well."

"What choice do I have? With all the attention Lila's giving me, and a half-dozen calls a day from Yianni, I don't dare disappoint them by *not* getting better."

"She's doing fine," Lila cut in. "So let me tell you what Mrs. Despotiko had to say." She took a sip of water from a refillable thermos. "She said her husband was shocked and appalled at Karavakis' son's attack on our family."

"Yeah," said Andreas, "killing cop families is a bad business plan."

"Let me finish, please."

"Please do."

"She wanted you and me to know that her husband had severed all ties with the father and is no longer doing business with him. I asked what that meant, and she said he's no longer in that hotel casino project with the father."

"Damn, if Despotiko's pulled out, that means Karavakis owns the whole thing." The sound of Andreas slamming his hand on his desk came vibrating through the speaker. "I guess having a kid who targets cop families isn't bad for business after all."

Toni jumped in. "Wait. I assumed Pepe's brother would be out of the deal now. Did Mrs. Despotiko say the hotel chain's still interested in the project?"

"It's Mykonos," said Andreas. "If big money can be made, business will find a way, and damn everything else."

Lila shouted, "*Stop*. Will you two please let me finish? You're jumping to conclusions before you've heard the facts." She exhaled. "What she said was that *her husband* is now the sole owner of the project. *Karavakis* is out, *not* Despotiko."

"Why would Karavakis do that?" said Toni. "Everyone agreed he had nothing to do with any of the murders or the attack on us."

"I haven't a clue," said Lila.

Silence.

"May I speak now?"

"Yes, dear, you may," grinned Lila.

"I think I have the answer to your Karvakis question. The prosecutor on the son's case told me that the son's about to confess to his role in three murders. Apparently, his father told him he had no choice."

"Do you really think the son had the brains to pull all of this off?" asked Toni. "Maybe someone was manipulating him to get at the father?"

Andreas paused. "From the way things turned out, I'd say it had all the hallmarks of the son's brainpower. Of course, there are those on the island who did not want the father's project to go forward, but for the record, the son's saying it was all his doing."

"What's his story?" said Lila.

"One of straightforward delusional narcissism at work. He said he convinced Pepe that the only chance he had at getting the club he wanted on Mykonos was to team up with him on bringing down his father.

"The first step was to get rid of the Colonel in a way that made it look like his father had set up Despotiko to take the fall for the assassination. So the son used his Bulgarian thug to pull it off, and that's about the only step that went as planned.

"The idea was to spark a war between Despotiko and his father. One in which the son could ultimately emerge as peacemaker and broker a deal with Despotiko, sending his father into retirement and giving the son the Colonel's protection business—with appropriate tribute paid regularly to Despotiko. He planned on using the Colonel's business model to squeeze every vulnerable club owner off the island and extract at least a piece of the action from the rest. Pepe's reward was to have his pick of whatever club he wanted."

"That sounds insane," said Lila.

"Sure does," said Toni, "but it's not that far off from what's happening on the island today."

Andreas continued. "The plan started off fine. The son had arranged for Pepe to talk to his father about security for Pepe's new club at a time when he knew Mrs. Despotiko would be at The Beach Club. That gave Pepe the opportunity to tell Mrs. Despotiko he was approaching her at Angelo Karavakis' suggestion, looking for a security recommendation from her husband. But Despotiko's wife never told her husband what Boy-pimp assumed she would. So Despotiko never got to thinking Karavakis had set him up for the Colonel's assassination.

"That's when the son had Pepe turn informer and take his made-up story to Interpol about the Colonel being assassinated over the threat he posed to *powerful interests* on the island. He thought for sure an Interpol investigation into the Colonel's assassination would expose his father's role in implicating Despotiko. What he hadn't counted on was how slowly Interpol worked.

"With nothing happening on the Despotiko front, and Yianni and me poking around, the son panicked and sent the same guy he'd used to take out the Colonel to take us out. When that failed, he used Pepe and Flora to 'take care of things' in the hospital, and that's when the wheels really started coming off. My guess is Pepe bribed the cop scheduled for hospital guard duty to call in sick. I also wouldn't bet against Pepe having bribed the local chief to assign the rookie to take the sick cop's shift. We'll never know for sure, now that Pepe's dead, because neither cop is going to admit to anything."

"What about Flora?" said Lila.

"The son doubts she even knew what was in the injection."

"No, I mean, has she turned up?"

"No. Boy-pimp claims he has no idea what happened to her, that she just disappeared."

"Likely trafficked," said Toni, shaking her head.

"As for Pepe, it's just as Yianni and I thought. After we dropped him off in Ano Mera, he called the son, who insisted they meet on his boat. The son was furious that we'd figured out he'd bugged the table at the taverna in Ano Mera. He made Pepe repeat everything he could remember we'd spoken about, then called him an idiot for admitting he knew the motorcyclist.

"Pepe got offended and told him the hospital hit only worked because of his thorough hospital reconnaissance. That's when Boy-pimp literally went ballistic, screaming at Pepe for being so stupid as to have done the recon himself, and without a disguise. He grabbed a shotgun he kept onboard, blasted Pepe, panicked, stripped off Pepe's pants, and dumped his body overboard."

Andreas swallowed. "Your decision to rescue Adina and Ino had unexpected consequences. He'd just blown away his last remaining collaborator on his crazy scheme for ruling the island. That put him in full-paranoia mode. Then came Ino's call admitting that she and Adina had just spent hours being pumped for information by the two of you. What sent his panic level off the charts was when Ino said they'd given you Flora's photograph. Until then, he thought Flora was the only person on earth who could bring him down. But now you knew too much, plus you were going to try to find Flora. That's when he decided to come after the two of you, and use his now-dead buddy in the concrete mixer to protect his flank."

"So the solution was to kill all of us?"

"Hard to know how that kind thinks. He's a narcissistic psycho, and they always need someone other than themselves to blame when things go wrong with their grand plans. His story to the prosecutor is that he was just trying to frighten you away from the girls."

"That's quite a tale he had to tell," said Toni.

Andreas sighed. "A combination of brilliant planning and utter stupidity in execution. Sometimes it's hard to tell which is which."

"But how does that explain why Karavakis turned over his interest in the hotel project to Despotiko?" said Lila.

"A father's love."

"Huh?" said Toni.

"I'm guessing Despotiko made it clear to Karavakis that what his son did was unforgivable, and being in business together with the father would stain Despotiko irreparably. Karavakis knew what that meant: whether free on the streets or tucked away in prison, his son was a dead man walking. So, Karavakis made a deal. He gave up his interest in the project in exchange for his son's life."

"Hmm," said Toni. "I never knew cold, hard cash removed stains."

Andreas laughed.

"Apparently it wasn't money that drove Despotiko to take over the project," said Lila.

"Why do you say that?" asked Toni.

"Because his wife told me that her husband has decided *not* to build the project, but leave the land as it is. Undeveloped."

"He's discovered a conscience?" asked Toni.

"I doubt that," said Lila. "More likely he realized his personal life would be unbearable if the project went ahead and his wife became queen of the new playground on Mykonos for billionaires. I can't even begin to imagine how much farther off the rails that sort of life would send her."

Toni nodded. "As a consolation prize she gets to claim that she and her husband are acting selflessly to preserve the island."

"Yes. Her husband knows what makes his wife tick," said Lila. "That sort of approach scores big points among island society."

"What about Karavakis?" asked Toni. "What will happen to him and all his dirty businesses?"

"Likely nothing," said Andreas. "If it isn't Karavakis, it would be someone else. The island wants his type, and as long as it does, his sort will flourish there."

"I get it," said Toni. "Supply and demand. Same as it ever was."

Lila shrugged. "I guess that as long as there are people chasing after vices, if you're willing to be the place on this earth where providers and a clientele can come together to freely do their business, you'll always make money, and family values be damned."

"If you're looking for a just ending, don't give up hope," said Andreas. "But also don't count on it being of the legal sort. In my experience these guys carry blood grudges, so I wouldn't be surprised if someday soon one of them whacks the other."

"I guess I should be happy that I confine my business dealings to thieves," said Toni.

"They can be dangerous, too."

"I'm sure, but I know of at least one thief who looks out for me."

"What's that mean?" said Andreas.

"He thought I was taking too many risks looking into Boypimp's activities, so he arranged for a guy with a motorcycle to keep an eye on me whenever—as he said—'Your cop boyfriend's not around.'"

"What a world," said Lila.

"On that observation, please allow me to hang up and get back to saving my small part of it. I'll speak to you ladies later."

"You're excused, my love. Bye."

"My, oh my, wasn't that enlightening?" said Toni.

Lila sighed. "Maybe this counseling idea isn't such a good idea after all. Perhaps being a mom is good enough."

Toni shrugged. "That's purely your call, but you really do have a natural talent for this sort of thing."

"But what sort of a difference did I really make? Ino turned on me the moment she left, and poor Flora…who knows what happened to her?"

"Two disappointing cases, for sure, but as the old Hank Williams Junior lyric goes, 'one out of three ain't bad.'"

"I thought that was Meat Loaf."

"No, he was, 'two out of three.' I guess Hank was more of an optimist. But the real point is, you did help Adina."

"Are you sure about that? We haven't heard from her. Who knows what she's doing?"

"I do."

"How do you know?"

"Her father came to visit me at the medical clinic. He wanted to pay me for helping his daughter. I refused. He persisted and I had to threaten to have him arrested if he didn't stop. That's when he told me about Adina. He said she's home, behaving, and psyched up about starting school. Then he handed me a letter." Toni reached into her pants pocket and pulled out a folded envelope. "I've been saving it for the right moment to show to you. I think that moment's now."

She handed it to Lila; it had been addressed to FRESH START.

Lila turned it over and saw a heart drawn where the flap met the envelope—the same spot where kids sometimes left a mark to indicate "sealed with a kiss." She pulled out a single sheet of paper, and read the letter aloud:

> *I never thought anyone cared about me other than my parents, and that whatever attention I received from others was because of my looks. I came to believe that I was only worth what I could earn off of them, and quickly found that they brought me more in a week than my parents earned with all their hard work in a season. I thought I'd found the easy way to a better life. But I was wrong, and I was trapped in a life I could not escape. I never thought I'd have a second chance. But now I have. Thanks to you. I shall not let you down. Or my parents.*
> *Adina.*

She'd signed off with a lot more hearts.

Lila set the letter down on her lap, tears welling up in her eyes. "You're right, Toni. One out of three ain't bad."